Thankfully in Love

Thankfully in Love

A Thanksgiving Anthology

Edited by

Lezli Robyn

CAEZIK

ROMANCE

ARC MANOR

ROCKVILLE, MARYLAND

SHAHID MAHMUD
PUBLISHER

www.CaezikRomance.com

ISBN: 978-1-64710-020-9

First Edition. First Printing.
1 2 3 4 5 6 7 8 9 10

CAEZIK
R O M A N C E

An imprint of Arc Manor LLC

www.CaezikRomance.com

CONTENTS

No Place Like Home

Anna J. Stewart

CHAPTER ONE

"*Y*ou missed your calling, Bro."

A firm hand landed solidly on Tripp Atsila's shoulder before the same hand smacked him lightly on the back of the head. Hammer poised, Tripp felt the amused smile curving his lips before he even thought about stopping it. Instead, he accepted his older brother's compliment and finished nailing the drywall into place. When he stepped back, he reached for his travel coffee mug only to find it completely empty.

"New pot's brewing across the street," Wade said with barely a glance. If there was one thing the Atsila siblings understood, it was coffee. "Should be ready in a few. What time did you get here, anyway?"

"Little after six." Tripp checked his watch. He'd been at it for nearly three hours already. At this rate, his insomnia was going to be the best thing that ever happened to his brother's deli expansion plans. "It's not a problem is it? Coming in early?"

Wade shook his head, waved away his concern, his dark eyes glimmering with humor. "Not as far as the neighborhood is concerned. Gran might have something to say about it, though."

"She's too busy finalizing the Thanksgiving dinner menu to worry about me." Even as Tripp said the words, he knew it wasn't true.

Ever since he'd come home to Woodville Springs, California, ten days ago, his grandmother had been watching him as if he were some kind of mirage about to vanish in the morning mist. After spending the last decade buried in his job as a federal cybercrime investigator, a job that had him rarely surfacing for air, he supposed he couldn't blame her. He'd been promising to come home forever. But now? He slipped his hammer into the loop on his tool belt. Now, he'd finally needed to. Woodville Springs was his solace of last resort.

Dealing with the darkest and seediest elements humanity had to offer didn't exactly lend itself to mental well-being. Or so the division therapist had told him during his last required session. The implication had been clear: take a break voluntarily or be forced on one. The choice was simple when one choice went on his permanent record and would no doubt affect any future promotions. The downside to time off? Too much time to think.

Far too much time.

"It's been a while since you've been back for the holidays," Wade said with that now familiar hint of curiosity in his tone. Wade and their three brothers had been gently trying to nudge information out of Tripp every chance they got, but were also happy to fill in the gaps in Tripp's familial knowledge. "Gran has this routine going. It'll be the weekend before Turkey Day before she finalizes anything and, even then, Hardy and Marshall will be looking for markets open on the day because some crucial ingredient hadn't been on her original list." He shook his head. "Poor guys." Then he grinned. "But hey, at least it won't be us scrambling to fill her list, am I right?"

"All the more reason to get this new restaurant slash grocery of yours up and running," Tripp said as he moved his tools out of the way for the local construction crew that began to trickle in. "You'll just have to hand her the keys."

"It's Brothers' Deli, remember? Hardy and Marshall can loan her their keys." Wade pointed to outside the window where, amidst the fiery foliage of the autumn-tipped trees, the new lighted sign would hang.

"On the other hand," Tripp added with an amused chuckle, "her having her own keys could mean Gran will take our brothers out of the picture completely and shop herself."

"You just had to ruin it." Wade sighed. "She'll rearrange every item on every shelf, but she'd be entitled, I suppose. She's been pushing us to expand the storefront for the last few years. Serves me right for taking so long to listen to her." He finished sorting through the mail, stopped when he came across a hand-addressed envelope. "That's weird." He set it aside.

"What?"

"Something for Parker." Wade shrugged, flipped it over. "Looks personal."

"Personal, huh?" The mention of Wade's attractive and very single assistant manager had Tripp's interest piquing. He'd spoken to her off and on since he'd been back. Nothing significant or deep, just small talk and an exchange of pleasantries. And smiles. Lots of smiles. She reminded him of a dark-haired tornado, spinning in and out of view faster than he could blink as she kept Brothers' Deli purring like a well-oiled machine. But he'd been around her enough that she'd made an impression. Enough that Tripp held out his hand to his brother. "I can deliver it to her. I'm going to fill my coffee anyway."

Wade's eyes narrowed to slits. "Just make sure getting coffee's all you're doing."

"What's that supposed to mean?" Tripp offered his best clueless and offended expression, neither of which passed muster.

"You know *exactly*. The same thing Marshall meant when he warned you about taking Sophie Sutterfield to the senior prom. Hands off Parker where any extracurricular activities are concerned."

"Sophie didn't have any complaints," Tripp grinned at the memory.

"Her brother did."

Tripp's humor faded. Why the sudden concern about Tripp's interest in Parker? "Marshall have something going on with Parker?" He wouldn't put it past their notoriously single—and happy to proclaim it—middle brother, Woodville Springs' leading accountant. He was a one-man dating app and Parker Rutledge was an eye-catching, single woman. But the Atsila brothers never, ever poached women from each other.

"Nothing that I know of," Wade said. "But she is the best employee I've ever had, and I don't want any of my brothers ..." he hesitated, no doubt self-censoring. "Just, be careful with Parker, okay? I don't know her story, but I know she has one. Something tells me it isn't pretty."

"Understood." That overactive protective gene all the Atsilas kids had been born with kicked into overdrive inside Tripp. He'd been the one to take that instinct further and made a career out of trying to keep people protected and safe. He'd been good at it. Really good. He repressed a shiver, a chill going down his back. Until he'd been too late.

Wade passed over his own empty travel cup. "Since you're going over to play mail carrier, get me a refill. And a breakfast sandwich. Essie's out of breakfast commission for the next few months. Eggs make her puke."

Not for the first time since he'd been home, envy sliced through Tripp. Wade had been the first of the Atsila brood to marry. He and Essie would be first-time parents come spring, an event the entire family was already planning multiple celebrations for; something Tripp was considering sticking around for. Gran had been knitting so much she'd be able to open her own store come the New Year.

Wade and Essie's pending arrival was probably to thank for their wayward sister Lilith's promise to come home for Thanksgiving for the first time in forever. She was bringing her boyfriend, a security expert named Quincy Lennox, who, at least to Tripp, sounded like an action-movie hero.

All the Atsila family under one roof? That might, Tripp thought as he exited the corner building his brothers had purchased for the expansion, be one of those signs of a pending apocalypse.

A November breeze kicked up, one tinged with the scent of autumn leaves, cool nights, and the warm aroma of apples and cinnamon. Crisp leaves danced and twirled their way down the sidewalk. The smattering of morning cars took up parking spaces while bicycles, minus security locks, leaned up against trees and storefronts. He eased his pace, remembering the promise he'd made to himself to slow down. So much of his life had been nonstop; endless work hours in front of a screen or holed up in surveillance vans or hotel rooms with less personality than a wannabe reality TV star. The rest of his time had been spent focusing on the worst humanity had to offer … child predators who hid behind computer monitors and within the loopholes of the law.

Woodville Springs, thankfully, was far away from all that. At least that's what he told himself. The small California town known for its hidden treasure wineries, collection of secluded, meandering rivers and streams, and an eclectic main street filled with cute touristy type shops interspersed with hobby and craft offerings, was peace personi-fied. The lack of chain stores and restaurants allowed local businesses to thrive and survive thanks to the steady weather and promise of one-day getaways from various larger Northern California suburbs. With Lake Tahoe and Sacramento equidistant from where Tripp cur-rently stood on the corner of Cedar Tree Way and Maple Lane, they were the "you have to know it's there" retreat for Californians looking for the ideal, relaxing vacation.

He crossed the street, holding up one hand in thanks to the car that stopped at the sign before continuing on its way out of town.

The aroma of fresh baked bread, roasting meats, fried dough, and sugar set Tripp's stomach to growling the second he entered Brothers' Deli. By now the thirty-seat delicatessen and take-out counter was filled with morning patrons on their way to work, grab-bing a quick lunch for later or a bite for breakfast. Wade's lifelong dream of running a neighborhood go-to place had come true more than five years ago, thanks to the eager investment of all the Atsila siblings, and had quickly become a popular eatery. Its offerings were different from the diner's down the road or the fare at the two pubs on either end of town, or at the burger joint close to the elementary and high schools.

The business had gotten a huge boost after being featured in a television spot highlighting small-town California eateries on one of those TV travelogue food shows everyone seemed to be obsessing over. With their "special recipe" homemade pastrami, fresh baked breads, and killer salads, they guaranteed there was something for everyone at Brothers'. Even those of the non-meat-eating persuasion couldn't resist, thanks to their brother Hardy's addition of vegan and vegetar-ian options. With the new, much larger location, the menu would no doubt expand again, this time to include dinner service along with a market and bakery. His brothers had thought of everything.

Including, Tripp thought as he wound his way around customers to behind the counter, employing the perfect staff.

Parker Rutledge stood behind the counter, her smile of welcome in place. First-time customer or long-time patrons, they garnered her equal attention, even as she filled orders, made sandwiches, and rang up sales.

He gave a quick wave to the three-person kitchen staff, then shimmied his way behind Parker who was quickly filling orders being flung at her by Misty, a twenty-something remote college student who had stars so bright in her eyes he had no doubt she'd never stepped foot out of Woodville Springs, let alone California.

It was Parker, however, who had caught his attention from the moment he'd first seen her. And okay, maybe it had a little to do with the way her curves filled out every inch of the very snug jeans she wore. She definitely had a rougher "I've seen and been through things" edge when compared to young women like Misty. An edge that came with a pretty smile but also tinted with a guarded, slightly suspicious expression. He'd taken a quick peek at her employment information and knew she was twenty-nine, only two years younger than himself. She'd previously worked as a waitress, a record keeper, and oddly enough, a self-defense instructor. He was extremely interested to know what brought about that professional combination.

"Careful." Parker glanced over her shoulder when he knocked his metal mug against the stacked cups near the coffee machine and nearly toppled them. "You break 'em, *you* tell your brother."

"Noted."

He hoped to catch her gaze, but she was already turning her attention back to the orders, making sandwiches at light speed, wrapping them up in parchment, and slapping a Brothers' Deli crown sticker on as a finishing touch.

She had cat eyes, Tripp thought. That stunning brown and amber combination that seemed to glint against the fluorescent lights. She wore her brown hair tied back, accentuating a round face devoid of most makeup save for a pale pink shine on her lips. She had a healthy figure, not one of those slight lives-on-coffee-and-oxygen builds, but smooth lines that made a man's hands itch to explore. The sneakers on her feet were well worn, but sensible; not one of those high-end brands that made you conscious about getting them dirty. Her chin reached his shoulders and their comparable height had him feeling the heat of her body radiating from just behind him, even as she buzzed up and down the sandwich counter, shouting out orders to the kitchen for the additional menu choices.

He took his time with the coffee, not in any rush to get back to the drywall his brother's crew would no doubt finish within the hour. It wasn't like he was being paid or being relied on. More like he was trying to keep busy and stop his mind from circling and obsessing over the work—and the lack of a life—he'd left behind with ICAC.

Even the acronym for the Internet Crimes Against Children team was enough to make him clench his fists against the panic of burnout. He stood there, trying not to shake as the noise around him faded. His back to the customers, hands gripping the counter, he closed his eyes and forced himself to breathe. In and out. Long breath in. Longer breath out.

Only when he pushed the darkness away could he feel his entire body begin to relax once more.

"Hey." Parker's soft voice had him jumping. Her hand on his arm had him opening his eyes and looking down. "Are you all right?"

"Yeah." He managed a quick, dismissive nod. Those moments were coming less frequently than they had been just a few weeks ago, but when they hit …. "Yeah, I'm fine." He saw Misty move away from the register and disappear into the back, where the sounds of voices and slamming of oven doors and clanging pots brought an odd sense of comfort.

"Maybe you should do decaf." Parker shifted, reached for his coffee, and dumped it into a paper cup, refilled from the second, less used pot.

"Decaf?" He looked at the drink as if it were toxic sludge. "Why is that even a thing?"

"Because sometimes our nerves need a break. Try it. It won't kill you." She stepped back, crossed her arms, and angled a look at him that was most definitely a challenge.

He sipped, prepared to cringe, but found himself frowning in approval. "That's good. Why is that good?"

"Cinnamon and just a touch of cardamom." She grinned. "My special touch. You need anything else?"

"Yeah. Wade wants a breakfast sandwich."

"No problem." She held up a finger, leaned over and shouted into the back. "It'll be a sec. How about you take a break?"

"Want to take one with me?"

"Awww, aren't you cute?" Her grin widened. "Hitting on me, are you? You know the employees have been taking bets. They have a pool going."

"Taking bets on what?" He wasn't sure he liked the sound of that. "Me hitting on you?"

"You hitting on anybody," Parker teased. "Rumor has it you used to be quite the serial dater back when you were growing up."

"Rumor has it, or my brothers are oversharing?" Tripp grumbled sourly. Sabotaged before he'd even taken a shot. Typical.

She smiled, and gave him a close-up look at that dimple in her right cheek.

"I refuse to reveal my sources. Can you confirm or deny said hitting has commenced?"

"That depends." He took another sip of his coffee. "Who wins if I say yes?"

She chuckled. "I'd have to check the sheet."

"For the record," he said when she started to move away. He liked talking with her. And he liked her teasing him. "I like my women fully formed now. Independent. Smart." He inclined his head and grinned. "Pretty."

"How shocking to confirm *all* the Atsila brothers have a certain charm about them." She patted a hand on his arm. "Too bad I'm immune." She grabbed the wrapped breakfast sandwich that came through the order window and handed it to him. "It was nice you tried, though."

"I take that to mean my offer for you to take a break with me is declined?"

"Afraid so. Don't take it personally." She reached across him for a pot of coffee. "I just don't tend to take my breaks. I need to refill people's cups. It was nice to chat you up, Tripp."

"Yeah." He nodded, then remembered the envelope. "Oh, wait." He pulled it out of his back pocket. "Sorry. Wade asked me to give this to you. Turned up in his mail."

"Oh. Thanks." She set the pot down, took it, and slipped her finger under to open it.

If he hadn't been standing so close to her, he might not have noticed the change on her face as she unfolded and read the contents. If he hadn't been a federal agent for the past ten years, he might

10

not have identified the flash of panic—and dread—on her face. The way her spine stiffened and her entire body tensed. The way she instantly tried to cover and pretend she wasn't upset, even as she closed herself off.

"Something wrong?" Stupid question, Tripp thought even as the color in her face drained. She folded the paper and envelope together, shoved both into her back pocket, and forced a smile when she looked at him.

"It's nothing." She scrubbed her palms against her jeans before she picked the coffee pot back up.

"You sure?"

"Yep. Very." The smile definitely didn't reach her eyes this time. "Thanks for playing postman." Her voice cracked, just a bit. Enough for him to wish he'd gotten a look at what was inside that letter. He watched her move off into the small collection of tables, belatedly grabbing his own coffees and Wade's breakfast. He headed back to the door, but couldn't help but look back.

He saw fear shining in her eyes.

Why wouldn't he just leave?

Parker could feel it. Tripp Atsila was watching her. His eyes were like two laser beams boring into her. She refused to give in and glance his way again; she'd just focus on her work, on cleaning the tables, filling coffee and ….

"Oh!" She spun and bashed right into Misty. She fumbled to keep hold of the plates and flatware, jostling them a bit but saved them from falling. She looked toward the door when the bell jingled and watched Tripp head back across the street. "I'm sorry, Misty."

"No worries." Her coworker frowned and swiped her hands down the front of her black T-shirt monogrammed with the deli's logo. "You all right?"

Thinking of how she'd just asked Tripp Atsila the same thing, she wondered if karma ever took time to breathe between strikes. "I'm fine. Just distracted I guess."

"Yeah, Tripp'll do that to a girl." Misty let out a soft sigh. "Let me take those for you." She hauled away the plates Parker all but clutched to her chest. "Things are under control here for a while. Why don't you get some fresh air?" She inclined her chin to where Tripp had gone.

"Actually." Parker untied the stained apron she wore around her waist. "I think I feel a migraine coming on. I'm going to run home and grab my meds."

"Sure, okay." Misty deposited the dishes into the tub by the back counter. "I might have something in my bag—"

"This is prescription," Parker cut her off as she hurried into the back for the designer hobo bag that her mother had given her as a graduation gift. "Hopefully, I can catch this in time before it … you know." She made explosive gestures with her hands.

"Tommy's been wanting extra hours. I can give him a call to cover?"

"Yeah." Parker shoved her hands into her pockets to keep them from shaking. "Yeah, that's a good idea. Thanks. I'll … I'll see you." Regret and sadness pushed in on her, forcing the air from her lungs. On impulse, she reached out and hugged Misty, a quick, burst of affection she couldn't resist. "Thank you, Misty."

It was the only way she could think to say goodbye. Without looking back, she hoisted her bag over her shoulder and hurried out of the deli. She forced herself to keep a steady pace as she passed the quilt shop that was just turning on its lights, the drug store on the corner. Then she crossed the street.

And ran.

CHAPTER TWO

"*Y*ou just had to mess things up, didn't you?"

"What?" Tripp pulled out his earphones and turned off the scroll saw. "What did I do?"

"I just got back from picking up lunch." Wade threw a wrapped sandwich at one of his crew, who quickly caught it and moved out of the line of verbal fire. "I told you not to mess with her. What did you say?"

It took Tripp a second to clear the buzz from his head. "Mess with who? Parker?" That warning in his gut tugged again. "What happened?"

"She's gone. She walked off her shift just after you left this morning. More like ran off from what Misty said. And it doesn't sound like she's coming back." Wade set the box of sandwiches down and stalked over, the anger in his normally easygoing gaze on full display. "Whatever you said, whatever you did, fix it. I need her to make this expansion work, Tripp. So make it right."

"I didn't do anything but deliver that letter," Tripp tried to explain but Wade was already walking away. "Hang on." He must have sounded as frustrated as he felt because the rest of the crew seemed to be paying attention now. Either that or they were really anxious for their lunch. "Wade, hang on a sec." He chased after his brother much the way, he thought, he used to when he'd been a kid. Wade had been his hero. His protector, guide, and sometimes conscience. He didn't like the idea, even after all these years, of having let him down. "Wade,

I can't fix what I didn't do. But I'll try," he added when Wade simply glared. "Seriously, I'll talk to her. Where does she live?"

The tension around Wade's eyes eased. "Off Poplar Way. The old Schlessinger house. You remember it?"

"Yeah. The one with the wraparound porch and white picket fence." Their sister Lilith had always called it the storybook house when she was little. "That's just a few blocks away."

"Then it won't take you long to get there."

"Okay, I get the message." Tripp stepped away and held up his hands. "She'll be back for her next shift, I promise." He cringed as he turned away. He hated making promises he might not be able to keep. And while he didn't know much about Parker Rutledge, he did know this: if she had her mind set on something, chances were he couldn't do anything to change it.

But he was going to have to try.

The adrenaline continued to surge through Parker's panic-loaded system as she dived up between the carved pumpkins on the porch stairs and through her front door. She dropped purse, cell, and keys on the table and started for the stairs, stopped, and backtracked to pull her suitcase out of the downstairs closet. After taking two steps up, she was down again, hurrying into the kitchen to retrieve the gingham-covered binder from the kitchen along with a box of protein bars before racing up to her bedroom.

It was almost noon. She'd lost time having to wait for the bank to open to empty her account. The ATM, which had been down for a week, was still out of service so she'd killed precious minutes at the pharmacy across the street, refilled her prescriptions and anything else she might need on the road. One bag, she reminded herself, falling into the old routine she'd hoped never to have to use again. One bag is all she could afford to take with her. Flipping the suitcase open on the bed, she dropped the binder and bars inside, followed by a drawer's worth of underwear, jeans, and shirts.

How had she let this happen? How had she let herself get so comfortable, so ensconced in Woodville Springs that she hadn't seen this coming? It had been almost a year, one perfect, blessedly uneventful year since she'd had to run. She'd landed the best job, made friends, had settled in as if she'd always lived here. What had she been thinking—believing she could ever outrun her past?

She stopped, hands in a dresser drawer, and stared at herself in the mirror. "Did I miss something?" She hated the fear she saw on her face; the wide-eyed heart-stopping anxiety that had her wondering how much time she had. She tossed the drawer's contents into the suitcase and pulled the letter out of her pocket.

They'd found her.

Maybe not where she lived, but where she worked—and that was close enough. Too close.

Give us the money.

Simple, concise, and terrifying. She tilted her head back, stopping the hot, angry tears before they could fall. Damn it!

Yet again she cursed her stupid, naive younger self for ever having fallen for "investment advisor to the stars," Chad Remington. He'd wined and dined, seduced and charmed her. He'd made her feel like Cinderella, minus the ashes and talking mice. He'd whirled her through a romance that ended with an impulsive elopement to Las Vegas before he'd taken her home with him to Los Angeles. Except it turned out Prince Charming wasn't charming at all. Her husband was nothing but a conman with extremely dangerous connections.

Connections who, even years after her husband's arrest and conviction, were convinced she'd been in on her ex-husband's schemes.

"Give them the money." She tossed the letter and envelope into the case and resumed cleaning out her drawers, then started on the bathroom. "Like it's that easy!"

The framed photos beside the bed, the only ones she had of her parents and sister, quickly joined her clothes, along with the few trinkets she'd added to her home in the past few months, including a picture of her with the staff of Brothers' Deli. If she was going to leave, she was going to take some memories with her. She'd be damned if Chad would take those from her, too.

In the silence of the bedroom, she heard a floorboard squeak. Parker froze, hand stilling on the zipper of the suitcase. Her body went ice cold as she strained to listen. The case landed with a thud on the carpet. Had she heard her name? Heavy booted footsteps.

Slow, even. Deliberate. Creeping through the house. Heading up the stairs.

She yanked open the nightstand drawer and pulled out her pistol, chambered a bullet, and heart pounding, soundlessly moved behind the door.

Well, she was here. Tripp lifted the strap of her purse. Or, at least, her keys and cell were.

Tripp stopped moving when the board under his foot squeaked. "Parker?" No response. The house was utterly silent. Eerily so. The skin on the back of his neck prickled and for the first time in weeks, he wished he had his service piece with him. He shifted his weight, walked down the short hallway, circled through the sparse living room and tidy, tiny kitchen.

The half bath off the pantry was empty and staircase leading down the basement was dark. He clicked on the light, called her name again.

"That just leaves upstairs, I guess." Why wasn't she answering him? He knew that his appearance would come as a surprise and no doubt his non-apology apology would as well, but the silence unnerved him. "Parker? It's Tripp. Tripp Atsila." He rolled his eyes as he climbed the stairs. *Hello, Captain Obvious.*

The bedroom to the left at the top of the stairs was open and empty while the door straight ahead was only slightly ajar. He stepped closer, pressed his fingertips against the door and pushed.

"Parker?" He saw the suitcase, the dresser drawers open and empty, the nightstand devoid of any ….

He spun at the breath of sound, hands going up as the door closed. Parker, gun in hand, stepped forward. "Don't move." She aimed the barrel right at his head.

"Not moving." He kept his hands up, took a step back until the backs of his knees hit the bed. After ten years as a federal agent, he could read people. He could see if someone knew—or didn't know—how to handle a weapon. Her stance, her grip on the gun, that steely look in her eyes … she knew. She wouldn't hesitate to pull the trigger.

"How did you get in?" She shifted to a one-handed grip and walked around him, pulled her suitcase closer then pushed it into the hall. "What are you doing here?"

He didn't think she'd appreciate hearing she'd left the front door not only unlocked, but slightly ajar. "I came to talk to you."

"Yeah?" She motioned for him to sit down on the bed. "What about?"

"Wade thinks I said something that made you quit. He doesn't want to lose you."

Parker snorted. "Try again. The truth this time."

He frowned. "It is the truth." Why else would he be here? "Parker, what's going on? Who do you think I am?"

Doubt flickered in her eyes.

"Whatever's going on," he tried again. "Maybe I can help. I'm a federal officer."

"I know." She didn't flinch. "Wade and Marshall filled me in. I've had *help* from the feds before. Doesn't mean I can trust you."

Now that stung. And raised more questions than expected. "You didn't have *me* helping you. This has something to do with that letter I gave you, doesn't it?"

"Yeah. The letter *you* gave me. The letter that happened to show up where I work. How convenient. Who are you working for?"

Tripp frowned. "I told you," he said slowly, his temper catching. He wasn't used to his word being questioned. Especially by a beautiful woman holding a gun. "I'm a federal agent. I'm just on vacation and visiting my family. Parker." He lowered his hands but left them in plain sight. "I grew up in this town, remember? It's my home." Even as he said it, he realized how true it was. "I wasn't sent by anyone. I just came home for Thanksgiving."

The doubt crept in again and this time settled in her face.

"How about you put the gun down and we talk?" Clearly, she had some things she might want to get off her chest.

"I don't have time to talk. I have to leave." She backed out of the room, reengaged the safety on the gun and shoved it into the back waistband of her jeans. "Tell Wade I'm sorry about running out on him. I just have to go."

She grabbed her suitcase in a fluid movement and was down the stairs in seconds, hefting up her purse. Tripp followed, carefully, watching every move she made as she patted her pockets, and searched her bag for her purse. "Damn it. Where are they?"

"Your keys? Right here." He held up the keys he'd pocketed on his way up.

She glared at him, those cat eyes of hers pinning him in place on her staircase.

"A half hour isn't going to kill you. How about we make some coffee and you tell me what's going on."

"You're wrong." She took a step back as he descended the stairs.

"About what?"

"A half hour *could* kill me." She looked out the front door's paned window and when she faced him again, the fear was back. "The longer I stay, the faster they'll find me."

"Parker." Whatever she was going through, whatever she was dealing with, it was clear she needed help. "No one is going to hurt you as long as I'm around. I promise. Thirty minutes. Give me that much. If, when we're done talking, you still want to go, I won't stand in your way. Deal?"

The moments it took her to respond felt like an eternity.

"A half hour?" Her expression was beyond skeptical. "You mean it?"

He could see the wheels turning in her head, no doubt debating if she truly could trust him. "I never say anything I don't mean." To prove he trusted her, he set her keys on the table, turned his back, and headed into the kitchen to wait.

She'd been so close, *so close* to getting away. She could still go. Parker stared at her keys, at the suitcase at her feet. It would be easy to just walk out the door and … the fluttering of hope beat inside her chest. Was it possible … after all this time, all these years, had she finally found someone she could trust?

"Unless you want me searching your cabinets for coffee," he called, "you'd best join me."

Irritation had her scrunching her mouth. Just who did this guy think he was? Okay, so he looked like he should be screen-testing for Hollywood blockbusters with that midnight-black hair that had a bit of curl to it and equally dark, deeply endless eyes that made her want to dive in. And yeah, he had the irascible charm of The Rock—including a smile that had no business sneaking past her defenses—not to mention a well-toned body that made her wonder just how many days a week he spent in the gym. A body that, for the last week, had definitely conjured up fantasies she hadn't allowed herself in ....

She stomped hard on the mental brakes. Heading down that road was only going to complicate her already massively messed up life. Tripp Atsila couldn't matter. So what if he slid back into life in Woodville Springs as if he'd pulled on a comfortable sweater? He had no business creeping into her house under the guise of being sent by his brother.

Parker caught her lower lip in her teeth. Knowing Wade, he *had* sent Tripp. She'd inadvertently made herself indispensable and he'd taken over the unofficial role of big brother; probably because that had been his role in life since the day he was born. Her boss had told her, multiple times, that he hadn't felt secure enough in the business to take a chance on expansion until she'd come on board. He'd given her a shot, a newcomer to town, helped her find this house to rent, paid her significantly more than minimum wage and ... and he'd become a friend.

And friends didn't leave their friends in the lurch.

So maybe she did owe him thirty minutes. Even if by proxy.

She set her purse down again, made sure to put her keys inside the front pocket this time, and joined Tripp in the kitchen.

The laugh that bubbled out of her caught them both by surprise. She covered her mouth, shook her head. "I'm sorry. It's just ... you take up so much space in here you look like you're stuck in a doll's house."

"That's kind of how I feel." He took a seat at the round table. "This place is definitely cozy. The timer starts when you sit down."

So he was already playing semantics. Parker sighed. Good to know. She set a pot of coffee to brew—she loathed those tiny pod things—and grabbed a package of Oreos out of one of the cabinets.

"You were going to leave these behind?" Tripp helped himself to a handful, shaking his head. "Clearly you aren't perfect after all."

Who on earth would ever think she was perfect? Parker folded her hands on the white-washed table. "If you expect me to just spill everything—"

19

"Let's start with your name. Your real name," he added when she started to lie.

Countless knots tightened in her belly. He'd asked the one question that would, indeed, tell him everything he wanted to know. But he'd given his word he'd let her go after a half hour. She set the timer on her watch and prayed she wasn't making a mistake. "My real name is Portia." She hesitated, then took the final leap. "Portia Remington."

It was like watching a slot machine pay off. Answers to questions he probably hadn't thought to ask dropped into place. "Well, hell." Some of the friendliness he exuded flooded away, but only for a moment. He popped another cookie into his mouth, and when he swallowed, gave her an approving nod. "You look amazing for a dead woman."

Thanks." Parker's lips twitched. He just couldn't help it with the charm, could he? Her heart was slamming hard against her ribs. She mock toasted him with a cookie, even as she dreaded the idea of starting all over. Again. With a new name. In a new town. With new friends and … she sighed. For the first time in three years, she didn't want to leave. She liked it here. No, she *loved* living in Woodville Springs. This small town of instant friends had welcomed her without question and shown her just how perfect a trappings-free life could truly be.

"Your husband—"Tripp began.

"*Ex*-husband."That was one distinction she wanted on the record from the start. "I started divorce proceedings the day after he was arrested."The day she'd learned her entire married life had been a lie.

She'd worked hard to put all this behind her. It wasn't easy, being reminded of the mistakes she'd made. Of how she'd just turned a blind eye and hoped by ignoring the signs it would all just go away. But life didn't work that way. The truth always came out. And the collateral damage was always extensive.

"Look, let's just cut to it," she said with a sigh. "As I told your fellow federal agents, I didn't know Chad was laundering money for the mob and other … entities. I had no idea he'd been using our personal property, holdings, and finances to do so. I married him when I was twenty-one and dumber than a box of hair color. He was older, rich, charming, and going places—and I wanted out of a town so small it makes Woodville Springs look like New York City." Her life in one seriously cracked nutshell. "It took me being married to him for four years to grow up and figure out that I was the only one capable of making my life what I wanted. Chad did what he did on his own. I might have spent his money, but I didn't have a hand in how he made it. And before you ask, no"—she took a deep breath and made sure Tripp was paying attention—"I do not know what he did with it."

He was quiet for a moment, looked at her for a good long time; all the while her pulse was so loud in her ears she was certain he could hear it. Finally, she couldn't stand the tension. "Well?"

"Well what?"

"Are you going to tell me what you're thinking?"

"I think"—he sat back and took a deep breath, then reached for another cookie—"that this is going to take a lot longer than thirty minutes."

Portia freaking Remington.

Tripp was fairly certain if he listened closely enough, he could hear what was left of his career being flushed down the toilet.

It had been more than an hour since she'd told him her true identity. An identity he knew for a fact was still floating around the white-collar division of the FBI in the hopes she'd lead someone—anyone—to the twenty million dollars Chad Remington had stashed before his arrest, trial, and conviction.

Coffee wasn't going to cut it as a coping mechanism, but as he'd recently given up drinking, it was going to have to do. Having watched her earlier, he set another pot to brewing, leaned back against the tiled counter, and pushed forward.

"So this letter you got at work—"

"The letter you delivered."

"Right." The letter that was useless as evidence now that half the town had touched it. "This letter. What exactly did it say?"

"Give me a sec." She ducked out of the kitchen and went back to her suitcase, unzipped it a fraction and yanked out the letter, then returned to her cup of coffee, handing the offending piece of paper over to Tripp.

"Give us the money." Tripp's eyebrows shot up. "Straight and to the point, that's for sure. Any idea who sent it?"

"I have a couple hundred names in mind. And there are probably a hundred more I don't know about. What are you going to do?"

"Do?" He was still focused on the letter, turned the envelope over, made note of the postmark.

"In regard to the FBI. I'm sure with that oath you took, you're pretty much obligated to turn me in. Don't you Atsilas have a code of honor or something?"

"We do. And under normal circumstances ..." he shrugged. The idea he didn't feel particularly remorseful about a potential end to his career told him far more than he wanted to admit. "I'm currently on leave from my job, so I have some buffer time to make up my mind. You and the FBI didn't get along very well, I'm guessing."

"We were going gangbusters until they realized I didn't know anything more than they did. Once they figured out I wasn't going to be any help, their offer to relocate and protect me was rescinded. That's when I decided it would be best for me if I just vanished."

"You faked your death by blowing up your car." He had to admit ... the action had taken some serious bal ... 'er, courage.

"Your point?"

He shook his head, turned to refill his coffee, then sat across from her again. "I guess I don't have one. How long has it been since your hus ..." he stopped at her harsh look. "Sorry, ex-husband's trial?"

"Three years. He was sentenced three years ago last month." She spit out each word as if it were glass. "Thirty years in federal prison."

Yeah, he remembered now. Tripp considered his coffee. Remington had refused to cut a deal; hadn't ratted anyone out, hadn't turned state's evidence despite multiple offers. It hadn't made sense then. It made even less sense now. "And you haven't gotten anything like this letter before?"

She glanced away, but not before he caught the slight cringe. "Parker?"

Surprise jumped into her eyes, as if she'd expected him to call her Portia. He wouldn't. He couldn't. That wasn't the woman he'd met. He'd met Parker. He didn't know Portia. He was getting to know Parker.

"There have been a couple before. They just said the same thing. One showed up about two weeks after I ... well, went boom. It was another eighteen months before I got another one. That time they tracked me down in Vegas. Really thought I could disappear there. Feds found me first, though, before I ran again."

"What made you land on Woodville Springs?"

"I didn't plan to stay. I was driving through, heading north to Canada." She shrugged, glanced out the window into a backyard filled with fall color. "Your brother had a help wanted sign in the window. I was low on cash; thought I'd take a couple of weeks, get flush again before I moved on. Then ... I don't know."

"You realized you didn't want to leave." He couldn't help it. He reached across the table and rested his hand on hers.

"Yeah." She tensed, but didn't pull away. "But now it looks like my time is up. Again."

"It doesn't have to be."

"Good Lord." Now Parker did tug her hand free, and rolled her eyes as she sat back. "If the threatening letter wasn't enough motivation, the feds just found me."

"*A* fed found you. One who wasn't even assigned to the case. Let's set that aside for the moment." He couldn't very well tell her she was right. At some point he was going to have to come clean, no matter what he decided to do about his own career. But for now ... maybe there was something he could do to help. "You haven't heard from your ex, have you?"

"I stopped communicating with him the day he was arrested. Everything went through lawyers," she said. "Wait—that's not true. There was an Agent McNally who asked me to try to talk Chad into taking one of their deals. It was the only time I ever visited him in jail. He couldn't say no fast enough. He didn't seem to care he'd get less time if he turned state's evidence."

"Or given back the money he stole," Tripp added and earned a shrug of agreement from her. "I didn't work the case, but I remember the details. He didn't just steal from his partners. He ripped off ordinary people, Parker. Good, hardworking people who invested their life savings with his company."

"I am well aware." She closed her eyes as if shielding herself against the memory. "I sat through the trial and the sentencing. I listened to every bit of testimony. Heard all those families ..." her breath caught; she turned her head as if that could help block it all out. When she pulled herself together; she looked at him, an unfamiliar, hard edge in her eyes. "I'm not the ice queen the media portrayed me to be. I was horrified by what he did. Horrified and disgusted. I testified willingly. Before I—"

"Disappeared," Tripp slid in, noting the slight physical differences between the woman he remembered from the press coverage and the woman sitting across from him now. Portia Remington had been blonde. Very blonde. And draped in designer clothes that would have cost him a month's salary. Pampered, perfect, and pretentious.

She was right. The media hadn't been kind, tagging her as an unwitting accomplice who must have known what her husband was up to. Some suggested she was Chad's motivation for his unending greed and deception. That might have been true of Portia, but Parker?

This woman sitting across from him bore little resemblance to the one whose life had been spread all over the tabloids, social media, and minute-by-minute ticker-tape news, and not just because she'd changed her hair color. He didn't see a hint of anything other than a fresh face, off-the-rack jeans and T-shirts, and a threadbare life within this house. A life she seemed sad to have to leave.

"Before I started over," she repeated as if each word were glass under her foot, "I had my attorney sell off everything of mine that had any value. Anything of Chad's I could get my hands on. Every home with my name on it, the cars. Investments. All that money went to the families. I know it wasn't everything they lost ...."

"But it let you sleep at night," he finished.

"Yeah," The tight smile she offered said otherwise. "I did what I could, Tripp. I just wanted a clean start."

"Bet that's hard to do with twenty million dollars floating around out there somewhere along with the rumor you have it." Twenty million Tripp knew the feds—and others—were still heavily invested in finding. She was a good liar. She'd certainly had him convinced she was just a regular, everyday, beautiful woman making a living at his brothers' eatery. He narrowed his gaze, tried to read her expression. Was she lying now? About any of it?

"I already told you." Her eyes sharpened like twin blades. "I don't know where that money is."

"Someone thinks you do." He'd have to decide later if he believed her. After he had some time to think all this through. "What does Chad think?"

"Chad thinks he's still going to get out of prison one day." Parker offered a mock toast with her mug. "I have no doubt he knows where it is. But unless he suddenly grows a conscience, it'll stay missing. None of which helps me." Parker pulled back the foil wrapping on the cookies and frowned after confirming it was empty. "So are we good?" She got up, threw the trash away, then began scavenging through her cabinets. "Why on earth did I buy these?" She held up a thin box of plain water crackers. "Do they even have any purpose?"

"Crunch factor," he said automatically. "They're good with Brie. Or a nice Camembert."

Her eyebrows went up. "Camembert?" She leaned back as if searching for something. "Is there a hidden camera somewhere in here?"

"I like cheese. Sue me." He got to his feet, plucked the box out of her hand and, after setting it down, ran his hand down her arm until he slid his fingers through hers. "You're trying to change the subject."

Her eyebrow quirked as she looked first at their linked hands, then up at him. "Seems I'm not the only one. What're you thinking now, agent man?"

"I'm thinking I should stop thinking so much." Screw it. He'd wanted this from the moment he'd seen her behind the counter at his brother's deli. He'd thought about it. Dreamed about it. And he was tired of waiting for it.

He caught her mouth with his, welcoming that gasp of surprise that shot through him like a lightning bolt. She tasted hot, like summer and ozone, sizzling his senses to the point he was incapable of thought. He wanted more. So much more. He wanted everything.

She surprised him, not by pulling away, but by pressing herself forward, into him, around him as she stretched up and twined her arm up and around his neck. The pressure of her breasts against him, the feel of her thighs and hips pressing into him, tantalized.

When she lifted her mouth back by a scant inch, he stared into her golden-brown eyes and found a hint of humor behind dazed and delayed passion.

"Thinking is definitely overrated," she murmured against his lips.

"I do have one thought," he managed, struggling to recapture his thoughts as she seemed determined to finish what he'd started.

"You thinking about how many half hours it would take for us to work each other out of our systems?" she teased, nipping at his lower lip.

"You are not as immune as you said." He gently set her back, then cupped her cheek in his palm. "I'm thinking maybe it's time you stopped running."

CHAPTER THREE

"*T*ripp, is that you?"

For the second time that day, Tripp halted at the foot of a staircase. "Yes, Gran." The simple response had him flashing back to his teenage years when his grandmother—the woman who had raised the five Atsila siblings after their parents' death in a boating accident—waited up until all her chicks were safely home. Some things not even time could change.

"Come into the kitchen, please."

The caffeine hadn't done its expected job on his nerves. Exhaustion had crept over him on his walk home from Parker's house; exhaustion he hadn't felt in ... he couldn't remember how long. His plans for a shower and an attempt at sleep would have to wait. When Aurelia Atsila requested your presence, you obeyed. He headed down the hall, halted in the doorway, and offered his grandmother a tired smile. "Evening, Gran."

"Wade dropped off your lunch." She pointed to the fridge and gave him "the look" before returning her attention to the countless handwritten family recipe cards spread out and covering the kitchen table. The small pile by her left hand indicated some had made the cut for Thanksgiving dinner. "Course it's nearing dinner time, now. You apologize to Parker for whatever it was you said? Convince her to stay?"

Because she'd harp on him if he didn't, he retrieved Wade's no doubt reluctant meal delivery. Aurelia Atsila was eighty-four years old and still spry and active enough to pass a federal agent's training obstacle course. Well, maybe not the entire course, but she was sneaky enough to try. She'd worked as a midwife and women's health advocate for most of her life, embracing and encouraging not only traditional medicine but also homeopathic and untraditional treatments. She'd straddled the worlds of science and faith her entire life—the latter from their family's partial Native American ancestry—and raised her only son, and then her grandchildren, to embrace both equally. She had been a presence in all their lives from the moment they took their first breath, ruling and guiding with strength, compassion, and love in equal measure.

And none of them, not even tempestuous, determined middle daughter Lilith, escaped Aurelia's sight and attention.

"Well?" Aurelia looked up at him from lowered lashes.

"Well what?"

"Did you speak with Parker? Is she staying?"

"Yes and I don't know." But he had a strong suspicion he'd been … persuasive. He'd no idea arguing with a woman could be so satisfying. Not nearly as satisfying as kissing her had been, but it came in a close second. He'd managed to counter every argument Parker threw at him, every excuse and reason why leaving town made sense. But it all came down to one thing as far as he was concerned: she needed to make a stand and claim the life she wanted, otherwise she was living under someone else's rules. And that had been his parting comment when he'd left a little more than an hour ago. "She's got a lot to consider," he added when his grandmother gave no sign of moving on.

Aurelia made one of her harrumph sounds and shook her head, pointing to the chair across from her. "Sit. Eat. Talk."

Tripp sighed, surrendered, and unwrapped the sandwich. His grandmother rearranged a few cards to give him space at the table. "I guess Wade came with more than a sandwich. I can't believe he ratted me out." That was so twenty years ago.

"Payback for you being the family tattletale," Aurelia said with a smirk. "You and your law-and-order ways. Didn't surprise me one bit, not one little bit, when you signed on with law enforcement. Would have been nice if you'd stuck closer to home, though." She sniffed.

"At least your brothers didn't stray too far. Most days it's nice having them close."

He'd never break his grandmother's heart by admitting getting out of Woodville Springs was one of the reasons he'd found the FBI so appealing. Now, the idea of home sounded like the best thing in the world.

"I think you can complain about that with Lilith more than me." Always happy to throw his sister under the bus, he took a large bite out of his sandwich, then took an extra beat to admire it. His younger brother Hardy definitely had a way in the kitchen. He'd trained as a chef at the CIA in Napa, but discovered a real love of charcuterie. Making his own homemade salamis, curing his own meats had fit in perfectly with Wade's dream of owning his own eatery. Throw in Marshall, their accountant big brother, and a business had been born.

Bonus? Thick prosciutto, salami, and ham and cheese sandwiches landed on Tripp's palate just about every day he was home.

"You leave your sister out of this," Gran said. "She'll be home soon enough. I'm more worried about Parker sticking around. You know Wade doesn't think he can run that place without her."

"From what I hear, Hardy and Marshall agree." Tripp bit into his sandwich, right through the crusty layers of bread baked fresh every morning and into the pungent, spicy meats. "Parker has some thinking to do. I pled my best case with her to stay." He'd promised to help, do what he could to smooth things over with the FBI. Flushing out whoever had sent Parker that letter was the right place to start. Getting his hands on the case file was at the top of his list to do, as soon as he managed to get some sleep. But he had to be careful. It was no secret the FBI had a vested interest in Chad Remington, not to mention the missing money. But he also wouldn't put it past his coworkers to throw Parker to the wolves if it meant achieving their goal. He *definitely* had to be careful. "I'm fairly optimistic," he added at his grandmother's doubtful look.

"You always could convince anyone to do anything you had your mind set on," Gran said. "She tell you her secret?"

Swallowing carefully, he chose his next words with caution. "What secret?" He picked up a recipe for cranberry and orange glazed turkey.

"Girl's got secrets," Aurelia said. "I saw that the second she walked into the deli. I was there that day, you know. Picking up an order for my book club. That young woman came walking in the door like an answered prayer. Didn't really give your brother a chance to say no, just dived right in." She plucked the card out of his hand and slapped it down like an Ace of Spades. "But I could see it, plain as anything. She came with secrets. Dark ones."

He retrieved a bottle of water from the fridge. He knew where this conversation was headed, and he wasn't a fan. "Now, Gran—"

"Don't you 'Now Gran' me," Aurelia demanded. "You know as well as I do that what I see is there. You just don't like to admit it."

What was it with the women in his family and their kinship to this ridiculous notion? "Intuition isn't magic, Gran."

"You keep telling yourself that," Aurelia told him. "One day you'll see it's true. Ask Lilith when she's here with her young man. I bet they know a thing or two about magic."

"I'll be sure to do that." Sometimes humoring his grandmother was the only way to move a conversation along. "As I said, Parker has some things to figure out."

"Well, hopefully having you to help her will help her think faster. Reminds me, you make sure to invite her to Thanksgiving dinner. I keep forgetting to ask Wade to do that, but just as well. He has enough on his mind with Essie and that baby on the way. What do you think about this one for the turkey?"

She handed him a newer recipe card for garlic-butter roasted turkey. The second he saw the handwriting, his heart softened. "This is one of Mom's."

"Keeps jumping to the top of the stack," Aurelia said. "I'll take that as a sign. I sure miss that girl. Never thought I'd ever meet someone who could handle your father the way she could, the way I did when he was growing up, but from the second she stepped foot in this house, she was mine. Instant daughter." The tears in her voice, even after more than fifteen years, were as evident as ever. "I miss your father, too. Parents aren't meant to bury their children. Losing both of them was like two knives in my heart. But I had you kids to look after, didn't I? Didn't have time to grieve."

No, she didn't, Tripp thought. But she'd made sure they did. And not a day passed where they didn't share a memory of their parents. "Thanksgiving was their favorite holiday. Mom used to do what you're doing now, going through all the family recipes …" he trailed off, understanding hitting him when his grandmother lifted her head to meet his gaze. "This was Mom's tradition. Going through all these cards. Finding the perfect matches, the perfect … but I always thought she got that from you."

"Your mother taught me a lot of things, Tripp—many, many things—but she taught one thing above all: the most important thing is love. And that's what Thanksgiving is to me and this family. It's all about love." She reached over and patted his hand. "Now just make sure you invite that Parker girl to join us. Something tells me she's going to fit in quite well with our brood."

Parker jerked awake. Her heart pounded like a bass drum, heavy and loud in her ears. She'd heard something. She reached for her phone. One A.M. She lay there, still as stone, straining to hear. Just when she thought she'd imagined it and drifted off, there it was again.

Thud. Thump thump.

She shot up, grabbed her gun off the nightstand. Barefoot, she hurried to the door, cringing when the doorknob squeaked as she pulled it open. If this was Tripp again ….

Cool air rushed past her, cutting through the warmth of the room. She shivered, stepped onto the second-floor landing. She peered over the railing before heading to the stairs, took them carefully, gun poised, finger on the side of the trigger. "Whoever you are, I've already called the police!" she shouted into the night. "I've got a gun." She clicked on the light before rounding the banister.

The front door stood open. The filmy curtains draping the living room windows billowed in the breeze. She stopped herself before stepping onto the porch. She was safer in the house. In the distance, she heard a car door slam. An engine started. Tires screeched briefly before fading into the night.

She stood there, clutching the door in one hand as she willed her heart to stop pounding. "Damn it!" Shoving her hair out of her face, she closed the door and locked up. Then, because clearly the deadbolt hadn't been close to successful, she retrieved a chair from the kitchen and shoved it under the handle.

She did a quick check of the house. Nothing seemed disturbed. Of course, there wasn't much to disturb. Everything that was hers was up in her room. "Waiting for me to finish packing," she muttered. Waiting for her to run.

Tripp had made a lot of good points, she told herself yet again. He made sense. Practical, logical sense. "Of course he did. He's a freaking FBI agent." Thankful the little cottage didn't have a back door to worry about, she double checked all the windows, tested the chair once more, then stomped back upstairs. Before she'd fallen asleep, she'd reconvinced herself that leaving was the only safe answer. For everyone, not just herself.

She'd planned to leave first thing in the morning. The only difference being she'd planned to stop and talk to Wade on her way out of town. It was the least she owed him. Only now ....

Anger simmered, hot and prickly under her skin.

They'd broken into her house!

She'd assumed since the letter had been sent to the deli that they didn't know where she lived. Obviously, that was wrong. The creep—or creeps—knew exactly where she lived and didn't have any qualms about jimmying the lock in the dead of night. They had to have known she was home; had to know she was sleeping. What was the point? What were they looking for?

Did they honestly think she had twenty million in cash stashed under the floorboards or something? She got back into bed, curled her knees into her chest and clicked on the TV for a distraction.

Tripp was right. If she ran again, she'd only spend the rest of her life looking over her shoulder. She'd never have the life she'd convinced herself she'd found here in Woodville Springs. She needed to make a stand.

And Tripp Atsila might be the one person who could help her do that. If she could manage to stay out of his bed. Just thinking about those few moments with him in her kitchen was enough to make her itch. She'd never been kissed like that. As if he'd starve without feasting on her. And she'd feasted right back. Passion. Attraction. A healthy dose of antagonism. They all added up to the perfect storm of emotions she wasn't entirely sure she could weather.

Wasn't sure she wanted to weather. She'd just have to stay in control, she told herself. She could manage a few hot kisses here and there, when they weren't too busy trying to figure out who was stalking her. In the meantime ....

"Might as well get this over with." She snatched up her cell, started to call him, then reconsidered. She really wasn't up for an "I told you so." Instead, she texted. Short and sweet. Two words. Then, because she didn't trust herself not to change her mind, she turned off her phone and fought her way back to sleep.

Considering Parker's terse declaration of "I'm staying," which had blipped onto his phone shortly after one this morning, Tripp had opted for the quick and ridiculously inadequate thumbs-up emoji response. Strangely impersonal, considering it wouldn't have taken much for that kiss they'd shared in the kitchen to result in far more distracting activities in her bedroom.

Not, Tripp told himself late that afternoon as he made the two-hour drive back home from Sacramento, the appropriate *professional* response.

And he was still a professional.

Whatever relief he'd felt at her decision was quickly squashed by the suffocating pressure of responsibility. He'd convinced her to stay. Talked her into fighting for the life she wanted to keep in Woodville Springs. Made her believe he was up to helping her find a way out of this situation that wouldn't result in her either arrested or in a body bag.

Yeah. Tripp scrubbed a tired hand across the back of his neck. "Nothing to it." His passenger turned jet-black eyes on him, let out a whimper of understanding that had Tripp reaching over and scratching him between his ears. "Just a bit shaky on the self-confidence, boy," Tripp assured the dog. "I'll get it under control, don't worry."

The dog woofed as if to say he'd better, and Tripp turned his attention back out the window and the cascade of falling leaves. As exhausted as Tripp was, he also felt that rush of excitement that came with the opportunity to make a difference in someone's life. Only this time, *this time*, he told himself, he wouldn't be too late.

Which was why he'd made the trip to Sacramento before the sun was even up. He had an old friend in the bureau who had been peripherally involved with the Remington case; a friend he knew he could trust not to broadcast Tripp's interest and let him know if he was poking some kind of hornet's nest. After that, he'd made one more stop, resisted the urge not to fill up his SUV with additional canine companions, and headed back home.

Home. Tripp found himself enjoying the welcoming peace of Woodville Springs. It really did feel like home.

He'd timed his return to town perfectly, it seemed, because he pulled into Parker's driveway just as she rounded the corner. Okay, so he'd called Wade to find out when her shift was over and maybe he'd hoped to be quick enough to pick her up, but this would do. He saw her hesitate upon seeing the car, a cautious, almost fearful look exploding into her eyes. But then it was gone, replaced with what he could only assume was irritation.

Irritation that made him smile.

"Don't tell me you're stalking me now, too."

It wasn't the greeting he'd hoped for as he climbed out of the car. But he'd take it. "I've got a present for you."

"A what?" She skidded to a halt at the back of his SUV, quickly backed away as he moved closer. "I don't think—"

"Some things you don't need to think about. Trust me. You'll love it. And if you don't, well, I'll just have to keep him myself." He walked around her to the passenger side of his vehicle, reached in and clipped the lead to the dog's collar. "Come on, boy. *Couche.*" He made a clicking sound and the dog hopped out. "Parker, this is Crowley. Crowley, this is the woman I've been telling you about. *Assis.*"

Crowley sat at Tripp's feet and looked up at him, then at Parker. "Oh."

Tripp glanced at her in time to see tears fill her eyes. "He's beautiful. But ..." She shook her head. "I can't have a dog. I mean, I've never ... even though I've always wanted ..." She waved her hand, as if her emotions didn't matter. "Tripp, I can't keep him."

Crowley whined right on cue.

"Sure you can. Wade checked with your landlord. She's fine with it. And I'd feel better about you having him around when I can't be. Only … there is one thing about him …."

"What's that?" Her voice cracked as she focused her attention on the dog.

"He only understands commands in French."

"French?" That had her gaze widening. "How does that happen?"

"It was a security precaution. He used to be a police dog." Tripp bent down, scrubbed his hands into the dog's fur and earned a significant lick on the face. He held out the lead. "He was injured on the job about a year ago. They have to retire them after that and a friend of mine down in Sacramento takes them in and finds them new homes. I called in a favor. He's all yours. I-s-i to make him come to you."

"*Isi*? Parker echoed and laughed as Crowley came over immediately and stood at attention, tongue out, tail wagging until she crouched down to give him a good sniff. "How old is he?"

"Three. Young for a retiree. His partner was a woman and she couldn't keep him. I thought you'd be a good match."

"Guess we're going to have to go shopping for some dog supplies, huh?" She dropped her purse on the ground and sank onto the grass, arms full of dog. "Oh, you're a beauty, aren't you?"

"With no ego at all," Tripp said as the dog seemed to puff out his chest in approval. "I took the liberty of getting you started with some food and stuff. I also did some grocery shopping for dinner tonight."

"Oh? You're going to cook?" Parker's eyebrows shot up.

"Or we can cook together." He opened the back and started unloading bags. "Speaking of which, I've been instructed to invite you to the Atsila Thanksgiving dinner."

"You have? By whom?" She pushed to her feet, caught the lead in one hand and hefted one of the bags out and followed Tripp up her porch steps.

"My grandmother. Which means you can't say no because if you try, she'll just hunt us both down and haul us over on the day." It was a good way to bolster her into saying yes. His cell phone buzzed. He set his bags down as she dug out her keys to open the door. "And it's probably best you commit now because in about a half hour we're going to be neck deep in paperwork." Still looking at his phone, he stepped inside.

"We're going to be what? Oh, watch out for that—"

His foot caught and he went sprawling face first onto her hallway floor. Crowley barked once, then padded over to sniff and nudge and verify he was all right.

"I'm so sorry!" Parker crouched beside him, holding the dog off.

Tripp rolled onto his back. "Well, that wasn't humiliating at all." He shoved up on his elbows, searching for whatever piece of furniture had attacked him. "That chair wasn't there yesterday."

"Ah, no." She cringed, sat back on her heels. "I used it to prop the door closed last night." She gnawed on her lower lip. "After someone broke in."

Temper, he told himself, would not help. But it was a struggle to keep it in check as he sat up. "Someone broke in here last night and you're just telling me about it now?"

She shrugged. "Didn't really have the chance to before and they didn't take anything. They woke me up—"

"They?" He pushed to his feet.

"They as in general terms. I didn't see them. I only heard them. And before you ask, I didn't see what they drove away in. They searched the place, that much I know, but there wasn't anything to find."

"Except you. Damn it!" He noticed Crowley sit at attention and go to full alert at his curse. "You should have called me. Or called the sheriff."

"Why?" She looked genuinely baffled as she stood up next to him. "Whoever broke in was long gone. I wasn't hurt. And actually, I did call. I just did it through text."

"That's why you changed your mind." So it hadn't been his arguments that had convinced her to stay. Or that kiss. "You got scared into staying."

"Hell no," she snapped, looking offended. "I got angry. I'm tired of being scared. I'm tired of worrying if some mobster is going to pop up on my front porch like some criminal jack-in-the-box and demand I turn over something I don't have. You were right. Somewhat. I can't live any kind of life I want with this hanging over my head. So I decided to stay. Now,"—she picked up the spilled groceries—"what are you going to fix me for dinner?"

CHAPTER FOUR

It shouldn't have surprised Parker that Tripp Atsila could cook. He was, after all, an Atsila brother and his siblings had repeatedly proved they were more than capable in the kitchen. What did surprise her was how much he seemed to enjoy the process. Either that or he was just trying to put her at ease with him.

Parker glanced over from where he'd put her in charge of the salad, a smile playing across her lips as he chopped and stirred and murmured under his breath, as if talking to the sauce that simmered on her stove. There was something sexy about a man in the kitchen. Something even sexier about a man in *her* kitchen. Who knew it took the aroma of garlic, basil, and the hint of red pepper spice to kick her hormones into serious overdrive?

Crowley lay patiently on the floor, between two of the kitchen chairs, no doubt hoping one of them would drop something edible in his direction. Enjoying the homey atmosphere, Parker chunked up a carrot and dropped it the dog's new food bowl. "You're as comfortable as your brothers are at the stove."

"Yeah, well." Tripp grinned at her over his shoulder and set every cell in her body to tingling. "Our mother had us helping in the kitchen from a pretty early age. It was second nature when we had to move to Gran's, so we took over a lot of the kitchen duties. When she let us," he added with a chuckle. "She might have worked full time, but the kitchen was—and still is—her first love."

Parker's hand stilled mid tomato slice. "Wade mentioned you all lost your parents when you were teenagers. I'm sorry."

"Thanks." That grin shifted to a smile of sadness. "It was hard. Still is sometimes. But we always took some comfort in the fact they went together doing something they loved. It was a boating accident. They got caught in a storm. Just didn't make it back."

The pang of loneliness that had been her constant companion for three years struck hard and deep. Sometimes—most days—she missed her parents and sister so much she actually hurt. But it had been the deal she'd made—and she'd known, even as she'd walked away from the burning car that had "ended" her life; it had been the only way to keep them safe.

Parker set her knife down, approached the stove, pushed her face into the luxurious steam wafting up from the pot. "Need a taste tester?" She rested a hand on his arm as a distraction so she could reach for the wooden spoon. He smacked her hand away. "Hey! I'm starving. It's my kitchen!"

"Currently under my control. Behave." At her pout, he laughed, then took pity on her and tore off a chunk of bread from the loaf he'd bought, dipped it into the sauce and held it to her lips. "Have at it."

She kept her eyes on his as she leaned in and nipped the bread from his fingers. Even as the spicy sauce excited her tongue, she saw his pupils contract and most of the humor fade from his gaze. "That's delicious," she murmured after she'd managed to swallow. "Your mom and grandmother would be proud. Although I'm betting they'd be disappointed you opted for dried pasta."

He reached out, brushed his thumb across her lips before he leaned down and pressed his mouth to hers. She jolted, not out of surprise, but at the bolt of attraction that speared through her. The kiss was brief, and held only a promise of the heat from their previous encounter, but it would tide her over until she could think through the possible ramifications of taking him to her bed.

"I save my homemade pasta for the second date," he murmured against her mouth, before he grinned and returned to his chopping.

Enjoying his teasing, she fell in step. "So that makes this our first date then? What would your brothers say?"

"Considering my brothers like you better than they do me, they'd say I have excellent taste." He seemed to hesitate. "Not to put a damper on the evening, but I do have some questions for you."

Just like that, her bubble of contentment burst. She should have known. Once an agent, always an agent. "I've told you everything I know."

"Maybe. But it could be you don't know what you know. You know?"

She snorted, surprisingly amused. "How about a quid pro quo." She wasn't about to pass up a chance to find out more about this man. "Question for question. And I get to go first because we've already delved into my situation."

"All right." He didn't sound particularly thrilled at the prospect and seemed to have taken an extra interest in the package of imported pasta.

"What division are you with in the FBI?" Guessing by the way his face relaxed, she assumed she'd surprised him.

"ICAC. For a little over ten years."

With that answer, suddenly a lot more about Tripp Atsila made sense. "Ten years working on child abuse cases?" Was that awe or worry she heard in her own voice. "Jesus, Tripp." She shook her head. "That's …"

"Yeah," he said when she couldn't find the words. "It is indeed. I've exceeded the burnout rate. Most agents make it two, maybe three years. Others, like my partner, made it almost twenty-five before the end. There's rarely anyone in the middle."

Something about the way he said "the end" had Parker taking a detour from her next question. "Please tell me it's at least sometimes rewarding." She didn't know how. From what little she knew about the role the internet played in child abuse, especially child sexual abuse and trafficking, she couldn't imagine there were many bright spots.

"It has its days." Tension had worked its way into his spine, his shoulders. His chopping motion stiffened, the knife striking the cutting board with more ferocity. "Most days it feels like trying to drain the ocean with an eyedropper."

"Tripp—"

"My turn. What other agents did you speak with during your ex-husband's case?"

She might have experienced whiplash if she hadn't been expecting the change of subject. "McNally was the main one. I think there were a few others. None that made any lasting impression. I kept notes on my laptop."

"Notes?" He stopped chopping and looked at her. "You kept notes?"

She blinked, all innocence. "My entire life blew up. Of course I took notes. Most of them are transcriptions from the meetings I recorded with McNally."

"But ..." Now it was his turn to blink. "That's illegal."

"Is it?" She pressed a hand against her heart. "Please." She rolled her eyes. "The FBI had every wire in and out of my house tapped. Besides, I wasn't sure who I could trust or what or who might turn around and bite me. And before you blow a gasket in that whirling brain of yours"—she tapped a finger against his temple—"you're welcome to read whatever you want."

"Oh. Well. All right then." He caught Crowley's eye as the dog wedged himself between them and let out a rather pathetic whine. "What's up, boy?"

"I think it's time for his real dinner." Parker backed away and selected a can from the bag Tripp had brought along with her new companion. "I'm betting that carrot didn't cut it. One quick question?"

"All right."

"I know you aren't married—"

"My brothers have big mouths."

She shook her head, digging out her rarely used can opener. Seemed those days were over now that she owned a dog. "I didn't need your brothers to tell me. You strike me as the kind of man who would wear a ring. But since you don't ... you aren't involved with anyone, are you? Girlfriend? Live in?"

"No."

"Good."

"Good?" His smile returned, almost reaching his beautiful dark eyes again.

"Definitely good." She scraped the dog food into a bowl, headed toward Crowley's designated eating spot, but stopped long enough to stretch up on her toes and give Tripp a quick kiss. "I don't sleep with men who are already spoken for. Come on, boy." She made a clicking sound and delivered Crowley his dinner.

It seemed, Tripp thought as he read through the documents and meticulous notes on Parker's laptop, he and Parker could very well be destined to continually surprise one another. Something he could live with, he supposed. He'd lived with a hell of a lot worse.

"Dishes are all done." Parker set a bowl of chocolate ice cream next to the laptop on the coffee table, then curled up beside him on the sofa. Crowley followed at her heels, then circled his bed near the fireplace and hunkered down. "Thanks again for dinner. That was fabulous."

He flicked a grin. "It felt good to cook again. I don't do a lot of it when I'm working."

"Speaking of working …." She licked her spoon in a way that had his brain fogging. "Why aren't you working now? You've been in Woodville Springs for almost two weeks. Rack up a lot of vacation time?"

"I do have quite a bit saved up." Because the question had been inevitable, he leaned back. This woman had not, as far as he'd been able to confirm so far, lied to him. He owed her the same courtesy. "I was encouraged to take some time off. To … reevaluate my career plans," he said, repeating the words the department's therapist had thrown at him. "The last year…." He struggled to put it all into a concise explanation. One that wouldn't dredge up the darkness again.

As if from a distance, he heard the gentle clunk of Parker setting her bowl down. "It's been a bad year," he began. "We had a case go bad. About as bad as it can get. We were following the lead on two young girls who had gone missing in Nevada. Circumstances were similar to some other cases around the country. Tracked them to this small border town, but local law enforcement leaked like a sieve. My partner and I were … too late." He nearly choked trying to swallow the rage and regret. "Human traffickers killed twelve girls, ages six to fifteen. One was still alive. Barely." He could feel the shakes starting as the memories came hard and fast. "She died in my partner's arms a few minutes after we found them. Three months later, he ate his gun."

41

Parker scooted closer, almost tucked into him as she drew her hand gently through his hair. "I'm so sorry."

He lifted an arm and wrapped it around her, drew her close until he could tuck her head under his chin. What was it about this woman that brought him such comfort? "I miss him every day. And I ask myself every day how I could have missed the signs." He squeezed his eyes shut, inhaled the scent of strawberries and spring from her hair. "I knew it was a hard case for both of us. He'd gotten close to the parents, had promised to do everything he could—"

"Because that's who he was," Parker whispered. "Men like him, like you, you have to believe you can succeed. That you can hold back the evil. And when you can't, you think you've failed." She lifted her head, then reached up to stroke the side of his face. "Is that what happened yesterday morning at the diner? When you were shaking? Did this all come back?"

"Yeah." He shook his head as if he could dislodge the thought. "It comes out of nowhere sometimes. Not sleeping probably doesn't help." He caught her hand, brought it to his lips. "I haven't slept in what feels like months."

Parker shifted and for a moment, he thought she was pulling away; that he'd said too much, revealed too much. She shifted and slipped onto his lap, straddling his hips, her arms twining around his neck as she brought her face, her mouth, close to his. "Maybe you just haven't had the right inducement," she murmured against his lips.

His hands trailed down her sides, cupped her hips as she kissed him. Slow. Deep. Soul searching. Heart healing. When she removed her mouth from his and trailed her lips down the side of his neck, he bit back a groan. "Parker."

"Yes?" He could hear the laughter in her voice.

"Isn't this ... too fast?"

"Maybe." She rose over him, lowered herself again, and as he sat up, her full breasts brushed against his chest. "I'm not really up to thinking about it too much. Come on." She slid off him, slipped her fingers through his and pulled him up and off the couch. "Crowley, you stay here."

42

The dog let out a canine sigh of contentment—much, Tripp thought, like he did as Parker drew him upstairs and into her bedroom.

"Tripp?" Parker murmured much later before she rolled away from him. "Your pants are buzzing."

"Tell me about it." He shifted, the mattress dipping as she struggled to hold onto sleep.

She'd never experienced such ... completion before in bed with a man. She'd never felt so wholly fulfilled, heck, even worshipped. Agent Tripp Atsila had some serious moves.

"Sorry," he murmured.

She pried open one eye. Only ten o'clock. She smothered a grin in her pillow. He'd worn her out. Considering the sleepy tone of his voice, she'd returned the favor.

"Yeah, it's Atsila," he said a few seconds later. His arm snaked out and under her, drawing her back against him. She didn't even try to fight it. Being near him, being *with* him, it just felt right. She'd known it from the second he'd almost toppled the coffee mugs at the deli the other morning. It was why she'd stopped at the drugstore on the way home for condoms. Just in case he didn't anticipate what she had. "Hey, Eamon. What's up?"

Eamon? Parker frowned. Odd name. She heard the other man's voice, but couldn't hear precisely what he was saying. But whatever it was definitely got Tripp's attention. He pulled away from her and swung his legs over the edge of the bed, leaving Parker feeling oddly cold. "You're sure about this? Yeah, no. We should definitely talk in person. I don't want to ...." He trailed off, pushed to his feet, and walked over to the window.

"What is it?" Parker demanded, dragging the sheet up and around herself. "What's wrong?"

"Nothing's wrong," Tripp assured her, before talking into the phone again. "Just ... give us a few minutes to—"

The doorbell rang.

Parker's mouth dropped open.

"Yeah, hang on, Eamon." Tripp disconnected, came over to the bed and leaned over, kissing her quick and deep. "My insomnia cure will have to be delayed. We've got company."

"*You've* got company, you mean," she grumbled, shoved her hair out of her face.

"I mean we. Eamon's from the San Francisco office. I met with him in Sacramento yesterday, asked him to look into some things on your ex-husband's case. And yours."

"Mine?" Parker stopped, T-shirt barely over her head. "But—"

"Yeah. That's a big but," Tripp said and ignored her glare as he dragged his jeans and shirt back on. "That's why he's here. He think he knows who's tracked you down. Come on. I'll get the coffee started."

CHAPTER FIVE

"**T**hanks for this." Eamon lifted his mug and leaned back against the kitchen counter. "I ran out an hour into my drive."

Parker glanced uneasily at Tripp. When he met her gaze, she could see his thoughts were running parallel to hers. Eamon must have found something pretty significant to make a late-night drive to Woodville Springs.

"We've got leftover pasta from dinner if you're hungry," Parker offered, wondering when she'd become an FBI pit stop. If someone had told her a month—heck, even a week ago—she'd have not one, but two FBI agents standing in her kitchen in the dead of night, she'd have wondered what they'd been smoking.

Still, she couldn't remember a better view. Two incredibly good-looking FBI agents from opposite ends of the physicality spectrum. Both Tripp and Eamon were exceptionally well built. Tall, filled out, and solid. But where Tripp had his stunning dark hair and equally dark eyes, Eamon had red hair, bright-green eyes, and a haunted look behind the spark that had her wondering what ghosts haunted the thirty-something man.

"I'm good, thanks." Eamon held up his hand. "Who's this?" He held out his hand to Crowley, who had wandered into the kitchen as if on patrol. He gave Eamon a good sniff, then sat back on his haunches, shooting an approving look in Tripp's direction.

"Crowley."

"Tripp thought I could use some added security," Parker added.

"Crowley, huh?" Eamon grinned. "Someone a *Supernatural* fan?"

"Who isn't?" Parker chimed in and earned an approving look from both men. "So …"

"Yeah, so." Eamon nodded and motioned for them to take a seat. "Before I get into what it seems I kicked into yesterday, I have a couple of questions for you, Parker."

Parker. Like Tripp, he'd called her Parker, not Portia. Some of the nervous knots in her stomach loosened. "All right."

"Can you tell me the last time you spoke with Agent McNally?"

"Oh." Not what she'd been expecting. "Sure. It was—"

"June seventeenth, last year," Tripp answered for her.

Parker shrugged. "Sounds right."

"I read through the notes she's kept on her laptop," Tripp explained when Eamon glanced at him.

"Yeah, he tracked me down in Vegas, shortly after I received a creepy note."

"How soon after you got the note?" Eamon asked.

"A day. Maybe two?" Alarm bells clanged in her head. "Why?"

"How did you leave things with him?"

"Quickly," Parker said. "He didn't seem particularly interested in helping, just kept asking me where the money was. He told me that the only way these people were going to leave me alone was if they got the money Chad stole from them. Didn't matter how many times I told him I didn't know where it was, he just kept pushing. The whole interaction didn't sit well with me, so I packed up my car and left. I haven't been in touch since."

"You want to tell us what we've stepped in?" Tripp asked.

Eamon took a long drink of his coffee. "Agent Ned McNally's been off FBI radar since last summer." He actually winced. "They can't find him."

Parker frowned. What did that mean?

Tripp swore. "Is OPR involved?"

"I don't like alphabet soup," Parker said, feeling completely out of the loop. "What's OPR?"

"Office of Professional Responsibility," Tripp explained. "It's like Internal Affairs for feds."

"And they were most definitely involved," Eamon added. "He was under a sixty-day suspension when he went underground."

"I am not liking where this is headed," Tripp said.

"Neither was my contact at OPR," Eamon said. "They've purposely tried to keep this under wraps because his being dirty jeopardizes a crap-ton of cases that are still active. Multijurisdictional cases. But here's the kicker. One of the last places McNally went before he went dark? He visited Remington in prison." He shifted his gaze to Parker. "June nineteenth."

"That can't be a coincidence," Parker said.

"I got a rundown on the case against McNally," Eamon said. "Just the bare basics, but suffice it to say there's no doubt he's working with your ex-husband, Parker."

"Remington bought him off, you mean," Tripp suggested.

"It wouldn't surprise me," Parker admitted. "Chad's talent was always identifying someone's desires and finding a way to hook them in." She knew from explicit experience. "I'm guessing with McNally it was money?"

"What makes you say—"

"I spent a lot of time with him and his partner during Chad's trial." To keep herself busy, she retrieved a new package of Oreos she'd seen Tripp stash in the cabinet earlier. "If he wasn't complaining about his mortgage, it was alimony. He was also obsessed with reading the racing sheets."

Eamon nodded in agreement. "She's absolutely right. The gambling had already put McNally on OPR's radar. He also got caught lying under oath, which is usually automatic grounds for termination but ..."

"But they wanted to see who was pulling his strings before cutting him loose," Tripp finished.

"They had to do something, which was when the suspension came down, but since then? Poof."

"I bet I know where he was last night," Parker sat back down and pried open a cookie. "Creeping around my house looking for something I don't have." Anger bubbled in her veins. "What is it going to take to convince anyone I don't have the money?" When Tripp remained silent, she glanced between him and Eamon. "What?"

"What if you do?" Eamon said before Tripp could respond. "I'm not saying you know you have it, but what if before Remington began to serve his sentence, somehow he put the money in your name or stashed it somewhere only you have access."

The back of Parker's neck prickled. "That would explain McNally's push for me to tell him where it was. If Chad told him I have it."

"Why would he do that if you didn't?"

"Because Chad didn't take kindly to me divorcing him. He saw it as a betrayal." It was a conversation she really didn't want to relive. "It was one reason I wanted him to believe I was dead. But if McNally was working for him, clearly, that never happened." Tears of rage burned the back of her throat. "I've lost the last three years of my life for nothing! I let my family, my parents and sister believe I was dead and all this time ...."

"All this time they were safe." Tripp reached over and took hold of her hand. "As long as you stayed dead, they weren't a threat to either Remington or McNally. Neither were you."

"You were also dead as far as the FBI was concerned," Eamon told them. "I read the report McNally filed. He said the plan to fake your death went wrong and that you were killed when your car exploded. So as far as we were concerned, you were out of the picture."

Panic blossomed anew inside of her. "What about now?"

"Now?" Eamon asked.

"What do they know now?"

"Parker—" Tripp squeezed her hand again, but she snatched it away.

"You had to tell them I was alive, didn't you?"

"Yes." She didn't see a hint of apology in Eamon's green-eyed gaze. "You're a material witness now, Parker. They can make a case against McNally with your help."

She snorted. "They had a corrupt agent handling my case and my safety. They haven't exactly earned my trust." As excited as she'd been to finally put all this behind her, she now knew that was never going to be possible. As long as she had any connection to Chad, to McNally, to the FBI ... to Tripp ... she was never going to be free.

"Have I?" Tripp asked.

She held the answer behind pressed lips and saw the light dim in his eyes. Whatever had been building between them began to crumble. As much as it hurt, as much as she wanted to keep him in her life, it wasn't possible. Putting aside the complications it created in her own life, what would it do to his career? Getting involved with a woman who spent the last three years lying to everyone she met, a woman who had been married to a convicted criminal, who had stood by while hundreds of people were robbed of everything they owned ... she wasn't worth it. Crowley let out a low whine and walked around the table to push his head under her arm. "Corrupt or not," she said after she cleared her throat. "I worked with you all long enough to know that you always have a plan. So what is it? No, wait. Let me guess." She reached down and sank her hand into Crowley's fur. "I'm about to be used as bait."

"He won't come back as long as you're here."

Tripp could have been completely deaf and still picked up on the irritation vibrating in Parker's voice. With Eamon on the phone in the kitchen, he and Parker had retreated to the living room where he scanned through pages of information Eamon had on his tablet and Parker paced. Crowley paced alongside, pivoting and moving in time with his new mistress.

"Then he won't come back," Tripp told her. "I'm not leaving you alone. I wouldn't have before; I'm certainly not going to now." The sun was beginning to peek up over the horizon, bathing Woodville Springs in its usual morning glory blaze. "You want me to call Wade or do you want to?"

"Call Wade for what?" She stopped moving, but she still had her thumb in her mouth from where she'd been gnawing on her nail.

"To tell him you won't be coming into work."

Something flashed in her eyes. Something Tripp couldn't quite put his finger on. He was really off his game these days. Maybe going back to work wasn't in the cards after all. If he couldn't even read the woman he was falling for ....

Falling for. His gaze skittered back to the screen, his mind a sudden jumble as he realized that was exactly what was happening. He

49

couldn't remember ever wanting or even thinking about sharing his life with someone, and yet … he took a deep breath. And yet from the moment he'd met Parker, that's all he'd been thinking about.

"Work. Right. I need to go to work," Parker said, glancing at her watch. "I need to get my mind off all this for a while at least."

"Then I'll come hang out while you're on shift."

"No." The denial came quick. Too quick.

Tripp frowned. "I'm not letting you go anywhere alone until McNally's in custody."

"I won't be alone at the deli," Parker argued. "The place is packed every minute of every hour. And if you take up a table all day, you're just going to tick your brothers off. I'll be fine."

"Then I'll drive you there and pick you up."

"Tripp, don't smother me. Just because we slept together—"

"Whoops. Sorry." Eamon came to a quick halt and pivoted. "Bad timing."

"You're fine," Parker said. "We're all adults here. Sex happens. What's going on?"

Eamon shot Tripp a look of apology before he responded. "I spoke with my superiors. They're sending a team of agents up here to talk to you and get an official statement about your interactions with McNally."

"All right." She rocked forward on her heels. "When?"

"Tomorrow. First thing."

"Perfect. Okay then." She smacked her hands together and earned an ear perk up from Crowley. "I'm going to go get ready for work. You two can do … whatever it is agents do while we're waiting for my life to completely blow up. Again."

Her smile was tight and didn't come close to reaching her eyes before she grabbed her laptop and headed upstairs, Crowley right at her heels.

"Sorry to interrupt."

Tripp waved off Eamon's concern. "Don't be. This thing between me and Parker, it's … new." Even as he said it, he knew it was more than that. So much more. "Still figuring things out."

"I like her." Eamon took a seat in the chair on the other side of the coffee table. "Not that what I think matters."

"It matters," Tripp said, surprised to find he believed it. "I appreciate you coming all the way up to help us deal with this. It feels good to be helping someone again." To not be too late this time.

"I was sorry to hear about Valdez. Losing a partner's never easy."

"No," Tripp said, biting back the grief, grief he knew Eamon understood. Not that his fellow agent had lost a partner. But he had lost a sister when they were kids. And waited over twenty years to find her killer. "No, it isn't. It's made me rethink my priorities, though."

"Understandable. Does she know?"

"Parker?" Tripp shrugged. "We haven't talked about it really. Like I said, this is all …"

"New," Eamon finished for him. "Want some advice from someone with no experience with a long-term relationship?"

"Why not?" Tripp sat back.

"Grab happiness where you find it. Even if it ends up not going the full distance, life's too short, Tripp. Spend as much of it as you can with someone you care about. That one up there?" Eamon pointed to the ceiling. "She gets this. She gets you. I can see it on her face. Don't walk away from that unless you don't have another choice." He held up his hands. "End of lecture. I'm going to head out. I saw a motel just outside town. I'm going to try to catch some sleep."

"No motel," Tripp said, reaching into his back pocket and pulling out his house key. "I've already called my grandmother. She has a guest room waiting for you." He rattled off the address. "She'll probably feed you first. It's what she does. But it'll be quieter and cheaper than a motel."

"Thanks." Eamon nodded in approval, taking his tablet as well. "That's great of both of you. I'll leave my cell on in case you need to get a hold of me."

"Sounds like a plan."

Parker continued her pacing in her bedroom, all the while trying to ignore the tangled, rumpled, memory-triggering sheets covering her bed. How could she be feeling so conflicted about this? She knew what she had to do. If McNally was watching her, he wasn't going to come anywhere near her with Tripp hanging around.

51

Crowley sneezed, then settled back down on the floor at the foot of her bed. McNally wasn't going to get near her with her new canine companion around, either.

She grabbed her phone and her purse, dumped out its contents and began rearranging, trying to figure out the best way to stash the cell so it could clearly record any conversation she might have. Getting him on audio recording would be a start. She pushed down the inserted pockets, ran her hands around the seams, looking for any way to keep the phone closer to the top. Her hand ran over a bump on the bottom, right near the small brass foot.

She flipped the empty bag over, her hands explored the soft leather, feeling the bump again. Strange. The purse was at least ten years old. Her mother had bought it as a gift for her high school graduation after Parker had been drooling over it online. It was designer, oversized, and at the time impractical, but its sheer capacity had been a lifesaver more times than she could count. Suitcases and clothes could be replaced, but her purse?

She pulled up the lining, looking for the strange … ah! There it was. She pressed her fingers around the small, solid rectangular object. Peering closer, she saw that the stitching had been redone. It was more jagged than the rest of the bag.

Parker grabbed the pair of manicure scissors she kept in her make-up bag and ripped open the seam. Out slipped a USB thumb drive. Her heart pounded heavy against her ribs. It was as if her body realized what was going on before her brain caught up. She pulled open her laptop, stuck the drive in and waited for the info to be recognized.

The window that popped up on her screen had her hands shaking. She clicked on the first folder, scanned the contents. Then the second, and the third. She'd never read so fast in her life and even as she did, she felt her life, once again, tilt off its axis. "Son of a bitch," she whispered, catching Crowley's attention. "That son of a bitch."

She heard footsteps coming up the stairs. Quickly, she closed the file, dropped the drive back into her purse, along with the rest of her items and darted into the bathroom. She'd just turned on the shower when she felt Tripp's presence behind her. "Hey." She scrubbed her damp palms down her jeans, forced a smile onto her face. "Sorry about being snippy down there."

"You're entitled." He moved toward her, caught her shoulders in his hands. "What's wrong?"

"Nothing." She didn't even convince herself, so she tried again. "Nothing other than finding out there's an ex-FBI agent out there stalking me. So you know, the usual." She managed a laugh. "I've got some time to kill before I have to be at work." The lie almost stuck in her throat. Almost. "You want to have pancakes for breakfast?" The very idea of food right now was enough to make her choke.

"Not really, no." He moved in, pulled her close. "Want to save some water?"

She reached up to his face, memorizing every feature, every bit of him to take with her. "I'm all for conservation," she whispered and lifted her mouth to his.

CHAPTER SIX

"*I* told you I didn't need a ride," Parker groaned later that morning when Tripp pulled his SUV into one of the spaces in front of the deli. "You know what's going to happen, right? One of your brothers is going to see us together and—"

"Morning, Tripp! Morning, Parker!" Wade pushed out of the deli and gave them both an almost absent wave, his cell phone up to one ear as he headed across the street to the new location.

Parker banged her head back against the passenger seat. "See?"

"My brothers know I have sex, Parker." He reached out a hand and brushed hers. "We've been competing in that area for most of our lives. Why the change? You weren't embarrassed with Eamon."

"Eamon isn't my boss," she said. "What's going to happen if this thing between you and me goes sideways? Wade'll feel as if he has to take sides."

"And he will," Tripp said matter-of-factly. "He'll choose you."

She snorted.

"He will. Because he'd be lost without you, Parker. You already said he didn't have any issues with who you really are. Why would he about this?"

"I don't know." Guilt pushed in on her again. She was back to where she'd been the other day—forced to leave a life she'd built for herself because she couldn't bear the thought of bringing the people she cared about down. Word was going to get out—if it hadn't already—of who she really was. She didn't want any of the Atsilas tainted by association. And she didn't want Tripp's career ruined by a past she could never change. "This is all just … weird."

"If dropping you off at work is weird, just imagine how it'll be when I pick you up." He laughed at her expression. "You're off at two, right?"

"Yeah," she choked out and nodded. "Two. You'll be okay with Crowley?" She turned in her seat and reached back to pet the dog.

"We'll be fine. We're going to go get some exercise just as soon as I check in with the sheriff and let her know the FBI's coming to town officially tomorrow."

And there it was. The final blow to any hope she had of staying. "Sounds like a plan." Because she couldn't resist the impulse, and because she needed to, she leaned across and kissed him. Kissed him like he'd kissed her that first time. Implanting what she hoped would be a powerful enough memory to get her through the rest of her life. "Goodbye, Tripp."

"See you at two."

"Yeah." She climbed out of the car and offered him one last smile. "See you then."

He'd gotten roped into Thanksgiving duty after all. The text message from his grandmother—one that included an implied dressing down for not having checked in with her last night—had him hitting three different stores for orders she'd placed on the phone. She was in precooking and décor mode, which meant he'd loaded up his SUV with variously sized and colored pumpkins, two bushels of ears of corn from a local supplier, and half a dozen bottles of wine that had him wincing at the dent the stop at the liquor store had left on his credit card.

Crowley had been content to stay in the car—window down, of course—casting a supervisory, if not suspicious, gaze across Woodville Springs.

Spending most of his morning and early afternoon on the streets of his hometown had also given him the opportunity to check with various managers and business owners if they'd seen anyone matching McNally's description. He'd couched his curiosity by saying he was expecting a fellow agent to come up for one of Woodville's special-recipe pumpkin-spice pies, but so far, he'd turned up nothing. Which left only the local sheriff's station on his mental checklist.

"One more stop, boy. Then we'll drop all this off at Gran's."

Crowley watched Tripp slide back into the car and heaved out a sigh.

"Maybe you'll come with me this time." Tripp rubbed the top of the dog's head. "I bet the sheriff would love to meet you."

Woof. Translation, Tripp decided: of course she would.

The sheriff's station, an old clapboard-sided building just off the main thoroughfare, was exactly as he remembered it, only with an updated cruiser SUV parked outside instead of the 1990s sedan reminiscent of his childhood. He parked, came around to let Crowley hop down, and headed inside.

The welcoming—and remodeled—atmosphere brought a surprised smile to his face. The warm, polished wood, modern desks, and even more modern computers on the trio of desks on the other side of the chest-high counter brought the Woodville Springs Police Department right into modern times.

"It's about time you swung by here to say hello." Sheriff Stephanie Capaldi pushed up out of her office chair and all but waddled over to him, one hand pressed into her back, the other guiding the very pregnant belly Tripp had no trouble believing needed help. "Finally, the last Atsila brother comes home." She lifted the pass-through and beelined toward him for a hug.

"Sheriff Capaldi," he said jokingly after she patted his back. "You're looking—"

"Finishing that sentence with any word other than 'fabulous' will earn you three days in lockup." She beamed, her copper-streaked brown hair tied back from her face. "Boy, it's good to see you. It's been too long. And hello to you." She stretched out her hand and almost bent backwards to let Crowley get a good sniff.

Steph had been one of his best friends in high school. Her father and grandfather had both been sheriff and, after having trained and served in the SFPD for a few years, she'd come home and assumed the role after her father retired.

"Slow business today?" Tripp followed her to her desk so she could sit back down.

"Thankfully. You here about the FBI visit tomorrow?"

Tripp cringed as he sat. "Sorry. Meant to get here sooner to tell you in person."

She waved off his concern. "No worries. No skin off mine if you guys want to come take charge of this renegade agent of yours. Buddy over there's at your disposal. Buddy, you remember Tripp Atsila? He's a big shot with the FBI these days."

Tripp shifted around to look at the younger man. The face was familiar. But the name ....

"Donny Buddington." The deputy walked over to shake his hand. "That's where the Buddy comes from."

"Right." Tripp remembered now. The kid had been a few years behind him in school. "Good to see you again. You two it for the department?"

"Yep. Haven't been able to fill the open spots, even though we need to." Steph pointed at her stomach. "Little one's due to break out in a couple of weeks, so we're just biding our time. Why? You looking to relocate? We could use you around here. Granted we aren't the fancy shmantzy FBI, but we do get our fair share of speeders and drunk and disorderlies."

He laughed, shook his head.

"Too bad. Any updates on this McNally guy of yours?"

"Doesn't seem to have made an appearance in town. No one's seen him, or at least remembers seeing him. This time of year it might be tough. Lots of new faces in and out for the holidays." He was probably laying low in one of those motels Eamon was going to bunk down in.

"True enough," Steph mused. "Still ... we could circulate a picture to our businesses. I don't want them engaging with this guy in any way if he's dangerous."

"He's not dangerous," Tripp said, "to anyone other than Parker Rutledge."

"You mean Portia Remington, don't you?" Steph's perfectly arched brow went up another inch. "Sorry. That's info that's already out."

Tripp sighed. "Figured as much. How bad is it?" He knew just how hostile small towns could get when rumors started swirling, even in a friendly place like Woodville Springs.

Steph shrugged. "It'll be news for a while, but people here don't know Portia. They know Parker. More importantly, they like Parker, so I wouldn't give it too much worry. It'll settle and be forgotten soon enough. How's the FBI treating you?"

He could tell, by that barely restrained glimmer of sympathy in her eyes, that she'd been brought up to speed. "Probably better than it should. Your dad enjoying retirement?"

"He's bored out of his gourd," Steph grinned. "And loving every minute of it. He's looking forward to being a grandpa."

Tripp's gaze dropped to Steph's very ringless hand. Not that that meant much these days. "You going solo on the mom thing?"

"Yep." Steph leaned back in an obvious attempt to get comfortable. "You remember Slade Decker from high school?"

"He's hard to forget." He'd racked up a reputation as a serious bad boy, especially when it came to drag racing on the mountain roads. Last Tripp had heard their former class president had been making inroads in Hollywood as a stuntman.

"He was here last winter, helping his mom after his dad died. Let's just say we redefined the term drive-by." Her smile was tight. "Whatever. I got the better end of the deal."

"You're going to be a great mom," Tripp said. Had Parker ever thought about kids? Did she want them? And whoa, where had that thought come from?

"You look like a goose just ran over your grave." Steph gave him an odd look. "Anything else we need to know about McNally?"

Tripp shook his head. "He'll pop out of whatever hidey hole he's in soon enough. Especially if we dangle Parker in front of him. Speaking of Parker, I should be heading over to the diner to pick her up."

"That woman is dedicated to her job," Buddy said, heading back to his desk. "You never catch me in here on my day off."

Tripp's blood ran cold. "Wait. Today's her day off?"

"It's Thursday, right?" Buddy glanced at the calendar on the wall. "Yeah. She's off Thursdays and Fridays. Says she likes it that way because weekends are always busy. Better tips. Something wrong?"

58

Tripp pulled out his cell phone, motioned to Crowley to follow. She'd lied to him. Beyond that, she'd deceived him. Maybe even played him.

"Tripp?" Steph called after him. When he didn't respond, she let out a shrill whistle that had him spinning around at the door. "You need us, you know where we are."

"Yeah," Tripp nodded as he waited for Eamon to pick up. "Thanks, Steph. Come on Crowley. Let's go find out what your mistress is up to."

CHAPTER SEVEN

"*C*ome on, it's freezing out here." Parker lamented her long-ago finished coffee, wishing she had the warm cup to keep the chill off her hands. Bundling up for a day in the park hadn't been an option. Anything other than her usual lightweight zip-up sweatshirt for a day at the deli would have tipped Tripp off. And she did not need him hovering when she was trying to lure McNally into the open.

She'd waited until Tripp's SUV was well out of sight range before she'd detoured away from her workplace and headed down Cedar Tree Way. Staying visible while trying to avoid the FBI agent she was sleeping with proved to be a little tricky. She'd almost run into him coming out of the liquor store. As it was, she'd had to hold up her hand to stop Crowley from barking at her. Twenty minutes later she took a seat on a bench in Teakwood Park, just far enough from the children's playground and Marco's Taco Truck to provide some privacy.

McNally was out there. She could feel it. "Or maybe you're just telling yourself that, so this doesn't feel like a complete waste of time." Her bag felt heavier today. Probably because she was carrying around twenty million in cybercash. All this time. All this time she'd been in possession of her ex-husband's stash. She gnashed her teeth together so hard she could almost taste dust. When this was all over …. If she *ever* got her hands on Chad ….

"Atsila won't be happy you ditched him."

She spun on the bench, nearly toppled off. Ned McNally, or at least she was pretty sure it was him, circled around from behind the aged oak. He wore an old army jacket with multiple pockets, jeans that looked as if they'd been dragged through the Old West, and a scraggly beard that had her remembering him instantly. Not from their many meetings about her ex-husband's case, but from the deli. Back corner table, the last three days for lunch. He'd had a ragged paperback open every time, but there was no mistaking her recollection. Or those piercing, stressed, blue eyes. It had been him.

"I can see the pieces falling into place in your eyes." His voice was tight, almost too controlled. As if he were anxious about something. "If you're expecting some TV crime series confessional, I'm not going to give you one."

So much for the record button on her phone. Still ... she shifted her bag, slipped her hand inside and grasped her cell phone.

"Don't ... do that." McNally's order had her jumping. The gun he withdrew from his jacket pocket had her swallowing hard. Anger had her staring back. "Just give me the drive."

It would be so easy, to just hand it over, to have him disappear and distract the FBI for her to vanish again. That had been the plan. It seemed the only way to protect Tripp and his career. She'd downloaded and saved all the information to her laptop, which she'd left on her living room table. Along with a note to Tripp explaining what she'd done.

But now ... seeing McNally, knowing he was the reason she'd lost three years of her life .... Knowing he'd set her up by making her believe the FBI didn't want her testimony after all, that she'd had no other option than to fake her own death, all so he could get his hands on her ex's stolen money .... Knowing she'd have to leave Tripp behind forever .... Now she wasn't quite so sure. "I didn't know I had it."

"Sure you didn't." McNally smirked. "You expect me to believe that? You knew exactly what you had back in Vegas when I tracked you down. That's why you disappeared again."

"Believe that if you want, but it's not true. I only found it this morning. When I realized ..." she swallowed, her dry mouth making it difficult. "When I realized you must have broken into my house looking for this." She hefted her bag, careful to keep her hand near her phone. "I normally leave it downstairs, but it was in my bedroom that night." Because she'd been planning to run then, too.

"Just give me the drive and this'll be over."

She looked at him. Really looked at him. And an odd peace settled over her. "That's not true, is it?" She got to her feet, backed away. "You're going to kill me no matter what."

"You're the last loose end. Once you're gone"—he released the safety on the gun—"there's no one left who knows where that money is."

"Chad knows."

"He *did* know. But like I said …" He inclined his head, and for an instant she swore she saw madness reflected in his gaze. "After you, there's no one left."

"We've got a problem." Eamon was racing down Tripp's grandmother's front steps when he pulled up in front of the house.

"I had the FBI ping Parker's phone," Tripp told him. "She's in Teakwood Park." He gunned the engine and screeched down the street. Crowley made a disapproving sound from the back seat as Eamon buckled in.

"We'd better get to her before McNally does."

"This I know."

"You don't understand. That problem? Chad Remington's dead. Someone shanked him in the shower two nights ago. Prison warden's saying it was a paid hit carried out by a drug dealer serving two life sentences. Guess who arrested that dealer in a federal sting?"

"McNally," Tripp ground out.

"Guy's cleaning house. Parker's the only one left who he thinks knows about the money."

"She does know." So much of the morning made sense now. How evasive she was after their shower. How almost sentimental she'd been in the car and how worried she'd been about them being seen together. It had all felt so forced, like she was trying to keep up some façade. He hadn't seen it then, probably because he hadn't wanted to.

Just like he hadn't seen how deep into depression his partner had fallen. He'd been too late to save Valdez. He wasn't going to be too late again.

"So she lied to us?" Eamon said, the disbelief evident in his tone.

"No. Not at first. I don't think she knew when this all started. It's been ... recent." He tried to flash back through the last day, wondered when she'd have had time to figure it out. "The only time she was alone was when she went up to her room. We can figure that all out later. For now, we just need to find her. Here." He handed Eamon his phone, told him to open the app. "Let me know what side of the park. We'll park out of the way, see if we can spot her." Three blocks from the park now. Three of the longest blocks Tripp had ever driven. When he got a hold of her he was going to ... who was he kidding? He was going to haul her into his arms and kiss her because that's what a man in love did.

"Ease up." Eamon said quietly. "Driving up guns blazing is only going to create chaos. You want me to contact the local sheriff?"

"No." The answer came snap fast. "No, we can handle this. I don't want Steph getting in the middle." He cringed. Call him a sexist ass, he wasn't about to have a friend, let alone a very pregnant sheriff, anywhere near Ned McNally. Especially now that they knew what the former FBI agent was capable of.

"I see Parker." Eamon motioned for Tripp to pull over to the side and park. "She's standing with someone just under that large oak tree."

Tripp shifted in his seat, looked in the direction Eamon now pointed. She was standing, clutching her bag to her chest. He couldn't read her expression, but he could see the tension in her body. She was coiled and ready to spring. "That's my girl," he murmured.

"What?" Eamon asked.

"She's not scared. She's pissed. That's going to work to our advantage."

"McNally's got a gun. And about a month's worth growth of beard from what I can see."

"I'll come up straight with Crowley. You circle around and behind while I keep him distracted."

"Got your back," Eamon confirmed and checked his weapon. "Be safe."

"Yeah, you too. Come on, Crowley. It's you and me."

Woof! *It's about time.*

"Just give me the flash drive, Portia."

Hearing her old name drop from his lips was enough to kick the fire back into her body. She released her cell phone, shoved her bag onto her shoulder and crossed her arms. "No."

His eyes narrowed. "You think I won't use this?"

"I have no doubt you'll use it. And get the attention of everyone within earshot." One thing she'd gotten good at the last three years—hell, the last eight years—was lying. And bluffing. "Woodville Springs isn't known for its gunshots. You might shoot me, you might even get the drive, but you won't get away. You can do that now though. Just turn around and go." The FBI would be on his tail soon enough. And she'd be able to stay and fight for the life she wanted in Woodville Springs.

Maybe even a life that included Tripp Atsila.

She saw the flash of red hair before she made the connection. The man was striding toward her, toward them, in his dark slacks and matching jacket, the narrow navy tie hanging in stark contrast to the white shirt. Even if she hadn't known Eamon Quinn was a federal agent, the way he approached, with his gun held low and those determined eyes of his locked on her, she'd have tagged him as one.

Panic seized her. If Eamon was here, Tripp wouldn't be far away. And she'd bet there was a reason why Eamon was the one approaching from behind.

"He's not going to get away in any case."

Parker closed her eyes, let out a frustrated breath. "Damn it, Tripp!" She turned, dropping her bag off her shoulder and into her hand. "I had this under control."

"That's what you call absconding with twenty million dollars?" The anger in his voice had her doing a double take. "Portia Remington, you're under arrest—"

"Stop!" McNally yelled. "Just stop!" He raised the gun, aimed it at Tripp as Tripp reached Parker's side.

Crowley growled and crouched, barked three times, sharp staccato sounds that had her wincing.

McNally turned the gun on the dog. Enraged, Parker spun toward him, swinging and arcing her purse directly at McNally's head. The second it struck, Crowley leaped, knocking McNally to the ground. The gun flew free of his grasp and landed on the grass at Eamon's feet.

"Get him off! Get it off me!" McNally screamed, his face muffled in the dirt as Crowley planted two paws on McNally's back.

"Crowley, cease! Dammit, what's the French word for stop?" She looked to Tripp for help.

"*Au pied*," He repeated it again and Crowley backed off, moving backwards to sit at his and Parker's feet. Eamon had McNally cuffed in seconds, but he left him on the ground. "Parker?" Tripp faced her. "You've got some explaining to do."

"I know. I know." She pressed her hands to her cheeks and couldn't help the smile that spread across her face. "I was going to give him the money and run. But ...." She looked up at him, then down to Crowley, who earned a big hug before she threw herself into Tripp's arms. "But I changed my mind. I don't want to go. I don't want to leave Woodville Springs. Even if everyone hates me."

"How could anyone hate you?" he murmured into her neck.

"I didn't want you to pay for what I am. What I've done." She stepped back to put some distance between them, so she could think. "I don't know if we can make a go of anything, if you can forgive me for what I did—"

"Excuse me." Eamon cleared his throat and disconnected whatever call he'd just made. "I think I can solve some of these issues. Where's the money, Parker?"

"Huh?" Parker blinked. "Oh, sure. Yeah, that would help, right?" She dug into her pocket for the flash drive. "I've had this purse ever since I left home. My mom bought it for me as a graduation present. Cost her half a paycheck, but ..." she shrugged and handed over the drive. "Anyway, it's the one thing Chad knew I'd never leave behind. He must have sewed it into the lining before he was arrested, then told McNally what he'd done. He said ... McNally said ... Chad?" She looked between the two FBI agents.

"I'm sorry," Tripp said and reached for her hand. "Eamon just got the call a while ago. He's dead."

Parker waited for something, any kind of emotion other than pity to surge, but nothing came. She'd been married to the man for years and yet .... "I'm sorry his victims won't get the justice they deserve."

"They might with this," Eamon said, indicating the flash drive. "Assuming it's all there."

"It's a list of accounts. Dozens of them in offshore banks. I made a copy on my laptop just in case."

"I'll make sure everyone knows you were the one responsible for retrieving the money, Parker," Eamon said.

Once upon a time that might have been all she'd needed to hear, but now? She didn't care who got the credit. As long as she had a future.

"Okay to take him to the sheriff's office now?" Eamon asked as he hauled McNally to his feet and pocketed the disgraced agent's gun.

"Yeah," Tripp said. "I'm sure Steph will make him very comfortable."

"Where are you headed?" Eamon asked as Tripp slung an arm around Parker's shoulders and brought her in for a hug.

Tripp looked down at her and she smiled, feeling free and happy for the first time in a long time. "Home," she said, gesturing for Crowley to follow. "We're going home."

CHAPTER EIGHT

"*T*hat smells amazing." Tripp slipped up behind Parker and wrapped his arms around her waist.

"My grandmother's triple apple cobbler." She leaned over and bathed her face in the steam, something Tripp noticed, she did frequently. "You're sure it's okay I bring this to dinner tomorrow? I don't want to step on your grandmother's toes."

"Not only is it okay, it's encouraged." His grandmother was already patting herself on the back knowing that Tripp and Parker had made what was shaping up to be a serious connection. "Bring your recipe book, too." He gestured to the gingham binder on the counter. "She'd probably be happy to snatch a couple of those for her collection."

"Happy to share. Have you heard from Eamon?"

"Yeah, he said to say thanks for the invitation to Thanksgiving dinner, but he's spending it with friends in Sacramento. Friends his sister grew up with." Tripp had told Parker about Eamon's loss and subsequent calling to law enforcement. "They consider him an honorary big brother, so he'll be with family."

"That's good. You two make a good team." She'd been hinting at trying to get a handle on his plans with the FBI for the past few days. But he didn't have anything to tell her. Nothing definite at least.

His cell phone buzzed.

"Don't tell me that's them." She turned and linked her hands behind his neck. "You get a few more weeks vacation at least."

"Leave," he corrected and kissed her quick. Glancing at his screen, he frowned. "That's weird. Why's she calling? Steph?" He answered.

"Hey there, Tripp. Guess who decided to make an early arrival."

"You've had the baby?" Joy and concern struck in equal measure. "Are you okay? Boy or girl?"

"I'm fine. I'm wonderful. And so is she." Was it possible to feel happiness over the phone? "My dad's holding her right now and I don't think I've ever been better."

He smiled. "Congratulations. I can't wait to meet her."

"I can't wait to decide on her name," Steph laughed. "So the reason I'm calling ... the other day when you stopped by the station, I asked if you were looking for a change. Rumor has it you are."

"Rumor?" He echoed. "Or Eamon?"

"I'm pleading the fifth. But seriously, as much as I love my job ... I'm going to be staying home for at least the next few months. I need to. For her and for me. I want to come back, but ... oh, hell. Do you want the job or not?"

"As sheriff?" Tripp's eyes went almost as wide as Parker's. "Uh, I don't know."

"Sure you do." He could all but see Steph rolling her eyes. "I already talked to the mayor. It's an appointment, not an elected position. Eamon and your superiors at the FBI all gave you glowing recommendations—"

"You talked to my superiors?"

"Of course I did. You think I was going to let you get away from us again? Tripp," Steph said, "this is your home. It's where you belong. We need you. *I* need you. The job is yours if you want it. And it doesn't have to be forever. I might change my mind and come back—at which time we'd arm wrestle for it."

"Steph, I ...." He didn't know what to say. But the idea wasn't completely a horrible one. In fact .... "Can you handle me being sheriff?" he asked Parker, mild disbelief ringing in his voice.

"Silly man." Parker angled a look at him, shook her head, and took the phone from him. "Hi, Steph, it's Parker. He'll take it."

"I can't believe you're here!" Tripp caught his sister Lilith in his arms and swung her around like she was ten years old again. She wasn't. In fact she was nearly as tall as he was, with the thick curly black hair their father had blessed them with.

"Stop spinning me or I'm going to puke," Lilith laughed. "I'm not even in the front door yet. Where's the welcoming committee?" She darted forward and into the arms of their other brothers, who each took turns doing the exact same welcome he'd given her.

The man standing out on the front porch appeared only slightly nervous. As expected, Quincy Lennox looked as if he could squeeze a watermelon with one hand—but he had a smile on his face. "Tripp Atsila. Welcome to the family, Quincy."

"Pleasure." Quincy returned the handshake. "I appreciate the warm welcome. She's been a little anxious about coming home."

"That's what happens when you spend so much time away." Aurelia emerged from the crowd to push past Tripp and take Quincy's hand. "My, you are a handsome one. You'll fit right in. Come in, let's get you something to drink. Tripp, have your girl open up that wine you brought."

"Yes, ma'am." Tripp maneuvered through his family, trying not to regret not having come home before now. But the time had been right. All the stars had aligned, as his grandmother would say. He'd come home when he was meant to.

Many poured wine glasses and passed appetizers later, the family began taking their seats around the extended dining room table that included the requisite card tables at either end. Already filled with serving dishes containing a stomach-stretching array of side dishes, vegetables, salad, homemade bread, and Tripp's personal favorite, macaroni and cheese, all that was missing from the table was the twenty pound turkey Aurelia had put in the oven before dawn.

With his grandmother at one end, Marshal, Hardy, Wade, and Wade's pregnant wife Essie on one side, and Lilith, Quincy, Tripp, and Parker on the other, that left three places empty.

"Who else is coming?" Parker asked for the hundredth time.

"I can't wait until next year when I'll have a high chair right here," Aurelia announced as if she hadn't heard Parker.

"I'm sure we'll be happy to let you deal with your great grandchild," Wade assured her.

With everyone seated, Aurelia returned to the kitchen to get the turkey. The doorbell rang.

Tripp had his hand already locked around a serving spoon. "How about you get that, Parker?"

"Me?" She looked shell shocked. "But I'm not—"

"You're not seriously going to say you aren't family, are you?" Essie said. "Please. Even if you hadn't hooked up with that one, you've saved my husband's sanity these last few months. For that alone, you earn Atsila status."

"Hear, hear," Marshall, usually the silent one of the bunch, toasted her with a beer.

"Go on now. Your first official task as an Atsila," Wade urged. "Although a ring would make it more official—Ouch!" He flinched when his wife smacked him on the arm. "What? You said it yourself this morning. Sheriff, I want to report a crazy woman in the house."

Tripp refrained from responding. No one needed to know he'd already found the perfect ring for Parker. For when the time was right. Eamon had been right. He'd found happiness with her. He'd found love. He wasn't about to let it go.

Parker seemed to be waiting for someone else to jump to their feet, but when no one did, she set her napkin on her plate and pushed back her chair. "All right then."

Everyone watched her leave the room. Seconds later they were all scrambling to their feet, Tripp in the lead, and watched Parker pull open the front door.

"Mom? Dad?" Parker gasped, then launched herself out the door. "Sammy?" She all but fell out of sight.

Tripp moved in, hushing his siblings as he joined Parker, offering a smile of welcome to the family she'd been convinced she'd lost. The family he'd tracked down and flown out as a surprise for the woman he loved. Greetings and introductions were exchanged. Parker couldn't stop crying and hugging and laughing and when she turned to face him, she had a toddler in her arms. "I can't believe this! You did this, didn't you?"

"We all did," Tripp said with a shrug. "Thanksgiving's about family and you deserved to see yours again."

"I'm an aunt," she cried. "This is Josiah." She smoothed dark blond curls away from his wide eyes. "My baby sister's a mama."

Baby sister, Sammy, taller and slimmer than Parker, came forward and hugged him. "You gave her back to us. We'll never be able to thank you."

"It was my pleasure."

"All right, let's bring this all inside." Aurelia waved the new arrivals in. "Rose, it's a pleasure to meet you in person," she said to Parker's mother. "That recipe you sent me for pomegranate salad is simply wonderful. It's also on the table and we're ready to eat."

Sammy retrieved her son and followed her parents and Tripp's family back to the dining room where the conversation started all over again.

"And I had thought this day couldn't get any better," Parker whispered as she wrapped her arms around Tripp and squeezed. "I can't believe you did this for me. Thank you."

"You're welcome." Seeing that look on her face, hearing that happiness surging out of her, would keep him smiling for holidays to come. "And Parker?"

"Yes?" She beamed up at him.

He kissed her, quick and hard. "Welcome home."

Second
Chances

Kayla Perrin

CHAPTER ONE

*M*iranda Cox smiled as the plane touched down on the runway at the Ottawa International Airport. She then retrieved her cell phone from her sweater pocket and switched it off of airplane mode. She punched in Matthew's number, anxious to touch base with her boyfriend and discuss their plans for the upcoming Thanksgiving weekend.

The phone made a weird clicking sound, and then went dead.

Miranda looked at the phone and frowned. She punched in his number again. Once again, the same thing happened. The phone didn't even ring. It just disconnected her.

That was odd. She checked her phone's signal strength, and it appeared strong. But maybe she should wait until she got into the terminal to call Matthew. Perhaps there was a connectivity issue out here on the tarmac.

Everybody on her early evening flight from DC was already on their feet, grabbing their overhead luggage, and lining up in the aisle. Miranda often wondered why people bothered to jump into the line just to stand and wait for five minutes until the plane was ready to open its doors. May as well sit and relax for the extra few minutes.

Miranda gazed out the window at the lights surrounding the airport. They looked like a myriad of stars in the darkness. Content, she sighed. She was glad that she was able to get the time off for her Thanksgiving holiday. Her work as an interpreter had her traveling the world, so she didn't always get the Canadian Thanksgiving off in order to visit her family. But here she was, arriving back home in Ottawa on Wednesday night. She was off tomorrow through Monday, and didn't need to be back to work until Tuesday morning.

And Matthew had committed to going to Toronto with her. He was going to be meeting her family for the first time.

She tried his number again, and again the strange nonconnection then disconnection sound happened. She decided to call Ruby, the friend who'd introduced her to Matthew.

When Ruby's number rang, Miranda was even more confused. It couldn't be a connection issue if her phone was working to call her friend.

Ruby answered after the first ring. "Hey, Miranda."

"Have you heard from Matthew?" Miranda asked without preamble.

"I'm fine, how are you?" Ruby asked, a smile in her voice.

"Sorry. I'm on the plane, just arriving from DC. I called Matthew but his phone is acting strange. I'm just wondering if you've heard from him."

"I haven't, but I can call him."

"That be great. I don't know why, but his phone keeps disconnecting on me and I can't even get through. So I don't know if there's a problem with his line, or if something else is going on …?"

"Let me call him right now," Ruby said.

"All right."

As Miranda disconnected the call, the line of people started to move. She gathered her belongings and stood to join the queue. She was off the plane and entering the airport when her phone rang. She glanced down, saw Ruby's number, and quickly answered.

"Did you reach him?"

"No. But his number rang normally for me. It rang and went to voicemail. I'm sure you'll get through to him later."

"Yeah, you're probably right. It's probably just a signal glitch here, and I've got to get my luggage, go through customs, and head home anyway. I'll try him later."

"Are we still on for drinks tomorrow night?" Ruby asked.

"You know we are!" Miranda took advantage of every opportunity to get together with Ruby and Anna, her two best friends, and relax with a couple of drinks. Especially when work kept her as busy as it did.

Hours later, Miranda still couldn't reach Matthew. His number continued to immediately disconnect when she tried to call him. She'd also sent him several text messages, but he wasn't responding. She tried him through WhatsApp, and all of her messages weren't going through. There was only one checkmark—not the two which would indicate that a message had been delivered—nor the blue checkmarks indicating that the messages had been read.

Miranda frowned, unhappy that she wasn't able to reach her man. He knew that she was coming back tonight. They'd talked about seeing each other, especially before the upcoming trip to Toronto.

The next morning rolled around, and Matthew hadn't gotten back to her, and her messages to him were still unread. She tried Facebook—something she hadn't thought to try the night before. When she went to find his page, she couldn't. That wasn't a good sign.

Glancing at her bedside clock, she was glad that it was only 9:33 A.M. Ruby was an animator at a local studio, and had a somewhat flexible schedule. She tended to start her work day later in the morning and stayed until after five. Ruby always preferred to sleep in.

Miranda called her. On the third ring, Ruby picked up.

"Hey, Miranda." Ruby sounded a little groggy.

"I hope I didn't wake you."

"No, I'm up. Just making a cup of coffee."

"Okay, this is really strange. Matthew's Facebook page isn't popping up. You think it was deleted?"

"Hold on." Several seconds passed. Then Ruby said, "I just pulled up his page on my phone. I can see it."

"You're kidding." What was going on?

As Miranda's gaze wandered to the window in her small bedroom, the truth hit her like a cold, hard slap in the face. Had he blocked her? Blocked her on Facebook, WhatsApp, and her phone?

"You don't think he blocked me?" she asked in a horrified whisper.

"I ... I don't know what to say."

The idea of him blocking her wouldn't have ever come into her mind, even now, if Matthew hadn't told her that he'd done that to a girlfriend in the past. He said when he'd wanted to end things with the possessive and irrational woman, he just cut her out of his life instantly. He never spoke to her again and gave her no way to reach him.

"But he never said we were having any kind of problems," Miranda protested. She bit down on her bottom lip, confused.

When Ruby said nothing, Miranda got a strange feeling. "Did he say something to you?"

"Well ..."

"What?" Miranda demanded.

"First of all, I never thought he'd do this. I never thought it was that serious. But he said .... He just said how you're always busy. That you're always traveling, never have enough time for him. He wasn't sure it was going to work."

"And you didn't think to tell me this?"

"I thought he was just thinking out loud. Complaining a little, but not going to take the route of blocking you and never talking to you again. Besides, I told him to talk to you about his concerns."

"But he's supposed to go with me to Toronto for Thanksgiving!" Miranda's brain was scrambling to make sense of this. Why would Matthew behave this way?

"I don't know what to say. Do you want me to try to call him?"

Confusion turning to anger, heat spread across Miranda's chest and rose to her cheeks. This was really happening. What kind of coward just cut you out of his life and never said another word to you?

"No," Miranda said. "I'm gonna go to his workplace."

"Are you sure you want to do that?" Ruby asked.

"The jerk may not want to be with me anymore, but he owes me an explanation."

Miranda heard Ruby's exhalation of breath on the other end of the line. "Ok, but ... keep your cool. Don't go crazy on him."

"You know I'm not going to do anything stupid. Though I could certainly get the attention of everyone at his accounting firm if I wanted. Spice things up in that boring office."

"Miranda ..."

"You know I'm not serious." Miranda frowned. She was a good person, wasn't she? Yes, she had a demanding career, but that wasn't necessarily a deal breaker. And if it was, just say that. "I only want to see him to let him know that he can't simply discard me and take the coward's way out."

"Okay, girl. Call me later. Let me know how it went!"

"I will."

Miranda ended the call with Ruby, then decided to call Matthew on her landline, one she often forgot about and barely used, so had never given the number to him. And lo and behold, his number rang and rang and then went to voicemail. What a jerk. He *had* blocked her!

Why wouldn't he just tell her that he wasn't happy? Why wouldn't he express his concerns to her?

Miranda didn't even bother with her morning coffee. She slipped into some clothes and was out the door in minutes. She reread Matthew's recent messages to her as she took the elevator down to the parking level in her condo building. *Can't wait to meet your family this weekend. We're going to have a great trip!*

Miranda's ire grew.

She exited the elevator and made her way through the door that led to her car. As she was nearing the sporty red Audi she'd bought as a present to herself on her thirtieth birthday, she stopped midstride.

What am I doing?

Why was she actually going to waste her time by going to Matthew's office? She was humiliated, yes, but was she really upset that their relationship was over?

Crossing her arms over her chest, she contemplated that question. Truth be told, she was sort of relieved. She realized her intense reaction was because of *how* he had ended it, not the simple fact that he had.

The pressure of Matthew heading to Toronto with her—the first boyfriend she'd be bringing home in years—had been getting to her. He wanted more, and she wasn't fully ready. She was open to falling in love with him, of course, but was he the one?

There were many times that she looked at him and wondered if they actually had a future, and there was a niggling thought in her mind that they didn't.

Honestly, wasn't it better that he broke things off before her family got involved? Before her sister started planning a wedding, and her mother started naming babies that would come in the future …?

Slowly, Miranda began to walk. She headed back upstairs to her condo, and there she called Matthew again from her landline. All she wanted now was closure on her terms. When his voicemail picked up, she said, "Okay, so you're ghosting me. That's fine. You could've just told me you were unhappy. Here's something to consider. Grown men talk to their partners, no matter what the situation. They don't run and hide like cowards."

Miranda ended the call, and smiled to herself.

And then she frowned. Now what?

Though she couldn't help feeling as though a weight had been lifted from her shoulders, she knew that when she got to Toronto there were going to be a lot of questions about why Matthew wasn't with her. It wasn't that she minded the questions, but the timing couldn't have been worse. Melanie was now engaged. Brandon and his wife were expecting their first baby. Everyone had amazing news to celebrate this Thanksgiving.

Everyone but her.

Instead, it was the same-old, same-old with Miranda. At thirty-four, she was now single with absolutely no prospects for marriage.

"But you have a great career," she said to herself, only half sarcastically.

Miranda headed into the kitchen and put a single-serve coffee pod into her machine. She loved her career as an interpreter, but she did wonder from time to time if she'd ever be able to fit love into her life. Real love that would last.

As she took her coffee cup to the sofa by the balcony window and looked out at the view of the Rideau River below, she told herself that never again would she settle. She would never end up dating another Matthew.

The next evening, Miranda was out at The Capital, a local bar for professionals in the center of the city. She was with her besties, Ruby and Anna. They had a round of cosmopolitans and were catching up on the week's events. Of course the hot topic was Matthew.

"Here's the crazy thing," Miranda said. "I don't even miss him."

"It's only been a day," Ruby pointed out.

"I know, but I feel like he set me free." Miranda fiddled with the slice of lime on the rim of her drink. "Honestly, part of me was faking it with him. Hoping for the best, yes. But I knew in my heart that he wasn't the one."

"Yet you were going to take him to Toronto?" Anna asked doubtfully.

Anna and Miranda had been friends since grade school. Anna could always sniff out Miranda's bull, and vice versa. They were like two peas in a pod, as close as sisters. In fact, people often thought they *were* sisters. Both were biracial, but Anna had long hair and loose curls, while Miranda's hair was naturally kinky and she'd been straightening it for years.

Miranda shrugged. "I would have, because I'd asked him. And I figured it would quiet my family from bemoaning my lack of a love life. But he did me a favor." Miranda sipped her drink. "What kind of professional man just ghosts you? I wish I'd never given him the time of day!"

Anna shot a glance at Ruby. "What?" Ruby protested, then tucked a strand of her blonde hair behind her ear. "I introduced them, but I never thought he'd do this. I'm not responsible."

When Ruby had introduced Miranda to Matthew, she hadn't dated in close to eighteen months. Matthew was the boy-next-door type, with sandy-blond hair and bright-blue eyes. Miranda had felt hopeful about him. He was attractive, intelligent, never been married, had a successful career. On paper, he checked all the boxes. But there hadn't been that spark between them that Miranda had been hoping for.

"Maybe you're gay," Anna mused. "White, Black, purple with pink polka dots—you're literally attracted to no man."

"I'm not gay." Miranda shot her friend a scowl before finishing off her drink. "I just haven't found the right guy." She shrugged. "I don't know. There's just something wrong with all of the guys I meet. They're either too clingy, not clingy enough, aloof, too arrogant …. Who knows? Maybe the right guy for me isn't out there."

"It's hard to find him when you're always working," Ruby stated. "You're addicted to your job."

"I'm not going to sacrifice my career for a relationship."

"And no one says that you have to," Ruby agreed. "But for goodness sake, if you want a relationship at all, you have to give a little."

Anna beckoned their waitress and ordered another round of cosmopolitans. Then she faced Miranda and said point-blank, "I know what the problem is."

"Oh?" Miranda asked.

"It's Taz, isn't it? You're still not over him."

"Taz?" Miranda's eyes bulged. "Taz Morrison?"

"Is there another Taz?" Anna asked.

Miranda scoffed. "You've lost your mind. You know that, right?"

"Who's Taz?" Ruby asked, her gaze volleying between Miranda and Anna. "Wait, is that the guy you told me about from high school? Your BFF?"

"So she told you about him," Anna said to Ruby.

"He was only ever a friend," Miranda explained.

"Yeah, but he's the only guy you really seemed to care about," Anna said. "In all the years I've known you, he's the only one who broke your heart—"

"We weren't even dating!"

"Do you have to be dating to love someone?" Anna countered.

Miranda helped herself to her second cosmopolitan as the waitress was lowering the tray. She took a liberal sip, then winced.

"You guys were best friends," Anna went on, making air quotes. "But you adored him. I admit, Taz seemed clueless, but I always thought he liked you. He made every excuse to hang out with you. But when he got engaged to Crystal Parker, I was as shocked as you w—"

"I don't want to talk about this. Why are we talking about this?" Miranda held up a hand. "Can we just stop now?"

Ruby leaned back in her chair and shot Miranda a questioning look. "Huh."

"Why are you looking at me like that?" Miranda quickly sipped more of her drink. "Okay, I had a crush on him, but that's ancient history. I haven't even been in touch with him in years."

"I'm just saying," Anna began, "he's the only guy I've ever known you to really care about. Your eyes lit up like a puppy dog's as you looked at him."

"Who is this woman you're describing?" Ruby asked with a hint of humor in her voice.

"She was smitten," Anna said.

"He's got to be on social media," Ruby said excitedly. "Are you still in touch with him?"

"Can you guys stop?" Miranda exclaimed.

Apparently not, because Ruby shifted her chair close to Anna's, and they both looked at her phone as Anna began to search.

As her two friends excitedly hunted for Taz, Miranda rolled her eyes. But strangely, her heart was beating a little faster, which irritated her. Because why should she feel anything when she thought of Taz? He'd only ever seen her as a friend. And then he'd married Crystal, part of the popular Queen Bee crowd at their high school. Miranda was still confused by what he saw in her.

And of course, she'd been wildly jealous. She had always had a thing for Taz, and held out hope that he liked her too. They always hung out together, worked on projects together—until late their senior year when Crystal had set out to win him. After that, Taz hadn't had much time for Miranda anymore.

Though Taz never reciprocated her feelings, as far as attraction and that *je ne sais quoi* factor, he had ticked all of the boxes for her. Literally a school girl with a big crush, Miranda had always been excited to be around him, even if she'd just been helping him with his French.

And once he'd started dating Crystal, Miranda had been crushed. Though her heart had been broken, she'd eventually put Taz in her rearview mirror and moved on. In the years between high school and now, she hadn't met another guy who inspired the same excitement in her that Taz had. Or maybe she was illogically expecting love to feel like she was caught up in a whirlwind of excitement. Heart pounding, spine tingling—maybe it was all nonsense and she'd turned away perfectly decent men because they didn't instantly give her that rush of excitement.

That thought was one of the reasons that she figured she ought to keep dating Matthew, even if she didn't feel a thrill when she looked at him or when he kissed her. Maybe she was never going to feel that rush of feeling again.

"He's only on LinkedIn," Ruby whined. "He's not on Facebook or Instagram. It says he's an architect in New York State."

"Are you guys done yet?" Miranda asked.

"He's gorgeous," Ruby mused.

Miranda was curious, but she didn't ask to see his current picture on Anna's phone. Taz was her past. May as well let him stay there.

CHAPTER TWO

*T*he next day around noon, Miranda was finishing up her packing for Toronto when her cell phone rang. Seeing that it was her sister calling, she quickly scooped it up from the bed and answered. "Melanie, hi."

"Hi, Sis. I'll make this quick. Doug and I just arrived at Pearson and we're about to get off the plane. I wanted to make sure that you picked up those Ottawa souvenirs I asked you to get."

"Yep, I have them." Doug, who was from Edmonton, wanted coasters and keychains that he would give to his family after the holiday.

"Thanks. It means a lot to Doug. He's hoping that his family will take a trip to Ottawa next year for Canada Day." Melanie paused. "What time are you and Matthew getting to Union Station?"

"Um," Miranda hedged, "the train arrives just before six thirty."

"Great! So we can all have a late dinner together. You *are* staying at the house, right? With Brandon and Tesha staying at an Airbnb, there's more than enough room for you and Matthew at the house."

"I wouldn't say *more* than enough room," Miranda said. "It'll be a full house."

"But it'll be fun!"

Miranda knew that Melanie just wanted an opportunity to sit and yap with Matthew, but she was never going to get that chance.

"No Airbnb," Miranda confirmed.

"Great," Melanie said. "You know I can't wait to meet Matthew!"

Miranda carefully lowered the jeans she had been holding into the suitcase. Though she was only going to Toronto for a few days, she was packing a variety of clothes. She always overpacked, but it was her philosophy that it was better to have too much as opposed to not enough. You never knew what the weather was going to be like, or if another situation would arise for which you needed something else to wear. With it being early October, there was a chill in the air in Ottawa, but Toronto was several degrees warmer right now.

"Sis? Are you there?"

"Sorry," Miranda said. Just the mention of Matthew had her distracted. Stalling was more like it. Everyone back home was excited about finally getting to meet the man who'd won her heart.

"Tell Matthew I say hello and I'm looking forward to seeing him tonight."

Miranda cringed. She knew that she should be telling her sister that Matthew wasn't coming. But she wasn't certain if she wanted to tell her family that Matthew was no longer in her life, or that he was just busy. Telling them the latter would be so much easier ....

"Okay," Miranda found herself saying.

She was being ridiculous. Why wasn't she just telling her sister that Matthew would not be coming?

Because it was too hard. Her family was so hopeful, and had begun calling him *Matthew-the-Great*—based on Miranda's descriptions of how perfect he was. She had been embellishing, given her sister's engagement and her brother's good news about the baby. Now she felt silly.

Besides, if she told Melanie the truth now, her sister would keep her on the phone longer than necessary, unable to wait until later to hear the explanation as to why.

Miranda knew there would be questions. But she would answer them when she got to Toronto.

"All right, Sis," Miranda said, "I've got to get ready to get out of here. Love you!"

"Love you, too."

Miranda ended the call, then put the last of her clothes into her suitcase. Originally, Matthew had planned to meet her at her place in an Uber, and then they would head to the train station. It was weird how one minute she'd been considering a future with him. Now, he was irrevocably out of her life.

And she didn't really miss him.

He hadn't responded to the voicemail she'd left him, but she hadn't expected him to. Further proof that he was a jerk.

It was the sting of rejection that hurt the most, and the callous way that he'd discarded her.

"Forget him," she told herself. Then she opened up her Uber app and scheduled a pick-up. This trip to Toronto was exactly what she needed.

Exactly on time, her train arrived at Union Station later that evening. The ride had been peaceful, and she'd taken the time to relax and read a novel. It was nice to have time off where she didn't have to think about work.

Miranda had snagged a seat on the upper level, a more interesting way to watch the world whiz by, as far as she was concerned. When everyone else began to disembark, she waited. She took her time so she didn't have to fight through the crowds of the other passengers. Toronto was clearly a popular destination this weekend, as the train had been nearly full.

After several minutes, Miranda exited the train and made her way to the stairs. She wrestled her luggage down the stairs. Maybe she'd packed *too* much. But she also had gifts for her family and her siblings' partners.

Once inside the main terminal, Miranda looked around the station with a sense of happiness and awe. It had gotten a face-lift. There were lots of shops and eateries and plenty of spaces to sit.

She scowled when she realized that to get to the street level, she was going to have to go *back* upstairs again. She could either struggle with her suitcase up the steps outside the building, or she could head to one of the elevators. There was only one option.

But first, she retrieved her phone and sent a text to her mother.

I'm here! See you soon!

Miranda headed toward one of the elevators. As she did, she was stuffing her phone back into her crossbody bag. She heard the "Whoa," just as she collided with someone.

She reeled backward, immediately embarrassed that she hadn't been watching where she was going. "I'm so sor—"

The words died in her throat when she looked up—and then her eyes widened in shock.

Could it be?

"*Taz?*"

His eyes narrowed. First, there was confusion. And then recognition flashed.

Oh, God. It *was* him. Her one-time best friend from high school. Her one-time crush.

His eyes lit up. "Miranda?"

A smile broke out on her face. She hadn't seen him in years, had actually tried to forget him, but now his friendly face had her feeling warm inside. "Yes! Oh my God, I can't believe I literally bumped into you at Union Station!"

"You know you're not supposed to be walking and texting," he playfully chastised.

"I know. Sorry about that."

"I'm not. If you hadn't bumped into me, maybe we wouldn't have noticed each other."

Oh, she would have noticed him. He was gorgeous. Skin the complexion of milk chocolate. His muscles had filled out and he was no longer the lanky kid he'd been in high school. He still had the same bright smile and perfect teeth, but now he had some facial hair. A small, nicely shaped beard that was mostly on his chin. Gone was the short afro he used to have. He was bald now, and it looked good on him.

Miranda's eyes lowered briefly, taking in the breadth of his chest beneath his open leather jacket. He was wearing a black T-shirt that hugged his skin. He had an easy sex appeal.

She quickly jerked her gaze back to his face. "What are you doing in town? I thought you lived in ... was it Seattle?" She felt flustered.

"Actually, I live in New York State now," he told her. "I'm here for the Thanksgiving weekend, to spend some time with my mother."

"Does she live in the same neighborhood?" Miranda asked. And strangely, her heart was beating a little bit faster. She tucked a strand of her hair behind her ear, suddenly self-conscious about how she looked.

"Yeah, she's in the same house. What about your family?"

"Yep. My parents are in the same house too."

"Is that where you're heading now?" Taz asked.

"Actually, yes."

"We can catch an Uber together."

"I'd like that."

"You ready now?" he asked.

Miranda nodded. "I was just about to head to the elevator."

"Then let's go." Taz had his own luggage, a small black suitcase plus a laptop bag that he had over one arm. But he reached for Miranda's suitcase, nonetheless.

"No, that's all right," she told him. "You have your hands full."

"You sure?" Taz asked.

"I'm fine," Miranda insisted. "Thank God for wheels, right? And elevators."

Taz led the way to the elevator and Miranda allowed herself a moment to inwardly freak out. Taz! She had just bumped into Taz Morrison! And he looked *good* ....

She entered the elevator behind Taz, giving him a little smile, as though her pulse wasn't racing out of control.

"Where in New York?" Miranda asked.

"Westchester," he told her.

"Why did I think you were in Seattle?"

"Because that's where I'd planned to go for college," he answered. "There's a lot we have to catch up on."

The elevator dinged, then the doors opened. As they stepped out onto the main floor of the terminal, Miranda gazed up at the high, arched ceilings, the long corridors, and the polished marble floors. At least the iconic look of Union Station hadn't changed on this level. She loved the old architecture that had withstood the test of time.

"I had just requested an Uber before you bumped into me," Taz said, glancing at his phone's screen. "Looks like it's already outside."

Together, they headed outside onto Front Street, which was lined with taxis and Ubers. Across the street was the Fairmont

Royal York hotel, where many visiting dignitaries had stayed. The sounds of honking horns mixed with the footfalls on the concrete. Crowds of people were moving through the street in one of the busiest areas of the city. The hustle and bustle was much more intense than it was in Ottawa.

Miranda inhaled the air deeply. Ahh, it was good to be home.

"That's our Uber. The black Escalade."

Taz hurried toward the car. Miranda followed him, and as she did, she couldn't help checking out his well-defined thighs. When had he gotten *those?*

Had he always been this sexy?

No, he was sexier now. A man, no longer a boy. His body had filled out in all the right places. He had strong, lean muscles. Everywhere.

As Miranda unabashedly ogled him while he helped the Uber driver put their luggage into the trunk, her stomach dropped. She remembered the very reason why she had pushed him out of her life.

Crystal.

Crystal hadn't been her high school nemesis or anything dramatic like that, but she hadn't really liked the girl. They didn't travel in the same circles, and Crystal would have never given Miranda the time of day. She was too cool for shy Miranda; Crystal probably hadn't ever noticed her as she'd walked by in the hallway with her gaggle of beautiful friends.

Miranda had especially disliked Crystal when she started to pursue Taz. Miranda's heart had started to crack when she'd realized that Taz was falling for her charms. The "Can you help me with my science?" line. Or the "Why don't you sit with me for lunch?" plea. Miranda hadn't dared to voice any objection to Taz, but she had been crushed to watch him start spending time with Crystal.

Guys always went for the confident, pretty girl. Not the girl who sat with her chin down and her eyes averted, barely able to look at the guy she liked.

Taz and Miranda had been friends since ninth grade when he'd moved to the neighborhood and they'd been in the same French class. He had hopelessly struggled through regular and irregular verbs, and, sitting next to her, he'd one day turned to her and begged her for her help. That's when their friendship had started.

All through high school, they'd been buddies. They'd work on high school assignments together whenever possible. He would help Miranda with her math homework. She would help him ace his English and French. But Crystal had come along during their senior year and made the moves on him.

Taz had even asked her for her advice regarding Crystal, wanting to know Miranda's opinion on what would make a memorable promposal. Oh, that had been a stab in her heart. By the time Miranda was in the eleventh grade, she'd started dreaming that Taz would take her to senior prom—and their love story would start.

Miranda could vividly remember her reaction. She'd pushed her chair away from the lunch table so fast, she had almost fallen over. "I don't know," she'd blurted out, then run from the cafeteria.

The tears had quickly followed. Tears she'd angrily brushed away. All this time she had been certain that Taz would realize he loved her ... but instead, he was into Crystal.

"You coming?"

Miranda's thoughts returned to the present. To Taz, who was looking over his shoulder at her.

She swallowed. "Yeah."

He held the door open and she climbed into the back seat of the Escalade. Then he settled in beside her.

Her stomach was twisting. She knew she should ask him about Crystal, if only to be polite. But she didn't want to know how many children they had nor how their life was going.

Maybe she *should* ask him so that she could rid herself of the strange feelings flowing through her. Flushed skin. Shallow breathing. A quickened pulse.

It was completely inappropriate and bewildering that just seeing him had her body reacting in a way she hadn't felt since .... Well, since the last time she'd seen him.

"I can't believe it," Taz said. "Miranda Cox. In the flesh."

Miranda angled her head to look at him. She grinned.

"You disappeared from my life after high school," he went on. "I tried to find you on Facebook, social media .... I never could."

"I—" Miranda hedged. Truth be told, she had specifically made sure that Taz *couldn't* find her. "I don't use my proper name. I just figure for work purposes that it's better to be anonymous on social media."

"Right. I get it." He paused. "You never looked for me?"

How could she tell him that she had never wanted to find him? The last thing Miranda wanted was to see pictures of him and Crystal on vacations, holding babies, sipping wine over romantic dinners, and laughing as they embraced each other. It would have killed her.

"I'm so busy with work, I'm barely on social media."

"I see."

Miranda turned to look out the window of the vehicle as the driver maneuvered onto the Gardiner Expressway. An awkward silence fell between them. There was so much to ask Taz, and yet she didn't want to.

"What's new in your world?" Taz asked after a moment. "I assume you ended up working as a translator."

"As an interpreter, actually. Though sometimes I freelance as a translator—translating French to English for various documents. Mostly, I travel and interpret speakers live."

"You always were good with languages. If not for you, I would've flunked French every year."

"I remember," Miranda said, smiling softly. "Can you believe high school was sixteen years ago? Wow, that sounds impossible."

"It's hard to believe," Taz agreed. "So much has happened."

Miranda didn't want him asking about her love life, or lack there-of, and she didn't want to hear about his. So she changed the subject. "How's your mom?"

Taz's expression changed. His smile fell, and his eyes filled with sadness. "She's not doing well."

Miranda looked at him with concern. "No?"

Taz shook his head. "She's sick."

"Cancer?" Miranda asked, fear in her voice.

"No, not cancer. Her kidneys. Kidney failure. The doctors don't know how long she'll survive without a transplant."

"Oh no! I'm so sorry. Is she on a waiting list?"

"She is, but nothing so far. I'm not a match, so I can't give her one of mine."

"What about your brother?" Miranda asked.

"He's been in Japan for years. And quite frankly, I'm disappointed with him. The first thing I would have done if I were him was get on a plane and come home."

"He hasn't?"

"He's got a demanding job. Suffers from an ulcer. His words." Taz shook his head.

Instinctively, Miranda placed a gentle hand on Taz's arm. "I'm sorry to hear that."

She remembered that Taz's younger brother was a bit weird. A homebody with very few friends. Owen had been into computers and programming and mostly stayed in his room when Miranda had visited the house.

"So I had to be here," Taz said. "Effectively, it's just me and Mom now. You remember my dad left us when we were in high school."

"Yes. Are you in touch with him?"

"Nope. I don't talk to him. He's got another life in Winnipeg with another family. Every so often he reaches out, but we don't have a real relationship."

"Ugh." What a sad turn of events in Taz's life.

"The bottom line is my mother has no one. She never remarried. I think my father was her one true love. Which is unfortunate."

Miranda nodded. She understood that, though—loving one man and not being able to forget him. Even if he wasn't the right one for you.

"No prospects for a transplant at all? No other family?"

Taz shook his head. "But we're always hoping. But you know how these things go. You just have to hope, and in the meantime Mom has to stay healthy enough to be able to be ready for transplant should the opportunity arise."

Miranda pouted, thinking suddenly about how much people took for granted. Life was short, and yet sometimes she was amazed that everyone she'd grown up with was still alive and well. Then other times it was clear that the very fact they were alive and well was a miracle. None of her close friends or family had succumbed to any sickness or tragic accidents.

"How are *you* doing?" Miranda asked him.

"As okay as is expected." He shrugged. "With each day that's passed, I'm trying more and more to resign myself to the fact that she might not get the transplant. But I don't want *her* to believe that. I want her to be as hopeful as possible."

"And is she hopeful?" Miranda asked.

"She's been pretty good, actually. But I wonder sometimes if she's just putting on a brave face for me when we talk."

Miranda nodded, then silence fell between them. This was a heavy conversation now. She looked out the window at the Lakeshore as they passed Woodbine Beach. It was dark now but the streetlights illuminated some of the trees, whose leaves had all turned a bright orange and red now that it was fall. It was so beautiful. A magical time of year. Miranda had always loved the fall and the brisk air and the bright colors.

Taz was also looking out his window, but Miranda suspected that he wasn't seeing anything of The Beaches neighborhood they'd enjoyed throughout high school. Once, they had been so close. They used to walk home from school and laugh and joke. By the end of their senior year, that had all stopped because of his relationship with Crystal.

She found herself glancing at his left hand. She didn't see a ring. Maybe he didn't like wearing one? Or—considering he was no longer quite the skinny kid who'd eloped the summer after high school, maybe he had gained weight and the ring no longer fit.

"We're getting close to my neighborhood," Taz said to the driver. "But if you don't mind, can you pull onto Hannaford Street, just a couple of blocks before my address? We can drop off my friend here."

The driver looked over his shoulder and nodded. "No problem."

Within a couple of minutes, the driver was turning onto her street. It was amazing how when she had been a child, the houses looked large and overwhelming. Now, they seemed normal sized. And in comparison to the new builds in the suburbs, these old houses in Toronto actually seemed small.

"It's number eighty-two," Miranda said.

She reached into her wallet for some money, but Taz immediately placed a hand over hers and pushed it down. "No. I'm not taking any money for an Uber ride."

"I was going to have to pay my own taxi anyway."

"And then you had the fortune of bumping into an old friend." He smiled at her. "Please, don't insult me by thinking that I would nickel and dime you a few bucks for this ride."

His words made her feel a little bit silly. Offering him money had been the right thing to do regardless. "Well, how about I take you out for a drink later this evening then?" The words had just fallen from her lips, unplanned and surprising even her. "After you spend some time with your mother, of course. We can catch up, maybe ten thirty?"

He looked curious. "Where did you have in mind?"

There were a lot of small mom-and-pop establishments and inde-pendent bars not far from their houses. "We could walk to Tommy's. Remember when we finally hit nineteen and we went there and had a beer? We felt so grown up." Miranda laughed.

"I remember," Taz said quietly.

That had been during their freshman year of college, when they had both returned home from school for Christmas. Miranda had been shocked to see Taz when he showed up on her doorstep. He'd been there to fulfill a promise—a drink at Tommy's to celebrate their nineteenth birthdays that had passed during the year. It was some-thing they'd talked about doing for years, after having tried to get into Tommy's at seventeen and being turned away. At the time, Miran-da had asked him about Crystal, and had been excited to learn that they'd broken up. But months later, not only were they back together, they were engaged.

Miranda pushed the memory out of her mind. "Ten thirty, then."

Miranda started to open the door, but Taz secured her by her wrist, preventing her from leaving. "Aren't you forgetting something?"

"Oh?"

"My number." He chuckled.

"Of course." What was wrong with her? She'd probably forget her name around him.

"Well, I *do* know where you live," she countered. I would have had a way to track you down if you stood me up."

Sheesh, why had she said *that*? As though she were flirting!

"Would you have thrown a rock at my window to get my atten-tion?" he asked.

Damn, his smile was still so sexy. No. It was sexier. The slight dimples in the chiseled jawline, the smooth, dark scalp. That small beard made him look all the more manly. Honestly, he was giving her heart palpitations. Which wasn't good.

"If I had to," she said, hoping that she'd come off as casual.

"Let me get your suitcase out of the car. And then give me your number and I'll text you."

He was just an old friend and they were going to get together to have a drink. But for a moment, she wondered if she was inviting something that was perhaps inappropriate. He was married. And yes, they went way back, but she didn't want him to get the wrong idea.

Still, after he took her suitcase from the trunk, she recited her number and he punched it into his phone. "Thanks," he said. "I'll text you."

She wanted to ask him why he had come alone. Why he wasn't with Crystal, or perhaps the rest of his family. Had he wanted to spare them the sadness of his mother's ordeal? And living in the States, they had the US Thanksgiving to celebrate in November.

Miranda started up the walkway to her parents' house. When she got to the base of the steps, she looked over her shoulder. His smile lit up the darkness.

"See you soon," he said.

CHAPTER THREE

*M*elanie threw the front door open with a definite sense of piz-zazz, her eyes searching expectantly, then narrowing in confusion. "Where's Matthew?"

"Good to see you too, Sis."

Miranda stepped forward and gave her sister a hug. Looking at her sister was like looking in a mirror, except that Melanie let her kinky hair grow naturally. It was a high, thick afro.

"Is he hiding?" Melanie asked as they pulled apart. "Come on, you know we're dying to meet him!"

"Um …" How much should she tell her sister right now? Heck, this was stupid. She just needed to acknowledge the truth. "He's not here."

Melanie's smile went flat. "Something came up?"

"You could say that," Miranda answered.

Doug was already making his way to the door, smiling brightly. It saved Miranda from having to get more into details.

"And you, Doug, my brother-in-law to be!" Miranda stepped toward him and threw her arms around him. She'd met Melanie's tall, sandy-blond-haired boyfriend a couple of times over the last year and half that he and her sister had been dating, and she really liked him. Melanie, who'd gone to Calgary for university and stayed there for work, had fallen for an actual cowboy.

"Yeah," Doug said softly. "I figured it was time I pop the question."

"Congratulations." Miranda reached for her sister's left hand and examined the engagement ring. It was a cushion cut diamond bordered by a rim of tiny diamonds, set in platinum. "It's stunning. Well done, Doug! I'm thrilled for both of you."

"Maybe you'll have some exciting news too in the near future?" he suggested.

Miranda smiled uncomfortably, and started for her suitcase, which was still on the porch, but Doug beat her to it. So she stepped farther into the foyer and bent to unzip her boots. She wiggled her toes when her feet were free.

"Where's Mom?"

"She's upstairs. She said she'd take the opportunity to catch up on her favorite soap opera, since we were all making too much noise while she was cooking."

Miranda went up the wooden steps, remembering exactly where each one creaked. The sense of familiarity warmed her heart.

She went into her parents' bedroom, where she saw her mother perched on the bed with her legs crossed at the ankles. Her mother was Italian, and though her face had aged, she was still a stunning beauty with her thick, dark hair set against her olive complexion. "Mom!"

"Sweetheart." Her mother's brown eyes lit up as she glanced at her, but then she quickly looked back at the television.

Miranda didn't let that stop her. She went straight to her mother, bent down, and embraced her, causing her mother to miss some precious seconds of the show. "Love you, Mom."

"You know I'm happy to see you," her mother said, "but Natalia is about to find out that her husband has been lying to her for years."

"You're never going to give this show up, are you, Mom?"

Her mother waved a hand. "Shh."

"Let me guess—Tom is still involved with Sylvia. Or is he back with Annalise?" Miranda shook her head, thinking of the storyline that alternated between Tom and two women. Invariably he was involved with one or the other, and no matter how many years passed and how many times he broke their hearts, the women were willing and happy to take him back when he chose them again. It was absurd.

"See you in a moment," her mother shushed her and waved her out of the room.

Ah, it was good to be back home.

Two hours later, Miranda, her parents, Melanie, and Doug were all seated at the table enjoying a dinner of roast beef, mashed potatoes, and glazed carrots. For as long as Miranda could remember, this was the meal her mother made on Friday nights.

"When is Brandon getting here?" Miranda asked. Her brother and his wife, who was now expecting, were coming in from Vancouver. Flights coming from the West Coast were often later.

"Their flight gets in late tonight," her mother said, echoing her thoughts.

"I guess I won't see him until tomorrow, then," Miranda said.

"We were hoping to see Matthew," her father commented.

"Yeah, I know."

"So, what happened?" her father continued. "Surely he's not working over the Thanksgiving weekend? Or did he decide to visit his family?"

Miranda's cell phone rang at that moment, saving her from answering. She was debating between outright lying and telling them the truth. Maybe she would wait until her brother got here, so she didn't have to answer the same questions again.

She swiped to answer the call, putting a finger up as she excused herself from the table. "Hey."

"How's the evening going?" Taz asked, his voice sounding incredibly sexy through the phone line.

Miranda wandered to the front hallway and the stairway that led to the second floor, allowing herself some privacy. "Good. We waited until my dad got home and we're just finishing up a very late dinner."

"Oh. You think you'll still be able to get that drink at ten thirty? That gives you forty-five minutes to finish up?"

"More than enough time."

"Good," he said, "because you owe me."

"I do?"

"For the Uber. Sorry, bad joke."

"Oh, right. I *do* owe you."

"Actually, I'm just really looking forward to seeing you."

Miranda's stomach lurched. "I see you're just as charming as ever."

Taz chuckled softly. "Should I come over at ten thirty?"

"I can be ready sooner. Gimme twenty minutes."

"Sounds good. I'll see you soon."

Miranda ended the call and went back to the table, her breathing a little erratic. This was silly, the idea of her even being excited at seeing Taz. But she was. She'd drink with him, reminisce about old times, and then come back down to earth. She wasn't going to cross any line with him. She wasn't that type of girl. But he'd always been her friend. There was no harm in hanging out.

Miranda speared the last morsel of her roast beef and stuffed it in her mouth. She ate it quickly, washed it down with a swig of cola, then said, "If you guys will excuse me ..."

"Who was that?" Melanie asked in a singsong voice. "Matthew?"

Miranda really ought to tell her sister the truth—and soon. She was going to ask a million-and-one questions about Matthew until he magically appeared.

"Actually, that was Taz," Miranda said.

"Taz?" Melanie and her mother said at the same time.

Miranda expelled a shuddery breath. "Yeah."

Her mother's eyes lit up. "Taz .... Well, that's a name I haven't heard in years."

"The nice kid you always hung out with in high school?" her father asked. He'd been in Canada for thirty-eight years, but he still had a Jamaican accent. People often said he looked like Harry Belafonte. There was no surprise as to why, as a young woman, her mother had been smitten with the handsome bus driver she saw every day as she headed to work.

"Yeah, Dad," Miranda said.

"I always thought you two would get together," her father went on. "I always liked him. He was a nice and respectful young man."

Oh, geez. Her father had thought that? Now she was glad she hadn't told them about Matthew, because Taz was coming to the door. Her family might start carrying on like a bunch of ridiculous matchmaking wannabes, if not for her now-fictitious relationship with Matthew.

"Why are you going out so late?" Melanie sounded suspicious.

"I ran into him at Union Station," Miranda explained. "We ended up taking an Uber back to the neighborhood together."

"How's he doing?" her mother asked.

"I think he's doing well. But unfortunately his mother is sick. Kidney problems."

"Oh. That's too bad," her mother commented.

"Yeah, it's quite serious. She needs a transplant in order to survive."

"Oh no!" Melanie's face twisted with disappointment.

"I feel really bad for him," Miranda said. "Sounds like he's really the only support for his mom. His brother's working in Japan, so he's not around."

"Maybe you should invite them over for Thanksgiving dinner," her mother suggested. "If they don't have any plans."

She hesitated for a moment, then chided herself for overthinking things. She had to try and learn to live in the moment. "Actually, that's a great idea," Miranda said. "I'll suggest it."

"Being sick, the last thing she's going to want to be doing is cooking," her mother continued. "And it's the last thing she *should* be doing. Tell Taz tonight. We'll have a full house, but we can add a couple more plates."

It was a good idea, and Miranda liked it. "Absolutely. I'll tell him."

No sooner than she went to the kitchen to put her plate in the dishwasher, the doorbell rang. Miranda's eyes bulged. She hadn't even had time to get ready!

Her sister jumped to her feet. "I'll get it."

Miranda took the opportunity to scurry upstairs so that she could freshen up a little bit. In the bathroom, she looked at herself in the mirror. She fluffed her short hair, which was longer on one side than the other. She tucked the shorter side behind her ear. She thought she might need to reapply her makeup, but she was satisfied with her appearance. She was wearing an off-the-shoulder gray sweater and blue jeans, and she looked cute. Besides, it wasn't like she was trying to impress him. They were just going to hang out for a little bit.

She got her purse and reapplied some lipstick, then dusted her face with powder. She smiled at her reflection. She was ready. Casual and cute. She didn't need to go for the sex vixen look.

Still, her stomach tickled as she headed down the steps. Melanie was at the door, animated as she was talking to Taz.

"I'm so sorry to hear about your mother," Melanie was saying. "Please give her my love."

"I will," Taz assured her.

"And you and Crystal …. That's a shock."

What was a shock? Miranda's eyes volleyed from her sister to Taz, but her sister stepped back at that moment, saying, "It was good to see you again, Taz."

"You too." He leaned his head into the door and waved at the rest of the family. "And good to see you all."

The family waved and echoed his sentiments.

Miranda slipped into her low-heeled boots and zipped them up. Then she turned and waved goodbye to her mother and father and brother-in-law to be, then stepped out of the house.

"You look lovely," Taz told her as she closed the door.

"Thank you." Miranda gave him a quick once over. He was wearing a casual navy blazer, a white shirt, and blue jeans. She couldn't get over how he had morphed into a sexy man from the teen he had once been. "You look pretty handsome yourself."

Taz offered her his arm and they went down the front steps.

Miranda swallowed, then asked, "What was that my sister was saying about Crystal?"

"Why don't we wait until we get to the bar. The story is best told over a drink."

"Oh?"

"Yeah."

Miranda was wildly curious, but they could wait the seven minutes it would take to walk to Tommy's.

"By the way, I told my mother about your mother, and she insisted on inviting you both over for Thanksgiving dinner. I agree. Your mother shouldn't be cooking right now. She needs to rest. Unless of course you have other plans …"

"No," Taz said. "Actually, I just figured I was going to have a quiet Thanksgiving with her. I was going to buy a cooked chicken tomorrow."

"You can't have a chicken on Thanksgiving," she admonished.

"It sounds like now I don't have to," he said, and looked down at her and smiled.

Taz had been tall in high school but he seemed even a bit taller now. Probably six foot two or three now, based on how he hovered over her despite her heels. He still dwarfed her, and she was five foot seven.

"If she's up to coming to our place for dinner, of course," Miranda said. "If she doesn't feel well enough, don't think you're obligated to come over. But we would love to have you."

A few minutes later, they were arriving at Tommy's. It was an Irish bar, with dark windows and the name written in a gold font that had faded over the years. It looked exactly as Miranda had remembered.

Ever the gentleman, Taz opened the door for her. She walked in ahead of him.

It was what many would call a dive bar. Nothing fancy, dark, and almost dingy, really. Tables that probably hadn't been changed since it opened. Chairs with brass finishings. There was a stage where musicians performed, behind which was tinsel decorating the wall. "Oh my God, I remember that tinsel from when we were here years ago. I can't believe they still have that."

"Some things never change."

That was for sure.

The place wasn't busy, so they walked to the far side and found a table. As Taz leaned an elbow on it, the table tipped to the right. Miranda couldn't help giggling. "To think we were so excited to be able to come here when we were younger, and finally legal."

"Yeah. It's humorous now that we think of it. But I like this place." Taz gazed at the various photos on the walls of performers who had been there over the years, and signs indicating who would be performing in the near future. "The beers are probably as cheap now as they were then."

Miranda picked up the plastic encased drink menu on the table. "Let's see."

She looked at the cocktails, but opted for a vodka cooler instead. Taz ordered a beer. At least the waitress who'd come around was friendly and quick.

"So how's Westchester?" Miranda asked.

"I like it. It's a good location. Close to New York City but far enough away to not be as crazy busy."

"Did you become an architect? That's what you were planning."

"I did. Sometimes I think about making a change, but I really do enjoy it."

"What would you change and do?" Miranda asked.

Taz shrugged. "Sometimes I fancy myself a guitar player. You remember I used to love playing music."

"Is that what you called it?" Miranda teased.

"I thought you used to enjoy my skills."

"I did. I'm just teasing you." She paused. "You used to be in that band with Dave and Jeff." Miranda smiled at the memory. "What did you guys call yourselves?"

"The Edge. We thought we were so cool."

"The Edge, that's right!" Miranda threw her head back and laughed. She remembered the times that she had gone to Dave's house to listen to them rock out in the basement. She had barely been able to handle all the noise, but she'd gone for one reason. To spend more time with Taz.

"Oh, to be so young and silly again," Taz said.

"Tell me about it." Miranda's laughter died. "What do you mean you *used* to love playing?"

"I gave it up. It was always just a hobby."

"You can still play for fun. There must be other hobbyists in Westchester."

"That was the plan. I even met with a group of guys and started playing with them on Friday nights. But Crystal didn't like it. She said I kept wasting time and not spending enough time with her, so you know." He shrugged. "I gave it up."

"Really?"

"Hey, it's fine. I was never going to be a music star. It was always just something to pass the time."

Even as he said that, Miranda could tell that he missed it. Obviously, it was a hobby, but a hobby that gave him enjoyment. He'd always loved playing the guitar in high school. She was surprised that his wife would make him give up something that brought him enjoyment.

The waitress arrived then with their drinks, smiling happily as she placed them on the table. "Would you like to order any food?"

"How about onion rings?" Taz suggested.

That had been their first order when they'd last been to this establishment. A couple of beers, and onion rings. As much as their student pocketbooks would allow.

"That's one of our most popular items," the waitress commented.

"It's like we're re-creating that first date," Miranda said as the waitress walked away. "Not that it was a *real* date, of course. Just our first time here. Except I had a beer then. I thought I liked beer. Until I realized there were other options."

She fiddled with the chilled glass, then decided to take a sip of the vodka cooler straight from the bottle. It was refreshing, and a way to shut her up. She felt like she was babbling.

Acoustic rock played over the speaker system. Miranda looked around the establishment, a way to avoid having to say anything. But finally she spoke, because her curiosity was getting the better of her. "So, tell me. What's this news with you and Crystal?"

"We divorced," Taz said succinctly.

Miranda's eyes widened. "What? When? Why?"

"Two years ago."

"Two years!" she exclaimed.

Taz took a pull of his beer. "We split, probably two and a half years ago, and the divorce was final around a year and a half ago to be exact. But yeah, we're not together anymore."

Miranda took a moment to digest that information. After a while she asked, "Did you have children?"

Taz shook his head. "No. And I'm grateful for that. She was never ready. She was an actor, you might remember. She was pursuing a career in theater. She did some off-Broadway shows but hoped to make it bigtime. She was never ready to have any kids."

"Wait, so she could pursue her artistic career but you couldn't pursue yours?"

"She always said we couldn't have two artists in the family. One of us had to make the money."

"That was convenient," Miranda quipped.

"It's expensive living in New York, as you might imagine."

"But still. It seems like quite the double standard to not even want you to pursue your music as a hobby while she's trying to be an actress."

He shrugged, shoulders a little stiff. "Like I said, we're divorced."

Miranda's heart was fluttering. Now she wished that she had dressed up a little more. Tried a little harder to look better.

"What about you?" Taz asked. "I don't see a ring, but that doesn't mean you're not married."

Miranda shook her head. "Nope. Definitely not married."

"No boyfriend?"

She took a swig of her drink. "Funny you ask. Until earlier this week, I thought I had one. He was supposed to come here with me, in fact. But now," she took another sip, "I'm single."

Taz looked at her through narrowed eyes. "There's a story there."

"There is."

He leaned back in his chair. "I'm all ears."

Miranda groaned. Suddenly, Matthew was the last thing on her mind. She'd gone from caring about him being with her here to thinking *Matthew who?*

"We'd only been together about six months. He's an accountant, I'm an interpreter. We both have busy lives, but next thing I know I'm coming back from a business trip and he's not answering my calls. Actually, correction." Miranda held up a finger. "His calls weren't going through. Then I couldn't find him on Facebook anymore, and he wasn't responding to any of my texts. So, long story short, he blocked me on everything."

"Wait, did you have a fight?"

"No. I went off to DC for my work trip, we talked a couple of times, made plans to see each other when I got back and finalize our trip to Toronto. And then the next thing, I'm completely out of his life."

Taz frowned. "He didn't even talk to you?"

"He talked to a mutual friend before he ghosted me. Told her I was too busy for him and he didn't think our relationship was working." Miranda shook her head, still unable to believe that Matthew had taken such a coward's way out. "Hey, it was better that he do that than head here for Thanksgiving with me and give my family hope—and having everybody like him and then him dumping me afterward."

"You seem to be taking it in stride."

"It wasn't meant to be," she said. She looked into Taz's eyes, held his gaze for a little too long. Something passed between them, an awareness that had her feeling a flash of heat.

She was still attracted to him. It made no sense, and yet it was true.

Taz raised his beer bottle. "A toast then. To reconnecting, after way too long."

CHAPTER FOUR

*T*wo hours later, Taz and Miranda arrived at her parents' house. She stopped at the end of the walkway that led up to the porch. Looking up at Taz, she said, "Well, that was fun."

"Yeah," Taz agreed. "I enjoyed myself."

"Maybe we can do it again sometime?" Miranda smiled bashfully, then averted her gaze. When would they have the time to do this again? She was just in town for the weekend and then heading back to Ottawa. Taz would be heading back to New York.

"Hey," Taz began softly. "Can I ask you something?"

"Sure," Miranda said, looking up at him again. "Anything."

Taz glanced at a passing car, then took her by the arm and guided her up the porch steps.

Did the curtain just move? Miranda wondered. She didn't doubt her sister was spying on them.

Now at her door, away from the window, Miranda said, "You were going to ask me something?"

Taz gently placed his fingers on her cheek and stroked down her jaw softly. Heat erupted in her body, while confusion clogged her brain. What was he doing?

"Can I kiss you?"

Miranda's eyes grew as wide as saucers. "What? Wait…. That's what you want to ask me?"

"You don't want me to? I kind of thought I was getting a vibe off you."

"No." Miranda realized what she'd said and then corrected herself. "I mean, yes. I'm just … I'm confused."

"I'm not." Taz's lips formed a little smile as his fingers reached into her hair. He eased her head backward while lowering his mouth to hers. Miranda could barely process what was happening.

And then his lips were on hers, moving with gentleness. After a few seconds of being stunned, Miranda expelled a breath. In reaction, Taz looped an arm around her waist, his lips picking up speed.

Sensations exploded inside Miranda's body; she didn't know how to react. She was too shocked. Was she dreaming?

Taz broke the kiss, and that wicked sexy smile greeted her as she looked up at him.

"I've wanted to do that for eighteen years," he whispered. "Good night."

"Good night?" He was going to kiss her like that and leave?

He started down the steps. "We'll talk tomorrow."

"Um, okay."

Miranda waved to Taz as he continued on his journey, thinking she might never wash her lips again. She was confused. She was excited. She was a mess.

Why had he done that? And the comment about wanting to do that for eighteen years? Her head was spinning.

Oh, she'd had the biggest crush on him then, but he had never ever crossed the boundaries of friendship with her. He'd never been even remotely interested. So where was that comment coming from?

Maybe he felt lonely and her familiarity warmed him? He had broken up with Crystal, maybe he hadn't been dating since, and suddenly there she was. She probably still looked at him with those pathetic puppy dog eyes. He'd picked up on her interest in him and of course he'd made a move on her.

Mystery solved; Miranda's shoulders slumped as she entered the house. She gasped in fright when she saw her sister standing in the foyer, eyeing her with delight.

"Is there something you're not telling me?" Melanie asked.

"Well …" Miranda hedged.

"First of all, you were out with Taz for quite a while. And didn't I just see him *kissing* you?"

Melanie had to have literally plastered her face onto the window to achieve enough of an angle to glimpse them together. "Yes."

Melanie squealed with glee.

"Shh. Don't wake Mom and Dad."

"We're awake, dear," came the voice from upstairs.

Miranda jerked her gaze to the top of the stairs. Her mother was standing there, securing the tie on her robe.

"We're waiting to hear that your brother has arrived safely," her mother went on.

"Oh, of course." Miranda had thought that they were waiting up for her.

"How did your evening with Taz go?" her mother asked.

"Your relationship just got complicated," Melanie whispered. "Didn't it?"

Melanie's gaze flitted from her sister to her mother. "Do you and Dad want to come down for a cup of tea? There's something I'd like to tell you all."

"Oh." Her mother looked concerned. "Everything okay?"

"Yeah. There's just something I need to tell you all. And I may as well do it now."

A few minutes later, Miranda, Melanie and their parents were sitting around the kitchen table. Both parents had declined the offer of mint tea; both were looking mildly concerned that they'd been summoned from bed.

Miranda hadn't planned to tell her family the news about Matthew at this exact moment, after midnight, but since everyone was still up and Melanie had seen her kissing Taz through the window, she decided it was best not to put it off any longer.

"Is everything okay, sweetheart?" her mother asked.

"Yes. That's the first thing I want to make sure you understand. I'm perfectly fine. But I do have a bit of news."

Beside her, Melanie was leaning forward, her lips curled in a sly smile. Oh, she'd always loved to be caught up in the gossip, and it must have thrilled her to witness Miranda's unexpected kiss with Taz and be the one who'd forced this impromptu meeting.

"Melanie, why do you seem so excited about whatever it is that your sister is going to say?" their mother asked.

Melanie tried to force a straight face, and mimed zipping her lips shut. Miranda gave her the side eye. She didn't know why her sister was acting with such glee.

"I know that everyone was looking forward to seeing Matthew this weekend," Miranda began.

"Yes," her father said. "I've been wanting to meet him for a while. Any man who has snagged my daughter's heart, I need to meet and have a talk with."

"Unfortunately, you won't be meeting him," Miranda said. "Not this weekend. Not ever."

Both of her parents looked instantly confused. "You broke up?" her father asked.

"Yes." And then Miranda explained the whole story to them, how they had broken up just this week, and that she was okay with it. And how in her heart she had known that Matthew wasn't really the one for her. She's been hopeful, but his cowardly breakup tactic had made it clear that they could never be together.

"And ...." her sister prompted.

Miranda looked at her, glaring. "And what?"

"And what was it that I saw outside? You and Taz ... reconnecting?"

"We're old friends," Miranda said, discreetly kicking her sister under the table.

"When a door closes ..." Melanie said.

"I haven't seen Taz in fourteen, fifteen years," Miranda protested.

"You know what I say," Melanie began, "everything happens for a reason. Maybe Matthew broke up with you right before you were heading home because you were going to see Taz, a guy you'd always had a crush on in school, and .... The rest is history."

"That's ridiculous," Miranda said.

"I always liked Taz," her father chimed in. "Decent young guy. And I admit, I always thought you two would get together."

"I thought the same thing," her mother said.

Miranda looked at each of them in turn. "Really? You know what, don't answer that. I ran into Taz at Union Station. We had a drink to catch up on each others' lives. No big deal."

Melanie kicked her under the table.

Miranda shot her a look, and she hoped that her sister would keep her mouth shut.

"So that's it, you don't get to meet Matthew," Miranda said. "But I'm okay with it. I'm not falling apart. I'm disappointed, but I'm not really upset."

"Well, that's good to hear," her mother said. "It definitely sounds as though he wasn't the right one for you."

"And I think fate has intervened," Melanie couldn't help saying.

Miranda shot her sister a feigned look of annoyance, but then her lips began to curl into a smile. Melanie, the romantic. Always looking for a silver lining. She couldn't be mad at her sister for wishing her the best.

"Are you sure you don't want any tea?" Miranda asked. Mint tea was a favorite in their family, a Jamaican tradition. They started the day with an Italian espresso, and ended it with Jamaican mint tea.

"No thank you," her father said. And then his cell phone, which was on the table, began to ring. "It's your brother," he said, then swiped to answer the call. "Hello? Oh, thank God. Do you need me to pick you up? Are you sure? Because it's no trouble."

Leaving her parents at the dining room table talking to her brother, Miranda headed upstairs. No sooner than she was in her room, so was Melanie. Her sister closed the door behind her. She still had that look of glee on her face.

"What were you trying to do?" Miranda asked. "Expose the fact that I shared a kiss with Taz and have Mom and Dad thinking that I've been having some sort of long-term affair with him?"

Melanie plopped herself down onto the bed. "Have you been?"

"No!"

"Then what was that I saw outside? You expect me to believe that you ran into Taz today for the first time in more than a decade and suddenly you're making out?"

Miranda wanted to tell her sister that it was her imagination. That Taz hadn't kissed her. But even as she remembered the feel of his mouth on her lips, the unexpected surprise and delight, she didn't want to deny it.

"Look at your face, the way it's lighting up. Seriously, have you and Taz been having a secret affair that you haven't told us about?"

"No." Miranda sat on the bed beside her sister. "Honestly, I don't know what got into him. I literally bumped into him at the train station, and that's the first I've seen him in so many years. We talked. It was like old times. And the next thing I know, he's kissing me."

"I always said it when we were young: you and Taz were meant to be together."

Miranda remembered her sister having said that often. Her sister the romantic hadn't been able to understand how Miranda and Taz could have simply been friends.

"He told me about his divorce, how things fell apart for him and Crystal. Maybe he's just lonely."

"Or maybe he's realizing that he made a mistake all those years ago. He should have chosen you."

Miranda didn't even want to think of that—in case it raised false hope—and waved off the suggestion. She wasn't about to read too much into the kiss. The way she saw it, it was probably a spur of the moment thing. If Miranda started fantasizing that it was something more than that, she was guaranteed to give herself heartache. She remembered how that heartache from Taz had felt as a teen. It was brutal.

"Look, I don't know what's going on," Miranda said. "It's just something that happened. Let's leave it at that."

Melanie squeezed the pillow that she had pulled onto her lap. "How was the kiss?"

Now Miranda couldn't help smiling. "It was amazing!"

The next morning, Miranda was heading down to the kitchen to make coffee. She was wearing her pajamas and rubbing sleep from her eyes when she saw her mother at the table with a beautiful bouquet of red roses. She was arranging them in a vase and looked up at her as Miranda approached, giving her bright smile.

"Morning, Mom." Miranda kissed her mother on the cheek. "Look at that. Dad is still so romantic."

"I can't tell you the last time your father got me flowers."

"Then you must feel even more special today."

"These aren't for me. They're for *you*."

Miranda's eyebrows shot up. "What do you mean they're for me?"

"Just what I said. I opened the door this morning and this bouquet was there. It had your name on it. Now, I didn't open the card or anything—"

"They're for me?" Miranda couldn't believe her mother's words.

"You must need me to make you an espresso," her mother said, smiling. "That'll wake you up."

Miranda looked at the stunning bouquet, then leaned forward to sniff them.

"Maybe they're from Matthew," her mother said. "Or maybe they're from Taz."

"Where's the card?"

Her mother lifted the envelope from the table and passed it to her. Miranda went into the kitchen, rested her butt against the counter, her heart beating fast as she debated opening it. If these weren't from Taz, she was going to be so disappointed.

"Well?" her mother asked, coming into the kitchen a minute later.

Miranda quickly opened the envelope. She withdrew the card, which read:

> It was an absolute pleasure running into you again.
> Maybe it's fate.
>
> Taz

Miranda's heart thundered in her chest. This was so unexpected and so thrilling! Taz had actually send her flowers.

"So?" her mother prompted.

Miranda tried to keep her voice even. "They're from Taz."

Her mother beamed. "Oh, look at that. You and Taz. I always liked him, I told you that."

"I can't believe he sent me roses."

"Why not? He's single now, you're single. And if you ask me, Taz would have been yours—if that other girl hadn't come along and stolen him away from you." When Miranda's eyes registered surprise, her mother went on. "You don't remember that time your father and I went to visit you in Ottawa and I could tell you'd been crying? You confided in me that you'd heard Taz was engaged to be married. You were heartbroken."

Gosh, that seemed like a lifetime ago. And yet, it also seemed like yesterday.

"I remember," Miranda said softly.

"What does the card say?"

Her stomach quivering, Miranda passed it to her mother. Watched the smile on her mother's face grow as she read it.

"Oh, my. Sweetheart, this is exciting!"

Her mother's excitement had Miranda allowing herself to feel the giddy sensation that had bubbled up in her. She went back into the dining room and once again checked out the array of stunning roses.

Maybe it's fate.

"Maybe this is just about him being lonely after his divorce. He ran into me and I was a friendly face from the past, and—"

"Maybe you need to stop overthinking this. Red roses mean love, plain and simple. You mark my words, sweetheart."

CHAPTER FIVE

*W*hile her mother set about making her an espresso, Miranda went upstairs and sent Taz a text thanking him for the roses, and promised that she would call him later. Though she was undoubtedly excited, she wanted to keep her heart aloof. She couldn't allow herself to regress to teenage Miranda, who could spend hours on the phone talking to him and still never want the call to end.

A few minutes later, Miranda heard the doorbell, and she knew her brother had arrived. He and his wife were coming over for a late breakfast, after having arrived in the early hours of the morning.

Miranda slipped into a robe and slippers, then headed downstairs. Brandon and Tesha were in the foyer, removing their jackets and shoes.

"Hey," Miranda said, joining her sister and parents in the foyer so that she could give her brother a hug. "Little Brother, how are you?"

She liked to refer to him as little brother, because the irony was that he'd grown taller than anyone had expected. He might be younger than Miranda by four years, but at six foot five, he was hardly "little."

"I'm great, Sis." He kissed her cheek. "Good to see you. You look beautiful."

Miranda moved to greet her sister-in-law. "And Tesha, so good to see you." She leaned forward to carefully hug Tesha without pressing too hard against her protruding belly. "I am so excited for you guys."

"Thanks, Miranda." Tesha was arching her back, showing off her belly bump with delight. "We're thrilled."

"Where's Matthew?" her brother asked. "I'm dying to meet him."

Miranda crossed her arms over her chest. "He's not here. I filled everyone in last night, so I'll tell you what's going on." She took a couple of minutes to give them the abbreviated version.

"But in the interim," her mother said, "Taz sent her that beautiful bouquet of flowers right there."

Brandon's eyes narrowed. "Taz?"

"Yes, Taz."

"The guy you had a crush on in high school?"

Was that the way her entire family saw her relationship with Taz? No one had seen them as strictly friends?

"He was my best friend," Miranda clarified.

"Taz is a good guy. He was always nice to me. What's he been up to? I thought he was married, no?"

Miranda filled her brother in on the latest with Taz, the fact that he was now single. That they'd met for a couple of drinks and now Melanie was already planning the wedding. She didn't tell him that Taz had kissed her on the front porch, and that she hadn't been able to stop thinking about that glorious kiss ever since.

"His mother's sick," their mother said. "I've invited them over for Thanksgiving dinner. You told him, right?" she asked Miranda.

"Yes. I did. I'm going to confirm with him today. Just tell me a time."

"I'd like to serve dinner at five. But they're welcome to come a little before that. Four, four thirty. Whatever's good for them."

"I'll tell him."

Then her mother was getting breakfast ready, bacon and pancakes and scrambled eggs. It was almost like old times when Miranda was a child. Her mother's face was lit up in a perpetual smile. She seemed thrilled to have a house full of people to cook for.

Everyone dug in, and soon there was chatter and laughter as everyone indulged.

"I haven't had a breakfast like that in a while," Miranda said. "Everything was delicious."

"Is that all you're having?" her mother asked. She was already reaching for the scrambled eggs and putting more onto her plate. "You need a bit more meat on your bones. Have some more eggs. And there's more bacon."

Miranda held up a hand to stop her mother as she reached for the homemade hash browns. Potatoes were Miranda's one guilty pleasure, but she simply couldn't eat any more. "Mom, I'm stuffed. I can't eat another bite."

"You've gotten so thin being out in Ottawa with no one to take care of you. Do you even eat?"

"Of course I eat." What was it with Italian mothers who were always feeding you, but the moment you put on any weight they were the first to point it out? Miranda couldn't help chuckling though. She loved her mother. It was good to be home.

To satisfy her mother, she ate one more hash brown and another spoonful of scrambled eggs, then pushed her chair back. She scooped up her coffee. "Thank you so much, Mom. I'm just gonna go upstairs for a little bit. I brought my laptop and I'm going to do a bit of work."

"This is a holiday weekend."

"I know. I just want to get a couple of things out of the way, then I'll be available."

What she really wanted to do was call Taz. She went into the bedroom and sat cross-legged on her bed, picked up her cell phone, and dialed his number.

Then she held her breath, waiting for him to answer. He answered after the first ring, as though he had been expecting her call. "Hello beautiful."

His voice was deeper than it had been when they were younger, and so very sexy. A shiver of delight danced down her spine. "I got the flowers," Miranda said. "They're lovely."

"I'm glad you like them."

"You're giving everyone here something to talk about, that's for sure."

"I couldn't help it. I was walking on the Danforth this morning, saw the lovely bouquet, and figured you should have them."

Miranda wanted to ask him about the card—and she didn't want to ask him. She didn't want to jump to conclusions. But he'd sent her red roses—wasn't there only one conclusion to make from that?

"Honestly, bumping into you at Union Station has been the highlight of my trip so far," Miranda said. "I keep thinking about high school and how close we were and everything we used to do. I feel kinda bad that we drifted apart."

"Me too. Though I'm sure we drifted apart because I married Crystal. And you went off to Ottawa, while I went off to the States."

"Yeah, but we should never have let anything come between us. We were such good friends."

Silence fell between them, and Miranda didn't know what he was thinking. She didn't know what *she* was thinking.

Yes she did. She was thinking that maybe, just maybe the kiss between them meant something. That it wasn't an off-the-cuff thing just to see how it felt. Maybe he was thinking about how he'd made a mistake by not pursuing her all those years ago.

"By the way," she began, "dinner's going to be at five on Sunday. You can come earlier with your mother. Any time after four. Will you be able to make it?"

"We'll be there. I talked to my mother, and she's super happy that you extended the invitation to us."

"Of course. I'm looking forward to seeing her as well."

"I just wish it were under better circumstances," Taz said softly.

"How is she?"

"Not as bad as I thought. She's really happy that I'm home, so maybe that's boosting her spirits and her pain threshold. I don't know."

"If there's anything I can do for you or your mother, just let me know. Anything at all."

"I appreciate that," he told her.

"I do mean it."

"I know you do." He paused briefly. Then he said, "I would try to steal you away again today for another drink, but you said you haven't seen your brother and sister in months, not to mention your parents. So I won't impose. But I'll see you tomorrow. Four o'clock."

Miranda wanted to tell him that she'd love to hang out with him for a bit and have another drink, but she was too timid. So she just said, "Sounds good. See you then."

Taz didn't text or call Miranda for the remainder of the day, but she thought about texting or calling him one hundred times. It was so weird, this nervousness she felt at the idea of even reaching out to someone who had always been a good friend. But it was that kiss. That kiss that had her wondering what was right to do and what wasn't.

The kiss also had the feelings for Taz she thought she'd buried rushing back. It was so clear now that what she'd felt for Matthew had been insignificant in the grand scheme of things. She'd liked him well enough, but there'd been no real passion between them. No butterflies, no excitement.

Yet seeing Taz again had Miranda feeling exactly that. Her heart was pondering, *What if?*

Sighing, she threw herself backward on the bed. Was she reading way too much into seeing Taz again and sharing a kiss? People slept together all the time and it didn't mean anything.

Still, the roses ....

Rolling over onto her stomach, she called Anna. Anna answered on the second ring. "Hey, girl. What's up?"

"A lot," Miranda said without preamble. "I have so much to tell you."

"Oh. That sounds intriguing. Let me just go into my room. James is here, but I have a feeling I'm gonna need some space and quiet for this one."

"You will."

Miranda could hear Anna shuffling on the other line, then a door close. A few moments later, her friend spoke. "Okay, what's going on?"

"You're not gonna believe any of this," Miranda said.

"Try me."

"Guess who I ran into when I got to Union Station? And I mean literally ran into—I bumped into him."

"Not Matthew?

"No, not Matthew."

"Dexter?"

"Why would you say Dexter?" Miranda asked.

"Because you want me to guess."

"No, not your ex-fiancé."

"I don't know what to think. Give me a hint."

"He went to high school with us," Miranda told her. "And you happened to mention him the other day when we were having drinks with Ruby."

"*Taz?*"

"The one and only."

"You're kidding," Anna said. "One day we're talking about him, the next you're running into him? What are the chances?"

"I know." Miranda blew out a harried breath. "I just want some perspective. Roses are normally a sign of romance, but from Taz he's just being friendly …. Right? Because he's an old friend?"

"He sent you roses?"

"Yes."

"What did the card say?" Anna asked, excitement bubbling in her voice.

Miranda read it to her, an odd sensation shooting through her veins.

"Wait, what aren't you telling me?"

"That we went for drinks and he kissed me," Miranda said in a rush. "And did I mention he's divorced?"

Anna squealed. "He *definitely* interested."

"But I haven't seen him in years. And he was never interested in me when we were young."

"Maybe he was." Anna's voice rose on a hopeful note. "You guys were such good friends. Maybe he didn't want to chance ruining the friendship by dating you, then Crystal came along and pounced on him."

Miranda bit down on her bottom lip. The last couple of days had been surreal. But reality was hitting her hard now. She raised herself up on her arms, pulling a pillow toward her to lean on. "I don't know why I even called you about this. It's not like it can go anywhere."

"Listen, you don't know that. Where there's a will, there's a way. If you and Taz are finally going to make something happen, no one's happier than I am. Maybe it's always just been an issue of timing for you guys."

Miranda frowned. She'd called Anna, excited to tell her this news, but now she knew most of all that she didn't want to be disappointed. What if this was just a rebound situation for Taz?

As she ended the call with Anna, she vowed to put Taz out of her mind as much as possible. To not take that trip down memory lane, because it was probably only going to end up in disappointment.

CHAPTER SIX

*T*he next evening, right at four o'clock, the doorbell rang. Melanie, who had been standing beside Miranda at the table to make sure all the place settings were just right, quickly shot her sister a look. "You want to get it?" Melanie asked.

"No, you get it."

Melanie smiled. "Have I told you how beautiful you look? That auburn sweater really looks good on you, and your black jeans …. Plus your makeup. You look amazing."

Miranda glanced away bashfully. Yes, she'd been trying to look good. Irresistible. She wished she could just say it was for the dinner, but it wasn't. It was for Taz.

Her sister hurried off to answer the door, and Miranda pretended she wasn't paying any attention. She smoothed out the napkins and the place settings, busying herself with the job that was already done.

"Hello," Melanie said warmly.

Miranda cast a furtive glance toward the front foyer, then stepped away from the table, brushed her palms against her jeans, and headed in that direction. She put on a bright smile as she saw Taz. He was dressed in navy dress pants and a pale-blue dress shirt that was open a couple of buttons at the collar. Miranda's eyes went from him, an image of absolute stunning perfection, to his mother. She had a gray sweater curled around her body, and she definitely looked frail. Her graying hair was pulled back in a bun. She was a lot thinner than Miranda remembered.

As her sister hugged both Taz and then his mother, Miranda made her way over to them. "Hi, Taz." She gave him a bashful smile as she noticed his eyes drink in her appearance. Then she quickly turned to his mother. "And Mrs. Morrison. So nice to see you again."

"Call me Camille."

"Camille it is," Miranda agreed. Then she hugged her. As she pulled apart from the woman she asked, "How are you feeling? Taz told me you're not feeling the best."

"I feel much better now that he's here."

"Of course." Miranda ran her palms down both of Camille's arms, and ultimately took her hands in hers. She squeezed them gently. "I'm praying for you. I think everything's going to go well."

"Thank you."

Miranda's own mother came down the stairs. She warmly greeted Taz and his mother. As everyone began to congregate in the foyer, introductions were made. Then Miranda's mother said, "Let's head into the living room. We can't keep the party in the foyer all evening!"

Once in the living room, everyone found their seat. Taz made sure that he helped his mother onto the sofa. Miranda watched him, seeing the look of worry etched in the lines around his mouth and his eyes.

Miranda's mother clasped her hands together. "I'm so glad you could make it. Typically, Thanksgiving is just us and extended family. But it should also be for dear friends."

Camille nodded. "It's amazing how time flies. I used to see you shopping on the Danforth sometimes. Now I barely run into you."

"I know, and I feel bad. I should've stayed in touch."

Miranda knew that when someone was sick, that's when people had regrets. They should have done this; they should have done that. Humans were so often taking the people in their lives for granted, as if there was endless time to be with them.

"Well," Camille said, "I'm here now. And I'm very glad that I don't have to do the dishes this year." She chuckled softly. "Or is that the price of dinner?"

Everyone laughed. Then they began to talk about old times, and what was new in their lives. Camille shared the story of how her older son was in Japan, which of course Taz had already told Miranda.

"Japan?" her father asked. "How does he like it?"

"It's a culture shock, but he fell in love, and that's where he is. I always hoped one day to be able to go there and visit him."

Taz took his mother's hand and squeezed it. "You will. I'll make sure of it."

Camille looked at her son with love in her eyes. Miranda could see in her gaze that she knew anything Taz could do for her, he would. Miranda's own eyes began to mist. She hoped that he could keep his promise to her.

With Brandon and Tesha's news about expecting a baby, and Melanie's news about being engaged, the conversation turned to happier things. Miranda was glad for that. She was especially glad because Camille was laughing a lot. Maybe when she was home, she only had time to sit and think about her predicament. But at least here, she was getting a reprieve from the reality of her life.

Miranda's mother excused herself from the living room. "Let me go check on the food."

"I'll join you," Miranda said. She hopped to her feet and followed her mother into the kitchen.

Once there, her mother looked at her with an expression filled with awe. "Wow. Taz is very handsome."

Miranda shushed her mother. "I don't want him to hear you."

"Everyone's talking in the living room. He won't hear me. I always liked him, did I tell you that?"

"Several times, Mom."

She and her mother set about checking the turkey and getting it onto the serving platter. Miranda got the potato salad and the green beans and the bread rolls. Together with her mother, she began to carry the food items into the dining room. Melanie came to join them, and exactly like their mother, she echoed just how gorgeous Taz has looked and mused that she hoped he would soon be her brother-in-law.

Miranda simply shook her head, but her stomach was tickling from excitement. He really did look good. He was gorgeous.

Was he really interested in her, or simply on the rebound? They really needed to talk about this at some point.

Forty minutes later, everyone's appetite was satiated. Miranda's father eased his body back and patted his robust belly. "Well, that was a meal."

"Does anyone want any more dessert?" her mother asked. She was already getting to her feet, prepared to go to the kitchen.

"I couldn't eat another bite," Camille said.

"Me neither," Taz echoed.

Miranda was bursting at the seams and didn't know if she'd be able to move. Doug, however, said, "Sure. I'd love some more of the pumpkin pie." His thin frame belied his huge appetite. "And if there's any more of your homemade tiramisu, I'll have a piece. I'll start my diet tomorrow."

Melanie looked at him and grinned. "You're always starting your diet tomorrow."

"Hey, when someone can cook this well, it's a crime not to eat the food."

There were chuckles all around. Then Miranda's father was standing. He clinked his glass, getting everyone's attention. "We have a tradition here in the Cox household," he announced. "Each of us takes a turn around the table to say what we're thankful for."

"I love that," Camille said.

"I'll start," her father continued. "This Thanksgiving, I am grateful that all of my family is here. My wife, all of my children and their partners. I'm grateful that there will be new beginnings, and life continuing. So much we take for granted, so this moment with everyone here able to smile and laugh I will always cherish."

"Here, here," Taz said, and squeezed his mother's hand. She gave him a wistful smile.

"I have to echo what my husband said," Miranda's mother stated. "I'm grateful that I have all of my children here. And I'm grateful that I have my old friend here. I'm reminded now that friendships and family relationships are the most important thing in this world. I never want to lose touch with anyone who's ever mattered to me." She looked at Camille. "I'm here for you, Camille. Whatever you need."

"I appreciate that," Camille said. "And I'd like to say something. I don't know if you have a specific order, but can I speak now?"

Her father waved off the concern. "Absolutely. Go ahead."

"I'm so thankful that my Taz ran into Miranda at the train station. As much as I love him and I love spending time with him, it's been an extra blessing to be here with all of you. Taz worries about me, I know. And while we would have made the best of the day, there might have been an overtone of sadness. But with you all, I've been laughing and reminiscing and not thinking about being sick. I don't know what tomorrow holds for me, but I'm really happy that in this moment I got to be normal. Not looked at with pity, but appreciation. I will always thank you for that."

"Well," Miranda's mother said, and dabbed at her eyes. "That was beautiful."

"Yeah, talk about making us all cry," Miranda echoed, wiping at her own eyes. Life was fragile. It was precious. Everyone should cherish every moment.

Maybe fate is *at play here*, Miranda thought, thinking of Taz's card. Life was short. Shouldn't she take a risk?

Taz cleared his throat. "I'd like to say something as well. You have all welcomed me and my mother with such warmth. I'm blown away, honestly. Your kindness and generosity have really made this Thanksgiving extra special. Sometimes I think life is about timing. Certain things happening when they should." His gaze landed on Miranda. "All I know is that I think I'm supposed to be here right now, with my mother. With all of you. It feels right."

Miranda's stomach was doing somersaults. He was throwing out major hints about his feelings for her. No, this was more than just a hint. He was being pretty obvious, wasn't he?

One by one, the rest of the family at the table spoke, all echoing similar sentiments. That they were grateful for the time together, that they were grateful for the promise of the future. They were appreciative of the love of friends and family at a time when some people didn't have that.

"Now, to change things up," Miranda's father said. "Every holiday gathering, we watch one of the Chevy Chase vacation movies."

"If you can call it watching," Miranda quipped. "The TV might be on, but we do more talking and laughing than watching. It helps that we've seen the movies a dozen times."

"So you're welcome to stay and watch with us," her father said.

"I'd like that," Camille said.

"Are you sure?" Taz asked her. "If you're not up to it, I can take you home."

"I'm having a great time," Camille said. "I'm not ready to go home yet."

Taz sat beside Miranda, putting some space between them. The movie, *European Vacation*, started and soon everyone was chatting and laughing. They paid attention to some of the movie, but otherwise they were entertaining themselves with humorous memories from the past.

Taz inched his hand across the vacant spot between him and Miranda and looped his baby finger with hers.

Miranda's eyes slowly shifted to look at Taz. He looked back and winked.

Miranda felt as though she were in the twilight zone. Was she dreaming? Maybe, because surely this wasn't really happening.

They stayed like that, secretly touching, everyone else oblivious. Seconds later, Miranda saw Melanie glance in their direction. Her eyes were like a hawk, and they went from Miranda's face to her and Taz's looped fingers.

Miranda quickly averted her gaze, trying to concentrate on the scene in the movie. Chevy Chase's character was cluelessly hitting the taxi driver with the various pieces of luggage as the family exited the taxi.

As Miranda had known, the movie played, but essentially no one paid any attention to it. Every so often eyes wandered to the TV to catch a joke and laugh, but their time together wasn't about watching the movie. It was about using the time together to connect.

Taz stroked Miranda's hand with his fingers. She met his eyes and offered him a small smile. He smiled back.

As improbable as it was, she and Taz were connecting.

Definitely.

CHAPTER SEVEN

*L*ater, there were hugs all around as Taz and his mother were leaving. "Thanks again," Camille said.

"We had a great time," Taz added. "Jeremy, I look forward to that tennis match when I'm back in town."

Miranda's father grinned, then shook Taz's hand. "You're on."

Taz and his mother headed out the door, then everyone waved. Once the door was shut, Melanie sidled up to Miranda. "I don't know, Sis. You're going to say I'm always the hopeless romantic, but I definitely saw and felt some sparks between you two."

Miranda simply looked at her sister and shrugged. "Oh, Melanie." But as Miranda headed upstairs to her bedroom, she couldn't help thinking the exact same thing.

Miranda was upstairs in her bedroom when her phone trilled. A text message had popped up. It read:

Look out your window.

Considering it was from Taz, Miranda was surprised. He'd left not even half an hour ago to go home with his mother. Nonetheless, she scrambled to her window and pulled aside the drapes. Looking down, she saw Taz on the street waving up at her. His smile was visible beneath the streetlights, that oh-so-charming smile. He beckoned for her to come downstairs.

"What's he doing?" Miranda asked herself. Then she quickly left the bedroom and bounded down the stairs.

"Where you going?" her mother asked as she began to open the front door.

"Taz wants to talk to me for a minute."

Miranda slipped into her sneakers and went out to meet him. He was still smiling. She grinned back. "Did you forget something?"

"Yeah, I did," he said, and took her by the hand and pulled her against him. She landed against the hard wall of his chest, a little moan escaping her as she did.

"What?" She asked.

"This."

Taz brought his mouth down on hers and kissed her. Unlike the first time, his lips were more urgent, his hands slipping into her hair and holding her head in place as his mouth ravished hers. His tongue tangled with hers and she raised her hands to his shoulders and gripped him tightly as the sweet sensations of the kiss were making her lightheaded.

His teeth sank softly into her bottom lip, and that's when Miranda pulled back. As she looked up at him, she could see the lust in his eyes. Sparks were definitely flying between them. She could no longer deny that.

"I've been wanting to do that all evening," Taz whispered.

"Why?"

"Because every time I look at you …." He skimmed her face with his fingers.

Miranda stepped back from him, nervous now. Unsure of what this was between them. If this wasn't real, she couldn't handle it. She didn't want to be a temporary distraction for anyone.

"The last I saw you, you were like my brother. At least that's how you treated me."

"Your brother?"

No, that wasn't quite what she meant. "You never saw me as anything other than a friend."

"Let's walk," he said.

Miranda glanced at the house, saw that she had an audience peeking through the living room blinds. Her mother, her sister—and even Doug, her sister's fiancé. She quickly walked with Taz to the end of the street, where they turned to the right.

"Obviously, I am hugely attracted to you."

"But where did this attraction come from?" Miranda asked. "You were crazy about Crystal."

"Please don't mention Crystal. She's a mistake I don't want to remember."

Miranda frowned. As they walked, they fell into silence. She wasn't sure where they were going, until Taz made a series of turns and they headed toward the park.

"Do you remember how we used to go here?" Taz asked. "We'd come after dark so the kids wouldn't be here, and we would play on the structure and on the swing. A bunch of giant kids."

A smile touched Miranda's lips. "I remember."

"So many days I wish I could go back to that time. So I could do things differently with you."

"What I remember about that time is that we were friends. Nothing more. And you were never interested in anything more."

"You didn't like me back then?"

Miranda's chest tightened as a sense of irritation filled her. What was he trying to say? That she had been had head over heels for him while he had seen her as nothing more? "Don't flatter yourself."

She looked away, but he placed his hands on her shoulders and guided her to the swing. "Sit." He guided her to the swing.

"Why?"

"Because. Don't you think back and remember how much easier life was back in the day? For just a moment, let's re-create that."

So Miranda sat and held the chains. Taz began to lightly push her. She raised her feet as the swing went up. After a few pushes, with the wind whipping around her, she began to laugh.

"There we go," he told her. "That's it."

Miranda dipped her head back and helped propel the momentum of her swinging. Soon, she was high in the air and squealing with delight. Taz pushed her a little harder than she expected, and she felt a moment of fright. "Taz!"

He quickly put his body forward to stop her momentum and as she swung backward, her body collided with his. She wriggled and twisted in the swing, but he put an arm around her waist and held her tight as the momentum subsided, and her body began to still.

Then he twisted the swing around so that she was facing him, and once again, he kissed her. Another kiss that left her breathless and confused.

"Do you think that way back when we used to do this that I never thought of kissing you?" he asked.

Miranda said nothing, but her head lowered.

"Because I did. All the time. I just didn't know how to make that move."

What was he saying? That he liked her back in high school?

He slipped his arm around her hip and pulled her upward, and Miranda slipped her body off of the swing. Then he pulled her against him, his hands now roaming over her back. He wasn't kissing her, but he was breathing heavily. His one hand went to the off-the-shoulder portion of her sweater and played with her skin. Then he pulled the sweater lower, exposing a portion of her bra. He groaned, his other hand slipped underneath her top, his cool palm caressing her flat stomach. She flinched against the coolness of his hand, but moments later, where he was touching her, she was suddenly warm.

"I always wanted to do this, but I was a shy kid who was clueless and thought you might reject me."

"Me, reject you?" Miranda asked, somewhat dazed.

His hands went upward, and cupped her breast over her bra. She sighed softly, wanting more.

"Yeah," he told her.

Miranda didn't know how to process this, not at all.

As Taz's hand slipped into her bra, he began kissing her again. His thumb caressed her nipple as his tongue flicked over hers.

Miranda broke the kiss and pulled backward. "This is so out of the blue."

Taz groaned softly. "I'm sorry." He ran a hand over his hair. "This is probably too much too soon."

Though on one hand Miranda wanted him to stop because she hadn't had any time to think about this new development between them, she was suddenly sad that he had. She'd had so many dreams about Taz touching her and kissing her as a teen, but all these years later her brain couldn't process the situation. Her heart was dancing with joy, but she was also wary.

"I feel a little chilly," Miranda said, wrapping her arms around her torso. "I should get back home."

She started to walk, and Taz had to fall into step behind her. He picked up his speed so that they were walking side by side. "I'm sorry. I … I don't want you to be upset with me. I moved too fast. It was just—"

"It's fine," Miranda interrupted. She was angry at herself for pushing him away, because part of her wanted to just go with the flow. Life was short, she knew that. And here he was offering her something she'd always wanted. But the truth was, her heart couldn't handle future rejection from him, so she was protecting herself from him now. She'd never been the kind of girl who could just fall into bed with someone if she didn't care about them. And Taz …. No, it would be too hard.

They didn't speak for the rest of the walk to her house, and Miranda didn't even pause to give him a proper goodbye. She just hurried up the walkway and the steps two at a time until she was at the door.

Then she turned and gave him a wave. "See you later."

Taz watched Miranda flee into the house. He was upset with himself. He'd overwhelmed her, and, in fact, had overwhelmed himself. He wasn't certain what had gotten into him. It was just that seeing Miranda, looking so beautiful and voluptuous, and remembering how close they'd been …. He'd been inspired to act.

And everything about their interaction told him that there was simmering desire between both of them. Maybe he would have taken things more slowly if he knew they were both going to be in town for the foreseeable future. But he wasn't, and she wasn't. They were both leaving soon. And something about his mother being sick had him thinking that he had to take any opportunity given to him to go for what he wanted.

He'd wasted so much time with Crystal. Time he could never get back. The only blessing was they never had children, something that would tie him to her for the rest of his life.

Crystal had been beautiful, vivacious, and a go-getter. She'd set her eyes on him and pursued him with all the confidence in the world. For an awkward guy like him, it had been impossible to resist her. Before he knew it, he had gotten caught up in a relationship he never wanted, believing what his friends told him—that he was lucky. They'd all been infatuated with Crystal, and he was the one who'd gotten her. One thing led to another, then suddenly Crystal was making plans for their life together. During the first year of college, they'd been apart and had broken up. But the next thing Taz knew, Crystal was moving so that she could be with him. She had this whole plan about them moving to New York, where he could pursue his career and she could pursue hers.

Taz had been about to break up with her when she'd announced that she was pregnant. He had been disappointed, but in the end he'd done the right thing. He'd married her. Only there'd been no baby. Crystal came home crying one day, telling him that she'd miscarried. Why hadn't she called him as she'd started to miscarry? He'd always had the niggling feeling that she had been lying about being pregnant. Something he could never prove.

At his house now, Taz made his way to the front door and went inside quietly, careful not to make any noise. He'd wasted a lot of time with the wrong person, and he had regrets over that. It had taken him some time to become the confident guy that everyone thought he was. He didn't like to hurt people, and maybe that was one of the reasons things had just escalated with Crystal. But he'd always thought of Miranda over the years, and when he tried to find her on social media he couldn't.

It had only been over the last few years that he'd started to wonder if maybe she'd been attracted to him, but that he hadn't been able to realize it as a dumb kid. Maybe that was why she'd never reached out to him on social media? And she seemed distrustful of his motives now. Could he really be held accountable for being young and stupid and unable to fully express what his heart knew?

The house was quiet. His mother was sleeping. Taz went into the house and up the stairs and got ready for bed. He'd done nothing but think about Miranda last night. He didn't know what she was feeling now or if she was thinking of him, but he did know that tomorrow he would see her. Because he had to. Before he went back to New York and before she went back to Ottawa, he needed to let her know how he felt and that it was real.

CHAPTER EIGHT

The next morning, Miranda woke up and immediately rolled over in the bed and picked up her cell phone. Her phone's screen showed a notification that she had at least one new text message.

She pressed the button on the bottom of her phone, and the screen lit up. Now she could see that the text was from Taz.

She quickly unlocked her phone to read the message.

> We had a great time last night. Thanks so much for inviting me and my mother. It meant a lot to her. And to me.
> What are you up to today? I'm hoping I can see you.

Miranda's pulse began to pound. She pinched her arm. Nope, she wasn't dreaming.

Everything with Taz was upside down. Not the way she remembered him at all, and not what she expected. It was as though she'd been thrown into an alternate universe.

She texted him back.

> What do you have in mind? I have no plans.

Taz's reply:

> Now you do.

A smile touched Miranda's lips. Despite her reservations and fears, this felt nice. This was not the Taz she had known in high school, the Taz who would always suggest they do things together, but only as friends. He'd never once leaned in for a kiss or tried to hold her hand or anything. He'd been her buddy.

But now, he was pursuing her in a way that was startling. Of course, he wasn't a teenager anymore, was he? He was a man. A man who suddenly wanted her.

Her body flushed at the thought of his hand under her shirt. That simple touch had electrified her body. If she were a different woman, she would have thrown herself at him and gone with him to find a dark alcove where they could get it on. She had friends who'd done similar things, and they claimed the thrill was out of this world. But she wasn't like that.

Miranda headed downstairs to make coffee, and almost everyone was already in the kitchen. Her mother looked at her, giving her a knowing smile. "What time did you get in, young lady?"

"Not as late as you think."

"What did you do?" her sister asked.

"We just walked around the neighborhood, reminisced about old times."

"It's really a great thing that Matthew didn't come," Melanie said. "Taz would have given him a run for his money—and it probably would have ended badly for him."

Miranda went to the coffee pot and poured herself a cup. "You really are too much."

"I don't know what's going on, but I can tell there's something different about you," her mother said. "There's a light in your eyes. I like it."

She wondered what her family would say if she told them that Taz had kissed her senseless in the park, and if she weren't a woman of more sound mind, she might have ended up naked, getting it on like a lust-filled animal. She'd come home and lain in bed and thought about nothing but Taz kissing her, and had imagined him doing more.

She'd awoken aroused, and sexually frustrated. When was the last time she'd actually had that kind of a fantasy about someone?

Never.

In just two days, her heart was already falling. And she didn't know if there was anything she could do to stop it.

Later, Miranda saw that she'd missed a message from Taz. He asked her if she could come over at six, promising dinner.

She quickly called him. "Dinner?"

"I've got a lot of leftovers here from an amazing dinner I had last night. However, if you don't feel in the mood for turkey and mashed potatoes, we can order pizza."

"I'll probably take some of the leftovers with me to Ottawa, so why don't we do pizza. Queen's Pizza?"

"Is there any other pizza in Toronto you'd rather have?"

She chuckled. "No." The pizza had been cheap, loaded with toppings and oozing with cheese, and had been a favorite of every high school student within walking distance. "How's your mother?"

"She's really in good spirits today, and that's great. In fact, she sounds brighter and more relaxed than I remember hearing her in a long time."

"I'm sure she's thrilled to have you home," Miranda said.

"Yeah, but it was also yesterday's dinner. It really did wonders for her. I can't imagine what it's like to sit around all day and just think about your life and your situation. There's nothing we can do about it, but I find myself just wishing she'd had a better life, you know? A man who truly loved her, adored her, wouldn't hurt her. A partner who would be with her right now as she's going through this disease."

"She does have a man who's there for her," Miranda said. "You."

"Thanks. I just wish I lived closer." He paused. "So …. Can you come over?"

"Queen's Pizza? How can I resist that offer?"

To much curiosity from her family, Miranda left the house and headed to Taz's place. She tried to look casual-cute again, and wore less makeup than the day before. She didn't want to appear like she was trying too hard. It was a fine balance between trying to look natural and look irresistible. Though why she wanted to look irresistible, she couldn't make sense of. Her brain and her heart were at war. Her brain kept telling her to calm down, to not read into things so much. To protect herself from any possible hurt. But her heart …. Her heart hadn't stopped dancing with glee since she ran into Taz at Union Station.

She got to his door, sucked in a deep breath, straightened her shoulders, and then hit the doorbell. She didn't realize she was holding her breath until Taz swung the door open.

And damn, didn't he look amazing? He was wearing an auburn-colored T-shirt that hugged those muscular pecs. Her eyes ventured down, beyond his jeans, and she saw that he was barefoot. Even his *feet* were sexy. They were long and well-groomed and decidedly male. The kind of feet that always turned her on.

Why was he so effortlessly sexy?

His face lit up with a smile. "Hello there."

"Hi." Miranda stepped into the house, looking around. It looked like a completely different place than she remembered.

"This doesn't even look like your house. There's a wall missing, and that floral wallpaper?"

"That wallpaper was the first thing to go! My mother was pretty much fine with the way things were, but she had a water leak from the bathroom upstairs. I figured that was the time to take out a wall, open things up a bit. Repaint. Get rid of that god-awful wallpaper." He shuddered.

"I don't even recognize the place."

It had an open concept. The living room and dining room were now one giant space. There was a sofa and an armchair, and a dining room table covered with a white, frilly edged tablecloth. It looked nice, but Miranda couldn't help thinking that it didn't feel quite so homey as it had years ago.

"Some days my mother tells me she misses the old place. She likes the changes, but misses the old look from time to time."

"It's different, but I like it." Miranda stepped farther into the house. "You know I've been salivating ever since you mentioned Queen's Pizza. Is it here?"

"I ordered it already, and it should be here probably in ten minutes or so. Let me show you the rest of the house."

He took her upstairs, which pretty much mirrored the downstairs. There had been three bedrooms before, but now there was one large bedroom and a second smaller one. "Maybe I lessened the value of the house," Taz said, "but I figured I'd give my mother more space, and the bigger closet she always wanted."

Miranda nodded. "When was this done?"

"Five years ago."

"It really does look nice. Like a completely different house."

The other bedroom was Taz's old room. Gone was the colorful knit bedspread, replaced with a simple white one. The blue and white striped wallpaper was also gone, replaced with slate gray walls. It looked nothing like the room where Miranda and Taz had spent time sitting on the bed and chatting, going over their homework.

"Let me show you the basement. You remember that?"

"I remember your music studio."

"I fixed that up too."

"I can't wait to see it."

Miranda followed him down the stairs to the basement, which had a low ceiling. Taller now, Taz's head nearly reached it. The basement had been brightened up with white walls and pale laminate flooring and floodlights in the ceiling. It had a single sofa, and in the corner was an electric guitar and speakers.

"Is that the same one you had before?" she asked, gesturing to the instrument.

"Yeah. I need to dust it off, though. I brought it back here after Crystal encouraged me to give up playing. I didn't want to get rid of it."

"You can still play?"

"Of course I can still play. I dabble a bit whenever I come home."

"Are you going to play something for me?"

Taz glanced at his phone. "We've got a few minutes. The Uber driver is now on the way with the pizza."

Taz went to sit on the stool. He tuned the guitar a bit, then started to strum the chords. "I'm a bit rusty," he said.

"I really hate that you stopped playing. There's no reason you should have."

"I know."

Taz began to play. What started low and slow turned into an intense rock-out session. He finished with passion, his entire body taut as his fingers vibrated over the chords during the rising crescendo.

"Woo!" Miranda cheered, clapping her hands. "You still got it!"

Taz grinned at her as he placed his palms on the strings to stop the lasting hum. "Thanks."

"You should really consider joining a band. You'll probably have lots of women throwing themselves at you. Isn't that one of the perks of being a musician?" she joked.

Taz got up and put the guitar down. "I was never like that. I don't need lots of women. I only need one."

His eyes held hers, and something immediately changed between them. Suddenly, there was a sexual energy in the air.

"There's a lot I wish I never gave up on," Taz went on.

Now Miranda was certain that he was speaking about her. And he was moving toward her with stealth determination. Her eyes widened and she extended her hands, placing them on his chest to stop him from advancing. "Where's your mother?"

"She's not here."

"I realize that, but did she go for a walk in the neighborhood? Is she coming back any second?"

"No."

Taz swooped his arm around her waist and kissed her. Something he was suddenly fond of doing. His hand splayed across her back as he held her against him, and her breasts flattened against his chest.

Miranda pushed herself away. "No, seriously. Where's your mother? I would hate for her to come into the house and find us like a couple of horny teenagers in the basement."

"Isn't it funny how you can regret something that never happened? I kinda wish we had been horny teenagers in the basement years ago—"

"Taz, stop this. Seriously. Nothing is going to come of this."

"Are you so sure about that? My trip here has already shown me that life can change in an instant, and for the better. My mother got in touch with one of her old friends this morning. Someone she'd been avoiding because she's been sitting at home mostly depressed. The friend was thrilled to hear from her. She invited her to her place tonight; my mother's going to spend the night there. Enjoying friends again. And honestly, I have you and your family to thank for that."

So they were alone. There was no chance that his mother was going to be come and interrupt them …. Miranda's stomach flipped with excitement—and nervousness.

"Was that the doorbell?" she asked.

"That's right!" Taz's eyes widened. "The pizza!"

Saved by the bell, Miranda thought.

CHAPTER NINE

*T*az's heart was beating fast, and it wasn't because he took the stairs two at a time to head to the door. He opened the door partially to the Uber driver, all too aware that he had a raging hard-on which he wanted to hide.

He smiled as he accepted the hot pizza box. "Thanks so much."

When he turned to head to the dining room, Miranda was standing there with her arms crossed over her chest and her lips pulled into a tight line. Taz blew out a slow breath. Did she have any idea how gorgeous she was? Even with that serious look on her face, she was irresistible.

She had a perfect hourglass figure, with shapely hips, a thin waist, and breasts that looked oh-so-tempting beneath the thin sweater she was wearing.

A very big part of him had wanted to kiss her senseless, until they were both ripping their clothes off in the basement and having sex on the sofa. The kind of thing he'd never have dared to do as a teen. Heck, not even with Crystal had he ever felt this burning desire to skip dinner, dessert, and head straight to sex.

He headed into the dining room, where he placed the pizza box.

"Oh, wow," Miranda said. "That's huge. I'll never be able to eat half of that."

"You don't have to." Taz offered her a smile. "Cold, day-old pizza is almost as good as when it's fresh."

"Almost," Miranda said.

"I've got red wine, white wine, and beer," Taz told her. "Which do you prefer?"

"Let's fancy up a bit and have wine," Miranda said. "Which one is best with pizza? Actually, I think I'd like the white."

"It's a Riesling. Not too dry."

"Perfect."

Miranda pulled out a chair at the table, and Taz went to get the wine. Moments later, he was returning with the bottle and two glasses. He opened the wine bottle, which had a twist cap, and then poured her a full glass. He did the same with his own.

As he sat beside her, he raised his glass. "A toast. To getting a second chance to make the right choice."

Miranda narrowed her eyes as she looked at him. "And what choice is that?"

"Us," Taz said simply. When her eyes widened, he continued. "You were always the one I should have chosen."

"Taz ..."

"Is this really so unexpected?" he asked her. "The only surprise is that we randomly bumped into each other. But I'd like to think that fate finally intervened to push us in the right direction because we couldn't get it right on our own."

A smile touched his lips, and despite her confusion, it warmed her heart. He was saying everything she'd always wanted to hear, but she was afraid.

Taz edged his glass closer to hers, and finally Miranda clinked her glass against his. Maybe she should just go with this moment. "To second chances," she echoed.

"Let's dig in." Taz opened the box. The cheese stretched as he pulled out a slice, and Miranda's stomach began to grumble. Oh, how she'd missed this pizza. There wasn't a place in Ottawa that made pizza quite as good as this.

She grabbed her own piece, a large one. Topped with pepperoni and sausage, there was steam coming from it. Miranda carefully took a bite. Then her eyes rolled heavenward. "Oh," she said around a mouthful. "This is as good as I remember."

Taz took a bite and began to nod as he chewed. "The best. They've got some pretty good pizza spots in Westchester, but this ..."

They ate, and drank. Miranda wanted to ask him so many things. This was like old times, but with a twist—the sudden desire between them.

Taz smiled. "This is like the good old days, isn't it?"

"Except our past doesn't include all this touching and kissing and," she waved her hand in the air back and forth between them, "whatever it is that's happening between us now." Miranda put down her slice of pizza and looked him dead in the eye. "Taz, I know that you're coming out of your divorce and maybe you've been single for a while, and I was always a great friend, and I'm … comfortable, but—"

"You think that's what this is about? That I'm lonely and horny and looking at my beautiful old friend and hoping to get laid?"

When he put it like that, it sounded a bit crass. "I'm not saying that. I guess … I just don't know what to think."

Taz put down his slice of pizza and came around the table. As he looked down at her, towering over her with all that manliness, Miranda was all too aware of just how sexy he was. She felt a thrill, wondering what he might do.

He leaned down, caressing her face, causing embers of desire to spark in her belly. Then he gently slipped his fingers into her hair and eased her head back. A few seconds passed, their heavy breathing the only sounds in the room. And then finally, he kissed her.

The embers grew into a full flame. Rising to stand tall, Taz simultaneously pulled Miranda to her feet. She rose without protest, clinging to his muscular arms. They made out right there in the dining room, his fingers teasing the skin along her neck, her hands exploring his broad shoulders. Her hands went lower to his chest, feeling, savoring. Wondering what he'd look like with his shirt off.

A groan rumbled in his chest, and Taz slipped his arm around her waist, tightening his grip on her. He began to walk her backward, his lips still on hers, until her body came into contact with the wall. Then he took one of her hands in his and extended their joined hands against the wall. She was trapped. And she loved it.

Her body was thrumming wildly. Her desire for Taz was consuming every inch of her. Though he was already touching her, she wished that his hands could be all over her simultaneously. Everywhere all at once.

She pulled one of her hands free and slipped it beneath Taz's shirt. As her fingers came into contact with his warm skin, his body quivered slightly. She made a soft purring sound, any thoughts of hesitation fully fleeing her mind. She wanted this. She wanted him.

"I want to make love to you," Taz rasped against her ear.

Miranda arched her body against his. "So do I."

Taz kissed her again, his mouth coming down on hers hungrily. Miranda's knees buckled, her legs feeling as sturdy as Jell-O. The onslaught of Taz's tongue teasing hers while his hand stroked her face, she was lost.

His lips moved from hers to the underside of her jaw, where he trilled his tongue along her skin. It made its way to her earlobe, flicking over the flesh there.

"Oh, God," Miranda moaned, remembering he had the house to himself for the night. Her breathing hitched.

"You're stunning," Taz told her, watching her as she tried to collect herself.

The words vaulted Miranda onto cloud nine. She knew he was attracted to her, obviously. But hearing him say the simple words made her feel incredibly beautiful—as though she were the only woman who would ever have his attention.

She stroked his face tenderly, letting him know that this wasn't just about the physical for her. His lips curled in the slightest of smiles, and then Taz took her hand and whizzed her through the dining room to the steps that led to his bedroom on the upper level.

Miranda couldn't believe that every teenage fantasy she'd had about Taz was about to come true.

CHAPTER TEN

*M*iranda awoke with a start. When she glanced at the bedside clock and saw that it was shortly after midnight, she gasped. How had she and Taz slept so long?

She bolted upright. "Oh, no."

"What?" Taz asked, his voice groggy.

"It's after midnight. I wasn't planning to stay. I—"

"I don't have to get my mother until the morning. You're free to stay."

"Yeah, but my family ..." She groaned, then placed her face in her palms. She had only been planning to see Taz for the evening, spend some time with him. But spending the night? What was she going to tell her parents? Her sister?

"Everyone's gonna wonder what I was doing. Why I didn't make it home."

Taz snaked his arm around her waist, pulled her into him, nuzzling her neck sleepily. "Maybe they'll think you're having the time of your life."

A shiver of delight coursed through her at the thought of just how incredible their time together had been. Though she wanted to make love to him again, she turned in his arms, faced him and said, "I don't want my family asking me questions about this when even I don't know how to explain it."

"How about I help you with that? Tell them that you and I finally did something we should have done years ago."

Miranda's mouth parted. "That's what you want me to tell them?"

"Absolutely. Because that's exactly what happened."

"Is it? This is something you wanted to happen years ago?"

"I was always attracted to you, Miranda."

Miranda huffed, settling back down. Was she overthinking things? That was one of her worst traits, she knew, but still. She knew he was attracted to her now, had feelings for her now—Taz was saying all the right things—but could she really believe that he was attracted to her in high school? He'd *never* shown any interest.

On one hand, she wanted to get out of Taz's bed, not listen to any more of his revisionist history. She didn't want to have her heart fall further for this guy when they were going to have to part ways. Because that's exactly what had been happening ever since she came back to Toronto and ran into him. Her heart had been falling for him. Little by little. Him saying all the right things wasn't making the situation any easier for her.

She had to acknowledge that their time together had been nothing short of amazing, but a sliver of doubt returned. Was he really attracted to her? "You don't have to say that," she said softly. "If this is just about a physical connection for you, it's fine. Two consenting adults can have sex if they want to."

"Who are you trying to convince?" Taz asked. "Me, or yourself?"

"Taz, this is so out of left field. You know it is."

"And yet I can't get enough of you."

His words, and the guttural tone to his voice, thrilled her, sending nervous butterflies fluttering throughout her body. Despite her own protests, she couldn't resist replying with a raised eyebrow and a teasing, "Is that so?"

"You tell me," he said, chuckling softly, inviting her to explore his resolution.

Emboldened by the enticement in his voice, Miranda slid on top of him, then leaned forward and began to kiss him. He groaned and wrapped both arms around her waist as he proceeded to show her just how much he wanted her.

It was shortly after five A.M. when Miranda woke up. She felt the arm draped across her waist, and in a nanosecond remembered where she was. And who she was with.

A smile spread on her face as memories from the night before flooded her mind. Taz had been an incredible lover.

But as the seconds ticked by, the happy memories led to a sense of anxiety. She was with Taz, and their night had been beyond anything she could have dreamed of. But what did it mean? A one-night stand? Surely given their circumstances it couldn't be more than that. They lived in two different cities in two different countries.

Pain stabbed at her heart. If she could slip out of his arms, she would sneak out of his bed and leave. It wasn't that she wanted to just bail on him—she would never do what Matthew had done to her—but she felt entirely *too* comfortable in his arms. And after making love to him for a second incredible time and then a third, she knew that her heart was fully open to the idea of loving him again. Maybe she'd never stopped.

Which was why she suddenly wanted to get out of there. This was the one man on earth who had the power to hurt her. She'd given him all of herself last night, no holding back, thinking only of her desires in the moment. Not about the pain that would come afterward.

Sure, he talked about always wanting to do this, but how could she believe him? And even if he had been romantically attracted to her before, many guys had thought of getting naked with female friends. That didn't mean anything emotionally to them.

Very carefully, Miranda tried to lift Taz's arm. But he stirred, and tightened his hand around her waist. Then he kissed the back of her head, and Miranda settled against him.

She sighed, somewhat sadly, somewhat contentedly. May as well enjoy being in his arms for a little while longer.

Later, Miranda's hope to escape had been foiled by the fact that Taz had awoken before her. As her eyes fluttered open, she could smell the bacon cooking downstairs.

There was a note on the bed that read: *There's a towel in the bathroom for you to shower. I hope you're hungry.*

Miranda went to the bathroom, showered quickly, and when she came out of the bathroom with the large towel wrapped around her, Taz was there. He had a tray with food, on which was a plate with bacon, toast, scrambled eggs; there was also a mug of coffee, beside which was sugar and cream.

"I don't know how you like your coffee, but I brought some sugar and some cream just in case. I hope you like scrambled eggs and bacon. I took the liberty of buttering the toast, I hope that's okay."

Miranda stared at him, wondering if this was for real. First of all, he was wearing boxer shorts only, exposing most of that absolutely phenomenal body to her. It was like waking up and having a *GQ* model bring you your breakfast. She almost pinched herself. She had to be dreaming.

"It all looks delicious and smells fantastic. What about yours? You didn't eat without me, did you?"

"I figured I'd bring this up to my sleeping beauty first. I'll bring mine up to join you."

He gave her a soft kiss on the lips, then left the room. Miranda's heart fluttered. Never in her wildest dreams had she expected something like this to transpire this weekend. *Ever*, actually. She felt such happiness in her heart, and yet there was also some fear.

When Taz returned with an identical plate to hers, they both began to eat. "We could just as easily eat downstairs," Miranda said.

"Or we could do something different. Like eat breakfast in bed. I feel that in so many ways I've lived my life playing by all the rules. But what has that gotten me?"

"A fabulous career?" Miranda offered.

"It's been great, sure. But it's also gotten me a failed marriage. Maybe I should have taken different risks."

Miranda's phone began to ring, interrupting the moment. "I'd better get that," she said. "I'll be quick."

She hurried off the bed, found her purse and fished out her phone. Melanie's smiling face was flashing on her screen. "Hey," Miranda answered cheerfully.

"Where are you?" her sister said without preamble. "Everyone's worried."

"I ... I'll be home soon."

"That doesn't answer the question."

"I'll explain when I get back." She paused. "You don't have to save any breakfast for me. I'm eating now."

"With whom?"

"Like I said, I'll tell you when I get home."

"Miranda—"

"Bye, Melanie." Miranda quickly ended the call.

"Your sister?" Taz asked.

"Yeah. I think they're losing their minds over there. I should have left last night."

"You regret staying?" Taz asked, meeting her eyes.

Miranda didn't regret it, so she said nothing, just shook her head.

"What are your plans for the rest of the day?" he asked.

Miranda's stomach lurched at the question. She sipped some of her coffee, then said, "Taz, this has been fun. Honestly, I never expected to reconnect with you this weekend and I really enjoyed myself. But ... I go back to Ottawa tomorrow morning and you go back to New York. I just don't think there's any reason to actually make something more ... you know .... Let's just leave this as it was. A fun time between two old friends."

For a moment Taz just stared at her, then something flashed in his eyes, something she couldn't read. And he didn't say what was on his mind.

Miranda's heart sank when Taz didn't say anything. He didn't protest her statement; he didn't tell her that she was wrong about what had happened. She was the one pushing him away, so did she really have a right to be unhappy?

She knew that she didn't, but irrationally, she was upset. What was wrong with her? She expected Taz to profess his undying love?

Suddenly, she was no longer hungry. The fantasy was over. They'd had a whirlwind weekend, and it was time to come back down to earth.

She got up from the bed and scooped up her clothes. "I'm going to change. I need to head home."

She disappeared into the bathroom, her heart breaking as she did.

A profound sense of disappointment washed over Taz when Miranda left his house. She barely looked him in the eye, desperate to get away as quickly as she could. And he'd let her go.

He wasn't sure why he hadn't responded to her statement. Why hadn't he told her that this was not a weekend fling for him?

But hadn't he been telling her that all along? He'd made it clear more than once that a relationship with her was something he should have pursued before. But she had rejected the idea every time.

She was overwhelmed, he knew. But maybe he was also wrong. He'd always thought there was something more between them besides a deep friendship. He'd been too shy to act on it, but there *had* been attraction, hadn't there? He'd been young and dumb, and perhaps so had she. Both of them afraid to ruin their relationship by being the first to express a romantic interest.

He'd settled for friendship, believing that she would always be in his life. But after Crystal, they'd grown apart.

Taz was a man now, no longer that shy, geeky kid. And seeing her again at this point in his life and knowing that life was short, he jumped at the idea of being able to pursue something with her.

But had he come off too strong? Or did she not feel the same way? Or was she just afraid?

Based on her comments, she didn't believe that he was genuine. If she was still saying that after they'd made love, how could he make her believe otherwise? They'd gone from building passion with the flirting and kissing, to fire between the sheets last night. And still she was hesitant.

So he'd let her go, and accepted her chaste kiss on the lips as she'd scooted through the door.

Now as he sat in the living room with his mug of cold coffee, he wondered if maybe she was right. They had their own lives, and it was possible that they would never be able to work out a relationship. He could travel and so could she, but would they keep it up? Maybe this *had* just been a one-time thing.

He sipped his coffee, winced, then set the mug aside. In his heart he knew that he didn't want this to be a one-time thing. Finally, he'd gotten a taste of what he could have had with Miranda, and he wanted more.

CHAPTER ELEVEN

*I*rrationally, Miranda felt glum as she filled her family in on the fact that she had been with Taz for the night. Though her mother looked at her with keen interest, her father surprised, she didn't tell them the truth about what had happened. She told them that they'd just hung out and watched a couple of movies—much like they had done as teens. But she'd had too much wine, so she'd stayed the night. No big deal.

Her sister, of course, did not accept any of what she was trying to sell, and wanted details. Once she was alone in her bedroom with Melanie, Miranda confided in her that she and Taz had slept together.

"Then why do you look so down?" Melanie asked.

"Because I got caught up in my emotions, and …. Obviously, this can't be anything." She frowned. "Why do other women say they feel good when they have a one-night stand? I feel so ambiguous."

"Because you're not just sleeping with someone hot you don't care about. You have feelings for Taz. And *he* has feelings for *you*."

Miranda's eyes widened. Her lips parted, but she didn't speak.

"Oh, come on. Don't give me that look. It's obvious. It was obvious years ago, and it's obvious now."

"Yes, I always liked him. But he was into Crystal."

Melanie made a face. "I don't believe that."

"But he married her!"

"Maybe you should have told him what you wanted back then," Melanie suggested. "Maybe you both would be together right now."

Miranda narrowed her eyes as she looked at her sister. "How can you even say that?"

"Because. You guys should've gotten together in high school. You were perfect for each other."

"But he didn't like me in that way back then. You *know* he didn't."

"Of course he did. I could see it every time he looked at you. And obviously, I could see how smitten you were every time you looked at him."

"And then he went and married somebody else," Miranda pointed out. "He never once said anything about liking me."

"Did you say anything to him?" her sister challenged.

Miranda's lips parted. She wanted to answer that, yes she had, but she knew she hadn't. She'd liked Taz, and she'd always been happy to spend time with him. Maybe she'd figured that he would *see* her interest, but she'd never come right out and told him how she felt.

"See?" Melanie said. "Maybe both of you were too afraid to say anything. Now there's no more Crystal and there's no more Matthew—not that he ever really was anything to you anyway. Timing is everything, Sis."

Her sister's words stayed with Miranda throughout the day. As she packed to leave, she thought about nothing but Taz.

She was heading back to Ottawa, and he would be heading back to New York. How could a relationship between them ever work?

Taz had called her, but she hadn't answered. However, during the afternoon she sent a message to ask if she could stop by to say goodbye to his mother. He agreed, telling her she could come by anytime.

Melinda went with Miranda, and she was happy to have her sister there as a shield of sorts. She just didn't want to be alone with him and end up discussing what had happened. A clean break would be best.

Miranda and Melanie went up the porch steps, and Miranda rang the doorbell. Moments later, Camille opened the door. Her face lit up with a bright smile. "Miranda, hello. And Melanie."

"I just wanted to come and say goodbye," Miranda said. "I head back to Ottawa shortly."

Camille moved toward her with her arms outstretched. "I wish you didn't have to leave so soon."

Miranda hugged her, and they swayed back and forth for a long while. "All good things come to an end."

"And sometimes good things spark," Camille said.

As if on cue, Taz appeared behind his mother. He looked at her, and she looked back, holding his gaze for a few seconds.

Breaking the hug, Miranda looked away. "My parents said they're going to stay in touch. They loved having you over for dinner."

"Good. I don't want to lose touch with them again. Life's too short."

"You're going to be okay," Miranda said to her, but she got the sense that Camille was resigned to her fate, that she accepted people's words of comfort but didn't fully believe them.

Camille smiled, but there was a hint of sadness behind her eyes. "No matter what the future holds, it's been a blessing to see you again. A blessing for me and for Taz."

"I've had a great weekend. I'll be praying for you." Miranda squeezed one of Camille's hands. "Know that."

"I hope you come back down soon to see me." She looked at her son. "And to see Taz."

He must have told his mother about her, which made her stomach twist a little. If he told his mother about her, then maybe he really did have deep feelings for her ....

Sometimes timing was everything, and sometimes you just couldn't get something right. Yes, she would love to explore a relationship with Taz. If they lived close enough to each other, she would. But things weren't going to change on her end. She was going to be as busy as ever, a complaint she'd heard from past boyfriends.

Stop making excuses, she told herself.

"And you, Melanie," Camille said and moved toward her sister.

Miranda sucked in a breath as Taz stepped toward her. "You're ready to leave?" he asked.

"Yeah. I'm packed and ready to go."

"Can I give you a ride to the train station?"

"I'm going in an Uber with my sister and her fiancé. I'm stopping at Union Station first, then they're going to continue to the airport."

Taz nodded. "I see."

Miranda nodded, not quite meeting his gaze. She could almost hear what he *hadn't* said: *You don't want to spend any more time with me?*

Miranda shifted from one foot to the other uncomfortably. "Yeah."

"I'm going to be staying here with my mom for a while," he said. "So if you get back to town …"

"You're not going back to New York?"

"Not yet. I figure I'll stay a bit longer."

Miranda's eyes narrowed with worry. "Taz," she said in a low voice. "Is your mom okay?"

"I just don't want her to be alone right now."

"Oh." Miranda frowned. Was he telling her everything?

"Taz," Melanie crooned, and she stepped between him and Miranda with her arms outstretched. "It was great seeing you again. A total surprise. And maybe I'll be seeing more of you in the future?" Melanie glanced over her shoulder at Miranda.

"Maybe," Taz said.

Miranda's heart beating fast, she glanced at her cell phone's screen to check the time. "We'd better go, Mel. Camille, take care and keep the faith. Taz, we'll be in touch."

Then Miranda all but ran down the steps.

Hours later, Miranda was on the train heading to Ottawa, looking outside but not seeing anything. There wasn't much to see except the city lights, as the reflection from the cabin lights made it impossible to see out into the darkness. She wasn't even sure how much time had passed; she'd been sitting there almost comatose.

She was experiencing a whole range of emotions. She was angry at herself. She was sad. She was wondering if she'd made a mistake.

Despite being certain that it was for the best to effectively end things with Taz, she kept going back and forth over everything that had happened with him. Yes, they'd just had an amazing weekend, but should he be occupying her every thought if she was convinced that they'd had a one-time fling?

So often she closed her eyes and relived every special moment they'd shared. The kiss at the playground. The kiss on the front step.

155

Taz pressing her body against the wall in his house …. Excitement rushed through her veins with every memory.

She'd put her phone to silent, not wanting to hear if Taz called. Perhaps it was childish, but she'd made her decision. Nothing could come of this relationship. Not at this point.

At least she would never have to spend the rest of her life wondering what it would have been like had she and Taz gotten together physically. She would know always that it was amazing.

It can continue to be amazing, was the thought that popped into her mind. She squashed it and closed her eyes.

Instantly, an image of Taz from earlier today flashed behind her closed lids. Just before she'd turned and left, there'd been something in his eyes that she couldn't quite read. A look that seemed to be pleading with her to give them a chance.

Miranda blew out a shaky breath. Why was she so afraid?

Miranda had hoped that heading home and getting back into her routine would help her forget about Taz. Instead, he continued to be on her mind almost all the time. She went to bed thinking about him, woke up thinking about him. She dreamed about their passionate lovemaking. This past weekend had been the best three days of her life.

Anna and Ruby both thought she was crazy. Anna point-blank told her that she'd blown it. "You finally get a chance with Taz and you tell him you don't want him? Is this about a power trip for you?"

"It's not, of course it's not. You know that, Anna."

"Then why would you do it?"

That was the question Miranda had been asking herself now for days. She had seen the distance as too big of a challenge, and yes, it would be an issue, but was it a deal breaker? And with Taz in Toronto right now, maybe he could spare some time to come visit her in Ottawa ….

Ruby also hadn't minced words. "Do you notice that you choose guys it's never going to work out with?"

"That's not true," Miranda had protested.

"Isn't it?" Ruby challenged. "They're guys you feel lukewarm about, and when things go south you just move on. I think you're afraid to put your heart on the line. From what Anna says, Taz was the only one who really had your heart. I can imagine you were crushed when he chose someone else, but that was years ago. If you want to be happy now, you're going to have to open up your heart to the chance of getting hurt. That's the only way. There are no guarantees when it comes to love."

Her friends were right. And Miranda was suddenly realizing that in a lot of ways she was a wimp. Taz had devastated her years ago when he chose Crystal, and quite frankly she'd never gotten over it. She'd put a wall around her heart as she moved on. She had been open to finding true love, but it just had never crossed her path. In the meantime, she had gone after guys who didn't challenge her and who didn't truly excite her. Maybe subconsciously she had known it would always be easy to walk away from men like that. No complications, no heartbreak.

But walking away from Taz now was proving hard. Every time she thought of him, her heart started to pound harder and her body got flushed. Oh, the memory of how he'd touched her, thrilled her, how perfect they'd been together.

But this would pass, wouldn't it? Just like she'd gotten over other men in the past. Maybe it would take a few more days or a few more weeks, but eventually she would forget him.

That's what she kept telling herself, but deep in her soul she knew her brain was lying to her heart.

CHAPTER TWELVE

*T*he following Thursday evening, Miranda was sitting on her bed with her laptop open when her cell phone rang. She glanced at it, saw Taz's face on her screen. Her heart lurched. They had texted a few times, and she'd kept their interaction cordial but not deep. Taz had followed her lead.

She picked up her phone and swiped to answer the call immediately. "Hey," she said, injecting a lighthearted tone to her voice.

"What's the chance you could head to Toronto this weekend?"

Her eyes widened at the question. She felt a rush of excitement. All her thoughts of forgetting him seemed a distant memory. Talk about being a hot mess!

"You want me to visit?" she asked.

"My mother's getting her transplant," Taz said, and Miranda could hear his happiness. "She's going into surgery tomorrow afternoon. If you can come to Toronto, I would appreciate it. And so would she."

"Oh my goodness!" Miranda exclaimed. "That's amazing!"

"Yeah, it is. We're so thrilled."

"Did you expect this?"

"No. Not at all. When I decided to stay in Toronto, I thought ... I didn't know if we had much time left."

"That's what I figured," Miranda said softly.

"But guess what—my brother came through. He showed up the day after you left, surprised her, got the requisite tests, and he's a match."

"What?" Miranda was flabbergasted.

"I sent you a text asking you to call me, but you didn't. I wanted to explain what was going on."

And now Miranda felt silly. She had been blocking him out of her life for the most part, and why? Because she loved him and was afraid that if she took a chance she'd get hurt? Yes. That was it exactly. Why was she such a coward?

"I'm sorry," she said. "I should have called. I just …" *I just thought you wanted to talk about us, and I was too scared to do that.*

"It's all right. I have you on the phone now."

"I'm astonished—and thrilled. I've been praying, but I didn't think a transplant would happen this soon."

"I know. It's a total shock that my brother stepped up. A real blessing. He had a couple of health issues that are resolved now. He wanted to get healthier to know that he *could* be a donor before getting tested and disappointing everyone."

"Wow," Miranda said. She knew that Taz had been frustrated with Owen, believing him to be uncaring about the issue. "This is the best news."

"God heard our prayers." Taz paused. "So, you think you can make it? I'd really like you here."

"Thankfully, I don't have to head out of town right now. I'll be there."

As soon as she had ended the call with Taz, Miranda called her mother, told her what was happening, and that she would be heading to Toronto for the weekend. "How wonderful!" her mother exclaimed. "I'm so happy for Camille."

So was Miranda. In fact, she couldn't stop smiling. There wasn't a chance she was going to miss out being there for her.

And for Taz.

When Miranda got to Toronto, she texted Taz and found out which hospital his mother was at, and exactly where to find him there.

"Your mom's here, too," he told her.

"She is?"

"Yeah, and I really appreciate her support. Your dad's working, so he can't be here, but he said he wishes that he could be."

A smile touched Miranda's lips as emotion filled her heart. This was what family and friends were all about. Having people in your corner when the going got tough. "I'm glad to hear that. I'll be there soon."

"Here, your mother wants to talk to you."

A moment later, her mother's voice sounded on the phone line. "Sweetheart, you're here?"

"Yep, I'm going to take a cab to the hospital." Located on University Avenue, it wasn't too far from the train station.

"We're waiting and praying. Owen's in surgery right now. Taz is being strong, but I know he's worried. I keep telling him everything is going to be fine."

"I'm sure it will be," Miranda said. "I'll be there soon."

It was no more than fifteen minutes later when Miranda joined Taz and her mother in the waiting room. The moment Taz's eyes met hers, his face that had been weary lifted with hope and happiness. She could literally see the transformation, and her entire body filled with warmth. Taz had just looked at her with love.

Yes, love.

He got to his feet and approached her, a smile on his lips. "Thanks so much for coming."

"I wouldn't be anywhere else," she told him as he wrapped his strong arms around her. She wanted to stay there like that with him forever. His arms wrapped around her, providing a sense of love and security. He could be that person in her corner she'd always been searching for.

But hadn't he already been that person? In high school, he had always been there for her. When John Dixon had been harassing her, he had stood up to the bully. He'd always found a way to make her smile if she was feeling down. And she had done the same for him.

She thought about her sister's claim, that Melanie had always been able to see Taz's love for her. Suddenly, the idea didn't seem so far-fetched.

She broke the hug with Taz to greet her mother properly. "Hi, Mom. How are you holding up?"

"A little hungry, a little tired, but mostly I'm hopeful. Owen's out of surgery, and it went well. They're working on Camille now. His brother's in recovery."

"You said you're hungry," Miranda said. "I can get you guys something to eat, maybe some coffee?"

"Why don't we go together?" Taz suggested.

Miranda looked up at him and offered him a small smile. "Okay. Let's do that."

They started to walk off, and Taz placed a hand on the small of her back. It was amazing how natural it felt to have him touching her, and how much she realized in that moment that she had missed him. For years they had not been in touch, but she suddenly knew that she couldn't go on with him out of her life.

She didn't want to.

"I'm really glad you came," Taz said.

"Taz, I had to come. Not just for your mother. But for you." She paused in the hallway and looked up at him. She saw hope ignite in his gaze. "I think I needed a little time to process everything. I'm going to admit this right now, I was a big scaredy-cat. There's only one man who's ever had the power to hurt me, and he did. *You* did. When you married Crystal and I lost you in my life." He opened his mouth to speak, but Miranda shushed him and placed a finger on his lips. "The one thing I always wanted was for you to tell me that you loved me, that you wanted me. Suddenly I was here and you were telling me you'd always been attracted to me and I couldn't accept it. Because when I really wanted you, I lost you. And the idea that you were just saying this, or that things might not work out …. I …." She drew in a deep breath, her pulse racing now. Even the idea that Taz might not be in her life at some time in the foreseeable future had her feeling stress. "You always were my everything, do you know that?"

Taz took her hand in his. "Miranda, you were always *my* everything. Who did I go to every movie opening with? How many times did I help you with your math and science homework? And do you think I really couldn't figure out all those irregular French verbs? To a degree, yes … but the harder it was for me to learn, the more time I got to spend with you."

Miranda's eyes narrowed. "You understood French better than I thought?"

"*Mais bien sûr,*" he said in French, meaning *But of course.*

She was incredulous. "You … you tricked me to spend more time with me?"

He grinned. "Guilty as charged." Slowly, his smile faded and his expression became more serious. "We both liked each other. We just didn't know how to take it to a romantic level. And can I clarify something? I never chose Crystal over you. I didn't know you were a choice. If I had, I would have chosen you. Absolutely. And I wish I did."

Miranda sucked in a breath, happiness warming her from head to toe. Everything she had felt for Taz years ago came rushing back. He was the one man she knew she could always look at without feeling bored or complacent. The excitement at just seeing him, the way her heart lifted when she saw his face light up …. He was the one she had loved in high school, and still now.

"I love you," Taz said. "Maybe I should have made that clear last weekend. It was so weird, seeing you, everything came rushing back. Our friendship. How close we had been. I suddenly realized just how much I missed you. I didn't want to let you go. I wanted to go all in with you. But I guess I was still little bit afraid to tell you how I really felt."

"And I was afraid to let myself feel what I had before." She glanced down briefly before meeting his eyes again. "I never really stopped feeling it."

Taz gently stroked her face, and she felt heat at his touch. But mostly, she felt love fill her heart. Her Thanksgiving trip had given her so much more to be thankful for than she could ever have imagined.

"I'm still afraid," she said softly.

"Please believe me—you don't have to be."

"But I'm more afraid now of *not* taking a chance," she went on. "I came to Toronto knowing that I couldn't live with myself if I continued to push you away out of fear. No matter what happens, I have to take a chance."

"I'm not going to hurt you, MirBear."

A smile tugged at her lips at the sound of her old nickname. "Mir-Bear, oh God. And you were Jazzy Taz."

"I wasn't a fan of that, but whatever."

Miranda chuckled. Then she got serious. "Can we really make this work?"

"If that's what we both want, absolutely." Taz's voice held no doubt. "I can get a new job. And as a Canadian, I can move back here any time."

"You don't want to live in New York anymore?"

"I want to be where you are. I'll move to Ottawa. I'm ready."

"You would?"

"I'm not going to let anything come between me and my happiness anymore. I saw that happen with my mother and I don't want that for my life. Whatever the challenges, we'll face them—together."

This all felt like a dream. Two weeks ago, Miranda would have never guessed that this could ever happen. It would have been as likely as her taking a trip to the moon.

And yet life had a way of surprising you. Sometimes for the bad, but sometimes for the good.

"We better get the food," she said.

"Wait," Taz said, taking her arm as she began to turn. "First, this."

And with hospital staff walking in the hallway behind them, he pulled her close and softly kissed her on the lips. "I love you, Miranda. I always have."

To say that Miranda was walking on air was an understatement. Even her mother had noticed her change in mood. She was happy, and Taz was happy. When they got to see his brother a couple of hours later, Miranda truly started to believe that all was right in the world—that love conquered all.

It was a couple of hours after that, well into the evening, when the doctors came out to give them an update on Camille. Taz got to his feet, and Miranda did as well, holding onto his arm to offer him comfort and strength in this moment. She could feel the tension in his body.

The doctor looked at all of them in turn, a serious expression on her face. But then, the edges of his lips began to turn up into a smile. "The surgery was successful," he announced.

"Oh thank God!"

"Hallelujah!"

"What a relief!"

They all spoke at once, their happiness erupting.

"I anticipate no complications," the doctor went on. "But of course she's in recovery right now. I'd advise you all to go home, get some rest, and come back in the morning. She'll be here, waiting for you."

"You're sure?" Taz asked. "She's going to be fine?"

"There are a lot of times I come out here and I'm not able to give good news. Sometimes that starts with not being able to find a donor. Or to say the surgery didn't quite go as anticipated. But what happened with your mother so unexpectedly and your brother being a perfect match .... Well, it's a miracle. This one is a win. Get some rest, because I'm sure she's going to be excited to see you all in the morning."

Miranda looked up at Taz and saw the tears slipping from his eyes. And she realized then just how much all of this meant to him. She knew he loved his mother, of course, but he must have been so terrified that he'd lose her. Instead, Camille had a second chance.

Within the span of a week, the world had changed for him. Owen had come through for their mother, Camille was going to live, and now Taz had her.

He looked down at her now and wiped at his tears. "This has been the best week of my life. Not just because of my mother. But also because of you. I want you to know that and never doubt it. Okay?"

Overwhelmed with emotion, Miranda's eyes began to mist. Was there a more perfect man in the world than Taz? Tall, gorgeous, sensitive, loyal, loving. She slipped her arms around his waist and held him close. And now he was hers.

"I'm never going to doubt it," she told him. "This week has taught me a lot about love and second chances. And fate."

He brushed away one of her tears as he gazed at her with love in his eyes. "Me too, baby."

"Does this mean what I think it means?" her mother interjected, and Miranda was surprised to see her standing so close. "Because I have to say, it's taken you both long enough."

Miranda started to giggle, and Taz tightened his arms around her, as though he never wanted to let her go. "It sure has, but we've finally gotten it right."

Dog - Gone
Holiday

Melinda Curtis

CHAPTER ONE

*T*hanksgiving used to be one of food critic and lifestyle blogger Claire Rothchild's favorite holidays.

Who didn't like turkey, gravy-soaked stuffing, and pie? Who didn't enjoy loading their plate with food without judgment? There were no presents to buy and wrap. No carols to sing. And for Claire, there was no column to write, no subtleties to detect, no presentation to critique. It was just, sit your heinie down and try everything—even have seconds!

Claire loved Thanksgiving so much that she'd planned to get married on that day.

And then the dish ran away with the spoon.

In this case, the dish was her bridesmaid Teri, and the spoon was her former fiancé, Stewart.

Nearly a year later, Claire still had six cases of California cabernet she was working her way through, a toddler she was battling custody for with Stewart, and a newly developed aversion to Thanksgiving. This Turkey Day, she planned to hide out at the coastal guesthouse of her married kid sister, Mary Jane Plutarch. No turkey, no gravy-soaked stuffing, no pie, and certainly no Stewart. She'd told Mary Jane she and Olly weren't going to be part of the fancy feast her brother-in-law was throwing. They'd be fine with fast-food burgers; Olly with his glass of milk and Claire with a glass of cabernet.

Knowing her sister, Claire was going to have to fight for her right *not* to party. Mary Jane was the family extrovert.

"Mommy, can I swim at Auntie MJ's?" Olly sat in his car seat behind her, sporting a black felt pirate hat and clutching his plastic pirate sword. His accessories and his love of all things pirate were a result of a trip to Disneyland last month with Stewart for his birthday.

"You can swim," she told him. Olly was a four-year-old fish in the water, just like his surfing champion father. "But it might be too cold."

"Daddy says pirates are *never* cold in the water."

Daddy says ...

Claire gritted her teeth, silently ruing the fact that the sun was out over San Diego today after an extremely wet and gloomy November. It didn't matter to Olly that the wind coming off the Pacific Ocean was gusty and cold this time of year. Stewart was fond of saying, "If the sun's out, the water's fine." And if his father said something, Olly took it as the gospel, even if it challenged his toddler balance and made his lips turn blue.

Mere blocks from Mary Jane's Del Mar home, Claire drove slowly past a construction crew working on placing a large pipe in a section of street in front of an undeveloped plot of land. Two men consulted what looked like blueprints as they faced the seemingly impossible-to-build-on slope. By summer, Mary Jane would have another neighbor.

"Can I, Mommy?" Olly was still focused on his swim.

"We'll see how cold and windy it is when we get there."

"Pirate sails need wind, Mommy. And I can wear a coat."

"In the pool?" Claire's laughter lifted her spirits.

Maybe they *would* go swimming. Maybe they'd thumb their noses at Thanksgiving and spend the week in the pool. Maybe she'd forget she had a life-changing decision to make by Black Monday. Maybe everyone would forget—Stewart, the family law judge, her lawyer ....

Claire turned her thoughts away from legalities as she turned into Mary Jane's gated driveway and entered the security code. With the windows down, the brisk coastal wind whipped in, bringing the tang of the sea and the sound of waves crashing on the cliffs far below. She rubbed her bare arms.

"I'm not cold," Olly said with the kind of thumb-your-nose bravery that Claire used to have.

The iron gates opened on silent hinges—because mansions on the cliffs of the Pacific Ocean, especially those owned by millionaire entrepreneur Luke Plutarch, didn't have creaky gates. She eased her SUV up the driveway, taking in the majesty of the two-story Spanish Colonial Revival looming ahead. Clean, white stuccoed walls. Grand arches. Red terracotta tile. It wasn't much different from the home she'd grown up in, but it was a big difference from her small condo miles inland and she couldn't stop a small pang of envy.

Before that small pang turned into an ache, Mary Jane came out the front door to greet them, flanked by a huge Saint Bernard. The dog was all white except for a brown mask over his eyes and ears. Compared to her short, petite sister, who counted every carb that passed her lips—even on Thanksgiving—the dog was the size of a small pony. She'd have to discourage Olly from trying to ride him.

Claire parked near the five-car garage and got out. Almost immediately, the wind tugged at her ponytail and she was given the smell test by the drooling Saint Bernard, which continued as she opened the SUV's back door. "When did you get a dog?"

Said canine pushed his way beneath Claire's arms as she ducked inside the back seat to release Olly. He stretched and sniffed and generally got in the way.

"Are we in the North Pole?" Olly asked in awe as Claire lifted him out. "That's a polar bear." The dog licked Olly's face clean, giving her son a fit of giggles. "Can I keep him? He'll make a good pirate."

"Sorry, Captain Olly. Snowy belongs to a friend of your uncle Luke's." Mary Jane crossed the driveway at a much slower pace in her heels and Del Mar "stay-at-home" attire, which Claire considered business-not-quite casual. "We're dog sitting. Can you believe it? Like I don't have a gazillion things to do with only days before Thanksgiving and Luke's investor party."

Only Luke would host financiers on a holiday.

The dog circled Olly, shedding white hair like a spring sprinkle.

"This doggy likes me, Auntie." Olly flung an arm around Snowy's neck, and buried his face in the dog's fur. "Take my picture, Mommy."

Claire traced the outline of her cell phone in her leggings side pocket but did no such thing.

"Snowflake. Snowy!" Finally having reached them, Mary Jane grabbed the dog's collar and wrestled him away. "I swear, this dog has no personal boundaries." But she rubbed his ears when she said it, clearly fond of him. "Come on. I'll help you carry your stuff to the guesthouse where you will *not* be spending Thanksgiving alone."

"I need a quiet holiday," Claire said firmly, giving her sister a one-armed hug. "I have a decision to make and papers to sign."

"Maps to read," Olly piped up, raising his sword. "X marks the spot."

"You know Stewart," Claire began.

Mary Jane stomped her high heel. Or it could have been that the dog rocked her off balance. "Don't bend to *his* demands." Him being Stewart.

"What choice do I have?" Stewart had told her this was his final custody offer before they gave up on arbitration and let the court decide for them.

His offer hinged on the way Claire made her living. If she continued as a food critic and lifestyle personality on social media, he wanted equal custody—from Costa Rica, where he and the dish had relocated. So ironic, given the pair also supplemented their income on social media—Stewart by surfing, Teri by rescuing wildlife. If Claire earned her living out of the spotlight, Stewart would settle for one week of visitation in the states every three months.

Claire's throat was thick with uncertainty. "My brand has evolved from straight food critiques to a luxury motherhood lifestyle." The latter was more lucrative. "And Stewart is demanding I stop posting photos of Olly or reference him in any way. If I do that, how will I put food on the table?" Especially when Stewart wasn't offering much in child support?

Olly knelt in front of Snowy, just out of range of a drip of drool, and touched one of the dog's large paws.

"This week, you can eat at our table," Mary Jane said, voice brimming with optimism. "And by the time we've eaten our way through leftovers, you'll know what to do."

"I hope you're right." Claire popped the hatch and hefted a large suitcase to the pavement, wheeling it toward Mary Jane before reaching in for Olly's smaller case. "But I'm determined to be a hermit in the guesthouse."

"Which explains your *small* weekend bag." Mary Jane arched a delicately shaped brow. "Did I tell you Luke invited some single men for Thanksgiving Day?"

"Let me fix one complication before you toss me another." Because Luke's idea of appropriate single men meant they were in their fifties and looking for a second or third wife. Claire gathered her purse, her laptop bag, and a small cooler.

Snowy rushed forward to sniff the cooler, making small, grumbly noises.

"I'm hungry, too," Olly told the inquisitive dog. "But that's not food. It's Mommy's special flowers."

"Flowers? Claire." Mary Jane's grip on the handle of Claire's suitcase was as rigid as her frown. "I thought you were joking when you said you were keeping them. This .... *This* is the reason I worry about you."

Ponytail tested by the wind, resolve tested by her sister, Claire wished she'd waited to take out the cooler and her wilted bridal bouquet inside until later. "I'm allowed one symbolic gesture, aren't I? It'll be ash in your firepit before your turkey is served."

"Can we have a fire and roast marshmallows now?" Olly thrust his face toward Mary Jane and grinned so hard he bared his teeth. "Plea-ee-ee-ese, Auntie."

Mary Jane knelt and hugged him. "We'll let your mom decide when to light that fire."

"Thanksgiving," Claire said tightly. "Come on. We can't swim until we unload."

Olly gave a shout of joy and started to run, dragging his suitcase toward the path to the guesthouse, trailed by Snowy. Claire and Mary Jane followed at a slower pace.

"Luke's good?" Claire was fond of her brother-in-law, but he wasn't the man she would have chosen for her sister. He was too much like their father, not to mention he was nearly their father's age, and his entire being was defined by his work and appearances.

Appearances? Wasn't Claire the pot calling the kettle black? Social media success was all about controlling impressions.

"Define good. Luke is Luke." Mary Jane's voice didn't turn dreamy or catch on a note of love. She talked about her husband matter-of-factly, which told Claire more about her marriage than her sister would have liked to realize. "As usual, he's researching investment opportunities. He should be on that *Shark Tank* show. Today, he's wearing socks made from recycled water bottles, wearing some belt contraption that the makers claim tightens your core, wearing a finger bandage with a mini-ice pack in it, and drinking seaweed protein shakes." And Mary Jane was left to manage an immaculate household and their social life.

"Never a dull moment," Claire said dutifully, wishing her sister hadn't settled for an existence like their mother's.

Olly and Snowy paused at the corner of the garage to wait for Mary Jane and Claire to catch up. The dog made a sound that was half groan, half whine.

"I know." Olly patted Snowy's broad head. "They're slow. We pirates walk fast."

"That boy and his imagination." Claire hefted her bags higher on her shoulder. "He tells me what his teddy bear is saying, too."

"That dog is no silent teddy bear." Mary Jane wheeled the suitcase forward. "Snowy thinks he's a person. I swear he knows what I'm saying. I talk and he yacks back in his own way. He's chattier than a dental hygienist during a cleaning."

On cue, Snowy grumbled to Olly.

"This?" Olly held up his plastic sword. "It's a pirate's cutlass."

The dog gave it the sniff test before leading the way on a winding path around the garage to the guesthouse, which was a two-bedroom cottage overlooking the pool and the ocean. Coming around the corner, the brisk ocean breeze hit them full force, whisking Olly's captain hat off and tumbling it across the ground. Before Claire could lunge after it, Snowy trotted over to pick it up, returning it to Olly.

"Ew, it's slobbery." Olly put it on his head anyway. "Good boy."

Mary Jane passed Olly and the dog. She opened the door to dark plank flooring, a gas insert fireplace, and cream-colored, wood-trimmed furniture—a designer's modern representation of Spanish Colonial Revival to coordinate with Luke's beloved main house. "Are you sure I can't convince you to come to Thanksgiving dinner? Olly, don't you want turkey and pumpkin pie?"

"Nuggets and fries, please." Captain Olly flopped onto the couch.

Snowy flopped on the floor next to him.

"Claire." Mary Jane made her name sound like a reprimand.

"Mary Jane," Claire parroted back. "Why would we want to leave all this?" It was tight quarters, but there was internet, a large-screen TV, and a blender to make milkshakes. She hung her purse and laptop bag in the foyer, taking the cooler into the tight kitchen.

"Why?" Her sister wasn't letting up. "Because you're lonely? But if you insist upon being the cat lady—"

"Minus the cats."

"—then I need a favor." Mary Jane wheeled Claire's suitcase into the main bedroom. "I need you to watch Snowy for me. He sheds like nobody's business and the caterer will have a fit."

Snowy grumbled, drooling and shedding even as he put his extra-large muzzle on his extra-large paws.

"No. We don't have a cat," Olly said, clearly relishing this game of talking with the dog. "Can we watch him, Mommy? Please? He can sleep in my bed."

Claire made room for her crumbling bouquet in the fridge. "He's not high maintenance, is he?"

The dog chuffed.

"He says he'll be good," Olly said solemnly.

"Snowy's no trouble." Mary Jane defended the dog, too. "And I've already put all his things in here—his bed, his kibble, his treats, a leash, and poop bags." She did her Vanna White impression in the small kitchen. "And before Margarite left, she baked you all kinds of cookies."

Claire set the remains of her paper-wrapped bouquet in the fridge and took stock of the provisions. There were enough holiday food cannisters on the counter to last all week, and the fridge had all the necessities to make turkey sandwiches if Mary Jane provided leftover turkey.

Snowy joined her in the kitchen, a leash dangling from his mouth.

"Wait. Snowy needs to be walked, too?" She'd overlooked that detail in her interest in food. Claire glanced through the windows at the extensive and immaculate garden. "I can't just let him outside to do his business?"

"Luke would die if he was entertaining and ..." Mary Jane's hand rolled through the air.

"But …" Olly frowned. "Everybody poops, Auntie. I have a book that says so."

Snowy grumbled around his grip on the leash.

"Everyone potties, Captain Olly, but not everyone wants to see." Mary Jane gave a forced chuckle. "Kids."

"Champagne problems," Claire murmured, hurting a little inside because Luke would never give Mary Jane children. She sometimes wondered if that's why her sister kept Olly at a bit of a distance, as if doting on him would only bring home he was something she could never have.

"Snowy will be no trouble," Mary Jane reiterated. "You'll hardly know he's here."

"I could say the same for us." Claire scratched behind Snowy's ears.

"But I won't let you." Mary Jane tossed a lock of hair over her shoulders. "You haven't been the same since last Thanksgiving. Sign the papers. Move on."

"And choose which option?" She'd gone over Stewart's demands with her sister last week.

Olly climbed onto a wrought iron barstool and surveyed the can-nisters. Watching him, Snowy leaned forward, licking his chops.

"How can I help?" Mary Jane smoothed her thumb over Claire's forehead, right where a crease had spent the past twelve months forming.

"You can't." Claire shook her head, shaking her sister's touch off. "Let me sulk a few more days."

The look Mary Jane gave Claire promised nothing of the sort.

"Pirates shouldn't walk so much." Olly marched next to Snowy a day after their arrival in Del Mar. His little feet dragged the sidewalk nearly as much as the jeans that were an inch too long. "And they shouldn't count steps."

"Pirates count steps to buried treasure," Claire pointed out, pat-ting the top of his felt pirate hat.

Snowy added in his two cents, emitting a deep rumble in his throat, as Claire eyed the horizon. Was that a thick fog bank? Or the rain clouds predicted to roll in this afternoon? With her luck, it was rain clouds, ones that would linger rather than moving inland. Luckily, Olly had gotten his swimming fix first thing this morning.

"Yeah. Mommy's right, Snowy." Olly trudged onward, flexing his overactive imagination. "She's always right. And she's not even a pirate!"

Claire chuckled.

A block ahead, a food truck with a colorful surfboard painted on the side turned into Mary Jane's driveway.

Snowy lifted his humongous nose and sniffed the air. And then he hurried forward, dragging Claire and Olly in his wake.

"What's your rush, Snowy?" Claire scooped up Olly as she tried to keep the dog from breaking into a gallop.

"He smells food." Olly held onto his pirate hat.

They jogged up the driveway as the driver of the food truck climbed out of the front seat, pausing with his back to them to check something on a clipboard. Tall and lean with shaggy, dark-blond hair, he could just as easily have been a surfer as a chef.

Claire's womanly radar pinged. Oh, yes. She had a type. At twenty-seven, she was getting too old to swoon for surfers.

Snowy chuffed, dragging them closer.

The man glanced at them over his shoulder.

Recognition had Claire digging in her heels and lowering Olly to the ground. "Drew?" Stewart's best man? Her high school nemesis? She hadn't seen him since the almost-wedding. And this was who her sister had chosen to cater Thanksgiving?

I'm going to kill Mary Jane.

Heel digging aside, Snowy pulled Claire toward Drew as if she were a stuffed animal attached to his leash.

Drew Barnett's icy hot, blue gaze locked on Claire. The man had a way of looking at her that both challenged and excited. "Well, look at what the dog dragged in. Like my new ride? I'm self-employed now." Spoken as if he'd finally made it in the world.

Claire tottered to a halt as Snowy reached Drew and began his nosey inspection with Olly not far behind. The ensuing chaos gave her time to regroup. "Well, Drew. What a surprise. Still unoriginal with your puns, I see." She gestured toward his truck's branding: *Surf's Up Seafood.*

"Still being dragged around instead of helming your own ship?" Drew stepped out of sniffing range, and tilted Olly's pirate hat at a jaunty angle. "Ahoy, Captain Olly. I haven't seen you since Disneyland."

"Ahoy, Uncle Drew. Cool van." Olly threw his arms around Drew's legs. "What did you bring me?" Because Drew was never empty-handed around Olly.

"Rations, like turkey and potatoes, Captain." Drew swung Olly to his hip. "There's a storm on the horizon and a feast to prepare."

"But did you bring me chocolate?" Olly whispered.

Drew spared Claire a mischievous glance that sent an unexpected thrill down her spine.

That did not just happen.

Drew whispered something in Olly's ear.

The nonhappening reaction happened again.

As if sensing her shock, Snowy sat down and studied Claire, silent for once. Meanwhile, Claire did a bit of silent cataloguing of her own.

In the year since she'd seen Drew, he looked no different. He hadn't gained an ounce. His shoulders weren't broken by betrayal. There were no worry lines emanating from his eyes or creasing his forehead. And why would there be? Drew hadn't been jilted last Thanksgiving.

Wishing she'd worn something other than a T-shirt and leggings, Claire sucked in her gut, pushed her shoulders back, and scrubbed a hand over her forehead, trying to wipe away that worry line.

"So …" Drew set Olly down, who ran to climb into the food truck's driver's seat. And then his attention was one hundred percent on Claire, blue gaze attempting to pierce her armor. "Instead of re-bounding into another man's arms, you got a dog."

Sarcasm. Classic Drew.

Annoyance gathered in her chest, generating heat as if she'd eaten too many jalapeños. She had to struggle to remain composed and keep her frustration from spilling into her words. "I am still—*thankfully*—a single mom. Mary Jane and Luke are dog sitting. Not that you should worry about anything as mundane as drool and dog hair getting in your turkey buffet—"

"*Buffet?*" Drew choked out, looking horrified.

"—I've been tasked with taking care of Snowy until you're gone." Which couldn't be soon enough. Next time he came, she vowed she'd have on makeup and do something more inspired than a ponytail with her hair.

They stared at each other the way they had in high school, through college, and during the activities leading up to her wedding day—like two territorial dogs tugging at the same chew toy: *Stewart.*

Wait a second. Was the animosity there? Drew didn't seem to be scowling but his gaze was just as intense.

Again, the jolt of attraction struck, making Claire frown harder. *I am* not *attracted to Drew.*

Drew sighed. "Do we have to fight?"

Claire almost said yes. With all the Stewart-induced drama in her life, she needed their familiar rivalry, not this unfamiliar tug of … something.

Snowy sighed and glanced up at Claire with what looked like disappointment in his big brown eyes. Eyes that seemed to say: *Make love, not war.*

Claire blew out a breath. She was getting as bad as Olly, attributing human thoughts and emotions to a dog. Speaking of which, she walked over to the van's open door. "Olly, what are you doing?"

"Eating buried treasure." Her son was unwrapping a chocolate coin packaged in gold foil. And it wasn't his first. His hands and face were smeared with chocolate. "X marks the spot!"

"Last one." Claire turned to Drew. Snowy sat down next to her, leaning against her leg as if lending her strength. "You knew we'd be here?"

Drew nodded, giving her that handsome half-smile he often gave to single ladies right before they propositioned him. He was that good looking. "Mary Jane gave me a guest list."

"Great. You had a heads up and I didn't." Not only her chest felt hot—annoyance thrummed through her veins. What else wasn't Mary Jane telling her?

"Well, I *am* the caterer. The Plutarch's chef for the holiday." Drew's smile went from half to full wattage.

Claire's heart stuttered. It was a powerful smile. A smile that both lured and alerted. It let a woman know that a relationship with him wouldn't be without challenges. But she couldn't let him dare her like this. She wasn't one of his easy conquests. They were friends, not ... never .... She stuffed attraction out of reach. "Titles mean nothing to me, Drew. Remember that Mrs. Chantilly liked my chocolate chip cookies better than yours."

Snowy's ears cocked and his big head swiveled from Claire to Drew.

"Claire." Drew *tsk*ed and his smile grew into a full-on, I-got-you-babe grin. "You can't hang your hat on accolades from our high school home economics teacher forever." He laughed as he turned and headed toward the front door.

Claire couldn't think of a retort. Drew got the last word in.

Or more accurately, the last laugh.

CHAPTER TWO

*C*laire Rothchild. Single and out of her element. It was a dream of his.

Part of him wanted to cut the bull and soften his edges. Part of him knew that if he did, he'd be in trouble. She was the woman he'd always wanted to be with. The woman he'd struggled to hide his longing for. Because for over ten years, she'd been dating his best friend.

Claire Rothchild. Even knowing she'd be here this weekend hadn't prepared him for the sight of her. That rich brown hair. Those intelligent brown eyes. An athletic body softened by motherhood. And a personality reflected in her awesome little dude.

Claire had always had the power to unsettle Drew. It was her fault he'd added too much flour to his chocolate chip cookies in home economics class. He'd been distracted by her laughter. It was her fault he didn't seriously date. No woman measured up to Claire. Not her beauty, not her smarts, not the way just being near her made his pulse quicken. No woman ever had. But during her tenure with Stewart, Drew couldn't let on that he was attracted to the princess of Del Mar. And he couldn't let on how he felt now that Stewart was out of the picture. Not today.

Because he couldn't afford to be distracted this week. The holiday feast he was making for Luke and Mary Jane was going to be a triumph. And when Drew served dessert, he'd ask Luke for a final decision—was he willing to invest in Drew and his restaurant in downtown Del Mar or not? Because Drew wanted to be more than a surfer who ran a food truck.

Over the years, he'd worked in the kitchen at some of the finest restaurants in San Diego. A year ago, he'd purchased a food truck but he was finding the income to be lean. He needed a brick-and-mortar restaurant to make the kind of money to support a woman like Claire, to provide employment and benefits, to make her proud.

"Hey, Drew." Claire's sister came down the front steps to greet him, looking like Del Mar royalty in a flowery red sheath and shiny black heels. Quite a contrast to Claire's dog-hair-covered leggings and wrinkled In-and-Out Burger T-shirt. "I'm so glad you'll be catering Thanksgiving. I told Luke we needed someone dependable. Last year, half of the chef's crew didn't show."

His crew …. Drew's head swung around as he searched for his brother. All he saw was Claire, Olly, and the big white dog disappearing around the corner of the garage. He fought the urge to follow as rain began to fall.

"Problem?" Mary Jane asked with a polite smile.

"No." *Where was Richie?* Drew's neck twinged. He moved beneath the porch to stay dry. "No problem. It's just—"

A car backfired at the entrance to the drive. His brother pulled in, his dilapidated "classic" Cadillac huffing and puffing at the effort it took to make it this far. Richie hopped out, dark-blond hair wet, as if he'd just gotten off a surfboard. "Look at me, Bro. Right on time, despite the crew working on the road down the block."

To Richie, "on time" was plus or minus thirty minutes. So, by his standards, his statement was true.

"They're always digging up something for that new house." Mary Jane smiled fondly at Richie. They'd been in the same grade together at school, three years younger than Drew and Claire. "I suppose you want to see the kitchen and put food away."

"Yes." When Mary Jane led them up the stairs, Drew gave Richie a charley horse in the arm.

"Ow," Richie mouthed but he was grinning. And smelling like the ocean.

"Behave," Drew whispered.

"I'm not five," Richie whispered back. He may not have been close to Olly in age, but Richie was closer to Olly in terms of the responsibility he was able to shoulder. If big waves were rolling in, Richie was a no-show at the food truck.

Not that Drew could fire him. He was family.

They followed Mary Jane through the grand foyer, down a long hall, and into a chef's kitchen overlooking the pool and the ocean. There was a feeling of spotless opulence, as if no one ever tracked sand in the house or even walked about barefoot. A showpiece, not a home.

"Sweet crib, Mary Jane." Richie did the head bop thing, which was so eighth grade.

Drew suppressed a shudder. There would be no restaurant unless he impressed Luke and his rich friends. Surfing, head-bopping assistant chefs were a liability, not an asset.

Drew focused on the positives—the eight burner Viking electric stove (he'd have preferred gas), the dual ovens (was two enough?), and the abundance of counter space (Carrera marble rather than stainless steel). It offered more square footage and better equipment than he had in his truck.

"Here's the final plan." Drew took the six-course menu from his clipboard and handed it to Mary Jane. "Food served over a six-hour span."

Mary Jane perused the list, a frown growing on her face. "There's nothing Spanish on here."

"MJ's right." Richie sat on a barstool at the large island as if he were a guest, not a worker. "No salsa. No aioli. No *sofrito*."

Drew's neck twinged again. "You told me Luke wanted to impress his guests. You told me they had particular tastes."

"Luke likes everything to fit a theme." Mary Jane mumbled something about the cuisine fitting the style of the house. "What can we do?"

"On such short notice …" Drew's gaze caught on movement.

Claire ran with Olly and the large dog to the guesthouse on the other side of the pool, dodging the rain. They disappeared inside. From that front window, she could see into the kitchen. She could see Drew while he worked. She could watch him in his element.

Drew sucked in air.

Claire was single. Stewart was a continent away. And Claire was single.

It had to be said twice because—

"Dude." Richie waved a hand in front of his face, nodding toward Mary Jane. "What adjustments can we make to the menu?"

"Winter squash agrodolce?" Mary Jane set the menu on the island. She had Claire's rich brown hair and delicate nose. She didn't have the stubborn set to her chin or a direct way of looking at a person. Her gaze swept the floor. "What is that exactly?"

"Winter squash *agrodolce*. It's a spicy, sweet squash." Drew tried to forget Claire and tried not to sound defensive. "You requested haute cuisine." Which he had experience with making in restaurants. His food truck tended toward more casual cuisine.

"Did I? Can you excuse me?" With a hand to her stomach, Mary Jane disappeared down a hall.

"Bro, quit being so uptight." Richie spun his barstool in a circle.

"I'm not." He was. Drew gritted his teeth.

"You are." Richie rolled his eyes. "You think you want this restaurant, but I don't think you realize you'll be chained to it night and day. Is that what you really want?"

"Yes. I'm adulting."

"That's what you said when you bought the food truck. How much adulting does one person need?"

Drew was annoyed to find he couldn't answer that question.

Outside, it began to pour. Down the hall, Mary Jane coughed.

The lights flickered and then went off. Strings of panic raced along Drew's nerves.

"Shoot." Mary Jane returned to the kitchen, which was gloomy given the storm clouds and the rain. "The construction crew down the road promised there'd be no more power outages."

"No more ...." Drew murmured. There had been other episodes of no power? "You have electric appliances." Not gas. And she didn't like his menu.

"Don't you have solar power, MJ?" Richie brought his barstool to a halt. "Or is that just over there?" He pointed at a large solar panel at the side of the house where Claire was.

There was power where Claire was.

Drew's head was shaking before the small word left his lips. "No." He couldn't possibly cook in the vicinity of Claire. He'd known she'd be here, but he'd assumed she wouldn't be in the kitchen or near enough to watch him. Much as he pretended otherwise, Claire Rothchild was his kryptonite.

Mary Jane beamed at Richie. "Luke only had solar installed at the guesthouse to see if it was worth the financial risk."

There was more at risk financially than the output of solar panels. Drew's future was at stake here. And Claire was inside that house. Unsettling, distracting Claire. Drew swallowed thickly.

"Would you like to check out the guesthouse kitchen?" Mary Jane asked sweetly. "And then we can talk about the menu changes."

"Lead the way." Drew clung to a smile. His van was filled with food based on the menu he'd given her. Good thing he'd come a day early with the nonperishables.

"It's just a precaution." Mary Jane hurried around the island to the French doors, grabbing an umbrella from a drawer. "I'm sure the power will come right back on."

"Thanksgiving is still two days away," Richie said good naturedly. "Plenty of time to restore power."

The trio traipsed over to the guest cottage in the deluge. Only Mary Jane stayed dry.

"Are you sure Claire won't mind the interruption?" Drew asked as they approached the door.

"Not at all." Mary Jane skipped up the steps and shook out her umbrella. "She has a big decision to make this week, but you know Claire, she loves people."

Before Drew could ask what the big decision was, Mary Jane opened the door without knocking. "Look what the cat dragged in."

The dog lumbered to his feet, staring toward the door with a low grumble.

"No cats, Snowy." Olly slung his arm over the dog's shoulders. "Just Auntie MJ and Uncle Drew."

"Don't forget Uncle Richie. Wowzer. Look at this spread. You have enough sugary treats here to mend a broken heart." Richie perused the cannisters on the counter and selected what looked like a gingersnap.

The dog padded over with a gentle, *ruh-row*. He sounded very Scooby Doo–like, as if eating the cookie foretold of trouble.

Claire *tsk*ed, staring at Drew's feet. "No one is heartbroken here."

"It was more like a crisis of confidence," Mary Jane said in a no-nonsense tone.

Drew sucked in his cheeks. He would not smile at Claire. He would not joke with Claire. He would not look at Claire's infinitely kissable lips.

Oops.

"We're here to check you out," he blurted. He smiled. He stared. He clarified, "Check out your kitchen."

Richie chuckled.

"What are you doing here?" Claire demanded of her sister, turning away from Drew and allowing him to breathe.

"Power outage. The guest cottage has solar and is therefore a back-up for the main kitchen." Mary Jane picked up a sheaf of what looked like legal papers.

Claire snatched the papers back, some of that fire Drew loved so much returning. "You can't cook here. We're dog sitting, remember?"

"Have you made a decision?" Mary Jane asked in a raised voice. "Signed anything?"

"No." Claire scowled. That scowl swung Drew's way. "Can we not talk in front of the enemy?"

"Are you …" Drew took a step back into more common ground, that of mock indignation. "You mean me?"

Richie laughed, enjoying the show far too much, and ate another ginger cookie.

"Yes." Claire shook those legal pages in the air. "You. Stewart's best friend. These are custody papers."

"Top-secret treasure maps." Olly had scaled a barstool and perused the spread of confections. His pirate hat was tilted at a jaunty angle. "Only Mommy touches them. Not for coloring."

"Stewart and I don't talk about you," Drew said. They talked about waves ridden and the low cost of living Stewart had found in Costa Rica. They talked about Stewart's social media following and endorsements. Sometimes they even talked about Drew. But they never, ever, talked about Claire. "I only see him when he comes back to visit Olly. And you know Stewart. He's not much for calling or texting."

Claire's mouth dropped open. Her gaze softened. "He left you, too?"

"Yeah. Kind-of," Drew managed to say because Claire was looking at him like he wasn't the enemy. And for once, his pulse pounded with hope, not under the burden of hiding the things he felt for Claire.

"Do you like what you see?" Mary Jane asked from behind Drew.

Yes, he did. He liked it too much.

"She means the kitchen," Richie said with his mouth full.

Concentrate. Drew moved into the small kitchen and nudged Richie out. "Double oven, six-burner gas range, microwave. This will serve in a pinch."

The dog grumbled, politely begging as he stared at Richie.

Drew's brother gave the dog a piece of cookie, which was immediately inhaled. "We won't be able to cook with this *mon-stah* in the house though."

"But you will be able to cook here?" Mary Jane asked seriously. "Give me a menu with a more Spanish-centric theme?"

"To match the house?" Claire sounded as horrified as Drew felt. "Really?"

"Yes." Mary Jane narrowed her eyes at her sister. "You got a problem with that?"

Claire tossed her hands in surrender.

Now that Claire wasn't looking at him, Drew recovered his professionalism. "We can adjust the menu, Mary Jane, but I prefer to cook in the large kitchen, away from the dog hair." And the distraction of Claire.

The dog stood and gave him a disapproving glance.

Drew opened the refrigerator. Front and center were the remains of a wedding bouquet. *Her* wedding bouquet. He recognized it from the ribbons she'd clutched a year ago. What did that mean? Was she hoping Stewart would come back to her? He frowned at Claire. "This will have to go."

"Never fear. It'll be ash soon." Claire's cheeks turned an attractive pink. "It means nothing."

In which case, Drew felt comfortable tossing out a tease. "Some people save the top layer of their wedding cake—"

"Presumably, people who get married," Claire groused.

"—while others save the bouquet they didn't get to throw."

"If Stewart hadn't fled the scene, Claire could have tossed it at his head." Mary Jane grinned. "I think we should have you prepare the meal in here, Drew. The power's been going on and off all week at the main house."

"What?" The color drained from Claire's cheeks.

"Better safe than sorry." Richie reached past Drew for a bottle of water.

"If you're here, we'll shut ourselves in the bedroom." Claire huffed. "We aren't attending the party anyway."

Aroo-who, the dog vocalized softly.

Richie jerked upright and glanced at Drew. "Did you say something?"

"No."

Olly giggled. "Snowy says if you cook here, he gets to watch."

"*To supervise,*" Richie muttered, staring at the dog. "I'm out." He scurried out the door into the increasing downpour.

He was gone when Drew returned to the van to begin unloading supplies.

"Power's back on in the main house," Claire announced as Drew brought in another a box of food. "You can—"

"I'm staying." Drew's chin jutted as he rearranged the cannisters of cookies and homemade confections on the counter, stacking and shoving them to the side. "Mary Jane wants me to cook from here. Here is where I'm cooking."

The rain had eased up to a soft pitter-patter. Olly was asleep, sprawled on his stomach on the couch. Snowy lay on the floor nearby, eyes on them.

"You said earlier you didn't want to fight." Claire kept her voice low, crossing the small living room to join Drew. "But we always fight."

"That's not true." Drew opened several cupboard doors until he found one that was empty. He began putting spices on a shelf. "We didn't fight until you started dating Stewart."

"That can't be right." She leaned on the counter, aware of everything in the kitchen she didn't need—sugar and Drew.

The gentle reach and extend of his actions engaged the muscles in his back, shoulders and arms, making her remember how fit Drew looked on a surfboard which was the only time she remembered not fighting with him.

"You don't remember." He faced her. She'd seen him wet and dripping as he emerged from the ocean, triumphant after riding a wave. He was wet now, and dripping. But triumph didn't line his firm features. His blue eyes were warm, tender. Increasingly, she felt as if she didn't know this Drew. "You don't remember sixth-grade band? You played the flute. I played the drums. Or seventh-grade science lab when we dissected a frog?"

"Yes. Sort of." She squirmed, embarrassed. "Those memories are vague."

"I remember." He leaned his elbows on the counter opposite her. "I remember holding you when Stewart disappeared from the wedding chapel." His voice was just a whisper now, smooth as silk and just as inviting. "I remember helping you and Olly into the back of the limo. Your cheeks were wet with tears. And I remember thinking ..."

Claire couldn't breathe. Not until he finished that thought.

"... that I never wanted to see you cry again."

Claire still couldn't breathe.

And then Drew reached across the counter, across the divide, across years of animosity, and touched her cheek. Just once.

Claire sucked in much-needed air. She should say thank you. She should say ....

She didn't know what to say. But she sure as heck shouldn't be staring at his lips.

Behind her, Snowy groaned softly. She glanced back. Olly's arm had fallen off the couch. His fingers speared through the fur around Snowy's neck.

The custody papers were where she left them on the coffee table. Those papers .... Everything leading up to them, starting with her ill-fated wedding day.

Her gaze swung back around to Drew. "Did you know? That day. Did you know Stewart was going to dump us?"

"No." Drew's voice was still low, but now it had a hard edge, a familiar edge.

For once, she liked his sharpness. "Did he tell you about"—this question was trickier—"his custody demands?"

"No." One word. How could it convey so much anger?

Claire wasn't sure if Drew was upset with Stewart's behavior or her for asking his opinion of it.

Drew stared at Olly. "When we talk, we don't talk about you two. And I wouldn't let him say anything if he tried to bring it up."

"You don't want to get in the middle." That made sense if Drew considered Claire a friend, which she still found hard to believe. "Why not take Stewart's side?"

Drew emptied the box, not speaking. "I'll be back tomorrow." He headed for the door, pausing with his hand on the knob. "What Stewart did wasn't right. You deserve to be with someone who'll treat you better." He gave Claire a look over his shoulder.

A look that said he knew who could treat her better.

And then he was gone.

Drew likes me? Drew wants me?

Impossible. Claire shook her head. She must have read his signals wrong.

Claire reached for a cookie tin, took out a ginger cookie, and ate it.

CHAPTER THREE

*S*_he needs her sleep._

"But I'm hungry." Olly's gentle voice permeated Claire's sleep. "We can't have cookies for dinner."

I can.

The male voice. It wasn't Drew. "Luke?" Claire cracked an eye open.

Olly and Snowy stood next to where she lay on the couch. She hadn't meant to doze off, only to rest her eyes. But those two darling faces …. They were picture worthy. She didn't reach for her cell phone the way she would have before Stewart had laid out his demands, because the temptation to post the heartwarming picture would be too great. And what did that say about her? Was she a proud mama? Or a woman using her son's cuteness? She preferred the former and Stewart was implying the latter.

"We're hungry," Olly said, breaking into her thoughts.

Claire sat up. "Where's Uncle Luke?"

Olly laughed, and she must have not quite been awake yet because she thought she heard an echo of older, male laughter. But it was just Snowy with them in the guest cottage, tongue hanging out of his mouth as he panted happily. Outside the window, the rain had tapered off and the sun was making a meager attempt at shining.

"We pirates want pizza." Olly slung his arms around Snowy's neck.

"We dog sitters need to go for a walk first."

Olly plopped down on the floor. "I'd rather walk the plank."

That's not nice.

"That's not ..." Claire got to her feet and walked quickly through the cottage. She could have sworn she heard a man mutter something. "Who's here?"

Olly and Snowy trotted after her.

Olly tugged her hand. "It's just us, Mommy. Hungry us. Let's walk. Snowy promises to hurry with his business."

"Snowy promises." Claire grabbed a lightweight jacket, helped Olly into a hoodie, and took Snowy's leash from a hook near the door.

The big dog held very still when she snapped his leash on, blowing out a breath that sounded like, "Thank you."

She was beginning to see where Olly got his imagination. "Let's go, boys."

Mary Jane met them on the driveway in a fancy pair of sweats and sneakers with rhinestones. "Any decision yet?"

"Yes. I decided to nap." Again, Claire heard the echoes of masculine laughter. She grabbed Mary Jane's arm. "Did you hear that? Is Luke home?"

"Luke home before seven on a workday?" Mary Jane chuckled. "I heard Snowy. I told you he's a talker."

There was a difference between talking and laughing and doggy sounds, but Claire chalked her off-kilter hearing to stress.

"Hurry up, Snowy." Olly ran ahead. "The sooner we walk, the sooner we eat."

Okay, okay, okay.

"That was Snowy panting, right?" Claire asked of her sister, who gave her a sharp look.

"Right." Mary Jane took Snowy's leash. "You need a break, I think. How did it go with Drew after I left?"

"It went fine. He was only there to drop off food." But the memory of his intense regard returned. "Wait a minute. What do you mean—how did it go? He's your chef. Unless ..." Why that meddler. "Mary Jane. What are you up to?"

Mary Jane scoffed. "I'm up to my armpits in preparations for Luke's guests, who arrive tomorrow."

Snowy paused to look at Claire, mouth open in that doggy grin, and Claire imagined she heard that laughter again.

"I don't believe you," Claire said. "Confess. You only hired Drew because of me."

"Yes." Mary Jane laughed. "I knew he'd be a shock to your system, which is just what you need when you're facing the biggest decision of your life. When Drew's around, you show the world you've got a backbone."

Now it was Claire's turn to scoff.

"Guys, hurry with your steps," Olly called from the gate, trying to leap up and hit the release button. "I'm so hungry, I could eat three cheese pizzas."

Wednesday afternoon, Drew spent an hour stocking Claire's kitchen with supplies from the food truck, provisions to slant the menu more toward the Spanish flavors Mary Jane seemed to want. Not everything, but enough to please both her and Drew.

By the time Drew was finished, he was soaked, despite his rain jacket, the hood of which was constantly blowing off.

"Uncle Drew, Snowy wants you to have a cookie." Olly handed him a ginger cookie, and then returned to sit on the floor in front of the television. "See? It's easy," he told the dog.

Drew chomped on the cookie. It was crisp, like biscotti but with the light flavor of gingerbread.

If Snowy really had wanted Drew to eat a cookie, he had a poor way of showing it. He watched Drew's every move, drooling.

Claire stepped between the two and handed Drew a hand towel. "Ready for tomorrow?"

Drew ran the towel over his head. "I'll be here bright and early." The storm brought big waves. Richie had been a no-show today. It was all coming down to Drew. He took another ginger cookie. "How come you haven't been posting on social media? You always post during the week."

Claire's gaze skittered away to those custody papers. "Maybe I needed a break."

Something wasn't right here. "Trouble with your sponsors?"

She shook her head, fingers tracing the back of a barstool. "Feeling uninspired?"

She shook her head again.

She's scared.

Drew glanced around to see who'd spoken. "Is there someone else here?"

"Did you hear something?" Claire turned around, searching as intently as Drew was. "I heard something last night. I'm beginning to think this place is haunted."

Snowy got to his feet and came into the kitchen, staring up at Drew.

She needs you.

"That's ridiculous," Drew said automatically.

"You don't have to sound so cold," Claire grumbled. "You're the one who pointed out we were friends once."

You should have been lovers.

Drew spun toward the door. The words had been spoken by a man. But he and Claire were alone, save for the Saint Bernard and Olly. "Did you hear that?"

"Mary Jane would say it was Snowy." Claire returned to the couch, sitting cross-legged.

"It *is* Snowy," Olly said, lying down on the floor. "He talks."

Claire and Drew exchanged glances. And then Drew stared at the dog, who coincidentally began moving his jowls.

She wants you to kiss her.

"Are you a ventriloquist?" Drew demanded of Claire. "That's not funny." But his gaze dipped to her lips. They looked soft and pink and perfect for kissing. "Pretending to put words in the dog's mouth."

Claire turned up the volume on Olly's cartoon.

She doesn't want to listen, the dog glanced over at Claire, *to me.*

Drew didn't either. He must be going insane. He dragged a hand over his face. "It's been a long day."

Amen. Snowy lay back down next to Olly.

A sound grew in the distance. A sound the likes of which Drew had never heard before. Louder than a boat. Quieter than an airplane. And the ground …. It seemed to tremble.

"Earthquake," he said snapped, moving toward Olly, intending to pick him up and hustle them all outside.

"No. Did you hear that?" Claire got to her feet and went to the window. "Earthquakes don't sound like that."

Drew wasn't going to admit he was hearing all kinds of things. "Claire, get outside." He gathered Olly into his arms, who shifted so he could see the television.

I heard it, too.

The dog pressed his nose to the window near Claire.

Not safe.

The lights in the main house went dark. The lights in the guest-house remained on. But the TV screen snapped to snow and static.

"Hey." Olly raised his head. "My show."

"Seriously, I heard a rumble." Claire glanced up at the dark sky.

"I heard it, too." He opened the door and it was like turning up the volume of the rain. "Earthquake drill. Let's get outside." A soaking was better than being crushed.

"It wasn't an earthquake." Claire moved slowly, shaking her head. "It sounded like a train without the whistle."

"Holy smokes!" Wearing a raincoat, Mary Jane scurried across the patio and into the guesthouse. She threw back her hood and panted, "Mudslide. Where that construction crew was laying pipe. Luke saw it from his upstairs man cave. He's on the phone with nine-one-one now."

"Richie." Drew set Olly back down inside the house and called his brother, who picked up on the first ring.

"I'm sorry, man. I meant to call. But you should see these waves. I'll head over to Del Mar now."

For once, Drew wasn't angry with his brother's priorities. "Don't bother." He explained about the slide and advised Richie to stay safe.

"Was anyone hurt?" Claire pulled Olly close as Drew hung up. "Did Luke see …?"

"Luke didn't think anyone was on the road." Mary Jane turned to Drew. "You'll have to stay here tonight, Drew. There's no way out past that slide and all our guest bedrooms are full."

Sweet. A romantic night in.

Snowy tilted his head up toward Drew, panting.

"Mudslides aren't romantic," Drew grumbled louder than the dog, earning sharp looks from both women.

And dogs don't talk.

"Wine?" Claire filled her glass with cabernet after Olly had gone to bed in her room, and they'd watched a local news report on the mudslide, one broadcast from farther down the hill.

"Please." Drew had changed into a pair of men's soccer sweats that Luke had loaned him. His damp clothes were in the washer.

The road report seemed grim. And the storm continued to make big waves along the coast. Good surfing waves. Drew wasn't sure his brother would show in the morning even if the road was clear.

Claire poured Drew a glass of wine without spilling a drop. "How are your parents?"

He could have done without her curiosity. "They're fine. The same."

His father was a captain in the navy. His mother a successful self-help guru and book author. Growing up, they'd pounded in the importance of perfection and responsibility, not realizing that their work ethics and trail blazing sent a different message: "Life is too short. Work hard at your passions." They just didn't understand their son's passions.

He opened a tin and removed a cookie. The smell of gingerbread filled the air.

Don't eat them all. Snowy inched closer to him, drooling on his bare foot.

"This is my cookie." Drew took a bite, ignoring Snowy's continued complaints as he took a paper towel and wiped up all the dog drool, including the drip on the dog's jowls. "Did you try these, Claire? They're so unusual." He gave her one and then took the wine glass, smirking at the dog, who definitely could not talk. Or so he kept reminding himself, so he didn't start seriously questioning his sanity.

Claire crunched on one end of the cookie before giving it to Snowy. "I tried one yesterday. It's good, potentially addicting if they weren't rock hard."

"Addicting?" He chuckled. "But you said you only had one."

"A lifetime of pressure to stay slim is harder to ignore than the siren call of sugar." She sounded melancholy.

194

He thought he knew the source of her sadness. Claire's father was a once-prominent real estate mogul, a man who'd lost a fortune in the crash of 2009. Up to that point, her mother had served on several charitable boards in the area. Whereas Drew's parents had focused on hard work and striving for their personal potential, Claire's emphasized the need to look good and move in the right circles. Mary Jane had taken to the lesson better than Claire.

"People will like you no matter your weight," Drew muttered. He'd like her.

She likes me, the dog seemed to say. *But she doesn't like hearing me.*

"*I* don't like hearing you either," Drew muttered.

Claire sat in one corner of the couch, drinking her wine. "I saw your mom had another book out."

She doesn't just like you .... Snowy came to sit next to Claire but his gaze was on Drew and his mouth moved as if he still worked a bit of cookie between his jaws. *She likes your mom. She's a keeper.*

Drew closed his eyes. Dogs do not talk, especially to sons of naval captains and self-help gurus.

He opened his eyes and trained his attention on Claire. On the soft curl of her brown hair. On the delicate bow to her pink lips. And that upright posture from the years her parents had kept her in ballet. She couldn't slouch if her life depended on it. Not even if her groom left her at the altar.

Say something nice.

Drew took another sip of wine, wishing he had something stronger. Maybe the dog was just a figment of his subconscious. Maybe deep down, Drew wanted to take advantage of Claire's availability and kiss her. Maybe the "dog," a.k.a. his subconscious, would go silent if Drew took his advice. "My mother always liked you."

Snowy tossed his head. *Good.*

Claire frowned. "She liked me even when we fought? I remember your eighteenth birthday party."

She'd shouted at him after he pushed her into the pool.

Drew set down his wine glass. "Can we forget that?" And all the other times they'd poked at and prodded each other.

"Why do we argue?" Claire leaned forward, brown eyes calm. "Tell me."

"Because Mrs. Chantilly liked your cookies better than mine in home ec class?" It was as good an answer as any. He wasn't about to tell Claire he'd been jealous of Stewart.

You need to drink more wine.

Drew made a sound that was more like a growl than Snowy was making. He grabbed his wine glass and took a generous drink. And then another. "It's like that dog can talk."

"I'm becoming better at ignoring him." Claire sipped her wine, attention still on Drew. "Because I could swear he inserts himself into every conversation."

"Are you good at ignoring Stewart?" Where had that question come from?

Claire buried her nose in her wine glass.

"I mean, ignoring his new 'more genuine' lifestyle." Drew ground out a laugh. "Living without the luxuries he so despises us for having and wanting. Glorying in his so-called relationship with nature and his authenticity like true millennials should."

The dog sank to the ground, resting his head on his paws, silent for once. If he had the intelligence to speak, he might have known that bringing up the topic of a woman's ex was the kiss of relationship death. Drew longed for kisses of another sort with Claire.

"Stewart despises luxuries," Claire said slowly. "That explains a lot."

"It does," Drew realized. Because Claire's sponsors were luxury brands and Stewart was positioning himself as the surfer dude who lived in a hut on the beach without fresh running water. Great place to raise a kid, even if Olly was enamored with pirates and nautical life.

"Do you think me taking pictures of Olly and posting them is exploitive?" Claire asked in a small voice.

Drew sat back in surprise. "I thought Olly liked being photographed." He was such a ham.

"He does, it's just ... Stewart disapproves." She grimaced. "I never thought of it on those terms before because it's like you said—Olly likes it."

Drew took a moment to think about the morality of the way Claire made her living. "You do post pictures of him using products he seems to like."

"I've never forced him to like anything." Her tone held hints of defensiveness. She swallowed and shook her head, and when next she spoke, the wariness was gone. "Sorry. I get touchy where Stewart's been attacking me. And then there's the fact that my endorsements pay the bills."

"You shouldn't listen to other people's opinions."

"I haven't heard yours," she reminded him.

Again, he took a moment to answer. "I think what you're doing is okay. He's only in postings for products he uses. And if Olly was unhappy, he'd refuse the spotlight."

She heaved a sigh of apparent relief. "Thank you. You're a pain in the butt, Drew. But I think we're more alike than we're like Stewart. Practically interchangeable in his eyes. We both came from wealthy families. And you were just perfect—straddling both worlds, his and ours."

"Only *just* perfect?" The wine was warming his chest, loosening his tongue. He set the glass back down.

Snowy was watching him without raising his head.

"The haughty Drew Barnett is fishing for compliments?" Claire's smile added warmth to his chest, making him sigh.

Making him want.

He wanted to hold all that softness and perfection in his arms.

Had he said that or the dog?

Drew frowned and rubbed his hands over his face. "I think …." What had they been talking about? He was staring at Claire's lips. "I think I need more wine." He got up and grabbed onto the wine bottle, refilling both their glasses.

"Chicken."

He didn't argue the observation. He drank, staring at the dog, whose eyes were closed. Drew wasn't fooled. Snowy's ears twitched every time Drew shifted in his seat.

"You should slow down on the wine," Claire said softly.

Drew took another sip. "Tomorrow is the biggest day of my career and it looks like all my dreams have slid down the cliff with half the road. If I impress Luke, he's going to invest in a restaurant with me. A high-end surfer joint in downtown San Diego. How's that for a truth?"

197

"You have everything here to make a wonderful meal to impress." She gave him a sly grin. "I should know. I peeked while you were in the shower."

He liked that she'd peeked.

"I haven't had your food in forever, but Mary Jane is desperate to fit into the mold Luke has for her." Claire rubbed her forehead. "You should stand behind your principles and your menu plans. Your food has always said a lot about who you are."

Wise words, the dog might have mumbled, had he been a dog that talked.

Agreeing, Drew ran his hand through his hair, instead of reaching over and running it through Claire's. "You want the truth about you and me?"

She nodded.

"There was more chemistry between the two of us than there ever was between you and Stewart."

Well played.

Drew lifted his gaze to Claire's face.

More like gone too far.

Claire couldn't breathe.

That was becoming standard operating procedure when Drew was around.

Outside, the eaves dripped. Inside, Snowy gave that soft grumble. And Drew? He said nothing. But he stared at Claire with those piercing blue eyes, waiting for her to say something.

Claire filled her lungs with air and set her wine glass down. "I think we've had enough to drink." And given each other enough to think about. At some point, she was going to have to make a decision regarding custody negotiations. But not now. Not with Drew looking at her like he thought she was the most beautiful woman in the world.

Snowy grumbled something that was thankfully unintelligible.

"Well, that's that." Drew heaved a sigh. "You always did have a way of kinking all my karma."

"Dude ... Dude, you just said we had chemistry." And he was right. It thrummed through her veins like truth. "And now ...." They were stuck in this small house together. With a fire in the gas fireplace and lots of good wine.

Drew shrugged. "It was just a … an observation. Like wondering how saffron might blend with harissa."

"Horribly." Claire knew enough about food to know that, even though the only thing she'd ever really mastered in the kitchen was chocolate chip cookies. But she couldn't let this chemistry thing be pushed aside. Because …. Because …. Her heart was pounding. "When Stewart and I began dating, you pointed out every misstep I took. It got to the point where I weighed every word, every outfit, against what you'd think."

"Blame chemistry," he mumbled. And then his gaze met hers. "I was an immature jerk. But because of that, you paid more attention to me than you did to Stewart."

"That can't be true." Was it true? Claire rubbed her temples. "I dated Stewart for nearly a decade. And I never felt …" *The desire to kiss you.*

That wasn't completely true. There'd been that night at the bar a few days before the wedding. Stewart had left early to take his cousin back to his hotel. She and Drew had been drinking martinis and snacking on chips and hummus, and …. She'd turned to look at Drew and leaned closer to say something. Only then she'd taken one look in his eyes and forgotten what was on her mind. Because …. Because she'd wanted to kiss him. It had felt so natural. She'd veered mid-lean and whispered in his ear, "I've had one martini too many."

She wanted to admit she'd had one wine too many tonight, but that wasn't true. She'd barely had one full glass. While Drew …. "Are you drunk?"

"I am … relaxed." His gaze dropped to the dog. He heaved a sigh. "Are we still arguing about chemistry?"

"No. But I still don't believe you about this going on for ten years."

He sighed. "We're still arguing."

Snowy made a rumbling noise.

"I know. I know. 'Stop arguing, Drew.'" He swiped a hand through the air. "It's like any other theory about compatible spices in a new dish." He lifted his eyes to Claire's, pupils so dark she imagined she could fall into their depths. "We can't talk in hypotheticals. We have to get in the kitchen and try it out."

Snowy grumbled, staring at Drew, who nodded and said, "Yep."

"What are you saying?" Claire whispered, although she wasn't sure if she was asking Drew for clarification or Snowy for a translation.

"Come here." Drew held out his hand, palm up. "Neither one of us is going to sleep tonight for wondering. Let's just get it over with. One kiss ought to do it."

"Now I know you've drank too much." But Claire's heart pounded and she knew she'd wonder about chemistry and Drew's kiss all night if they didn't conduct this test. And yet, she couldn't scoot across the couch cushions to do anything about it. Pride held her back. "What if there is no spark."

"Oh, there are plenty of sparks." Drew ran a finger across the empty couch cushion between them. "This is a line. Inch on up to it in that careful way of yours. Only our lips are going to cross that line."

Snowy grumbled.

"I don't care if it's not romantic." Drew looked at the dog. He tossed another hand the way he tossed parmesan cheese on an alfredo dish. "There's a difference between fast food and fine cuisine, the same as there's a difference between lust and love."

"Lust?" *Love?* Claire had been about to inch forward but she froze at the L-words.

"Lips, Ms. Rothchild. Focus on lips." He tapped his with a finger and sat on his side of the middle cushion.

There was danger here and it wasn't from the thunder and pounding rain outside. It was from Drew and the risk he presented to her heart. But she'd never backed down from one of Drew's challenges. She wasn't going to start now.

Claire eased herself from the safety of the couch corner into the neutral zone in the middle of the couch. "Just lips," she reiterated, more for herself than for Drew. She needed some courage.

"Just lips." He leaned forward.

She leaned forward, her gaze lowering to his hands resting on either side of the cushion. The length of his fingers. The bunch of muscle in his upper arms. Her heart was pounding. Her hands were knotted in the soft fabric of her T-shirt.

"Lips," he whispered. "I can't get to yours when you look down."

"Oh." There was no escaping this moment, this test.

Their lips met, tentatively. His were warm, firm, welcoming. His tongue traced the shape of her mouth, which opened on a sigh. She missed kissing and being held. But it wasn't Stewart she was thinking of. It was Drew. She tilted into his kiss, into him, and it was fabulous and hot and decadent.

And only their mouths were touching.

Without warning, Drew pulled back. "Whoa."

Stopping wasn't what Claire would have chosen. She was breathing hard and realizing it was her turn to say something, to save face and what little friendship they had between them. "There was no chemistry there at all."

"None," Drew agreed. And then he kissed her again, slowly, as if their kiss was something to be savored.

She pulled back from him, with reluctance. "Hold up." It was Claire who brought a halt to the drugging kisses this time. "No sense continuing when we know the outcome."

She was right. Their chemistry was dangerous.

Because it was combustible.

He reached for her again.

CHAPTER FOUR

On Thanksgiving morning, Claire made coffee, fed Snowy, and took him for a walk before Olly woke up.

Drew knew this because he listened to Claire from the smaller bedroom in the guesthouse.

He hadn't heard the dog talk all morning.

Thankfully.

And they hadn't done more than kiss thrice last night, but his theory about their physical compatibility was correct. Which was too bad. Because today, of all days, he couldn't afford the distraction of Claire. He needed to look like a respectable man with a future if he was going to win her heart.

Not that he had time to ponder his attraction to Claire. He had a six-course Thanksgiving feast to prepare and a dream of restaurant ownership to salvage. He dressed and made his way to the kitchen.

Olly stumbled out. "What's for breakfast, Uncle Drew?" He mashed his pirate hat on his head.

"Breakfast quiche in an hour or your Cheerios."

"Cheerios, please." Olly laid his head on his hands and yawned.

A few minutes after he'd served Olly a bowl of cereal, Claire came through the door with Snowy. They stared at each other. Mostly, Drew stared at Claire's lips because they were fabulous, and he knew their soft texture by heart already.

Before he could figure out what to say, the oven beeped, having warmed to the desired temperature to cook breakfast quiche.

I am a chef. I have people to feed.

And yet at the sight of her, all he wanted to do was play with Claire's chemistry set.

Drew cleared his throat. "For food safety, I need the dog outside or in another room." *Please go with him so I'm not distracted by either one of you.*

"He and I will happily quarantine in the bedroom after I burn my wedding bouquet," Claire said in a husky voice. She grabbed a book of matches from a drawer and went outside, heading toward the firepit and its haphazard stack of wet wood, flanked by Snowy and Olly. Drew returned his attention to the eggs he was whisking in a bowl.

A few minutes later, Claire stomped back inside. "I need paper. The fire won't light. It's my wedding day all over again. A dud. I was so hoping for fireworks."

"Me, too." Olly shrugged deeper into his hoodie. "Or TV." The cable was still out.

"Don't panic." Drew handed Claire a mug of coffee and one of the ginger cookies—because when he thought of Claire and fireworks, he thought of kisses and sweetness, and the cookies were sweet.

Eyeing the exchange, Snowy grumbled. Grumbled, not talked. Conclusion: the wine last night had made it seem as if Snowy had the power of speech.

Drew would have patted the dog on the head if that hadn't meant he'd have to wash his hands again. "Out of the kitchen, Snowy."

Claire dipped the cookie in the coffee mug and took a bite. "I can't figure out why these are so good. There's too much brown spice." She gave Snowy the rest of hers. "And they're too crunchy."

"It's elegant tasting," Drew countered. "Nothing as plain as a chocolate chip cookie."

"Don't rain on my skills, Chef." Claire disappeared into her bedroom, returning with a delicate pashmina scarf. "This will burn, won't it?"

"Sure, but …. Isn't that the scarf Stewart gave you for Christmas one year?"

"All the more reason to burn it." She headed toward the door with her scarf, her bouquet, Olly, and the dog.

Drew followed, revised menu in hand, but he only went as far as the door. This felt like something Claire had to do without him. He watched through the window.

She set the bouquet on a patio chair. Olly and Snowy stood beside her, as any good wedding attendants would. Claire struck a match. The wind from the ocean extinguished it before the sulfur tip had burned, before she was even able to hold it to the scarf.

She struck another. And another. "The universe wants to save this bouquet!" Claire shouted at the blue sky.

Snowy sniffed the air. Olly tugged the brim of his hat over both ears.

Drew opened the door a few inches. "I have a gas lighter. Mind if I do the honors?"

After a moment's hesitation, Claire nodded.

She'd put the scarf on top of the wood. He handed it back to her and then shoved his menu underneath the kindling. A few clicks of his gas lighter and the menu caught, sheltered from the wind. And then the kindling caught flame. Soon the pyre was crackling, and so was Claire.

"Yes!" she said.

Mary Jane came out the kitchen door to watch, dressed in pumpkin-colored slacks and a cream-colored sweater. Fancy, compared to Claire's black leggings and lightweight sweater. But Drew much preferred Claire.

Claire placed the bouquet on top of the fire. It shriveled in on itself with one small burst of flame.

"No fireworks." Claire's gaze lifted to Drew's.

Oh, he knew how to make fireworks if she wanted some.

Not now, Chef.

He returned to his kitchen and tried to push all thoughts of Claire from his mind.

"I got the bedroom TV working in my room, Captain Olly," Drew announced. "It is internet compatible, whereas the living room TV isn't."

Olly didn't need Drew to tell him twice. He ran off to his cartoons.

"Thanks." Claire fisted her scarf, grateful Olly had been distracted before begging to swim. It was still nippy out. "We'll get out of your hair now." She and Snowy turned toward the guesthouse.

"Hang on, Claire. Before you head to quarantine ..." Drew reached the door ahead of them and held it open. "... how are your food-prep skills?"

"Is Chef Barnett asking me if I can peel potatoes?" Claire chuckled as she went in.

"Hey, you're always promoting those ready-to-cook meal boxes, so I wasn't sure if you still remembered how to use a knife or a peeler." Drew entered the small kitchen. "The only way Richie is making it here today is if he gets dropped in by helicopter. And that's not happening."

"So, you're asking me to take pity on you?" Their teasing was almost as good as his kisses last night. Better even. She had no trouble drawing a breath this morning, although that half-smile of his still had the power to send butterflies fluttering in her chest.

He washed his hands in the sink. "I'm asking for help. A good leader knows when to ask for help. And a good person knows when to be gracious about stepping up to the plate."

"You want me to be gracious? And forget about the line we breached last night?" That earned her a mischievous smile, one that had Claire shaking her head in defeat. "Okay. Gracious it is. Snowy, go watch cartoons with Olly in the bedroom." She took Drew's place at the sink when he was done and washed her hands.

Before she could even ask what Drew needed, he was laying out vegetables on a cutting board. "Dice the red peppers. Coarsely grate the carrots. Peel potatoes." His list went on and on. In the midst of it, he handed her another ginger cookie. "You'll need sustenance." A coffee mug appeared at her elbow. "I've been gingered up all morning."

Claire sighed, dipping the cookie into the coffee.

From the doorway to her bedroom, Snowy grumbled softly.

"No," Drew said cryptically. He turned his back on Claire, dropping sausage into a frying pan. "And when you're done with that cookie, you'll need to wash your hands again before you start on the vegetables."

"Yes, Chef." Claire dunked the cookie deeper in the coffee this time. Drew was right. It was much better softened by strong French roast. "This isn't how I envisioned today going. A few days ago, I was trying to boycott the holiday, planning on eating burgers and drinking wine while binging on mindless television."

"And I interrupted your binge watching of Hallmark movies?" He moved on to dice onions, operating at enviable efficiency. Half an onion joined the sausage. "Do you know what good chefs leave at the door?"

"High heels?" She wore sneakers, although she had applied make-up and hair gel.

"Their troubles. Nothing comes between you and the food." Drew ground fresh pepper over the frying pan.

"I'll like that statement better when I'm sitting down with a plate in front of me."

Drew scoffed. "What happened to burgers and wine?"

"A mudslide." Geez, that was obvious. His staff couldn't get in and she couldn't get out.

"You can eat my food if you don't critique my food." With a flourish, Drew added a bit of dry white wine to the skillet. "No pictures or postings either."

"It's not entirely your food if I help make it."

"It's entirely my food." Drew sent her a glance that her heart categorized as steamy, even though it was a short-lived flicker of eye contact before he returned his attention to the skillet.

He's flirting with you.

That masculine voice. Claire chuckled. "Talking about yourself in the third person now, Drew?"

"A little more chopping, a little less talking." Drew's knife moved so fast over a tomato and against the cutting board that it was hard to hear his words.

You should smile more. He likes it when you smile.

Claire spun around, expecting to see Luke at the door. "Who said that?" Because this time she was sure it hadn't been Drew.

"More chopping," Drew repeated, pausing to glance at Claire. "Problem?"

"No." She was hearing things but that was to be expected. The main house was full of guests. Except no one was outside on the deck between the two houses.

Kiss the cook. Isn't that what they say?

Claire set down the knife and went to check on what Olly was watching. She stepped over Snowy, entering Drew's room. Olly was watching the Disney Channel, cradling his cutlass. Claire darted into their room and grabbed her phone and earbuds.

"I need those peppers in thirty seconds, Claire," Drew said when she reemerged. "Earn your keep."

"On it." Claire turned up Imagine Dragons, drowning out the voice.

You were with the wrong guy all along.

"Mary Jane, is that you?" Setting down her plate with Drew's first course, a fluffy quiche with spicy chorizo, Claire looked toward the door and then around at the living room coffee tables. "Are you talking to me through Alexa? If so, you need a new app. You sound like a ninety-year-old man."

He's the one.

"Not funny, Mary Jane." Claire turned up the sound on the television and the Thanksgiving parade, thankful the cable was back on. And then she took a moment to appreciate the beauty of Drew's quiche. It was photogenic and delicious. She regretted the promise she'd made not to share her opinion of it.

He likes your legs.

Snowy was staring at her, licking his chops. Or maybe moving his jowls while he spoke.

Olly had gone with Drew into the main house.

I caught him looking.

"Very funny, Drew." He must have put jalapeños on Snowy's tongue before he and Mary Jane left with the brunch trays. She took Snowy's muzzle in her hands and gave him some loving. "You have quite the personality, mister. But dogs don't talk."

Snowy muscled his big nose next to her cheek.

You were with the wrong man all along.

"You ..." Claire shot to her feet. She'd attributed him communicating with her yesterday to his basic sounds coming off like basic sounds—laughter, short words. Not sentences. "No. You *aren't* talking. It's Luke or Mary Jane. Or ... or Drew." She was being pranked. Claire hurried out the door and across the pool deck to the main house, buffeted by the crisp ocean wind. She barreled into the kitchen and into Drew's arms.

"Slow down. What's the matter?"

Down the hall in the dining room, the conversation was boisterous. Despite their jovial mood, no one stood waiting to claim responsibility for Snowy "talking." She could hear Olly recounting the difficulty they'd had with the bouquet burning.

Drew's arms pulled her close, soothing her fears over something that couldn't have happened. "Did Stewart call?"

"No." Claire was upset all over again, only this time for an entirely different reason. She twisted in his arms, tilting her face up to his. "I was alone. And I thought …." *The dog talked to me.* She swallowed. She couldn't say it.

Those eyes stared at her with an unfathomable expression. And then Drew pressed a kiss to her forehead. "Did you finish food prep?"

"Is that all you think about? Food?" she grumbled as sorely as Snowy, which only reminded her that someone must have wired the dog for sound. "Where's Mary Jane?"—the person who'd insisted she dog sit ….

"She's with her guests. I've got a job to do. I can't have you stealing the spotlight. And neither can Mary Jane."

"Stealing the …" She elbowed clear of his embrace. "Is that what you think I do?"

"Sometimes," he allowed, checking his watch. "Come on. We're already four minutes behind on the second course."

"Maybe I don't want to help you anymore."

He *tsk*ed, guiding her out the door. "Claire, you're many things, but you're a woman of your word."

How she wished he weren't right.

You're very good at ignoring me.

Snowy sat in the doorway to Claire's bedroom, whining softly.

Drew heard both the whine and the words, but he refused to acknowledge either. He was behind schedule, short-handed, and already distracted by Claire's presence. They did a polite dance around the small kitchen as they worked, and he was hard put not to touch her hand, slip his arm around her waist, or kiss those lips.

Olly climbed onto a barstool. "Do you like my mommy? Snowy says yes."

"Of course, I like her. We've known each other a long time. Since before you were born." Drew finished making the dough for his rolls, covered the bowl, and put it on top of the refrigerator to rise. "What brought this on? That's not what Snowy said just now."

I never get ignored.

"I'm not ignoring you," Claire muttered.

Drew's head jerked around. "You hear it, too?"

"What's that?" Claire removed an earbud, sending soft music between them.

"Never mind." Drew returned his attention to his pile of supplies. "I know I'm forgetting something."

Cranberry sauce.

Olly reached for a ginger cookie. "He says—"

"Did you remember the cranberry sauce?" Claire tapped Drew on his shoulder, earbud out.

Drew pointed at Claire and Olly, pulse pounding in his temples. "You both hear him?"

"I've been telling you ..." Olly took a cookie and broke it in half. He touched it with his tongue and made a face, climbing back down out of the chair. "Snowy talks."

Drew faced Claire. "You hear him?"

You're so tense.

"Shut up," Drew and Claire said at the same time, turning toward Snowy.

"You hear him." Drew placed his hands on the countertop and hung his head. "I thought I was pushing myself too hard."

"Same here." Claire came to stand next to him, so close her shoulder brushed his.

They both reached for a ginger cookie as Olly fed Snowy pieces of the one he carried.

"It's the cookies," Olly said. "They're magic."

Claire tossed her cookie on the counter, untouched, and then slapped Drew's cookie from his hand. "They're drugged with a hallucinogenic. Olly, no more cookies .... Except ... if they've been tampered with, why are we all hearing the dog say the same thing?"

209

Drew saw his entire career and his hopes for a future with Claire going down the toilet. *She's going to think their whole holiday experience together had been induced by drugs.*

They're just cookies, Snowy said between crunching his treat. *But they increase my volume.*

"I could hear him from the start." Olly knelt next to Snowy. "Pirates have good ears."

"What does this mean?" Claire moved a hand over her stomach. "Is there a cure?"

Snowy rolled over on his back, feet in the air. *It wears off eventually.*

"I don't have time for this." Drew grabbed the bag of cranberries.

Luke says that all the time. Luke says, "I can't invest in that" all the time.

Luke, who held Drew's career in his hands. "You hear Luke?"

Snowy chuffed. *I sniff everybody.*

That much was true. Drew leaned forward. "Do you have to be in the same room? You know, to hear him?"

"How else is he gonna sniff someone?" Olly tossed his hands in the air.

"Drew, what's going on? What are you thinking?"

He grabbed Claire's upper arms and turned them away from the dog. "You heard him. He's been giving us love advice the entire time."

Because you should be together.

Claire's cheeks pinkened.

Drew pointed at the dog—the talking, mind-reading dog! "He can let me know if my dishes are furthering my cause with Luke. I can adjust some things on the fly, really personalize it to his taste. If I have an inside man ... er, dog."

"Do you hear yourself?" Claire asked, eyes wide. "Forget about the dog. I can just ask Mary Jane."

Drew shook his head. "I've asked your sister and—don't take this wrong—I don't think she knows what Luke likes. But a talking dog ..."

Snowy rolled back over. *You're sending me on a mission? Like Dad.*

"Dad?" Now Drew had doubts.

"His owner's a Navy SEAL," Claire explained. "He probably goes on missions all the time."

"Thank heavens." Drew bussed Claire's cheek. There was so much to do and so little time. "Yes, Snowy. You're being recruited for a top-secret mission. But first, I've got to make cranberry relish."

CHAPTER FIVE

"*I* need you to split and pit those cherries next." Drew turned a burner on and took bacon out of the refrigerator, looking calm and collected.

Olly and Snowy were on a recon mission to the main house. It was just Drew and Claire in the kitchen. Claire wasn't calm or collected.

"And then slice the cabbage. I'm making bacon-wrapped cherries on a small bed of cabbage."

"You're making a bad decision." Claire wasn't worried that Drew would manipulate her brother-in-law. She was worried that, "You're hinging your career hopes on a dog."

"And on you." Drew's gaze stroked her, and that was smokin' hot. "But mostly, my future hinges on me. I'm good in the kitchen, Claire. The dog is just … insurance. Part of my team. Haven't you ever stretched yourself and been grateful you had a team behind you? I'm grateful for you and Olly."

Her heart warmed. Maybe this was a dream, one where she realized she and Drew could have something together. What harm was there in playing along with a dream? "Snowy said the cookies amplify his thoughts. You need to eat them regularly." Claire glanced at the handful of cherries. "I don't have very many of these to split."

"Each person gets one. And one piece of bacon."

"One? You're serving each guest one cherry?" She gave him a dubious look.

"I'm making six courses today, Claire. I don't want people to stop eating after the third course because they're full."

"There's a method to Chef Barnett's madness." She took a moment to stroke a hand down his arm. "But honestly, no one turns down food on Thanksgiving, not even me."

"Back up. I like it when you call me Chef." There was that heat again, along with his devastating smile.

He likes me. And I like him. More than like, she realized, stopping herself from putting another label to it. Claire had to work slowly as she split the cherries so that she didn't ruin them.

Olly and Snowy tumbled into the front door.

Olly rolled onto the floor. "Auntie MJ kicked us out." But he was laughing about it.

Drew wasn't amused. "Before you had a chance to sniff Luke?"

He likes your food. Snowy glanced out the window toward the main house.

"He said it was good trucker food." Olly stood on his toes and pressed his nose to the edge of the counter. "Are those cherries?"

Drew moved to the end of the counter, back to Claire and Olly. "Trucker food? Diner food? Food truck food? What did he mean? Was he disappointed?"

He's worried.

"About my food?" Drew demanded.

Claire went to Drew, holding onto his shoulders. "Focus on the menu, Drew. Not on Snowy." When the dog glanced her way, she gave him a gentle smile. "No offense."

No cherries. The dog sniffed the air.

"I love cherries," Olly said.

As one, Claire and Drew spun around.

Olly had his mouth stuffed with cherries. Bright red juice dripped from his mouth and fingers. And the counter where Claire had been prepping them? Only pits remained.

"Oh, no." Claire clutched Drew's arm. "I am so, so sorry."

"Don't be." Drew's face paled. "This always happens."

"What?" Claire wet a paper towel and washed the cherry stains from Olly's face and fingers.

"When you're around, things tend to fall apart." Drew spoke absently, as if to himself. "It's over."

His words washed over her like that mudslide had smeared itself down the cliffside, wiping away the beauty of kisses and hopes. "Nothing is over unless you let it be." But she knew now what Drew thought of her.

Mary Jane had claimed Drew gave Claire a backbone. She felt it now, lifting her shoulders, if not her spirits. For a few hours, he'd made her forget the hard decisions ahead. For a few hours, she'd felt love was possible again. But the truth was all around her. Drew still found her lacking.

"Okay, so I have to scramble." Drew was still in self-centered shock. "I need something to replace cherries."

"They were good cherries," Olly said happily.

Pirated. Snowy panted widemouthed, the way he did when he laughed in her head.

"Quiet please. I'm trying to think." Drew stared at the sizzling bacon, oblivious to those around him.

Claire couldn't stand to be in the same room as someone who thought so little of her. "Come on, Olly." She took his hand and headed for the door, calling for Snowy.

"Where are we going?" Olly lunged for his pirate hat, which had fallen to the floor when he entered.

"For a walk with Snowy."

But .... Snowy moved away from the window, away from the door, standing in the middle of the living room, squarely between Claire and Drew.

"But what about being spies?" Olly glanced over his shoulder at Drew.

"You're not spies. You're a pirate and his furry first mate, sailing off on an adventure to view a mudslide." Which from a distance would be better than watching Drew's meltdown and hearing his hurtful words. "We don't want to get in Uncle Drew's way any more than we already have."

Drew had no buts, no objections. He stood in the kitchen and watched them leave. He was probably grateful they were gone. And

Claire .... She didn't think she could have been hurt this deeply again. On Thanksgiving, no less.

They made their way around the garage to the front of the house, where there was a parking lot of luxury vehicles boxing in Claire's SUV and Drew's food truck.

"Hey, where are you going?" Mary Jane hurried out the door, heels clicking on the pavement as she approached. "Is Drew okay by himself?"

"He'll have to be." Claire stopped her griping. She hadn't seen Mary Jane since the bouquet burning. "What did you do to your hair?" It was swept up and twisted in place with a hairnet.

"It's some product Tom Randall is pitching Luke today. He wanted me to model it and ..." Mary Jane's face fell. "It's hideous, isn't it?" She fell into Claire's arms. "I feel like some underappreciated hotel concierge."

"I get it." Claire clung to her. "I feel like an undervalued sous chef."

"Men," Mary Jane mumbled into Claire's shoulder. "Luke's oldest is just five years younger than me and ... I'm pregnant, Claire." She began to cry.

Claire clutched her sister closer, certain those weren't happy tears. "It's okay. He'll be shocked but it's okay."

"What's wrong with Auntie?" Olly tugged on Claire's blouse. "Did somebody die?"

Snowy was circling them, a concerned look on his furry face. Since Claire hadn't eaten more than a bite or so of ginger cookie, her internal hearing aids didn't seem to be catching the dog's thoughts.

"Sometimes you just need to shed a few tears, Olly. Even if you're happy." Claire pulled back from her sister and made a grab for the hairnet. "We'll be fine. *You'll* be fine." This last was directed at Mary Jane.

"Don't." Mary Jane dodged out of reach, dabbing at her tears with her fingertips. "I'll take care of it later, along with ... everything."

Claire raised her brows. "And talk to Luke? This is a blessing, Mary Jane."

"My critique will be dramatic, I assure you." Mary Jane continued to dodge the issue. "I just have to figure out how to reject this hairnet without embarrassing the idiot who thinks this will be all the rage."

"I suggest you slingshot it at Tom across the dining room table. And quit pretending you didn't just admit—"

"Claire." Mary Jane scrunched her eyes shut, as if holding back the tears. And then she opened her eyes and rolled her shoulders back. "I think just putting it onto his hair might do the trick."

"Mary Jane." Claire grabbed onto her sister's shoulders and gave them a little shake, aware of Olly watching them, her heart breaking for what lay ahead for Mary Jane in what should have been a happy time. But she had a choice—continue to press her sister about the pregnancy or be a team player and go along with focusing on this hairnet business. "Do you want us to come inside? For moral support ... when you take that hairnet off?"

"No." Mary Jane scoffed, features relaxing. "It's my bed, so to speak. You go on. Enjoy your walk."

Enjoy wasn't a word Claire would have chosen when her heart seemed to be falling in pieces.

But she'd learned a lot in the past year. One of which was to keep putting one foot in front of the other.

That is a disaster.

That was Drew's voice in his head, not Snowy's. Didn't matter who spoke the words. Thanksgiving was a disaster. And the second course hadn't even been served!

For several minutes after Claire left, Drew stood in the kitchen.

Bacon sizzled in the frying pan, browning to the point it wouldn't wrap around anything. Water was boiling in a saucepan on the back burner, waiting for the chutney ingredients to be added. Time was ticking. Everything was headed for ruin. He felt like he'd cut his surfboard too quickly in the underside of a big curling wave and now it was crashing on him. He was tumbling, forced to the bottom. And it was all Claire's fault. And Richie's. And ...

That's not true.

Everything was his fault. Who was he going to blame next? Mother Nature?

He rewound the careless words he'd said to Claire, cringing inside. How could she possibly love such an egotistical jerk?

Bacon popped, sending a drop of grease on his arm. A stinging reminder that he had to finish what he'd started today. He took a handful of cranberries and dropped them into the boiling water. And then he began removing nearly burnt bacon from the pan.

The door opened.

"I'm sorry," he said without looking up.

"Sorry for what?" It was Mary Jane. Her hair was swept off her shoulders in something that looked like a hairnet and she wore pearls. Someday, she'd grow into that look. But today, she just looked out of place, like it was a look she'd adopted too soon.

Too soon. That's the way he felt suddenly about venturing into restaurant ownership. He still had a lot to learn about money and management and love. Because he loved Claire and all he seemed good at was hurting her. He needed to invest in himself and the love he had for Claire.

And he needed to get through the day without totally biffing the works.

"Mary Jane." He rushed on. "I'm a few minutes late with this next course."

"Don't blow this." She came over to lean on the countertop, choosing a space in between the two barstools that was directly across from him. "Don't blow this with Claire."

"With Claire?" Drew was stunned. "Don't you mean with Luke?"

"No, I mean Claire." She frowned, touching the net holding her hair. "I'm not much good at the games Luke plays. He draws people in with the promise of potential fortune. I didn't ask you to cater to give you a break with Luke."

Understanding dawned. "There was never any power outage in the main house. You flipped a breaker."

"That's right." She looked sad to admit it. "I wanted you to have a shot with my sister. She needs someone like you." Mary Jane glanced over her shoulder to the stack of legal papers on the table. "Someone who won't use Claire and Olly—or a perceptive, caring dog—to make themselves look better."

Shame clawed at Drew's gut. But since they were getting things out on the table .... "Luke doesn't want to invest in me." Not that he'd blame him.

Mary Jane shrugged, an elegant movement that barely shifted the fall of her sweater. "He might. But this isn't the best chance for you to shine, what with the road being closed and you having no help. Luke and his friends are watching football. You can leave the turkeys in the oven. I'll muddle through the rest." She backed out of the small space and headed for the door.

Another wave crashed around Drew. Tumbling his emotions. Failure. Shame. Disappointment. His father would say he wasn't handling adversity well. His mother would tell him that nothing easy was worth having. "I'm not quitting."

Mary Jane paused, turned, looking as surprised as Drew felt.

"I said I'd put on a fabulous meal, and I will. It might not be the menu as planned but it will be good." A Thanksgiving spread that would impress not just Luke but the woman Drew loved. The woman who used to love the holiday.

Claire might never be his, but he wanted to give her back this holiday, at least.

"I ..." Mary Jane removed the hairnet. "We should all do our best every day. And be our best with each other. Good luck, Drew."

He felt like he needed to wish Mary Jane the same. But she left before he could respond in kind.

CHAPTER SIX

*G*rowing up near the coast, Claire was used to the push and pull of coastal winds.

She wasn't used to the push and pull of emotions toward Drew.

He'd always been a man who couldn't sit still. His parents set high expectations for him, wanting him to go to college or join the navy. He'd chosen another path, first as a competitive surfer and then as a chef. He was great with Olly, great with her, great with dogs ... until he wasn't. He was prickly but he was also working in a high pressure field. And he had a lot at stake today.

The big man had been felled by *cherries*. Go figure.

The wind tugged at her hair, pulling from the scalp. Nothing about living near the coast was easy. Costs were high. The sun was often out, but the wind wasn't always gentle. If she followed the growing feelings she had for Drew, it wouldn't be easy either.

They rounded the bend in the road and approached the yellow caution tape, wrapped from one mailbox to the other. Where there had been a slope and pipes laid, there was a huge gouge in the hillside. The road was hidden beneath several feet of mud and rock, and it continued down through someone's backyard, wiping out fences and shrubbery on a path to the ocean cliff.

Claire felt sorry for whoever had been trying to build a home here. Their dreams had slipped away.

"No ships out there." Olly clutched his pirate hat with one hand. The fingers on his other hand were curled and held up to his eye like a spyglass.

Snowy stood next to him, nose into the wind.

For the first time in days, Claire pulled her cell phone from her legging pocket, and snapped a shot. She studied the photo. Best friends looking over Mother Nature's devastation toward the horizon. It was poignant, adorable, and had great color composition. And look, Olly was wearing his favorite hoodie, the one made by one of Claire's corporate sponsors.

"Olly, can I post this picture of you online?" Claire angled her screen so he could see.

Olly shrugged. "Sure. But why do you ask? You never ask."

"Because …" Claire knelt next to him, gently tugging the sleeve of his sweatshirt. "The people who make this will pay me money if enough people see your picture."

"Pay?" Olly frowned. "Like a job?"

"Yes. My job."

"But I'm doing the work." Olly held the material away from his body, glancing down at the logo. "I'm wearing it."

Snowy nudged Claire's arm, grumbling a little. It wasn't hard to understand what he was trying to say. Olly had a good point.

"You're right, honey." Claire straightened his sweatshirt. "When you're in the picture I post, you should be getting paid. How about this? I put your money in a treasure chest—" a bank account "—until you turn eighteen."

His eyes widened. "Really?"

"Really." It was the perfect solution to Stewart's concerns. She could make sure Olly visited his father in civilized, safe living conditions, no matter what they agreed to in terms of percentages shared. Her body coursed with relief.

"I love you, Mommy." Olly wrapped his arms around her. "Wait until I tell Daddy. *X* marks the spot!"

"I love you, too, honey. But let me tell Daddy first."

Claire, Olly, and Snowy hadn't returned from their walk for hours.

Drew assumed they'd found a place in the main house, away from rude chefs and insensitive love interests.

He'd found a solution for the cherries, substituting cranberries. And he'd served a third course of fried Spam and shrimp tacos, and a fourth of various vegetable dishes, including winter squash *agrodolce*. The only courses left were the stars of the show—turkey, mashed potatoes, and rolls, and then dessert.

Drew darted into the main house for the vanilla gelato Mary Jane had said she kept on hand when he heard his name.

"Drew, join us." Luke's invitation wasn't a request. The older man waved to him from the family room down the hall.

Drew hesitated, calculating how much time he could be away from what he had on the stove and in the oven.

"Come on. We're drinking whiskey sours." Luke offered one up. "All the bowl games are at the half and we were just talking about how great all the food's been today."

Drew came down the hall, accepting the drink and the accolades of the other six men in attendance. Middle-aged men, all. And Mary Jane was nowhere to be seen.

"I'm impressed by your talent in the kitchen." Luke gave Drew a pat on the back. "There's some money to be made, I think. But some details to be worked out."

Drew made a sound of agreement and sipped his whiskey sour. Far be it from him to close a door that had unexpectedly opened. But he was listening with a fresh pair of ears, more aware of his priorities in life than before.

"Running a restaurant is different than running a food truck." Luke had the smile of a salesman.

Drew nodded. "What's the catch?" He had food to tend to.

"Claire," Luke said plainly. "Her Instagram business fell off last year after the wedding fiasco, and Stewart is hamstringing her further. My wife is concerned about her, and frankly, so am I. She needs a job with a steady paycheck."

"She doesn't want to work in a kitchen," Drew said carefully when what he wanted to do was shout that what Claire did for a living was none of Luke's business.

"Claire might change her mind. She likes you." Luke winked. And that wink said a lot about the man and what he thought of Drew. It said Luke didn't take the work of women seriously. It said Luke didn't take Drew seriously, either. "Claire is a princess, like my wife. She's better off with a man in her life."

Inwardly, Drew cringed. *Better.* He'd used that word with Claire the other night. But in a different context.

"I think you could be that man, Drew." Another backslap. Another wink. "Two birds with one stone, eh? This deal is too good for any of us to pass up. Me, you, Claire."

Before Drew could respond, movement on the nearby stairwell caught his attention. Claire stood there, wide-eyed, holding the end of Snowy's leash.

Uh-oh. Snowy whined.

And then Claire fled down the stairs and out the door, dragging the dog behind her.

Claire was halfway down the driveway when she heard Drew call her name.

Snowy cocked his ears, glancing over his shoulder.

"Keep walking, Snowy," Claire said.

"Claire, wait!"

"No." She pressed the gate release button, annoyed that it moved so slowly. "Go back to your turkey, Drew. This princess needs her royal space." She would not turn around. She would not look at him. She would not see the pity in his eyes. Not that she believed Luke. But it would be painful if Drew agreed. He'd pointed out all her flaws for years, after all.

He looks like he's sorry.

She glanced down at Snowy. "You can't be talking to me. I haven't had a cookie since this morning."

Chuffing, Snowy sat down and watched Drew approach.

Claire kept her back to him, grateful that Olly had stayed upstairs with Mary Jane. It was hard enough to keep the drama of the divorce from spilling over onto her son. She didn't want him to witness her lashing out at Drew.

"Claire." Drew turned her to face him. It was a crime how handsome he was, even with the tight lines of tension drawn on his face. "Honey, we need to talk."

"Don't." She brushed off his touch. "I know how Luke works. He's been married to Mary Jane for two years. He's old school. *I'm a mother and therefore I need a man.* I don't care if you need his money to start a restaurant. I'm not part of the deal."

"Claire, I—"

"We have chemistry, Drew, but we don't have a relationship. This is a great opportunity for you, but you've got to go back in there and suck up with Luke to close the deal. Without me. Tell him I'm impossible. Tell him I'm too entitled. That's what you used to think of me, isn't it?"

"Claire, I—"

"Reassure him that things will be smoother without rainstorms and mudslides or princesses from Del Mar."

"Claire." Drew placed a hand over her mouth, igniting heat within her just with that touch. "I have gravy on a warming burner and turkey in the oven. If you aren't going to walk back with me, hear me out. Please. I'm different than Luke, even if I'm not perfect, even if I sometimes put my foot in my mouth. Will you listen? Please?"

Claire nodded slowly, curtly.

His hand dropped to her shoulder, down her arm, came to rest in her hand. "Do you know what running a restaurant and running a social media career have in common?"

"No." And why were they having this conversation? Why wasn't he talking about Luke's stupid idea?

"Popularity. That's what they share." His hold on her was gentle, not so much a tether as a gesture of unity. His eyes pleaded for patience and forgiveness. His blond hair lifted in the wind, begging for her fingers to smooth it back in place. "It's hard to capture the imagination and loyalty of a following in either case. You can make mistakes but only a few before things start to sink. You and I .... We face many of the same obstacles."

She nodded, but only because he'd paused and seemed to expect her to react. She was caught in this limbo—angry with Luke, worried for Mary Jane, annoyed that Drew hadn't been quicker in his rejection of Luke's conditions, swifter with an apology about her role in the day's challenges, hastier to get to the point.

Drew cupped her cheek in his palm, again, so gentle. "And because running a restaurant or a social media empire is fraught with pitfalls, you shouldn't jump in until you're ready." He drew a deep breath. "I just don't think I'm ready to open my own restaurant, Claire. There are other things that are more important at the moment. Namely, you and Olly."

And there went the air in her lungs.

Drew's smile was incredibly tender. His embrace wonderfully tentative. He was waiting for her to tell him what a jerk he'd been and push him away. Or perhaps he expected her to tell him this was a once-in-a-lifetime opportunity with an investor and that nothing should stand in the way of his dreams.

"Claire, honey, I need you and Olly in my life, but I've never been in a serious relationship and I'm scared to death I'll make a mistake and go sliding off a cliff, just like the hillside down there."

"When it comes to love," Claire held on tighter, "you need an incredible amount of practice." But her heart pounded with joy at the idea that he wanted to take that step with her and that he was honest enough to admit the road ahead wouldn't be easy.

Snowy made a small noise and butted his broad head against each of their legs.

"Yes," Drew said as if in answer to the dog. He leaned forward to whisper in her ear, "I need to learn the limits of my patience and skill in the kitchen. And the give and take of a relationship with you. I'm so sorry for what I said to you earlier, about blaming you for things going wrong. You are both my balance and my undoing, because when you're around I feel like I can take on the world, if only I could stop thinking about kissing you."

Claire drew back, liking that the wind teased up the fringe of his hair, enjoying the strength of his arms around her, and loving the compassionate look in his blue eyes. "I don't want to be a distraction. Relationships are about give and take, support and challenge."

"And today, I failed." He pressed a kiss to her nose. "Tell me we can make a proper go of this. Tell me you want to explore a relationship with me, Drew Barnett, food-truck owner, surfer, and wannabe restauranteur."

He was no longer her nemesis. No longer the enemy. He was the man she could see growing old with. "I do think there's something here, Drew. Something love can build upon. But first, we need to establish boundaries for you. I want to know what you're comfortable about me posting online because I think I've crossed too many lines in my relationships in the past, when it came to Stewart and Olly." She'd learned that much in the past year. "Just like you need boundaries in the kitchen. There should be no more cherry surprises."

Snowy made that happy, panting sound that immediately made her think of laughter.

"I'd hoped you'd understand." Drew gathered her close. "That sounds perfect. Boundaries to keep our work safe. Boundaries to protect our love."

"Love," she whispered in his ear. "Yes, I like the sound of that." She'd like to hear that over and over.

Snowy bumped their legs with his shoulder, grumbling.

"Snowy wants some love, too." She reached down to give him a pat.

"He doesn't want me to burn the turkey." Drew grabbed onto her hand and tugged her toward the path leading around the garage. "Oh, Claire. I am going to fill your plate with all your favorites. This is going to be the best Thanksgiving ever. You'll see."

She did see. She saw many Thanksgivings stretching out before them, days when they paused to give thanks to how far they'd come and how much still lay ahead. And love, they'd be thankful for a love they shared, one that needed proper tending to allow it to thrive as they grew old together.

CHAPTER SEVEN

*F*our adults, one child, and one dog gathered around the kitchen table of the main house, while six men lounged in front of the television down the hall.

"There is nothing like pumpkin pie on Thanksgiving." Luke's chair was right next to Mary Jane's. His arm was draped over his wife's shoulders. He hadn't let her out of his sight since she'd told him she was pregnant. "Or good news. I can't believe you would think I wouldn't be happy to be a father again, Mary Jane."

She buried her head in his shoulder, beaming at Claire.

They'd all been wrong about Luke's reaction to becoming a father once more.

Claire was bursting with happiness for her sister.

"There's nothing like *family* on Thanksgiving," Claire amended Luke's statement. She had Olly in her lap and her chair just as close to Drew's as Luke's was to Mary Jane's. "It's not a holiday where food comes first."

"Are you knocking my food?" Drew teased, making Olly giggle.

"No. Your food was fantastic." Claire nudged him with her elbow. "I'm saying Thanksgiving is a day when you should be grateful for the people *and relationships* in your life." She tilted her head to touch Drew's shoulder. They couldn't seem to keep their distance from one another.

Drew had held Claire's hand earlier when she'd called Stewart and told him about the changes she was going to make in the way she conducted her social media business. Stewart had agreed that was the best for Olly, and had agreed that prolonged periods out of the country weren't in their son's best interests. Monday didn't loom so black.

Claire sighed happily. The day had been full of ups and downs, but they were all coming together on a high note. "And a way to celebrate being thankful is to take the time to make—and eat—all the dishes you don't normally make."

"Nice sentiment, Claire. Drew, your food was exceptional. Are you sure you don't want to take me up on my offer to help launch your restaurant?" Luke kissed Mary Jane's temple.

"You'll be the first to know when I reevaluate my priorities." Not to be outdone in the public display of affection department, Drew kissed Claire's temple and then stole Olly's pirate hat, depositing it on his own head.

"Hey." Olly tapped his thumb against his chest. "I'm the captain."

Snowy pushed himself up from the floor into a sitting position, grumbling and groaning as was his way.

"You're right." Drew took the hat and made as if to place it on Olly's head. At the last moment, his arm shifted its trajectory and he placed it on top of Snowy's. "Everyone deserves a turn at being captain."

Everyone laughed, even Olly. Snowy panted happily.

Drew leaned in and whispered to Claire, "Olly's going to need practice if he's going to be a good big brother."

"There are a lot of moving parts in getting a relationship right," Claire agreed. But her heart sang with joy and optimism because she couldn't have asked for a better man to share that journey with.

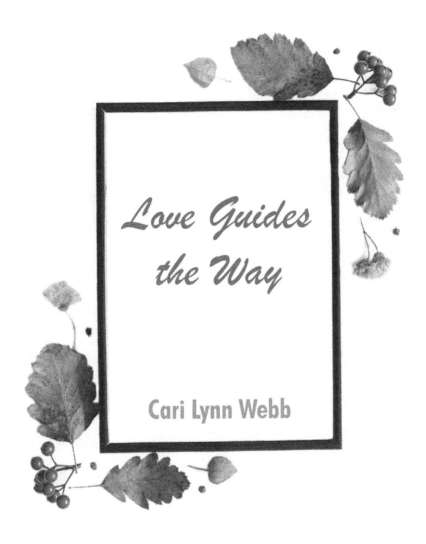

Love Guides
the Way

Cari Lynn Webb

CHAPTER ONE

"*I* don't want a cure." Kelsey Thomas lowered her camera onto the bar counter of the Blue Orchid Grotto and gave her full attention to the two women filling the video chat window on her phone screen.

Her mom gasped. "Kelsey, you don't mean that."

"What if I do?" Kelsey arranged yellow plumeria flowers around her chilled bottle of cider and rearranged her irritation. "Would you two stop then?"

"You can't give up hope." Her mother ignored Kelsey's question and turned her firm words into adamant. "You simply *can't.*"

If Kelsey was to be truthful with herself, she *did* want a cure. She just wished she didn't *want* a cure. It only made the reality of not having one available to her all the more painful.

"Never give up, dear." Her grandmother, Gem, allowed a small smile to soften her caution. "Never."

"Hope doesn't prepare me for what is to come." Hope wouldn't prepare her family either. Everyone had to accept the facts. First and foremost, in five years, Kelsey would be completely blind.

It was not the future Kelsey had envisioned for herself as a child. Or the one her family had dreamed for her. Nor the one her ex-boyfriend had wanted. But this was Kelsey's reality now. She had to face it—eyes wide open.

"We found a doctor …" her mom started.

"No." Kelsey shook her head at the phone screen and tamped down her frustration. The last two trials had never lived up to their promise. "No more interviews. No more medical inventors. No more trials."

"But …" Gem's eyebrows pulled together.

"Please," Kelsey interrupted. "We're going to be celebrating Gem and Harland's love and Thanksgiving here in the Caribbean at this incredible island resort. Can't that be what this upcoming week is about?"

"Of course, we want it to be all about family." Her mom smoothed her fingers over her eyebrow as if Kelsey's refusal had smeared her makeup. "And it will be."

"I'm asking for one week." Kelsey held up her forefinger. One week to pretend she was like everyone else. A week not to worry or lose sleep over her uncertain future.

"We just want …" Gem began.

"I know you want the best for me," Kelsey finished for her grandmother. She adored her family. Knew she would need to lean on them. But she wanted to prove she could rely on herself first. "And I love you for it."

"We love you too." Gem kissed her hand and pressed her fingers toward the phone's camera screen. "So very much."

"Then please promise me," Kelsey pressed.

"We promise." Kelsey's mom shrugged and lifted both hands in surrender.

Kelsey narrowed her gaze and leaned into the video camera on her phone screen. "Promise what?" Both women could be crafty and sneaky—never to be mean, only ever to get their way. They just firmly believed their way was always the right way. Another reason Kelsey adored them.

"Kelsey, really, be serious," her mom said.

"I am," she said.

Her mom and grandmother glanced at each other, then at the camera. Her mom tapped her finger against her chin and grinned. "We promise not to talk about possible cures for the whole week."

"That also includes upcoming clinical trials," Kelsey added. "And new treatments and new doctors."

Her mother's finger stilled. Gem lifted both eyebrows. Kelsey held her gaze. Finally, Gem nodded. Then her mother.

Kelsey relaxed and picked up her camera. "I'm going to go now and take pictures of the sunset."

"From your bungalow," her mother suggested. "There isn't a long twilight there like we have here on the east coast. You're closer to the equator. It'll get dark quickly."

Hiding inside her bungalow proved nothing. Not to her mom or to herself. "I can be out alone and be fine."

"Perhaps you might meet someone to take pictures with," Gem offered. "Now that you're single and all."

Her mom frowned. "Kelsey's suite is really the safest place for her."

Kelsey drummed her fingers on the bar counter. She wasn't any closer to convincing her mom she hadn't lost her independence. Just her boyfriend and a large portion of her night vision.

Her mom continued, "Kelsey, did you remember your motion lights?"

"We've packed extra lights, if you need them Kelsey." Gem lifted a teacup and smiled. "Harland and I have come to really like them at our house."

"About the lights in your suite, Kelsey?" Her mom added a new definition to relentless. "I really wish you would've waited and flown out with us in a few days."

Kelsey curved her fingers around her cider bottle. Anita Thomas loved her two daughters to depths some would consider just shy of smothering. Darren had used similar words about Kelsey's mom over the years. But her mom's heart was always in the right place. Her dad had often reminded Kelsey of that vital fact. *Better to have more love than you can handle, than to always be begging for the smallest scrap of affection.* Those words Kelsey had launched at Darren's back ten days ago after he'd ended things and walked out of her life for good.

Kelsey sighed. "The lights are already plugged in at my bungalow."

"Do you have your cane?" Her mom sipped from a teacup.

"Folded inside my backpack." Not that she intended to use it. Usually, Kelsey left her older sister Meagan to test their overprotective, overanxious mother's patience, but this was important. Independence had to be earned. "I'm going to go and enjoy the sunset now. Maybe even stay out after dark."

"Keep away from the water." Her mom balanced her teacup on a saucer and leaned forward. "You don't want to walk into the water and a school of sharks by mistake."

Kelsey touched the bruise on her shin. She'd walked into a metal luggage cart at the airport. In full daylight. Nothing her mom needed to know.

She was feeling restless, ready to start living some of those five years of independence she had left. She glanced over at the gentleman sitting on the stool beside her, minding his own business. She had to squint to note his lack of a wedding ring. As for his wind-tossed hair, she wanted to sink her fingers into the wavy strands, tousle his hair and take his picture. That inappropriate urge she blamed on Gem for suggesting she find someone to take pictures with. Kelsey had never once tousled Darren's hair. Never really had the urge.

She caught the man's attention. "Do you happen to know if there are sharks in the lagoon?"

"Only reef fish, lionfish, and the occasional eagle ray." He pushed his dark-tinted sunglasses up on his nose. His one-sided grin, set inside unshaven cheeks and a strong jaw, disarmed and distracted her.

Kelsey forced her attention back to her phone screen. "The gentleman beside me says there are no sharks. Looks like I'm safe to play in the water tonight."

"That's not what I meant." Her mom's disapproval wrapped around Kelsey.

Kelsey doubled down. She disliked disappointing her mom, but she wanted to earn something more valuable: her independence and her family's acceptance. "Good night. I love you both. Now I have a sunset to enjoy."

"Don't forget to catch more than fish." Gem grinned and lifted her hand to her mouth as if sharing a really good secret. "Life is always more fun with two."

Kelsey shook her head, ended the video call, and flipped her phone over onto the bar. Catching a guy wasn't as simple for her as it had been for her outgoing sister and adventurous cousin. Vision issues aside, Kelsey had always been more reserved, more comfortable watching the world around her from behind a camera lens, rather than stepping into the spotlight like her relatives. Even her grandmother had declared she was greedy and that she wanted to fall in love again, so she did.

Kelsey considered the guy beside her. He wore printed surf shorts and a plain white T-shirt like most islanders and tourists. Still there was something about him that drew Kelsey to him. Made her look and wonder. Strong shoulders always appealed, but even those weren't always reliable. Darren had proven that much. Still, something about her bar companion made her redefine the boundary between stranger and acquaintance. And reconsider Gem's suggestion.

But she hadn't flown in early for a fling.

The gentleman greeted the bartender by his first name and shifted toward Kelsey. "Do you have a fear of sharks or doctors? Sorry, it was hard not to overhear your conversation."

Kelsey blinked and straightened. Her mother had taken to raising her voice as if Kelsey's failing eyesight also affected her hearing. She pointed to her headphones on the bar. "My apologies if we were too loud. Batteries died on my headphones. And it's my mom with the fear of sharks."

He nodded.

A cold local beer and bowl of lime slices appeared in front of her bar mate. No order required. She smiled. "Come here often?"

"This is my third night here." He squeezed a lime into the beer bottle. "I usually sit on your stool and always order the same thing."

"Why this stool?" she asked.

"It has the best view of the sunset." He motioned toward the ocean.

"You can watch the sunset from every other stool at this bar." Doubt eased into her tone. There were over two dozen stools bordering the circular bar situated between two beach entry pools. A lazy river joined the pools and two thatched bridges offered the only access to the bar.

"Actually, I have." He laughed. "You've got the best seat aside from the beach chaise loungers."

"You've tried all those too then." She sipped her cider, convincing herself it was the crisp sparkling taste, not his easy laughter, relaxing her.

He shook his head. "I leave the chaises for the couples."

She swallowed more cider, rinsed away her rush of excitement and warned herself he could be one half of a couple. Besides, she wasn't interested in reeling in a man. Never mind she didn't know how to do that exactly. She'd promised herself she'd remain single, and her heart safe, after Darren had walked out. "Anywhere else I should or shouldn't sit?"

"That depends on what you want to see," he said.

Everything. She wanted to see everything. From a ladybug on an orchid petal to every color variation in the sunset. She wanted to see everything before she saw nothing. "Dolphins. Sea turtles. Manta rays and a hammerhead shark."

"You'll need to take a seaplane to the southernmost island for the hammerheads." He tapped his fingers against his beer bottle. "The others should be a local tour boat away."

"Have you been diving with hammerhead sharks?" she asked. He looked confident enough to swim with sharks.

"Not me." A small smile creased his cheeks. "My cousin is the scuba diver in the family. He's the reason I know about this resort."

"And is he here?"

"Not this trip." He shoved his sunglasses onto the top of his head and settled his steely blue-eyed gaze on her. "I'm here alone for the week."

"I'm alone too." She bit down on her lip. Now was probably the time someone shouted: cut bait and run.

He set down his beer bottle and wiped his hand on his shorts then reached out. "I'm Noah—"

"No. No last names." Then he couldn't learn more about her than she wanted to reveal. Couldn't read the newspaper articles or the well-meaning online interviews her mom and grandmother had arranged to help Kelsey find a cure.

"Then it's just Noah."

"Kelsey." She set her hand inside his and held on. Nothing slowed the steady stream of excitement rushing through her. She wasn't looking for a one-night romance. But she wasn't ready to be alone yet either. "Now we can get to know each other like they used to before the internet searches and social media stalking."

"Then it doesn't matter if I tell the truth or not." Humor lifted his grin into a smile.

"But it does matter if we want to see each again."

"Do we?" The interest in his words spread into his sharp gaze. "Do we want to see each other again?"

Definitely. He seemed … interested. How bold could she be? Suddenly Kelsey wanted to find out. Wanted to test the limits of her courage. "Let's find out."

"In the interest of keeping to decades-old social habits, let's skip the usual conversation about what we do and where we live." He ordered them both another round of drinks. "What brings you here alone before a holiday?"

"I won't be alone in two days," she said. "My family will be here for a reunion and my grandmother's commitment ceremony. I came in early to explore and do things I wanted to do." And prove she still had her independence.

"Why not a wedding?" he asked.

"A marriage complicates the family trusts both my grandmother and her boyfriend have set up. It's a wedding without the legal recognition."

"Shouldn't you have a date for this wedding that isn't a wedding?" he asked.

"I had a date until two weeks ago." She wiped the condensation off her bottle and the bitterness from her voice. She should've been the one to walk away. She should've been stronger, recognized she hadn't needed Darren to lean on. She could rely on herself. "He ended things because my family was overbearing and expected too much out of him."

His eyebrows drew together. "What did your family expect?"

"The usual love, loyalty, and commitment." She lifted one shoulder. "They expected him to be loyal and committed once he told me he loved me."

"And did he?"

"Tell me that he loved me?" She lifted her cider bottle up in a mock toast, the bite of irony in her voice far from fake. "Every single day."

"Yet he's not here now." Confusion narrowed his gaze.

"No, he's more loyal to his internet affairs. More committed to playing the field." She finished her cider and her walk down memory lane. "How about you?"

"This is my third Thanksgiving here at the resort." He centered his bottle on the bamboo coaster. "I came here the first time after my wife left me. It was supposed to have been our vacation to reconnect and strengthen our bond."

She recognized the layer of disdain coating his words. Did he regret not walking away first too? "What happened?"

"I drank more than I care to admit and barely remember much about my stay." He frowned and tipped his bottle toward the other side of bar. "I do recall claiming the barstools over there every night."

She'd spent her first night alone packing up Darren's things. By sunrise she had his entire life stuffed into a dozen boxes stacked in the hallway outside their apartment door. "And your ex-wife?"

"Cited irreconcilable differences." He swallowed a deep drink of his beer. "Apparently, she had difficulty reconciling her idea of who she thought I was with the reality of the man she'd married."

"You're a secret service operative, aren't you?" She lightened her voice into playful. "You walk around looking like a carefree surfer during the day. Then hunt the bad guys in camo at night. Your ex hated that you put your life at risk and couldn't handle the stress."

"Would you like me more if I said yes?" He grinned at her.

She already liked him enough. More than enough for an unconventional conversation between strangers at a bar. "Where is your ex now?"

"Married to a renowned cardiologist and living the life she always imagined for herself," he said. "What about your ex?"

"I'm not sure. I changed the locks, blocked his number, and moved on."

He lifted his beer in a toast. "Here's to moving on and letting go of the past and the people not worth holding onto."

The finality in his tone hinted that he'd let go of his past and his ex. Still, she searched his face. "Yet you came back here."

"I returned last year to correct my previous stay." His grin returned as if he closed and locked the door on his memories. "I intended to see the island and relax."

"And did you?" she asked.

"I spent more time on conference calls and my laptop inside my bungalow than out in the sun."

From the wince around his eyes and cringe in his voice, it hadn't been the vacation he'd planned. "So, this is your third try to get it right."

"The third time is supposed to be a charm." His warm gaze drifted over her face.

The sudden speculation in his voice curled inside her like a tempting lure. She cleared her throat. "And has it been charming?"

"It is now." He tapped his bottle against her cider and leaned closer. "You should know my phone and laptop are currently turned off and in my room. I intend to get it right this time."

She picked up her phone and powered it off. "Then I'll join you."

"Want to dance?" He held out his hand.

Her gaze skipped to the setting sun, just starting its dip into the ocean on the horizon. Her daring dipped too. Still, she set her hand in his, wrapped her fingers around his. She'd believed once before in steady and strong. Vowed she'd never mislead herself again. "One dance."

"Is this like Cinderella?" he teased. "One dance and you run before night falls and reality returns."

He was entirely too close to the truth. Only Kelsey lacked a fairy godmother, a magic wand, and her vision at night.

One more reason she'd vowed to remain single. A blind girlfriend was more of a burden. More of a responsibility. Her ex had reinforced that truth after he had broken up with her. He had blamed her overbearing family, but that was only code for her bleak future.

Darren had been beside her in the doctor's office for the devastating news weeks ago. He'd even held her hand as the doctor had explained the time line for the progression of her vision loss. He'd been beside her until he'd bailed.

She straightened. She'd face her future on her own terms. Alone and stronger for it.

But right now, she stepped into Noah's arms, determined to have one perfect week. One week not centered around her vision or her future. One week to pretend she was like everyone else.

She imprinted the scent of the ocean breeze, the salty air against her skin, and the curve his arms around her waist in her mind. She added one more moment to her collection.

After all, she would still remember, even after she couldn't see.

CHAPTER TWO

"*D*id you meet her?" Jason Parks asked.

"Last night at the bar." Noah steepled his hands, set them under his chin and stared at his assistant's face filling his laptop screen.

"And she agreed to the trial?" Excitement rushed Jason's words. He leaned into the camera as if preparing to reach through the screen and hug Noah. "Of course she would agree. She meets our criteria perfectly."

"Well, we haven't quite gotten to that point …." Kelsey had agreed to get to know him better. Even now, two cups of coffee into the morning, Noah wasn't even certain if Kelsey had decided she even wanted to see him again or not. If he broached the trial with her, she definitely would bolt.

Last night, the song had ended. Kelsey had thanked him, turned, bumped into a nearby table, then had kept on walking away. She'd never looked back as if she had been as captivated by Noah as he had been by her.

Captivation was not a requirement for acceptance into his trial. He only required her consent. Noah rubbed his hands over his face.

"I know you'll secure the funding to save your father's dream." Jason nodded like a sage subject-matter expert.

Jason was the best assistant Noah had worked with, but even the best could be wrong. And Jason was too young to have earned expert status yet. "I haven't met the investors. They arrive in a few days."

"That's just paperwork and signatures." Jason adjusted his slim, black-framed glasses and flicked his wrist. "Nothing you can't wrap up in an afternoon, then you'll be free to enjoy your vacation."

"Right." Noah scratched his cheek. He still had to work out how to get Kelsey to sign onto the trial.

Jason leaned in as if he too had heard Noah's lack of conviction from across the Atlantic Ocean. His fingers tapped against the key-board. "You *do* remember how to have fun, don't you?"

Noah hadn't arrived to have fun. Or vacation. He'd traveled to the Caribbean to save his research and development company, Optical Ovations, Inc. The very company his father had started and invested his entire life into. And the one his father would let Noah run, if Noah proved he could secure the family legacy.

Now Noah had a potentially unwilling candidate for his trial. Yes, he had listened in on most of Kelsey's conversation with her mom, Anita Thomas, and grandmother, Elsie-Mae Yates, last night at the bar. Elsie-Mae—or "Gem," as Kelsey called her—and her fiancé, Harland Scott had offered to become Optical Ovations angel inves-tors. All for the simple guarantee that Noah would cure the failing eyesight of Elsie-Mae's granddaughter, Kelsey.

Noah couldn't guarantee anything if Kelsey refused to even speak to him about his retinal eye chip and the upcoming trial. Kelsey had been more than clear with her mom and grandmother: no doctors and no inventors and no trials for an entire week. Noah represented everything Kelsey did not want. Panic constricted his ribs.

"You're too quiet." Jason stopped typing. Even the camera couldn't disguise his assistant's critical regard. "What's wrong? What did I miss?"

"Nothing," Noah said. No point bursting his assistant's happy little bubble until he at least tried to get the enigmatic Kelsey to sign up. "I'm thinking about my agenda for the day."

"Suntan, snorkeling, and celebration," Jason offered. "Simple. You're in the tropics on vacation."

Jason stretched out the last word as if Noah required another re-minder. Noah had no time to doze off on a chaise lounge. The future of his family company was at risk. He had employees to consider. Not to mention medical devices that patients needed. But to bring those devices to market, he needed money. And fast.

First, he needed Kelsey's agreement to join his trial. Without that, he doubted her family would agree to become his angel investors. Frustration made his words sound terser. "I don't tan."

"Wait." His assistant's mouth thinned. "You don't know how to, do you?"

Noah pulled back. "How to what?"

"Be on vacation." Jason's eyes widened behind his glasses.

"That's ridiculous." Although, it is true he didn't take vacations on purpose. He always chose work. Always chose his family's company. He knew his priorities. That hardly meant he didn't know *how* to vacation. He had just failed to put work aside the last time he was at the resort and had resolved to do better this time. "I danced last night on the beach."

"That's a start." Jason adjusted his glasses. "Was Kelsey Thomas as pretty in person as her pictures?"

"Even more stunning." Kelsey's long brown hair and dark brown eyes were an attractive combination. It was her smile—natural and infectious—that transformed her face. Her wide smile seemed to capture joy itself and promise everything would be better if he only followed her lead. "I never said I danced with Kelsey."

"You're going to restore her eyesight," Jason said. "Of course you would choose to dance with her."

She'd danced with Noah, the guy dressed like a surfer. Not the doctor. Or the inventor. Or the designated Lawson family savior. How long had it been since he'd been known as just Noah?

He couldn't deny the appeal. Or the freedom in the lack of expectations.

"Are you seeing her again today?" Jason's mild tone failed to disguise the thread of interest in his voice.

"Obviously. She's a candidate for our trial." And thinking of her as anything else muddied already murky waters.

"There's nothing wrong with spending time with her simply because you want to," Jason said. "You could use a little more work-life balance."

"There's nothing wrong with my life," he argued.

"Let's agree to disagree." Jason grinned. "But my advice, go find Kelsey before someone else fills her dance card." With that suggestion, Jason ended their video chat.

Noah opened his email and stared at the offer from Elsie-Mae Yates and Harland Scott, Noah's only truly viable investors left. His last option.

Their investment would allow Noah to keep the research and development company open and operating for the next twenty-four months. Noah had only to guarantee he would cure Kelsey's failing eyesight.

Guarantee.

The word cut through Noah like a dozen dull scalpels.

There was no guarantee his retinal chip and customized eyeglasses would communicate flawlessly. They were near the final phases of the device's hardware and software development. Code had been rewritten and enhanced. The design modified, reengineered, and fine-tuned. And Noah believed in all of it. Still, there were hurdles: clinical trials to complete, FDA approval to be granted. *Nothing* was guaranteed.

Not even Kelsey's consent.

He closed his laptop and walked outside. A school of fish swam under the glass floor of the balcony. The bungalow was perched above the lagoon, granting the guests panoramic views of the colorful life inside the crystal-clear waters. If only Noah's choice was as crystal clear. He wanted an investor to believe and buy in without the strings attached. But without the money ....

He walked into the connecting bedroom and yanked on his running shoes. Noah needed to get out of his head. The fitness center and a long run on the treadmill would reorganize his thoughts and help him develop his plan to change Kelsey's mind.

A woman leaned over the railing at the entrance of the dock. Her professional-grade camera aimed toward the beach where the sand and water mixed. The warm breeze caught her ponytail, lifting her brunette hair over her shoulder.

Kelsey. His dance partner—and reluctant, unknowing trial candidate—had a bungalow that shared his same dock. *How convenient.*

Six private bungalows stood between Noah's suite and the end of the dock that exited onto the beach. Right where Kelsey stood.

Noah picked up his pace, stepped up to the railing and leaned over beside Kelsey. "Good morning. What are we looking at?"

She gasped and swayed toward the water, clutching her camera.

"Sorry." Noah set his hand on her lower back and grabbed her arm, steadying her. "Didn't mean to surprise you into falling."

Her grip secured on her camera, she stood up and exhaled. "That was me. I didn't realize how far I'd leaned over."

Noah peered over the railing again, searched the sand and frowned. "What was down there and where did it go?"

"It wasn't anything." She adjusted the thick camera strap around her neck.

He studied her. "You almost toppled headfirst over a railing for nothing?"

"It was the light reflecting off the water-logged sand." She tapped on her camera screen and turned it toward him. "It was the feeling I wanted to capture."

He looked at the screen, then lifted his gaze to her face. He was more interested in the enthusiasm he saw there. More interested in the feelings she stirred inside him. Not that he'd do anything about those. He definitely had no interest in filling up his own dance card. "What did it make you feel?"

She turned as if suddenly shy about her feelings and picked up her backpack. "Warm, curious, and excited. Like an invitation to escape into a really cozy moment."

He wanted to take her camera back. Look again at the picture of sand and water and feel the same passion she expressed. Then ask her to tell him one of her secrets.

He drifted a step farther from her side. He wasn't offering to be her dance partner for more than a stolen moment. And their secrets were best left unspoken. "What do you have planned for the rest of your day?"

"A hike." She aimed her camera at him, clicked, then grinned. "Capturing more feelings."

He wanted to capture the sunlight in her smile. What was wrong with him? Jason tended toward the poetic, not him. "Should you be hiking alone?"

Her eyebrows pulled together. The sunlight on her face dimmed as if a cloud passed over, but the skies were clear. "The bartenders told me about a waterfall not in the tourist guides. There's a trail and they drew me a really good map."

He ran his hand through his hair, willed himself to stop talking. He'd already made her grin fade. Not a good start to winning her over so she might then participate in his trial. "But is it safe?"

"It's less than a two-mile walk." She patted the pocket of her shorts. The tilt of her chin tipped into a defiant angle. "I have my cell phone fully charged."

"That's probably for the best." Just as it was for the best that he left her to her hike. She wasn't asking for his escort. He wasn't offering. But her smile—he wanted one more glimpse. "I have to confess, I'd most likely push you in front of me if we ran into a snake or scorpion. Poisonous reptiles and things like that tend to freak me out."

She chewed on the corner of her lip. "There are no venomous snakes on the island. I already checked."

"Just like that, I'll sleep better tonight." He walked beside her off the dock.

"What are you doing today?"

"Remember, I'm supposed to be vacationing." He motioned to the sign indicating the lobby and fitness center. "Thought I'd start with a long run."

"Inside?" She frowned.

"It's a state-of-the-art fitness center," he said. "The cardio equipment is top of the line."

"The beaches here are some of the most beautiful in the world. White sand and clear waters are perfect for running." She stopped and spread her arms wide. "It's a paradise that should be experienced."

"The treadmills have a full view of the ocean. It's like you're right on the beach."

She tipped her head back and laughed. "You don't *know* how to vacation do you?"

"You're the second person to tell me that today." He crossed his arms over his chest. There was nothing wrong with gyms. He used the small gym they'd built in one of the empty offices at work daily. There was also nothing wrong with his style of vacationing.

"Is it nature or being outdoors that repels you?" More laughter twitched across her cheeks.

"I like nature just fine." He had some kind of cactus that bloomed on his office desk and there were succulent gardens that Jason and the staff had planted in colorful pots on nearly every window ledge around their office building. "My work keeps me inside, not my fear of the outdoors."

"Got it." She shifted the strap of her backpack. "You should come on the hike."

He eyed her, his pulse increasing despite his practiced nonchalance.

"Not because I need an escort," she stressed, "but because you need to get out."

"And experience nature." Whatever that meant.

"Exactly. Don't worry, I'll show you." She turned toward the paved path leading to the resort lobby. "We'll take it slow."

Just as he planned to slowly ease her into changing her mind about medical trials. One short hike at a time. "Do you have any extra room in that backpack?"

"What do you want to put in here?"

"A few essential supplies." He walked beside her into the lobby.

She confirmed the directions to the waterfall with concierge staff and Noah purchased water bottles, granola bars, and fruit from the hotel pantry. Supplies secured in her backpack Noah swung the bag over his back.

"What are you doing?" She reached for the strap.

"I didn't fill it up to make you carry it." He settled the backpack around his shoulders. "Now, you'll be free to really immerse yourself in the nature on the trail and take your happy snaps."

"Thanks." She nodded, slow and deliberate as if reassessing his words. "That's really thoughtful."

"Don't tell me your ex never carried your backpack?" Noah frowned and followed her outside. Her ex and past relationships were none of his concern.

"There were a lot of nevers with my ex." She brushed a stray hair off her face and smiled at him. "But I'm not interested in talking about him."

"That makes two of us."

She laughed and bumped her shoulder against his. "So, tell me Noah, where is someplace your family and friends would be surprised to find you?"

Anywhere outside his research and development lab. "On a nature hike on a remote island in the Caribbean. What about you?"

"On a dance floor. I step on too many toes." The disapproval in her voice made her admission sound more like a criticism.

"You didn't step on my toes last night." He rolled up onto the balls of his feet to prove his point.

"We were in the sand." Her smile relaxed her face and her shoulders lowered as if she'd released her inner guard. "I think we swayed more than danced."

And it was perfect. Too short. If she hadn't just told her family she didn't want to do more trials, it would've been even more perfect. "Well, I'll sway with you anytime."

Pink tinged her cheeks. From the sun, the humidity, or because of him, he wasn't sure. He moved closer, pretending to be more interested in the map she held than in her.

"It's that way." She pointed to a trail between a cluster of palm trees.

He walked beside her across the parking lot, content to follow her lead for now.

"What would be your hobbies, if you made the time and had the money?" She handed him the map and adjusted her camera lens.

He paused at the entrance of the trail and turned toward her. "Why do I feel like you searched out unique get-to-know-you questions on the internet?"

"Well, I couldn't search out your profile." She laughed and snapped another candid shot of him. "I had to search *something* in case we met again."

"Then you wanted to see me again?" He lost the tease in his tone.

"I had hoped to." She aimed her camera toward the fronds of a tall palm tree. Pictures taken, she tucked her chin and eased around him.

Not before he noticed a very appealing, very real blush sweeping across her cheeks.

His own smile stretched wide, revealing the good mood spreading through him. He could learn to like vacationing if he wasn't careful. Just as he could learn to like Kelsey, too.

CHAPTER THREE

"*I* figure you're trying to capture the light through the palm leaves and trees on our last few stops?" Noah scratched his fingers over his cheek. His eyebrows pulled together. "Now, I'm stumped. You're aiming your camera at the tree trunk."

"And the iguana balanced on the curve between the truck and branch." She zoomed in.

Noah motioned for her camera. "Let me see."

Kelsey lifted off the strap around her neck and handed the camera to Noah, thrilled he hadn't uttered one complaint about their slow pace. Or encouraged her to hurry. Or muttered that she'd already taken more than enough tree photos. For most of the pictures, he'd stood beside her and fixed his gaze in the same direction as her lens, as if interested.

"That's amazing." Wonder curled around his words.

And joy wound through her. Both for her picture and his company. She hadn't fallen or tripped, thanks to their careful pace. Noah remained beside her, not because she needed assistance but rather to see what she saw through her second pair of eyes.

"It was mostly luck." And the fact that she used her lens to bring the distance into better focus. "I've also been training myself to be patient and search for the details. All the little things most people overlook in a normal day, or are too busy and too preoccupied to stop and feel. Or to record."

"You've trained yourself well." Noah gave her camera back and checked the map. "We're almost there."

"I can hear the water." She felt triumphant. She'd hiked to a waterfall! Not completely alone, like she'd planned, but her secret about her poor vision remained safe and she'd guided Noah. There was triumph in that knowledge.

He turned in a slow circle, his head moving from one place to another.

"What are you doing?" she asked.

"We can't rush." He set his hands on his hips and looked at her. His tinted sunglasses blocked his eyes, but not the insistence in his words. "We might miss another iguana. Or a bird. Or some rare flower."

She dropped her camera. "You're serious?"

"Completely." He raised his arms. "Today you showed me things I would've marched past in my rush to get to the destination."

And suddenly she didn't want to miss getting to know more about Noah. She snapped several pictures of him, releasing her camera as well as her curiosity. "I have more questions if you're up for the challenge."

He folded the map and stuck it in his pocket. "Don't have one. Pizza connoisseur. Morning."

"Don't have what?" She gaped at him.

"Favorite color: I don't have one. Favorite food: I consider myself a pizza connoisseur. And I'm a morning person, not a night owl." He glanced at her. "Your turn."

"It's a tie between blue and purple for favorite color. Every kind of taco with extra guacamole." She slowed and eased into Noah's side, unsure if the trail dropped off ahead or if her eyes misled her. "Definitely a morning person too."

Noah stopped and studied the trail. "This is the fork in the path, according to Emmitt's notes on your map. We have a choice."

Her eyes hadn't deceived her. She hadn't lost all trust in her vision. The disquiet—a constant companion since her diagnosis—eased. "Does one trail lead to fame and fortune and the other to happiness and contentment?"

"You could be famous for jumping off the waterfall into the pool below, I suppose." He pointed into the trees behind her. "Or if heights aren't your thing, you might be happier weaving through the foliage to reach the lower pool for a swim."

"Are there sharks?" She managed to flatten her grin.

"Not here. It's fresh water." He stepped around her toward the foliage. "I myself could use a snack and a swim, but I'm happy to cheer you on if you decide to jump."

"I think I'll let you dive in first." She followed him onto the smaller trail, which was narrowed by tall grass and elephant leaves. "Just to confirm your no-shark theory."

"That's very selfless of you." His laughter wrapped around her. He reached back and wiggled his fingers. "Hold on. The trail isn't much of a path now."

Grateful for his assistance and his hunger that kept them from hiking farther up the hill, Kelsey grabbed his hand and let him guide her. Then wondered how he'd feel if he knew his cautions to watch her steps and his firm hold were more than simple courtesy for her.

She bit her lip and concentrated on arriving at the base of the waterfall without falling. Or confessing.

She wanted to remain simply Kelsey with Noah for a little while longer. After she explained her condition, her disability would come first, not her. As it had for most of her family, her ex, and her friends. Friends introduced her as, "My blind friend, Kelsey," not simply, "My friend, Kelsey." Her impending blindness often led to conversations making it appear her visual impairment was her only defining feature.

But right now, she remained Kelsey. A single woman on a hike with her camera and a handsome guy. A woman tempted to swim and flirt and steal a different kind of moment.

"We're here." Noah released her hand, removed the backpack, and set it on a moss-covered rock. "It's like our own private piece of paradise."

Private. Enticing. Tempting. Kelsey raised her camera, zoomed in on the tree roots reaching into the waterfall like fingers beckoning her closer. Sunlight glinted off the pool and sparkled as if sprinkled in pixie dust.

Beside her, Noah removed his shirt and jumped into the water. He swam to the middle of the pool, no larger than a baseball diamond, and floated on his back. She adjusted her lens, focused on the bliss on his face and clicked.

He shifted positions and tread water. His gaze fixed on her camera, but his intense focus fixed entirely on her as if he stood in front of her, not feet away. He swam forward, never releasing her from his sight.

Her breath caught inside the double beat of her heart. Awareness fired along her nerves. And a different wish caught her—one that involved forevers and confidantes and hearts.

Noah stepped onto the shore. "It's time to put down the camera and join me."

"This is how I capture feelings." She hesitated, then lowered the camera between them.

"Let's try something different. A new way to experience feelings." A warmth infused his gaze, an invitation in his words. He held his hand out.

Kelsey held her breath. Told her heart to back down. Her pulse to slow. One swim. One stolen moment wasn't ....

"Look out below!" That shout came from the top of the waterfall and rattled through Kelsey like a well-timed lecture on the fallout of bad decisions.

The teenager's worthy splash into the pool and the subsequent boisterous cheers of his friends still gathered at the top of the water-fall doused their private moment.

Noah shaded his eyes and gazed at the waterfall. "Guess it's not as private as the bartenders led you to believe."

Two teenage girls held hands, stepped off the top of the waterfall and released twin squeals. Kelsey raised her camera and caught their open-mouthed, closed-eyed entry into the water. "Well, we can eat and watch. Remember what it was like to be young and fearless."

Noah sat on a smooth rock and pulled two red apples from the backpack. "Were you ever that daring?"

"I pretended to be." Just as she had a moment earlier. Pretended she was bold enough to take Noah's hand and let herself have one stolen moment.

But she wasn't made for moments. Her heart always intruded and wanted more. Expected more. And that only led to heartbreak. Better she never find out what she was missing. Better she never learn the feel of Noah's embrace or the taste of his lips. Better she never discover the conditions of his love. "My sister and cousin have always been the fearless ones in the family. I tried to be like them growing up."

"What did they do?" He bit into his apple, stretched out his legs until his feet touched the water.

"Always accepted the dare, never the truth." She referenced that popular campfire game of her childhood while she set her camera on her lap and wiped her apple on her shirt. "It was exhausting coming up with more and more outrageous challenges. Then we became teenagers and I started to win for a while."

Several more teens jumped into the pool and started a splash war with their friends. Noah grinned. "Only a while?"

"I came up with dares that involved boys from school and in our neighborhood." She laughed at the surprise widening his eyes. "Nothing outlandish. Knocking on the neighbor's door and introducing yourself. Calling a boy from school and telling him you liked him. Those kinds of things."

He bit into his apple and chewed. "Let me guess. They refused at first."

"Then used the dares as a way to break the ice." Kelsey shook her head. "And it worked. My cousin Fran got her junior prom date out of a dare."

"How did *you* break the ice?"

Kelsey didn't. She waited on the sidelines. "I was more of the wallflower type. Never really put myself out there."

"Yet you asked me about sharks and here we are." He grinned around the last bite of his apple. "I consider that an effective icebreaker."

"What about you?" she asked. "How do *you* break the ice?"

"I sit down beside the prettiest girl in the room, hope she isn't taken, and wait for her to ask me a question I pray I can answer." He shrugged, his voice and face neutral, but she realized he was teasing her.

"Come on." She pushed on his shoulder. "Be serious. How did you approach girls in high school?"

She imagined more girls had approached him, than vice versa, given his wavy dark hair, intense eyes, and his all-around appeal. An appeal that kept drawing her to him as if he'd hooked her.

"Believe it or not, that *is* how I did it." He dropped his apple core into a paper bag and shoved it inside the backpack. "I don't think our companions are leaving any time soon."

Three girls had claimed the sunniest spots to tan. Four boys appeared at the top of the waterfall. And the others threw a beach ball around in the pool. "They seem to have settled in for the afternoon."

"We can head back to the resort and see what other parts of nature we can capture," he suggested.

"You haven't had enough of the outdoors?" She put her apple core in the paper bag.

He held out his hand to help her up. She set her hand in his, accepted his assistance—and her attraction. Not that she intended to make it into anything more than it was: what her teenage self would've labeled nothing more than a harmless crush. Nothing she couldn't control. Or handle.

Now standing again, he tugged her into him. His hand landed on her waist. Her heart landed in her throat.

"Just to be clear, it's you." He reached up, tucked her hair behind her ear and brushed his fingertips across her cheek. "I haven't had enough time with you."

Before she could unravel her voice, he released her, picked up the backpack, and waved goodbye to the teenagers.

Just to be clear, it's you. Noah's words echoed inside her, but the promise layered through his voice leveled straight into her heart, dismantling her defenses.

Two miles. She had two miles back to the resort. Two miles to keep her footsteps steady on the trail. Time enough to remind herself of all the reasons love couldn't be trusted. All the reasons her heart was better off in lockdown.

CHAPTER FOUR

"**K**elsey." A high-pitched voice bounced around the quaint lobby. "Kelsey!"

Noah set his sunglasses on the top his head and blinked several times to get his eyes to adjust to the dim, cool interior of the resort lobby. Kelsey hooked her sunglasses on the collar of her tank top and turned away from Noah.

"Kelsey. Darling." A woman dressed in wide, flowing flower-print pants and an even wider brimmed white hat waved at them from near the guest services desk. "Over here."

"Mom." Kelsey started forward.

The tropical heat pressed down on Noah, stifling and suffocating.

Too late, Noah noticed the knee-height table in her path. Kelsey's left knee clipped the square edge, knocking her sideways. Noah jumped to Kelsey's side, catching her before she fell on the floor.

The woman gasped and rushed across the lobby. An older woman spun around from the guest-services desk and scrambled toward them.

"I'm good." Kelsey patted Noah's arm. The one he'd anchored around her waist. She patted him harder and added, "You can release me."

Noah focused on Kelsey. And on breathing and remaining calm.

"Well, I'm good, except for my pride." She sighed into his T-shirt. "But that's been dinged before. It's nothing that won't heal. So really, I'm fine."

Noah removed his arm and stepped back. Too bad he couldn't step all the way back to the dock and his bungalow. Still, he remained close enough he wouldn't have to lunge to catch her again.

"Kelsey, you are not fine." The woman barreled toward them and snatched Kelsey's right arm. Alarm and panic saturated her voice. "You are bleeding."

Bleeding. Sweat dampened his neck, dripped down his spine, and sealed his entire T-shirt to his skin. He brought her back injured. *Injured.*

The older woman, her pure-white hair tinted pink and her rhinestone cat-eye glasses slightly askew, dashed into the fray. She set her hand—the one with the diamond larger than her knuckle—over her heart and the lettering of the word, Bride, in jewel print on her polo. "Haven't sprinted like that in an age. Certainly gets the heart pumping something fierce."

"Hello to you too, Mom. Grandma." Kelsey pushed her hair out of her face and motioned between the two women. "Noah, this is Anita Thomas, my mom. And my grandmother, Elsie-Mae Yates, affectionately known by everyone as Gem."

Noah acknowledged Kelsey's family with a quick nod. After one swift glance—one second of direct eye-to-eye contact—recognition flared between him and Gem. But his interest promptly returned to Kelsey's wound. "When did this happen?"

"You just let her bleed." Anita rounded on him, anger in her narrowed gaze. "What kind of ..."

Doctor was he? "Not a very good one," he acknowledged, disrupting Anita's outburst.

How had Noah missed such an obvious cut on Kelsey's arm? The blood was dried. And she'd draped a towel around her neck. He'd assumed for the heat. The dried blood on the towel proved that original theory incorrect.

He'd been too busy looking at nature's details, something she had taught him to do, to focus completely on his trial candidate. On the walk back from the waterfall, he'd noted four stumbles, and one slip, all of which Kelsey had recovered from quickly. He'd kept close to her, prepared to intervene if she'd fallen. He'd caught her just now, but that hardly made up for his oversight of her cut.

Now her family considered him a sham of a doctor.

Shams didn't take over companies. Or save family legacies. *Prove to me you have what it takes. Prove to me I should trust you with my life's work. Promise me you won't let me down, Son.*

Noah shoved all that aside. What was wrong with him? Kelsey wasn't simply a test subject logged into a computer database. She was ….

"Noah didn't know." Kelsey tugged her arm out of her mother's grasp and retreated. "I was in the brush, on my hands and knees, not on the trail just now. Wait until you see the pictures I got."

"You let her wander off some path by herself?" The dozen shiny silver bangles on Anita's wrist slid toward her elbow, clinking against each other as if stacking up her accusations against Noah.

Noah focused on Kelsey. He set the backpack on a small table, pushed Kelsey into the nearby chair, then examined her cut closer. Not deep enough for stitches, but several sections were gouged more than he liked. She obviously had an impact to her peripheral vision. To what to degree, he wasn't quite certain. The cut extending from her wrist toward her elbow proved his initial assumption correct. One more box checked on his candidate qualification checklist.

He stroked his thumb over her warm skin, registering a normal body temperature and a softness that distracted. That tempted.

"Surely this qualifies her for the trial." Gem kept her hand pressed against her chest and raised the other one as if she prepared to take an oath. " 'No more tests required.' That's was the last I was told."

He opened the backpack and dug around for the first-aid kit he'd seen earlier as well as seeking a suitable reply. One that wouldn't out him to Kelsey, yet. He had to speak to Gem and Harland first about the stipulations of their investment. As of right now, his future, and the future of their invention, depended solely on Kelsey.

"What are you talking about, Gem?" Kelsey lifted her uninjured arm like a crossing guard at a busy intersection. Her stern tone demanded silence. "I invited Noah to join me on a hike to the local waterfall. I cut my arm. It's not that bad. Tell them, Noah."

"You don't need stitches." He opened the plastic box and dumped the contents out on the table. "But you need a good cleaning, antiseptic cream, and bandages."

"I can do that in my suite." She tugged on her arm.

Noah tightened his hold and refused to release her.

She muttered, "I can take of it myself."

"You should let Noah take care of you." Gem squeezed Kelsey's shoulder, her voice soothing.

Noah gave the older bride-to-be a quick, warning glance and dismissed the speculation in her gaze. If they wanted Kelsey to buy into his procedure, they had to keep his identity a secret from her a bit longer.

"It's not like he's a doctor." Frustration filtered through Kelsey's words. She inhaled loudly, nudged her sandal into his thigh. Once. Then again.

Finally, he lifted his gaze to hers. He'd never been good at deceit. His mother had always claimed his fidgeting gave him away. *Close this deal, Son. Whatever it takes.* He pressed his palm against the cloth he'd placed on Kelsey's arm to stop the bleeding, secured his hold and his dishonesty.

Kelsey tipped her head. Suspicion worked through her gaze. "*Are you a doctor?*"

"How do you *not* know whether he's a doctor or not?" Anita threw her hands up in the air and paced behind her daughter's chair.

"I don't even know his last name," Kelsey charged. She twisted around to look at her mother. Her words dropped like angry sparks around her. "Where he lives. Where he works. Or if he has a dog or cat or a pet fish."

"No pets," Noah whispered. "Always wanted a big dog."

"Me too." Kelsey shifted, sagged against the chair, and grinned at him.

Not the wide, contagious smile he preferred, but something quieter and more potent that spoke of connections and confidences shared. Another time. Another place. Maybe ....

Gem pressed her hands to her cheeks. That speculation spread into her words. "But you two obviously know each other."

"We met last night at the bar," Noah explained. "Kelsey wanted to keep things unconventional."

Her mother took off her white sun hat and fanned herself with the wide brim. "What exactly does that mean?"

"We didn't have a wild night in my suite, Mom," Kelsey declared. "But if we did, that would've been okay. I'm a grown woman who can take care of herself, remember?"

Noah bit back a grin he had no right feeling. She was a woman. That much he had been noticing since he first saw her last night. Confidant. Poised. Courageous. Those qualities would serve her well during the medical trial.

Her mother whipped the hat back and forth faster and faster. Her cheeks drew in further and further, tightening her expression.

"I do have first-aid training, by the way." Noah opened a second antiseptic cloth and wiped the last of the dirt from Kelsey's cut. "Does your mother faint often?"

"She can be overdramatic," Kelsey muttered. "But not to the level of fainting. Not usually anyway."

"Then what did you two do last night?" Gem was the calm to her daughter's theatrics, despite Gem's pink-tinted hair, glittery toenails, and colorful, heeled sandals.

"We talked like two adults about interesting things. Then we danced." Kelsey paused for a beat. "On the beach, even."

"Then Noah escorted you back to your suite," Gem offered, her smile acknowledging his manners and something more.

Noah cringed. He let Kelsey bleed today and walk home alone last night. Now he looked like an impolite sham of a doctor. Hardly reassuring.

"No, he did not escort me anywhere." Kelsey shook her head. "I walked back to my bungalow. Myself."

Not that he hadn't wanted to dance longer with her. Not that he wouldn't have escorted her anywhere she'd requested, if she hadn't dashed off. He should be more grateful. After all, if she discovered he was a doctor with a trial, she would've walked away much sooner.

"That wasn't a smart choice." Her mother's hat suddenly stilled. "We talked about that on our call yesterday."

They'd also pledged not to discuss cures or trials or doctors for the entire week. Was that what kept Gem quiet now? She'd given their word to Kelsey. He'd thank her later, after he changed Kelsey's mind and the investment contracts had been signed and notarized.

"Yet, here I am." Kelsey lifted her legs straight out and wiggled her toes. "No broken bones. No more bruises than usual. All in one piece."

"Except Noah is wrapping a bandage around your arm from wrist to elbow." One of Anita's penciled in eyebrows arched.

Kelsey frowned. "Let's just move on and let it go."

"I have an idea." Gem waved between Kelsey and Noah. Her voice drifted into lyrical as if she wanted to break out in song. "Noah can be your plus one for the week, Kelsey."

Plus one? That hadn't been written in any fine print on any communication or contract between Noah and Gem. He couldn't keep lying to Kelsey for a week. If he did ....

"Oh, Noah can't ..." Kelsey's voice leveled up from concerned to outright alarmed.

She rejected him. Never hesitated.

Her mom touched her earring. "Noah, do you have family arriving for the holiday?"

His family hadn't celebrated the holidays together since Noah had been in grade school. After his parent's divorce, his mother had displaced her festive holiday spirit. Thanksgiving had simply become another night for Chinese takeout and movies in his bedroom. Noah cleared his throat. "I do not."

"Then it's settled." Gem clasped her hands together and squeezed her arms against her sides as if giving herself a quick hug.

What was happening? This had *not* been part of the plan.

"Kelsey has a date now." Kelsey's mom looked as if she wanted to shimmy in celebration too.

"*Nothing* is settled," Kelsey interrupted. "Noah and I didn't agree to anything."

Noah tied off Kelsey's bandage, but not the anticipation seeping inside him. He would have unprecedented access to Kelsey. He could possibly discover something useful from his interactions with her to help another patient. That wasn't something to easily dismiss. "I don't want to impose. This is your time for family."

"And friends," Anita assured him.

A hawk tracked its prey with less intensity than Anita watched him. Anita might not be the final decision on the investment money, but she could become a very strong influencer.

"Two things you need to know about the women in our family." Kelsey tucked the stray end of her bandage away and rose. "They rarely accept no for an answer. And strangers become friends after first name introductions. And friends become family after a meal together."

He had a family already. One that expected better of him than deceiving a potential patient.

Gem touched her watch. "Dinner is tonight at our villa. Appetizers at six o'clock. Dinner to follow at seven."

"You won't want to be late. We've arranged for a local private chef." Her mom shifted her attention to Noah. "Now, Noah, where do you live?"

"Outside of Raleigh," Noah said.

"That's convenient. We live near Raleigh too." Her mom's voice slipped several notes above delighted. "Kelsey lives north of Charlotte. Not too far away."

"And we've been telling her to move closer to home." Gem tipped her perceptive gaze on Kelsey. "Then you'd be closer to Noah, too."

That was bold. Location wasn't a requirement to participate in the trial. What was the older woman up to now?

"It's just a week, not a lifetime." A warning rang through Kelsey's voice.

"Every lifetime together started from one day," her grandmother pronounced.

And every successful business started from one idea and the willingness to do whatever it took to thrive and prosper. Even if it meant accepting the role of plus-one.

Now he had more access to Kelsey, like he wanted, but the deception left a taste of bile in his mouth.

Everyone looked at him. He tried to smile, but it felt more like a grimace.

CHAPTER FIVE

"Kelsey, you're early." Gem stood in the open doorway of their two-story villa and peered around Kelsey. "Where's Noah?"

As if Noah were the only answer. He'd certainly featured in Kelsey's afternoon daydreaming about a family. A girl could dream, right? Dreams were allowed in her perfect week.

Kelsey stepped inside the villa, hugged her grandmother, and followed her into the stainless steel and marble kitchen. "Noah is meeting us here later."

"Kelsey." Her mom checked her watch. "The chef hasn't even delivered appetizers or dinner yet."

"But the wine is chilled." Her father removed his fedora-style straw hat, revealed his bald head, and his welcoming smile. "I'm opening a bottle of wine. Care for a tall glass?"

"Please." Kelsey hugged her dad, grateful for the one person in the family who had agreed to let her be as she was—a woman ready to have fun on vacation.

Harland greeted her and took several wine glasses out of the cabinet.

"I wanted to take pictures of you all before the sun sets." Kelsey had agreed to design Gem and Harland's wedding photograph memory book. She wanted to start the memory collecting tonight.

Yet she hadn't invited Noah to join them early for pictures. She knew after one day spent together that Noah would fit into her family. But she didn't want to hurt him by including him in family pictures in what, for her, was only a week to pretend and perhaps daydream.

Nothing more. She looked at her family. "And I also want to set some ground rules."

"I hope those rules involve no more unsupervised hikes." Her mom frowned at the bandage on her arm.

"How is your injury?" Her dad touched her shoulder, his grip steady and encouraging.

"It's fine." Although the bandage Noah had wound around her arm seemed a bit much. "The ground rules have to do with Noah. And me."

"More rules." Her mother hid her scowl behind her wine glass.

Wine glasses filled, Kelsey led the foursome outside onto the patio. A series of river-rock waterfalls flowed under a bridge into the villa's private backyard pool. She pictured the foursome on the arched bridge; the ocean, cloud-free blue sky, and the sun barely beginning its descent a beautiful backdrop. A perfect setting for the start of Gem and Harland's wedding-week adventures. "We'll start at the bridge."

Her grandmother wrapped her arm around Harland's waist and squeezed. "What about Noah, dear?"

Kelsey checked her camera lighting and took several tests shots of the empty bridge. "Please don't tell Noah about my condition at dinner tonight."

As expected, the foursome broke their positions, scattering around the patio like windblown leaves. Confusion and disapproval displaced their smiles.

Her mom set her hands on her hips and frowned. "How can Noah not already know about your vision issues?"

"Simple." Kelsey set her camera on the teak outdoor dining table. She'd expected her request to disrupt the photo shoot, but not end it entirely. "I never told him. He's just a date."

For the week. Not the future.

And she relied on a simple truth. A lot of people looked at her, saw normal brown eyes and assumed her vision was the same as theirs. As if there was a certain "look" to a blind person. Something obvious they could point to and prove Kelsey was different.

Harland pulled out chairs for the three women and motioned for them to sit. He took a seat beside Gem.

"Are you waiting to learn more about Noah before you tell him? You haven't said what he's like." Gem brushed her pink-tipped bangs off her forehead and settled back into her picture-worthy smile. "Is he the kind of man who'd turn in a wallet to lost and found?"

"You certainly want someone like that." Her mom lifted her shoulder in a delicate shrug.

"Or someone you can count on in a crisis," Gem added. "Is Noah someone like that? Someone you could share the truth with."

Too much speculation lingered in her grandmother's gaze. Kelsey straightened, instantly on alert. *Wait a minute.* Gem lived for romance. Thrived on love stories. And contended she'd been something of a premiere matchmaker in her day.

Kelsey eyed Gem, her voice mild. "You aren't matchmaking, are you?"

"There's nothing wrong with wanting you to be settled and happy." Gem twisted her diamond wedding ring around her finger.

Happy. She wanted that for herself too. Her grandmother's calm voice tangled Kelsey's conviction, seeding in doubt. Kelsey glanced at her dad. Surely, he'd step in. Her dad settled his straw fedora on his head and winked at her as if he approved. *Winked.*

She had to stop her grandmother and her family from matchmaking. It was bad enough she'd already been daydreaming about Noah earlier. "No guy wants a blind girlfriend. I don't check any boxes for top girlfriend material."

"True love isn't about checking boxes. It's more powerful than that." Gem took Harland's hand. "Together, you push each other to be more than you ever thought possible."

"I couldn't agree more." Harland smiled, lifted their joined hands, and kissed Gem's knuckles.

But the key words was "true love." And the only love Kelsey had known came with conditions. Her grandmother and Harland could have their own love. Kelsey was better alone.

She ran her palms over the pants of her jumpsuit. She'd chosen the deep red color to remind herself to be bold. Confident in her choices and her decisions. "Can we just agree not to tell Noah, please?"

Her dad kissed her mom on the cheek, refilled the wine glasses, and said, "Love aside, if I can't tell Noah about who are you today, I'll just have to tell him stories about who you were."

Kelsey bit down on the retort that being blind was not *who* she is, but *what* she is, and sipped her wine. At least they'd moved on from true love and matchmaking.

"I can tell Noah about the time you and your sister decided to cut each other's hair. What were you? About five. You told your mom you thought you could just pull more hair out of your head like you did with your doll." Her dad tapped his glass against hers. "I laughed for a month."

"I was not as amused as your father." Her mom grimaced.

Meagan and Kelsey each had dolls that magically grew more hair. They'd quickly discovered there was no magic to immediately growing back their own hair. "Maybe you could pick another story."

"I prefer the time you declared you would win the school spelling bee and carried around the dictionary for the entire school year," Gem offered.

She'd lost the spelling bee but toned the muscles in her arms. Still, her family liked to overcomplicate things. She had one simple request: not to mention her vision. Now she wondered if she needed to give them a list of approved topics of conversation. "We should probably skip awkward childhood stories too."

"We'll leave those to your sister and cousin." Her dad grinned. "Meagan and Fran have much better storytelling skills than we do, and they'll be here tomorrow to entertain us."

Worry tipped through Kelsey. She hadn't planned to tell Noah at all. But more family was arriving. More chances someone else could mention her vision issues to him.

"There's nothing wrong with letting Noah see who you really are, dear. You may realize there's nothing to fear." Gem watched Kelsey as if she read her mind.

Her mom asked, "Wasn't there something else you wanted to talk about?"

"Yes." Kelsey snatched the crystal wine-charm dish away from her mom.

"I was picking out a charm for my glass," her mom said.

"I need you to pay attention," Kelsey said. "This is really important."

"We've already agreed not to tell Noah about your eyes." Her mom settled her floral-print silk wrap around her shoulders as if Kelsey's curt tone chilled her. "And we all promised not to discuss cures, trials, or doctors."

Kelsey inhaled and went all in. "That's what I want to discuss."

"Really?" Hope spread from Gem's perceptive gaze to her low voice.

Her mom straightened and centered her attention Kelsey.

"It's going to be a short conversation." Kelsey searched for the Thomas' trademark smile, faltered, and pushed her voice into upbeat. She hated disappointing her family. "I'm not going to do any more trials. Ever again."

Silence, the oppressive uncomfortable kind, swept across the table.

"You can't be serious about this." Her mom pressed her finger into the side of her mouth as if stalling her deep scowl.

"Yes. I am." Kelsey leaned forward and held her mom's gaze. "It's *my* eyes. *My* decision."

"That's giving up." Gem shook her head. "We don't give up."

"There's a difference between giving up and acceptance," Kelsey said. "I'm choosing acceptance."

"But there are new breakthroughs all the time," Harland offered. "New technology revealed practically every month."

"And I have very good doctors, specialists." Kelsey stressed. "They will tell me if I should consider something."

"Doctors miss things. They're not perfect." Worry pinched across her mother's face from the creases around her eyes down to her pursed lips.

"I have to trust the doctors I have to know what's best for me." Just as she had to learn to trust herself too. "The doctors know what will work and what won't for my particular condition."

"Is that the requirement then?" Gem asked, her expression unreadable from the shadows created by the setting sun. "A doctor's opinion. That will change your mind about whether or not to participate?"

"It's not about changing my mind." Kelsey gripped her hands together on top of the table and held tight to her resolve. "It's about not missing out on my life because I spent it chasing down a cure. It's about you all not missing out on your lives."

"But we want to help you." Her mother's voice cracked.

Her dad reached for her mom's hand. Tears pooled in his eyes. "We want to help so very much."

"I appreciate it. I really do. And I love you all the more for it." Kelsey settled her hand over her parent's joined ones, then reached for Gem and Harland with her other. "But it's time to stop. You all need to focus on other things."

"What will you do?" More anxiety from her mom.

"I have my photography business. And I've been asked to teach photography classes at the local college." Nothing really ever lessened her mom's concern. And still Kelsey tried. Pride intensified the defiance in her words. "There is much more to me than my blindness."

"Of course, there is, dear." Gem patted her hand. Her voice gained strength. "Kelsey has given us her orders. Now we need to get prepared for dinner and a wonderful week with our family."

"That sounds like a Gem command." Her father laughed and stood. "What are our new orders?"

"Harland and Wayne show the chef and his assistant to the kitchen when they arrive." Gem finished her wine and rose from her chair. "Anita can touch up her makeup and Kelsey can take those pictures."

The group dispersed, leaving Gem and Kelsey alone on the patio. Kelsey walked around the table and hugged her grandmother. "Thank you for understanding."

"I can understand and not agree." Her grandmother touched Kelsey's cheek and smiled. "Besides, your mind can always change."

CHAPTER SIX

*T*he front door of the two-story villa swung open before Noah could knock. Gem eased out and quietly shut the door behind her and kept her voice low. "Kelsey refuses to consent to any more trials."

Every light looked to have been turned on inside the house. However, the porch remained dim. Better to conceal his shock. "Kelsey told you that?"

"Earlier this evening." Gem glanced over her shoulder as if to make sure they were alone. "This does not just mean your trial. It's *any* medical trial now or in the future."

Noah rubbed the back of his neck and paced a slow circle around the wide front porch. No consent. No investment. He failed his father. And there was Kelsey. He *wanted* to help her now.

Other medical trials existed. Other options for her. He could convince her not to turn her back completely. He'd taken an oath as a doctor.

"It's unacceptable, of course." Irritation thinned Gem's mouth and words.

Noah paused in his pacing and stared at the older woman. "It's her choice to make." He liked Kelsey. Wanted her to have the right to her own decisions. But he *could* help her. Yet, once she learned the truth about him, she'd walk away, not speak to him again.

"It's our choice to try and change her mind." The resolve in Gem's words weighted her voice into firm and unyielding. "And that's what we're going to do."

How simple that sounded. Nothing was that simple, especially now. "You have a plan?"

"I've been married twice to the loves of my life. That's no accident." Gem brushed her fingers through her hair, touched her diamond earrings as if putting herself back together. "I raised three children and have ten grandchildren, and soon, another fifteen step-grands. All of whom come to me for advice and guidance. Again, it's no accident. Of course, I have a plan."

"We'll tell her tonight who I am." Noah rubbed his chin and nodded, settling into his strategy. "I can show her the device, the data, and the testing. You have the sample I gave you, right?" He could talk to her about other trials.

"You'll do no such thing," Gem ordered.

"She should know who I am," Noah argued. "What I can do for her."

"And she will," Gem said. "All in good time. Tonight, you're her plus-one."

Noah stared at her. His mouth opened and closed. Deception couldn't be her suggestion. Kelsey was her granddaughter. "So, that's the big plan. Continue on as we are, leaving out important details. She's going to get hurt."

"You have to earn her trust," Gem said. "This is the happiest I've seen her in a long time.

"You want me to earn her trust," Noah scowled, "and then break it once I reveal the truth about who I am. She won't be happy then. She won't sign up for my trial."

"This is important." Gem stepped forward and gripped his hand, her hold tight, her voice fierce. "You have to change her mind."

"I can do that." He squeezed her fingers, pushing certainty through his tone. "If I can use my data. Scientific evidence. Studies."

Gem's head swayed from side to side. "She won't hear you. She won't listen to your data or science facts."

"But that's what I have," Noah whispered. In spreadsheets and slideshows. Case studies and functioning prototypes.

"This is about more than science. This is about my granddaughter." Gem set her other hand over their joined ones. "I want her to see the tears in her groom's gaze as she walks down the aisle on their wedding day. I want her to see her child's first smile. First steps.

Read a bedtime story. I want her to experience everything life offers and more. I want her to have hope."

Noah wanted that too. His team wanted that. Kelsey and patients like her were the reason Noah spent so many hours in his research and development laboratory.

Whatever you do in life, Noah, make sure it matters. Touch another life—that's the greatest gift you can leave behind.

Wise words. Not from Noah's father, but from retired Lieutenant General Marvin Rivers. His mom and Noah had moved in next door to Marvin after his parents had divorced. Marvin had given that advice to Noah on the day Noah had left for medical school.

Gem clutched his hand. "If Kelsey realizes what losing her sight really means after this week, she'll be a better candidate for your trial. A willing one, if you do this."

He wanted Kelsey's consent. He also wanted her to have hope. He looked into Gem's tear-filled eyes. "I won't tell her who I am yet, and I'll try to talk to her."

"You'll get her to change her mind." Gem's words came out more like a command.

He had no idea how. His chin dipped slightly. His smile refused to relax across his face.

It was enough for Gem. She squeezed his hand one last time and released him. "Now, let me get inside then ring the doorbell."

He blinked at the older woman. "What?"

"The doorbell." Gem pointed at the soft-lit button on the door frame and whispered, "Ring it as if you've just arrived."

Gem slipped inside and closed the door. Gem believed he could convince Kelsey to change her mind. But even if he succeeded, she'd dislike him for his deception. Still, if he could convince Kelsey not to give up, to research other possible trials, he would have made a positive difference in her life. That should be enough.

He pressed the doorbell and pushed back his discontent.

Kelsey opened the door and stepped outside. Her hair was twisted on top of her head, several loose, wavy strands dancing around her cheeks. Her dark-red jumpsuit skimmed her curves and exposed her shoulders. Effortless and eye-catching.

And he wanted her to be his. For more than a week.

He caught his breath and his wayward heart. Prepared his confession. "You look stunning."

"Thanks. You clean up quite nicely as well." She tucked her hair behind her ear and reached out her hand. "Still want to be my plus-one?"

Always. He wrapped his fingers around hers, stepped inside the villa, and silenced all the reasons he should have retreated.

CHAPTER SEVEN

*D*inner dishes cleared, cleaned, and put away, Kelsey and Noah rejoined her family on the patio. Her dad had shared two entertaining childhood stories and her grandmother one about Kelsey and her older sister. Then the conversation had drifted between the arrival of different family members the following day and the schedule for the remainder of the week. The Thanksgiving menu had been finalized and commitment ceremony details discussed.

Noah was included in the conversations as if he'd always been a part of their evening dinners. No awkward silences had intruded. Neither had any mention of Noah's profession, the medical trial, or Kelsey's impaired vision.

And the beats of restless unease tapping through him came from the replay of Gem's voice inside his head. *Look how happy she is. She hasn't been this happy in so long.*

Noah pulled out Kelsey's chair for her. Once again joy overtook her smile as it had most of the evening. Look how happy she was.

"I thought this year, since we are traveling for Thanksgiving, our traditions should travel too." Kelsey reached under the table, set a cloth shopping bag on her lap, and pulled out a nonstick cake pan.

"That's the castle pan." Her dad set his wine glass on the table and grinned. "Did you pack it in your suitcase?"

"I had to take a larger suitcase." Kelsey hugged the cake pan and laughed. "But it's worth it for Double-Chocolate Thomas Castle Cake."

"I've been looking forward to another piece of that cake since last Thanksgiving." Harland touched his stomach and glanced at Noah. "One of the best you're ever going to taste. I can promise you that."

But could Harland promise that Noah would become immune to Kelsey's laughter? To the vibrance of her smile? Could Harland promise Noah his interest in Kelsey was simply a reaction to the humidity and welcoming spirit of the islands? Merely a result of enjoying his vacation?

"I worked with the catering staff here." Delight colored Kelsey's words. "And I have all the ingredients to make our cake."

"Why are we sitting out here then?" Gem waved to the sliding glass doors. "We need to get baking."

"I'll make it." Kelsey stood, the cake pan cradled against her. "I have a copy of the recipe and I even practiced last week."

"How was it?" Gem slanted her gaze at Noah as if to point out her granddaughter's enthusiasm.

"Burnt." Kelsey waved her hand as if wiping away that admission. "But the chocolate glaze was delicious on my vanilla ice cream."

Her dad reached over and touched her mom's arm. Anita set her hand against the front of her throat as if catching her response. Worry trembled across her mouth. Her fingers lowered and curved around the gold heart locket she wore.

Noah wasn't certain if Anita held her own heart or her family's in her fist. But he understood. Kelsey's family loved deeply and unapologetically. Approve or criticize their methods, their choices, their decisions—at their core, it was love that guided them.

Noah had never let love lead him. Rarely had he made decisions based on what his heart wanted. He scooted his chair back, flattened his spine against the teak chair frame. His skin twitched. His muscles tensed. That was the discomfort of an imposter.

Love did not drive him. He had no place at their family dinner table.

"I think you should try baking it again." Her dad's smile reached across the table like an encouraging hug. "It's the only way to learn how to get it right so you can make it for your own family one day."

Family. Also at their core. Their very foundation.

Noah's own father had traded his family for work. Noah had followed his father's example. After all, Noah had wasted too many childhood wishes trying to repair his broken family.

Noah glanced at Kelsey. A tremor worked across her bottom lip. Her cheeks paled.

She blew out a small breath as if collecting her words. "I want to get the cake right for you all this Thanksgiving."

But not for her future family. Noah sat forward, dismissed the dull thud in his chest. Surely Kelsey wasn't saying no to more than the medical trials. He shouldn't be bothered either. Whether Kelsey wanted to have a family or not wasn't his concern. But he did care. Too much. He had to stop.

"We can help." Anita finished her wine. "That's the first cake I learned to make after your grandmother threatened to take the recipe to her grave."

Gem tapped her wine glass against Harland's. "Got her to learn real quick too. She'd been married for almost fifteen years."

"I admit it." Anita refilled her wine glass. "Your cake always tasted better than mine."

"It's from the joy." Gem tapped her chest. "Have joy here and you can taste it in every bite of the food you cook."

"I always thought it was because your oven cooked more evenly than mine," Anita laughed.

Harland nodded, his smile notching wider with the continued up-and-down motion. "Kelsey, remember, bring only joy into your kitchen."

"Right." Kelsey's eyebrows pulled together.

"I can assist." Noah stood, then ground his teeth together. He knew nothing about bringing joy to the kitchen. Or to his food. He cooked to satisfy his hunger. And to bring joy to another person. He intended to do that through medical advances.

Kelsey tipped her head and studied him as if she too questioned the joy he'd bring. "Do you cook?"

"I know my way around the kitchen." He tugged on his polo, clearing the wrinkles from his shirt and the doubt from his words. "I can't claim to know much about the baking side of things."

"That makes two of us." Kelsey chewed on her lip.

"We can figure it out together." *Together*. He liked that idea a bit too much. Cooking one cake wasn't a relationship starter. But he could start another conversation. One about opening herself back up to medical trials without tipping his hand that he knew.

"Then it's settled. Kelsey and Noah will bake together." Gem clasped her hands together. "We'll wait out here. You don't want too many cooks in the kitchen confusing things."

"As it happens, I have another tradition that traveled to the islands with us." Her dad set two decks of playing cards on the table.

"You brought the poker cards." Happiness swished through Kelsey's voice.

"It's a family tradition." Her dad shuffled the deck. "We'll just play a few hands and get ourselves warmed up."

"I packed the poker chips." Gem rose and grinned at the table. Her eyes sparkled behind her glasses. "I was hoping we might find time to play. Hurry and get the cake in the oven, you two, so you can join us."

Noah massaged the back of his neck. He'd packed clothes and his overnight kit. Kelsey's family had packed holiday traditions. Poker and chocolate cake. Nothing wrong with that combination. As for Noah joining in—that felt wrong. He owed Kelsey the truth about who he was. Yet, that he *wanted* to join in felt entirely too right. Which was completely wrong.

The more time he spent with her family, the more he liked them. The more time he spent with Kelsey, the more he forgot where he belonged. Where he *wanted* to belong.

He walked into the kitchen. He'd thank her for dinner, wish her a goodnight, and then leave. Leave her to her family and her baking joy. That was the right thing to do. "What can I do to help?"

Wrong words. Still he couldn't find the right words to correct himself.

"Grease the pan." Kelsey set a stick of butter and the cake pan on the counter in front of him. "Get the butter into every crevice in the pan."

Noah buttered the baking dish and smeared over his guilt. Promised himself tomorrow he'd remember his priorities; put the family business and his father's expectations first.

Kelsey opened several cabinets and set more baking supplies on the marble island. Then she organized every ingredient into rows: one for dry ingredients, one for wet. Her mixing bowls were placed into their own row. The recipe she moved across the counter next to the stand mixer.

Noah finished prepping the cake pan and washed his hands. "What's the tradition behind this cake?"

"Chocolate is its own food group in our family." She put butter in the mixing bowl then paused to stare at the counter.

Noah glanced at the recipe and shifted the sugar container into her sight line.

"The recipe has been passed down through so many generations, the story is that it was first made in a castle." She scooped out the sugar and leveled it with a butter knife. Determination creased a line into her forehead. "My sister and I always made up stories about our family members who lived in a grand castle overlooking the ocean."

"Impressive." He scooted the salt out of her view before she picked it up again.

Her gaze narrowed on the printed recipe. Tension flattened her mouth. The joy Gem had wanted in the kitchen was slowly displaced by Kelsey's intense, almost grim concentration. She'd have a headache, not a blissful sugar rush if she continued.

He added, "My family comes from a long line of sheepherders."

She cracked an egg into the mixing bowl and peered at him. A tiny smile cracked across her face. "Is that true? Sheepherders?"

He shrugged. "My mom always threatened to send me to the mountains to herd sheep when I misbehaved."

Her grin splintered into a full smile. "Did you start behaving?"

"I did until I discovered cowboys and decided I could be a cowboy sheepherder." Noah handed her the flour container and took the powdered sugar jar. He skipped over correcting her mistake and continued, "Then my mom told me herding sheep can only be done on foot."

"Is that true?" She turned on the mixer.

"I have no idea." He put the eggs back inside the refrigerator. "But it was enough for me to get in line and follow the rules."

273

"Now that's impressive parenting." She sprinkled cocoa powder around the greased pan then frowned. "Do you think too much cocoa matters?"

Noah glanced inside the pan. Clumps filled most of the crevices. "More chocolate never hurts anything does it?"

"My thoughts exactly." She shifted her attention to the mixing bowl. "Will you use the sheepherding punishment for your own kids?"

His kids. He opened one of the chocolate bars she'd set on the counter, cracked off a piece and stuffed the candy in his mouth. "I haven't really thought about it."

"Kids or parenting styles?" she asked.

"Both." He snapped off another piece of chocolate. Kids. A family. He'd have to find a wife first. A partner in life. He was used to being alone. Nothing wrong with being single. And yet there wasn't anything completely right about his life either. His gaze tracked to Kelsey and stuck as if he were lost and she'd guide him home. "What about you?"

"Me?" The mixing bowl slipped in her grip.

He grabbed the bottom, held it while she scraped the batter into the cake pan.

She tapped the spoon against the cake pan. Sincerity fell into her voice. "I imagine I'd like to be a parent like Gem, if I was one."

If. He heard the emphasis she pressed into the one simple word.

She returned her attention to the cake pan and returned the conversation back to him. "What's your family Thanksgiving like?"

"Chinese take-out and a sci-fi movie marathon." He dipped his finger inside the empty cake bowl and scraped a taste from the side.

"Take-out?" she asked.

"My parents divorced before I was ten." He sampled the batter. Nothing bittersweet about the cake mix, only his tone. "Mom was a nurse. She worked holidays for the extra pay. The Chinese restaurant delivered for free."

"Where was your dad?" she asked.

"Dad wasn't around much after they divorced." He snapped off another piece of chocolate and blamed the candy for the truths breaking out of him. "Or before, for that matter."

I'm building a legacy, Noah. I must focus. You want your dad to succeed, don't you?

Every child wanted their parents to succeed. Every child wanted to matter to their parents, too. Noah set the candy back on the island and brushed off his hands.

Kelsey put the cake pan in the oven, reached for Noah's hand. He liked how easily she reached for him, like her own parents reached for each other during dinner. The same way Gem and Harland offered silent support to each other with touch as well as words. He curved his fingers around hers and held on.

"I'm sorry your dad wasn't there for you growing up." She curved her fingers around his.

"It's in the past." He stared at their joined hands. He was more interested in the future. Maybe one with her. But futures started with clean slates. No secrets. No lies. "Kelsey ... I ..."

She looked up. Her gaze fixed on his.

And he lost his voice. Lost himself in the warm, steady comfort of her touch, the compassion softening across her face. And her kindness. He set his palm against her cheek, wanting to learn more. Feel more of everything she stirred inside him.

She moved toward him, lifted her arm.

The sliding glass door slipped open. The sea-infused breeze swept around them carrying Gem's animated voice. "How much longer? I'm losing out there and need some cake to change my luck."

Noah jerked his hand away and jumped away from Kelsey, unable to decide if Gem's arrival was fortunate or not. Kelsey spun around and checked the oven.

He had no business kissing Kelsey, yet he couldn't deny it had become something of a priority. But he'd never lost focus before.

CHAPTER EIGHT

"*W*hat can we order you for lunch, Kelsey?" Her dad studied the menu board outside the Hidden Cove restaurant on the private island they'd just docked at.

"Nothing." Kelsey adjusted her sunglasses and glanced around, looking for Noah.

Her sister and cousin, along with Harland's family, had arrived that morning. By noon, the extended families, tallying close to thirty people, had boarded a charter boat and set sail for an afternoon water adventure. Introductions completed ten minutes into their cruise, Kelsey and Noah had settled in beside Meagan and Fran and their husbands Brad and Marcus. Childhood stories had been told and the conversation quickly detoured to dares and bets like old times.

Kelsey had even accepted one.

Her mom adjusted her wide-brimmed hat. "You really should eat something."

"I'm snorkeling, not eating." Kelsey scanned the group heading toward the beach for Noah.

"Not out there." Disapproval weighted her mom's words.

"It's not allowed in the restaurant." Kelsey eyed her mom and stiffened her shoulders. "And the turtles are out there."

"According to the captain, you have to swim quite far past the reef." Her mom chewed on her bottom lip.

Her mom disliked any water where her feet couldn't touch the bottom. Kelsey reminded herself not to take on her mom's fear.

Or her mom's reserve. "Yes, past the twin rocks and then hook left."

Her sister and cousin stood on the shore, snorkeling masks on their heads, fins in their hands. Meagan motioned with her free hand and hollered. "Hurry up, slow poke."

"Get a move on, Kels," Fran yelled. "You don't want to be the last one to the turtles."

Her cousin set her hand on her husband's shoulder and worked her fins on her feet. Hands clasped together, the couple headed off into the surf—a team ready to conquer their lives together.

A pang pulsed inside Kelsey's chest. A shard of envy, and even more, that persistent wish to have the very same for herself.

Her sister and her husband disappeared in the surf together, too. Just as Kelsey expected her dreams to disappear. Wishes and fantasies had no place in her real world back home. Still, she wanted to believe ....

"Do you think snorkeling is a good idea after your last experience?" Her mom stepped in front of Kelsey, blocking her view of the ocean and the happy couples.

"It's fine." Certainty coated her voice. Still, a hint of worry skimmed over her like a soft breeze.

"The last time you snorkeled certainly *wasn't* fine." Gem eyed her.

"You haven't forgotten, have you?" More anxiety from her mom.

Kelsey was losing her eyesight. Not her memory. "Stepping on a sea urchin is hard to forget."

"What about the other urchin you knocked your arm into?" her mom pressed.

"I remember that one too." Kelsey rubbed the back of her elbow and the scars there.

Accepting her cousin and sister's snorkel challenge on the charter boat had been instantaneous. Noah had been beside her. His strength and support had emboldened her. With Noah next to her, she believed again.

But he wasn't beside her now. Doubt crept in.

A hand landed on her lower back, steady and secure as if bracing her backbone. Kelsey lifted her chin and glanced at Noah, now beside her again. "I'm going to find the turtles. Want to join me? Unless you've had enough of the outdoors."

His smile hitched one corner of his mouth. "I haven't had nearly enough."

Kelsey relaxed. She hadn't had nearly enough time with him either.

"Noah, don't let her drift too far away," Gem suggested.

Noah took Kelsey's hand, wrapped his fingers around hers. "We'll avoid sea urchin encounters and stick together like magnets."

How much of their conversation had he heard? Kelsey tightened her hold on Noah's hand and felt as if he tightened his grip around her heart. This week had been nearly perfect. She couldn't allow her heart to get away from her now.

They moved farther from her family. Snorkeling masks and fins on, Noah handed Kelsey a disposable waterproof camera. "This is for you. Now you can capture more of those feelings you like so much."

"You bought me an underwater camera!" Kelsey lost her grip on her heart, threw her arms around Noah, and anchored herself to him. Caught one more perfect moment.

The hum of the boat's engines surrounded Kelsey and Noah. The spray from the ocean waves dusted her skin. But Kelsey wasn't moving. They were alone on a bench at the back of the charter boat.

The rest of her family sunbathed topside and others gathered inside away from the sun's rays.

Her disposable camera—the film full of sea turtles, manta rays, colorful fish, and vibrant coral reefs—was tucked inside her bag. Her hand was tucked inside Noah's, her head rested on his shoulder.

Noah squeezed her fingers. "You good?"

"Better than good." For the first time in a long time. "I never did thank you for the camera."

"Just make sure you share those pictures with me."

Her heart wanted to share so much more. She bit into her lip, reminded herself to live only in the moment. No peeking into the future. No worry about what ifs. Not right now. "There's something that would make this day perfect."

"What's that?" He shifted on the bench.

"Something we never got around to last night." Kelsey raised her head, leveled her gaze on his and risked. "Something I don't want to regret missing."

His gaze sharpened, centered on her. Her heart kicked up its pace. She curved her hand up around the side of his neck, dipped her fingers into his damp hair. His hand moved up to frame her cheek, gentle and tender. She leaned forward. He met her halfway.

Finally, their lips met. Two breaths became one. The moment became theirs.

And for the first time since her diagnosis, she believed anything was possible.

CHAPTER NINE

*K*elsey hummed and washed the bowls she'd used to mix the family cornbread muffins. Her parents and Harland had left to check on additional Thanksgiving meal prep happening in the other villas. Gem and Noah were outside, rearranging patio furniture to make room for the thirty-plus guests arriving soon to spend Thanksgiving together.

A burning smell wafted around her.

Kelsey spun around, rushed to the oven and yanked open the door. The tops of the muffins had turned black and billowed smoke. *No. No. No.*

Panic filled her. She searched the counter for the potholders. Every second charcoaled the muffin tops more. She grabbed a hand towel and reached for the pan. The heat seared through the towel, deep into her fingers. She clutched the pan with her other bare hand and yelped.

The pan smashed to the floor. Muffins scattered across the tile.

Both hands throbbed. Her heart ached.

She'd ruined a family tradition. Ruined it completely.

Noah and Gem hurried into the kitchen. Gem turned off the faucet. Noah approached her.

"I couldn't find the potholders." Kelsey raised her throbbing hands in front of her face. "I put them on the counter. They were supposed to be on the counter."

Noah bent and picked up the potholders from the floor. Right below the oven. "Can I see your hands?"

"It's not my hands. It's my eyes." She'd knocked the potholders on the floor and never noticed. She'd gotten too comfortable and started to believe again. "I ruined the muffins."

She ruined the perfection.

"Never mind the muffins, dear." Gem stepped toward her, concern creasing around her eyes. "Let's take care of your hands."

"We can make more muffins." Noah scooped several muffins into the trash, his voice and movements calm.

"But I can't make more." Her fingers stung and ached, the pain of the truth pulsing in her head and singeing her heart. "Me. All by myself."

The list of things she wouldn't be able to do seared through her, cracking her composure. Shattering her fantasy week like broken glass. She spun around, stumbled out of the kitchen, down the hall, searching for a place to fall apart.

She collapsed in one of the twin tall-backed chairs in the alcove of the villa's main bedroom. A pair of unusual black-framed glasses sat on the thin round table between the chairs. She wiped her damp cheeks and leaned forward. *Optical Ovations* was typed in oversized bold lettering on the paper inside a clear plastic folder.

Gem and Noah walked into the bedroom and slowed.

"What is this?" Kelsey flicked her hand over the presentation and glasses on the table. "Who is Optical Ovations?"

"We can discuss that later." Gem scurried around the room, avoided looking at Kelsey. "I need to find my first-aid supplies. You need to put your hands under cold water. Everyone will be here soon."

Kelsey scowled. "Grandma, you promised."

"You and I haven't discussed cure, trials, or doctors." Gem walked into the bathroom and returned with supplies.

"You have a presentation and sample sitting next to your bridal jewelry." Kelsey dropped her throbbing hands on her lap.

"You could've changed your mind." Gem handed the first-aid kit to Noah. "We wanted to be prepared."

We?

Noah shifted into her view, knelt beside her to examine her fingers. They could've been a *we*. If she was someone else. Her fingers ached. Her body ached.

"Have you changed your mind?" Gem paced behind Noah.

No. Love entailed too many conditions. Too many risks. Kelsey set her head on the chair back. "I wanted one week. One perfect week full of perfect memories."

"We all want what's best for you," Gem offered.

"For you or for me?" Kelsey raised her head. "If you cure my vision, I won't be a burden. A constant worry. A disappointment."

She could have a chance at that *we*.

God knows what Noah thought of her now. As defective, probably. For that is how she felt.

"Kelsey." Gem pressed her hands to her cheeks and shook her head. "That's not fair. You've never been any of those things to any of us."

Noah finished applying ointment to Kelsey's left hand and switched to her right. Nothing dulled the pain in her chest.

"Then what's all this." Kelsey ramped up the presentation. "You've ramped up your cure search. It's all anyone focuses on, even at your wedding. During our family holiday. Aren't you exhausted?"

"No." Gem set her hands on her hips. Determination hardened her voice. "I'll never stop fighting for you. Never."

"What if I want to stop?" Kelsey ignored the tears pooling in her eyes. "Stop and learn to live as I am. To be accepted as I am, broken eyes included. Why am I not good enough as I am?"

"You are," Gem said.

Noah nodded and added, "You're more than good enough."

"That's not true." Noah didn't know the real her. Kelsey shook her head, dislodged those tears. "Or you'd never have found another doctor. Another trial. Another opportunity to fix me."

"What if it works?" Noah finished tying off a bandage around her four fingers, covering the worst of the burns.

"Every other doctor has believed their fix would work too." Kelsey exhaled, accepting the pain and releasing the truth. "Now I'll lose my sight completely in five years. Nothing has worked."

"This trial could be different." Noah gathered the first-aid supplies.

"It only takes one successful trial," Gem offered.

"You can't be so certain." Kelsey shook her head.

"I can about that one." Noah angled his chin toward the table. His face remained neutral, his tone impartial.

Kelsey eyed him. He was too contained, almost defensive.

He settled his gaze on her. His mouth thinned. "I'm the doctor that invented it. I am Optical Ovations."

No. Kelsey sucked in a breath as if she'd been burned again. She squeezed her eyes shut. He'd been the reason for her perfect week. He'd made her believe she could just be herself. Her heart dropped. He'd played her. The same as her grandmother. "I should have known."

"Did you enroll me in his trial already?" She glared at her grandmother.

"Only you can do that." Noah folded his arms over his chest, his face and tone impassive.

Where was the man who she'd spent the week with? Where was the man she'd fallen for? *No.* She hadn't fallen for Noah. The week was all pretend, her feelings and his interest. "You already knew my full condition. Probably read my medical file too."

"Only you can grant me full access to your medical records." She heard even more of his indifference as if he'd detached.

She wanted to shout, to rattle him. She'd granted him full access to her heart and now he locked her out. Anger crushed against her chest and hurt—she hurt everywhere. She hurt so much. "Who approached who?" She lifted her bandaged hand and stopped their replies. "Never mind. I don't want to know. It doesn't matter."

"I should have told you." Noah ran his hands through his hair, unsettling the strands, yet disturbing nothing more. "I planned to tell you after the hike. Then your family arrived. Then at dinner, but …"

Always her family interfered. Convenient. Her ex had blamed her family too. What if he had been right and it had not been an excuse? "What was the new plan? Wait until I fell in love with you, then confess. After all, I couldn't be too mad since love always prevails."

"You don't …" His voice dropped away. His face hardened.

"Love you?" she spat out. Now she understood the truth of a broken heart. The numbing pain that suffocated, stealing joy and her voice. "No. You're safe."

"What does that mean?" Finally, a hint of emotion fractured his voice.

"You don't want to be in love." Neither did she. Not like this. Regret rooted inside her heart. "You want the perfect trial candidate."

He flinched. "I won't deny you meet every qualification."

"Now you're going to tell me that this was about more than work." She never eased the bitterness in her tone.

He opened his mouth as if he wanted to deny her claim. Instead he retreated. "It's always about work."

"For me, it's always about trust." Kelsey paused, held her breath long enough to gather her pride. "I need you both to leave."

"Kelsey." Noah stepped forward.

"Please." She raised her bandaged hand. "Just leave."

The bedroom door closed behind them and Kelsey finally broke. Tears spilled over her cheeks. The doorbell rang. Voices filled the entryway outside the bedroom door. She had to get out.

Her knees swayed as she stood. Her bandaged hands slipped over the handle of the patio doors. Pain radiated up her arms. She couldn't even escape on her own.

Pathetic.

She slid down the glass doors and curled into a ball.

Minutes or hours passed; Kelsey wasn't sure how long she lay on the floor. Long enough to believe her heartache would be timeless. The bedroom door eased open. Two women eased inside, closed the door, and rushed to her.

"What can we do?" Meagan knelt beside her and brushed Kelsey's hair off her face.

"Anything," Fran wiped several tissues across Kelsey's cheeks, "you name it."

"Get me out of here." Kelsey lifted her limp hands and defeated gaze to her sister and cousin. "I can't do this tonight."

Fran and Meagan never hesitated. Never paused to convince her to change her mind. Never offered their own opinions on what was best for her.

Meagan helped her stand, simply wrapping her arm around Kelsey's waist, transferring her own strength to her sister.

Fran peeked outside the bedroom and closed the door. "Too many people that way."

"Back patio it is." Meagan guided Kelsey in the opposite direction.

Fran headed to the sliding doors. "Let me go first and check out the best route."

"It's like sneaking out of the house as teens all over again," Meagan whispered.

Kelsey set her head on her sister's shoulder, grateful for these two incredible women in her life.

"Don't worry." Fran turned toward them and gripped Kelsey's shoulders. "We didn't get caught back then, we sure as heck aren't getting caught now."

Ten minutes later, the trio walked in the door of Kelsey's suite.

Fran lifted a wine bottle out of a canvas tote bag. "Figured we could toast our successful getaway."

"When did you get that?" Meagan grinned.

"When I paused at the bar to talk to Uncle Travis and Aunt Trina as a diversion." Fran picked up the wine opener from the small bar.

"That was well done," Kelsey said.

"I know." Fran filled the three wine glasses Meagan set on the counter. "I'm quite proud of it."

Meagan looked at Kelsey. "We're here until you tell us to go."

Fran stepped closer. "For whatever you need."

"I love you guys." Kelsey wrapped her arms around her sister and cousin. Then finally broke down completely.

CHAPTER TEN

*N*oah opened the door for room service. Not exactly the Thanksgiving dinner he'd anticipated. He tipped the server, and while his meal waited on the sofa table, Noah answered the video call on his laptop from his cousin, Brent Bishop.

Noah and his cousins had spent their holidays together until Noah's parents had divorced and he and his mother had moved away. Still, Brent, his younger brothers, and Noah spoke every Thanksgiving and Christmas. Without fail.

"Where are the others?" Noah glanced into the camera, noticed Brent sitting in his office alone.

"Corralling their high-maintenance dates." Brent laughed. "It's why I spend my holidays as a happy, single man."

Noah lifted his whiskey glass. "Here's to being alone."

"You don't sound or look happy." Brent leaned into the camera and frowned. "In fact, you look and sound more and more like your dad."

"Thanks for the compliment." Noah sipped his whiskey.

"It wasn't meant to be one." Brent rubbed his chin. "Want to tell me what's going on?"

Brent and Noah had traded stories about their fathers over the years. They'd forged a bond around the weight of heavy expectations. They'd bonded more during the challenges of medical school. "My trip to the islands was a bust."

"You really need to pick a new island," Brent said. "It's time for a change."

For a brief moment, Noah believed he'd discovered a different kind of change. One that involved Kelsey in his life for more than the trial. "The candidate for the trial is a no-go."

Same as his personal life.

Brent nodded. "Maybe your father will accept our offers now."

"Offers?" Noah straightened and stared at his cousin. "What offers?"

"The ones we've extended over the past two years," Brent explained. "To fold Optical Ovations into our parent corporation."

Noah lowered his glass onto the table and ran his palms over his shorts. Noah's Uncle—

Brent's father—owned one of the leading, cutting-edge medical companies in the nation. For years, Noah's father had been seeking to outshine his former brother-in-law. As if the Bishop family and their success had somehow stolen his. "Why wasn't I told?"

"Because your dad expected you to fix his own mistakes." Brent scowled. "Same way he expected your mom to fix their marriage."

"What do you mean?" Noah rubbed his forehead and the headache building there. He recalled snippets of arguments between his mom and dad. His mom had constantly shouted at his dad to fix the mess he'd made. His dad had always challenged her to work harder.

"Your dad expected your mom to work more shifts at the hospital to finance his company and his dreams," Brent added.

"What about what Mom wanted?" What about what Noah wanted?

"It's never been about anyone but your dad." Brent winced. "Sorry for the truth slam."

And Noah was following in his father's footsteps. Otherwise, he would have been searching for the right solution for the retinal eye chip. Searching for the most effective way to bring the eye chip to the market to help patients worldwide, regardless of his own personal gain. Regardless of his own recognition—or his father's.

Noah picked up his tumbler and swirled the ice around in the amber liquid. However, nothing diluted the acid twisting in his gut. "Don't be. I think I've known the truth about my dad all along."

"No one wants to admit their own father is greedy and selfish," Brent said.

"I don't want to become like him." Noah stared into the screen. "We need to meet when I return. I want to discuss your offers."

"How about Monday?"

"I'm on the red-eye," he said. "I'll call you when I arrive in Charlotte."

"Head to the offices." Brent nodded. "I'll be there."

"Don't you have a full schedule of meetings already?" Noah asked.

"I always have time for family," Brent replied. Quick and simple. End of discussion. Family first.

Family. Kelsey had shown Noah the true meaning of family. She'd invited him into her family's world, then treated him as if he'd belonged. Brent and his brothers had always accepted Noah. Also treated him as if he belonged. It was past time he saw his cousins and reconnected with his true family.

"Now about the woman ...." Curiosity lengthened Brent's words.

"Who said anything about a woman?" Noah poured more whiskey into his glass.

"You have room service untouched on the table beside you, but the whiskey bottle is opened." Brent laughed. "What's her name?"

"Kelsey." Noah launched into the specifics from his first meeting at his labs with Gem to the fallout an hour earlier with Kelsey. All the while, Brent listened, smiled, and laughed, then frowned and considered.

Finally, Noah paused and finished off the whiskey in his tumbler.

"You know what you are?" Brent looked into the camera as if he wanted to examine Noah closer.

"I am on my way to a whiskey-induced good night's sleep." Noah tipped his glass toward the computer screen. He could wish, couldn't he? Yet he feared Kelsey would haunt his dreams, asleep or awake.

"Well, that too ..."

He fell for the bait. "So what am I, then?"

"*You* are the blind one. You're in love. I can't say I ever thought you'd *fall* in love."

Love. Noah's glass clunked against the table. He would know if he were in love. Besides, he'd refused to fall in love. "I was married before. I should know."

"That wasn't love." Brent laughed and flicked his hand in front of the screen. "That was you pretending. Doing what everyone else expected. Date the so-called perfect girl for you. Get engaged. Get married."

Expectations. There they were again. Had Noah ever set any goal for himself? Or had he been following the ones set for him by his father and everyone around him? It was expected that he work in the family business. It was expected that he follow in his father's footsteps. It was expected that he ensure the family legacy.

But was it right? Was it what Noah wanted? He massaged the back of his neck, rolled his shoulders. He hadn't asked himself what he wanted in entirely too long.

"So, what's the plan?" Brent's voice broke the silence.

He wanted Kelsey. That much he knew. No hesitation. No doubts. He smiled into the camera. "The plan is to go get the girl."

"Good luck." Brent grinned. "See you Monday."

"Definitely."

"By the way," his cousin said. "It looks good on you."

"What does?" Noah asked.

"Love."

CHAPTER ELEVEN

"*I*t's open." Kelsey never moved from her chair on the patio. The sun had barely greeted the day and she knew only two people, besides herself, who preferred such early mornings—and Noah wasn't coming to her suite. She sipped her coffee and waited for her grandmother to step out on the porch. "There's more coffee in the pot."

"It's my wedding day." Gem lowered into the chair beside Kelsey. "I'm already jittery enough. Never thought I'd be doing this again."

"Why are you?" Kelsey stared at the blur of the horizon, closed her eyes then shifted her focus to the fish swimming underneath the glass patio floor.

"Because love is precious. It should be celebrated and cherished." Gem set her feet on the padded footrest. "And life is short."

"Is this about love or a cure for me?" Kelsey clenched her coffee mug, unsure what she preferred to hear.

"Love was always the plan." No apology slipped into Gem's voice. "You asked us to accept your condition. I don't believe that accepting your condition sentences you to a life spent alone."

"Did you know that the doctors give you a diagnosis and an expiration date on your dreams?" Dreams like marriage. Her own kids and family.

"The dream might look different than you imagined," Gem said. "Doesn't mean your dreams have no value. No significance. Dreams are still worth pursuing."

"To what end?" Kelsey leaned her elbows on her knees. "I'm going to need so much more help." Sooner than Kelsey wanted to admit.

"You have a courage that humbles me."

Courage? Not her. Kelsey rocked back in her chair. She'd flown to an island to spend a week in denial. That wasn't courageous. Or brave. "Grandma, you're the bravest woman I know."

Gem's mouth flattened into a thin line, her head shook. "Easy to be brave when you aren't faced with challenges."

"You've been challenged," Kelsey countered.

"Not like you are being challenged now." Gem leaned toward her and touched her arm. "And you're facing it with grace and confidence."

"Aside from my meltdown yesterday in your villa." And the one she'd had after she'd left the doctor's office several weeks ago.

"You're entitled to each and every one of those moments." Gem tightened her hold on Kelsey and the conviction in her tone. "It's how you rise up and move forward that defines you and makes you into the person you were meant to be."

Who *did* she want to become? She wanted to be defined by more than her blindness. Wanted to build a life worth remembering. And she wanted to build that life with Noah beside her. *Noah.*

Her heart tripped inside her chest; the dream snagging inside her. Dare she reach for it? "What about children. How can I raise a child? I won't even know if my clothes match."

"Parents don't come in a standard one-size-fits-all package." Gem rubbed her arm. "You work out the parenting challenges and hurdles with your partner, together as a team."

Team. She'd never been in a team relationship, even before her eyesight problems. But she'd felt like a team with Noah. He'd given her an underwater camera and she'd hugged him like he'd given her a priceless gift. And he had: he had bestowed his understanding. Noah understood her in a way no one else ever had.

But would he want her—a not-quite-one-hundred-percent Kelsey Thomas? Was it too much to ask of him? "What about all the little daily things that I know I'll need help with, like grocery shopping, driving, cooking dinner? I won't be able to contribute."

"You'll work that out together too," Gem urged. "That's what two people in love do. Work together to build a stronger, safer foundation for each other. To make each other better. Happier."

Kelsey stared into her empty mug as if an answer lingered in the last drop of coffee. "We have so much to work out."

"So, because it's too daunting, you walk away? Call it quits since it's just too hard?" Gem rose and pressed a kiss against Kelsey's cheek. "You give up on Noah *and* yourself."

"It's not that simple," Kelsey whispered.

"Before you decide, consider this," Gem said. "You might be giving up on what could be the greatest journey of your life."

Kelsey's heart, bruised and battered as it was, encouraged her to take the risk. Her mind shied away, listed all the cons she brought to a relationship. Could love really conquer all?

Gem walked to the open patio doors and turned back. "If you give up now, it could become the greatest regret of your life."

CHAPTER TWELVE

*K*elsey slipped on her sandals and stiffened her backbone. No regrets, she repeated. *No regrets.*

Her grandmother had been right. She had to find him, talk to him. She had already forgiven Noah his deception, realizing she had, in a way, set the scene for it by not allowing anyone to talk about medical trials for a week. Had he done wrong? Yes. But she'd had time to think about it, and she could tell his heart was in the right place. As was her family's.

If she'd have known what he did for a living from the start, she would have never given him the time of day. She would have never seen what he had to offer her life—and her heart.

Kelsey had to take a risk, both in her life and in love. She walked outside her bungalow and headed to Noah's.

She'd face her life challenges as they came. And she'd fight to make the most of the life she'd been given.

As for love, she'd face that now; she'd face the risk now.

She knocked on Noah's door, heard the movement inside his suite, and locked her knees. No more running away.

The door swung open. Noah stared at her, surprise on his face and in his voice. "Kelsey."

She cleared the tremor from her throat. "Can I come in?"

He opened the door wide and motioned her inside. She paced into the suite, turned, and found him rooted in the entrance.

"Here's the thing," Kelsey smoothed her hands down her halter dress and jumped all in. "There's a wedding and I could use a date."

"Is that right?" He leaned against the closed door and eyed her.

"Yeah," she said. "I *had* a date."

"What happened?" He crossed his arms over his chest.

"The usual." She lifted one shoulder in a slight shrug. There was nothing offhand about the thumping of her heart, the racing of her pulse. "Got scared. Kept secrets. Both of us were too afraid to trust in what was between us."

"What was," he repeated.

"Or what could be, if we agreed to second chances." She lifted her hands, her fingers fluttering in front of her like those butterflies in her stomach. "Everyone deserves those, right?"

"I like to think so." He pushed away from the door and closed the distance between them. "Are there rules for this second chance?"

She lifted her chin, leveled her gaze on his. "No secrets."

"Agreed." He stepped fully into her space, held himself a deep sigh away. "Twenty-four hours is too long to wait to apologize."

"I'm sorry," she said.

"No." He touched her cheek, the barest caress of his fingertips across her skin. Tender and sincere.

A shiver skimmed over her. Warmth arrowed into her core.

"It's all on me. I can't begin to tell you how truly sorry I am." He tucked her hair behind her ear and locked his gaze on hers. "I should have been honest about who I was and what I did from the beginning. You deserve better."

"We'll be honest from here on out." She reached between them, laid her hand over his heart.

He nodded and wrapped his fingers around hers, capturing her hand against his chest.

"I don't know how this will work." She exhaled, stepped fully into her truth. "I don't know what my life will look like in a few years and I'm terrified."

"None of us can see into the future. There's fear in that and it can overtake us if we let it." His grip tightened. "But we can face anything together. As long as we're together, we can win."

She searched his face. "You really mean that?"

"With all my heart." He framed her face inside his hands. "I can't guarantee that I'll ever be able to restore your vision fully. But I can guarantee I'll love you for the rest of my life."

"Say it again," she said.

"I love you," he said. "It's you. Perfect vision or not—I love *you*, Kelsey."

She closed her eyes and allowed his words to seep into her heart. Mend all those broken pieces. Fill all those empty places. Chase away all those fears.

She curved her arms around his neck. "I can't guarantee I'm not going to have bad days or be difficult to live with, but I won't ever give up on us. Or our love."

He dipped his head. She lifted toward him. Their lips joined. Their hearts merged beneath a kiss that promised a love of a lifetime. A love that conquered all. A love that endured.

Kelsey sighed and leaned back in Noah's embrace. "About that wedding date? Will you be my plus-one?"

"Always."

Vows recited, the commitment ceremony a touching success, and the reception concluded, Noah and Kelsey walked along the dock toward their bungalows. "I have a surprise for you."

"When did you plan a surprise?" she asked.

"Before you arrived to ask me to be your date," he said. "You didn't think I wasn't going to fight for you, did you?"

"Obviously, I just got to you first today." She smiled. "I like knowing you would've come for me."

"I'll always be there for you." He opened his suite door. The interior was lit like daytime. The TV had been set to an easy-listening music station. "I borrowed some lights from Gem and Harland."

"Why?" she asked.

"I wanted you to be safe," he said, "and not miss anything."

She pressed her hand to her chest. "What are we doing?"

He lifted several stainless-steel covers off the plates arranged on the small dining table. "Having our own Thanksgiving."

She stepped to the table and studied the collection of plates and bowls. "Those are all my family's dishes."

"I borrowed the leftovers from yesterday." He stacked the metal covers and rubbed his hands together. "Fran and Meagan helped. Gem too."

"And are those egg rolls?" She laughed.

"I may have added a few new items to the menu." He pointed to the pot stickers and honey-walnut shrimp. "A merging of sorts."

"The beginning of our own traditions." She picked up an egg roll and sampled it.

Their own traditions. His own family. "I like that a lot."

"What should be our first tradition?" She set the egg roll on a plate and wiped her hands on a napkin.

"A dance on water." He led her out onto the glass-floored patio, wrapped his arms around her waist, and pulled her close. The soft music drifted through open sliding doors. The ocean breeze played with the strands of her hair that had fallen loose around her shoulders.

She peered up at him. "Harland and Gem told me about the potential investment today."

"I turned them down." He turned her in a slow circle.

"Why?"

"Because I love you." He kissed her, softly and soundly, then pulled away. "It took me falling in love to realize what was important to me. To decide what I really wanted."

"What about your medical trial and your prototype?" she asked. "That's important too."

"Very much so," he said. "I spoke to my cousin. We're meeting next week to discuss a merger of our company into his."

"What about your dad?" she asked.

"That's just it," he said. "It's about more than me and my dad. It's about doing what's right for the patients we want to help."

"People like me." She kept her chin high.

"Definitely," he said. "Can I ask what changed your mind about us?"

"I realized I couldn't live as if I was facing a death sentence," she said. "I realized I'll still be able to hear, touch, taste, even if my sight can't be fixed. I'll still be able to feel. There's a gift in that. A life I can't waste."

"I don't want to waste one minute of our lives together." He anchored her against him, slowed their dance into more of a swaying motion on the patio.

"I'm so thankful for you." She leaned up and kissed him, stole his breath and the rest of his heart. "I think this is the perfect start to our future."

THE END

CPSIA information can be obtained
at www.ICGtesting.com
Printed in the USA
JSHW020826230920
8123JS00006B/1